Praise for Jenny Hale

"Jenny Hale writes touching, beautiful stories about people and places I love visiting."

—RaeAnne Thayne, *New York Times* bestselling author

Summer at Firefly Beach

"A great summer beach read."

—*PopSugar*

"A perfect beach read about rediscovering oneself, second chances, and the power of healing."

—*Harlequin Junkies*

It Started with Christmas

"This sweet small-town romance will leave readers feeling warm all the way through."

—*Publishers Weekly*

The Summer House

"Hale's rich and slow-building romance is enhanced by the allure of the North Carolina coast... North Carolina's beautiful Outer Banks is the perfect setting for this sweet, poignant romance, and authentic characters and a riveting story make it a keeper worth savoring."

—*Publishers Weekly* (Starred Review)

"Like a paper-and-ink version of a chick-flick... gives you the butterflies and leaves you happy and hopeful."

—*Due South*

Christmas Wishes and Mistletoe Kisses

"[A] tender treat that can be savored in any season."

—*Publishers Weekly* (Starred Review)

"[Jenny] Hale's impeccably executed contemporary romance is the perfect gift for readers who love sweetly romantic love stories imbued with all the warmth and joy of the holiday season."

—*Booklist*

summer
by the sea

ALSO BY JENNY HALE

Christmas Wishes and Mistletoe Kisses
The Summer House
It Started with Christmas
Summer at Firefly Beach
A Christmas to Remember

summer
by the sea

JENNY HALE

FOREVER
NEW YORK BOSTON

Forever
Hachette Book Group
1290 Avenue of the Americas, New York, NY 10104
read-forever.com
twitter.com/readforeverpub

Originally published in 2015 by Bookouture, an imprint of StoryFire Ltd.
First Forever Edition: June 2021

Forever is an imprint of Grand Central Publishing. The Forever name and logo are trademarks of Hachette Book Group, Inc.

The publisher is not responsible for websites (or their content) that are not owned by the publisher.

The Hachette Speakers Bureau provides a wide range of authors for speaking events. To find out more, go to www.hachettespeakersbureau.com or call (866) 376-6591.

LCCN: 2021933933

ISBNs: 978-1-5387-2058-5 (trade paperback),
978-1-5387-5471-9 (hardcover library)

Printed in the United States of America

LSC-C

Printing 1, 2021

summer
by the sea

Chapter One

Faith stopped the car in front of her favorite lunch spot in the Outer Banks: Dune Burger. It was a tiny shack of a building—a little rectangle that sat so close to the beach that the sand from the dunes blew across the street, covering the curb on windy days. The insignificantly sized building was painted a bright red, with stark white trim, and the walk-up windows across the front were all open. Faith got out of her car, and the heat of summer assaulted her. She remembered this heat from her childhood when they would come here to North Carolina and spend two weeks at the beach every summer. Just as it did now, the sun had warmed her all the way through. She walked up to the window to place her order, noticing how this time she could reach the counter without a problem. As a kid, the counter had been too high to see over. She'd grabbed onto it, dangling by her arms until her mother had shooed her away, telling her gently that it wasn't meant for that. As they waited for their order, her mother, Martha, would swing her around in circles. She remembered how the building would blur in her dizziness, the rush of ocean air in her ears.

"What would you like to order?" A woman greeted Faith from behind the counter, bringing her back to the present.

"I'll have a cheeseburger with ketchup and mustard, please," she said to the woman before rummaging in her handbag for her change purse.

Faith was early, after driving all the way there from her home in South Carolina, so she'd decided to stop and have a little lunch before heading to the cottage. As she waited for her burger, she noticed a small crowd of people standing around one of the windows at the other end. They were surrounding a tall, dark-haired man, clapping him on the back, chuckling, and making jokes.

When her burger was ready, she took it over to a red picnic table that was painted to match the building. It had an equally bright red umbrella, but, even tilted toward where she was standing, the sun overpowered its shade, and she got no relief from the heat when underneath it except for the sea breeze coming from the shore. She slipped her sunglasses on, sat down, and spun her legs under the table.

The sky was a perfect, cloudless blue, and the sound of the waves crashing just over the dunes was the only sound apart from a passing car here and there. It had been a long time since she'd been here, but this spot had hardly changed.

Before she met her family today, Faith had promised herself that she'd drive a few blocks down from Dune Burger and see the area of beach where their family cottage had stood. It had been leveled by a hurricane when she was a teenager, and, ever since then, they hadn't been back to the Outer Banks as a family. Not until today. She remembered the cottage as if she'd just been there. She could almost smell the earthy scent of it. The exterior had been the same brown color as driftwood—like most of the older cottages that sat on Beach Road. It was tall, on stilts to protect it from the high tides during storms; it had a small porch that went around the outside, and a driveway that led through the stilts and under the house.

On the porch, there had been two rocking chairs and a bench swing. If she closed her eyes, she could almost feel the sand on her feet as she hugged her knees on that swing, her cheeks throbbing from too much sun, her dark blond hair so golden from the summer spent outside that it looked yellow against her tan skin. Her sister, Casey, was taller than she was, and she could push against the floor hard enough to make the swing sail backward and then forward, the rocking motion tickling Faith's tummy, but her favorite times on that swing were when it was still, the breeze pushing her hair around her shoulders and cooling her skin. She liked the quiet moments on that porch, the serenity of it. She'd always been that way.

The sound of a car parking pulled her from her memories. The crowd by the window had gone now, the man with dark hair still there. Getting out of his car, the driver called, "Jake! How are ya?" and walked over to shake the man's hand. When he did, Faith got a good look at the man named Jake. He certainly seemed popular. He greeted the other man, and Faith noticed the sincerity in his smile and how striking his features were as he got a little closer. He had a strong jawline, but there was something gentle about the way his expressions moved around his face. He was wearing some sort of work clothes—painter, maybe?

His dark hair was windblown, his shoes spotted from whatever it was he did for a living, but there was something about him that seemed juxtaposed to what she could see. He had an authoritative presence—squared shoulders, a strong, intense look in his eyes, but at the same time, he seemed genuinely friendly. He had a firm-looking handshake, and appeared so at ease with himself; just watching how he interacted with people made Faith want to see what he'd do next. She looked down at her burger to avoid staring at him.

The two men talked for a while—she couldn't make out their conversation, and she didn't want to eavesdrop, so she just ate her burger and enjoyed the solitude. It was maybe the last moment of quiet she'd get for a while. Soon, she'd be with her entire family. They were coming together for two weeks to celebrate her grandmother's ninetieth birthday. She hadn't been with them all together in quite a while. She just couldn't face Casey. Faith had been able to make excuses up until now—parent-teacher conferences at school, report cards to be completed, field trips—and it was time she faced her. She'd seen Nan and her mother, but she'd always avoided Casey. Seeing her sister had been too complicated, with too many feelings surrounding the two of them. Just thinking about Casey had been painful, but staying away from her was painful too. She missed her sister terribly, but she couldn't deny what Casey had done, and it was enough to make her want to stay away. Faith worried that seeing her might bring back the sting of Casey's betrayal, but she finally felt like she was strong enough to face it head-on. She couldn't have done that earlier, but now she could, and there was no way she would've missed her Nan's birthday.

Faith couldn't wait to see her grandmother. Nan had been her rock growing up. It was Nan who had planned their childhood visits to the beach, who had watched them when their mother was working, who had picked them up from school and had taken care of them at home when they were sick. While she was eager to be back here and with her family, it was Nan who she was the most excited to see.

Faith's thoughts were as wild as the sea wind as she came back to the present. The man—Jake—began walking toward her, carrying his burger. He seemed to be heading straight for her table. Was he planning to sit with her? He paused a few steps from her table for just a moment, just a breath, and smiled. It was a polite smile, the kind one would offer to a stranger, but yet there was something so approachable about him. As he started to walk toward her again, his blue eyes on her, that intensity she'd witnessed now directed at her, she was taken with how attractive he was, and she wondered what her hair looked like—she'd driven there with the windows down the whole way. Did she have any makeup left on her face? Just when she was thinking he was actually going to ask to sit with her, he continued past her and sat at the table next to hers. *Silly*, she thought. *Why would he sit with a complete stranger?*

Faith ate the last bite of her burger and balled up the paper. Then, walking past Jake's table, she threw her trash away and got back into her car. She pulled onto Beach Road, and with the man in her rear-view mirror, she headed toward the lot that had held the cottage from her childhood. As she drove, she thought about that moment she'd had when the man named Jake had smiled at her. She could've easily mentioned the beautiful weather or asked him about the best shopping spots in the area. She could've said anything, but she hadn't. Her sister, Casey, would've. Casey had an easy way about her. She could talk to anyone. Faith often felt that opportunities came Casey's way just because she was so easy to talk to. Faith was the quiet one. She had just as much to offer as her sister, but she had a harder time getting that across to people. She knew what she wanted to say; she just didn't feel comfortable blurting it out. Just like now. If there had been any chance to have a conversation with a friendly, handsome man, she'd missed it. She shouldn't have missed it. In her adult life, she was very confident.

Faith's confidence had grown through her work. She'd been a kindergarten teacher for the last five years, and she'd loved it. She'd learned so much about personalities from the children she taught, and she realized, as she taught them, how being quiet could also mean being strong. She threw herself into her job and gave it everything she had, and her strength grew as she made friends with other teachers in her school. The children inspired her, and she finally felt in control of things. She loved the idea of preparing instructional lessons the way she wanted to and seeing the results when the children learned the concepts easily as a result of her preparation.

The kids looked up to her; they listened to her. She had to know how to be with the kids, and they were brutally honest. What Faith had found was that, in her quiet way, she taught them how to trust her. She'd found that they liked her—she made them giggle. And, crucially, they learned.

Last month, she'd received the best news—she was Teacher of the Year for her school. She'd had a big party with all her friends, and the school had recognized her accomplishments with a banquet. So many of the parents of her students came out for it that it touched her. This was her year. She was finally the person she was meant to be. And, for the first time in her life, she was happy. So, when Nan called about this beach trip, knowing Casey would be there, Faith felt strong enough to see her sister.

The one thing that was still niggling at her was the fact that, while both sisters were very successful in their own right, Casey still had something that Faith didn't: a family. Faith had spent so many years building her self-confidence and working to make her life what she wanted that now she was worried she'd waited too long. Dating people had always come second to her job, and at the time, she felt she couldn't help that. Now, looking back on it, she wondered if she'd been right. She'd had two long-term relationships that had ended because of her constant working. When her first relationship ended on that note, she'd just considered it a difference of opinion, that perhaps they just weren't right for each other. But then, when her last relationship with a man named Patrick had ended for the same reason, she started to take a look at her priorities.

Patrick had been a great guy. He knew how to treat her, and she enjoyed being with him. But when he wanted to take things further, and he mentioned her pulling back a little on her work, she'd dug in her heels. She felt at the time like he was trying to take away her control. But now, she wondered if perhaps she should've given a little. Because, in the end, the children in her classroom would go home to their parents, but she would go home to an empty house, with no children of her own. Unlike Casey, who had a wonderful husband and a beautiful daughter named Isabella. She couldn't help but feel sad at the thought. But she wouldn't let that spoil this vacation.

Faith's long, dark blond hair chased the air as it rushed in and out of the open car window. It felt good to be out of her usual skirts and button-up shirts. Her sunglasses and dangly earrings were casual like the shorts she had on and the flip-flops on her feet. She'd painted her toenails a beachy pink, and she was ready to have a little fun. Teaching children was hard work, and she needed the break. She wondered if Casey would welcome the slower pace. Her sister was a lawyer for a firm in Boston and from all she'd heard, it seemed that she worked all the time these days too.

Apart from her sister's job, which Faith would never want, Casey had everything. She had an amazing family and a house full of photos and reminders of the travels and adventures they'd had. As a kid, when Faith had thought about what her life would be like when she grew up, she'd imagined a house full of children, a loving husband,

and a job that she loved. She was too young to grasp at the time that those things weren't guaranteed. Faith's personal life was a little like the empty lot she was going to see: a blank spot just waiting for something to be built on it.

As she drove toward the empty lot where the family cottage once stood, the sun warm on her face, she thought about why her life had ended up different than her sister's. Faith wanted to know what it was like to hear the patter of feet around the house, and look into the eyes of her child, to see the perfect mixture of her and the man she loved. She wanted to spend her days passing on her family traditions and making new ones. She'd wanted to begin that chapter of her own life, but, once again, Casey had taken the lead, marrying her husband, Scott, and having a baby together.

When Scott's job had taken them to Boston, Faith was actually relieved. She could finally see Nan and her mother. Seeing Casey and Scott together reminded her of the family that she still didn't have, the happiness that she knew had to be out there waiting for her that she still hadn't found. And it reminded her of the sister who had betrayed her. Who didn't care enough for her and could hurt her terribly without even a second thought.

When Faith had left to go to college, she felt her life was a clean slate, and she was optimistic that she'd fill it up at some point. She wasn't upset anymore, but she was still carrying around the hurt that Casey had caused. She'd been away from Casey for so long now, and she'd made something of herself, so she was ready to see her.

Faith pulled the car up into the drive to the empty driveway, and she had to close her gaping mouth. Right there in front of her was a blast from the past. Like a ghost, sending waves of laughter and memories through her mind. She blinked to be sure she wasn't hallucinating. Without warning, a lump formed in her throat as she got out to look at what was in front of her. The rush of coastal wind pushed against her as she made her way through the sea grass and over the dune. With a hand over her eyes to shield the sunlight that was too bright for even her sunglasses to manage, she let her eyes roam the new structure in front of her. It was tall, sitting on stilts like the old cottage had been, brown, shingled siding, with a porch going all the way around. It was magnificent.

Every cottage was given a name, and that name was displayed on the front of it to assist renters in finding their vacation home. This one had a wooden sign centered below the roofline of the house that said "Better Together." She blinked away the tears that were clouding her vision as she thought about how much better life had been when they were all together here. The new cottage—looking so much like Nan's had looked—stood, looming like a ghost of happier times.

There was nothing to indicate that someone was living in the cottage—no cars, no beach towels on a clothesline or hanging over the railings like they'd done when she was a kid—so she walked closer to have a better look. There were manufacturer stickers on the windows and a pile of lumber and flooring propped against one of the posts. This was a brand-new cottage. She knew she probably shouldn't, but, since no one was there, she decided to climb the steps to get a look from the porch.

With every step she took she felt like she was going back in time to her childhood cottage. Her heart pounded as she anticipated the view that she'd spent so many years seeing from that old porch swing. The cottage had been in her family for generations. It had belonged to Nan. She'd only found out as an adult that just before it was destroyed Nan had told Faith's mom she could no longer physically manage the upkeep on the cottage or make the journey to board it up every hurricane season. Martha, a single mother, couldn't take it on, so, sadly, when the house was leveled, Martha suggested they sell the lot, and, given its location, they'd make a ton of money. Martha had confided in Faith once that she'd cried when Nan told her the cottage was gone. But, given the burden it placed on Nan, it had been for the best.

Faith walked across the brand new wooden porch floor and leaned against the railing on her elbows, the tide relentless like her memories. She remembered the sandcastles she'd built in that sand, the hours swimming in the ocean with Casey, the way the salt tasted on her lips. This had been a place of nothing but happiness for her, and as she stood there, the ocean view was a reminder of the time in her life before the burdens of adulthood had settled in, before Casey had torn them apart. Faith's life was split into two distinct parts, and this place represented that first part. Just seeing it again pulled her toward that happiness she'd had as a child and made her want to feel that again. Tears welled up in her eyes, and she brushed one away as it escaped down her cheek.

She could see the thin, gray line of the horizon, where the two shades of blue met, and the silhouette of a sailboat. As a child, she'd watch the sailboats out at sea and wish she could have a ride on one. She'd never been on a boat before. She closed her eyes to remember happier times and take in the briny air. This beach was perfection, and, if she tried hard enough, she could almost go back to that time before her sister had hurt her. Almost.

"Hello," she heard from behind her and nearly jumped out of her skin. She'd been so taken with the view and the memories of her childhood that she hadn't heard the sound of the truck as it had pulled in or the footsteps of the man behind her. She was glad for her sunglasses to hide the tears that had filled her eyes. As she tried to clear them, she turned around and was startled yet again to see the man from Dune Burger standing there. For a second she worried about being there, but he was smiling, those blue eyes as warm as the midday sun. "It's a good view," he said, walking toward her. He held out his hand in greeting. "I'm Jake Buchanan."

"Faith Summers." She shook his hand, the feel of it as commanding as she imagined it to be, yet gentle, as if he were holding back because she was a woman. He was even more attractive up close, his smile reaching his eyes, making her feel as if she were the only person in the world at that moment. It looked as though he was drinking her up, like he'd been waiting all day just to see her, yet it was clear by the slight distance he'd created between them that he was a perfect gentleman. He made her feel totally at ease and safe.

"Are you all right?" he asked, and she felt a pinch of worry in her chest. Apparently, her sunglasses hadn't hidden as much as she thought they had. His question—the fact that someone else was aware of her pain when no one had ever been there to share it with her before—caused more tears to surface against her will. She sniffled. It was all so complex.

"I have a lot of memories here. Good ones from my childhood. But I'm not a kid anymore, and life changes, doesn't it?" she said, realizing then that her statements probably made no sense to him. She smiled through her tears. They were subsiding now. Talking out loud to someone was helping. It was nice just having someone there to listen. "Sometimes I still feel like I have to prove myself to people. I know I don't, but it still feels that way." She'd never admitted that to anyone, so she didn't know why she just had to Jake. Perhaps it was the fact that he was a neutral party, or that he seemed kind. Maybe it was his understanding eyes—she didn't know, but she felt as if she could talk to him.

"What do you have to prove?"

By his question, it was clear that he was paying attention. This man she'd only just met was listening to her, and she really liked that. "That I'm happy."

"It's funny that you say that. I know exactly how you feel."

How could he know? Had he had someone hurt him like Casey had hurt her? Did he go home alone every night and wonder if he'd made the right choices? "You do?"

"Yeah. I don't need someone to show me how to be happy; I can do it by myself. I'm finally doing that." He smiled.

Faith stood there for a moment, taking in what had just transpired. Here they were—two complete strangers—sharing thoughts that she knew were not the kinds of things that strangers shared. Why? It made her feel that, perhaps, he was a lot like her, and he felt, for whatever reason, able to share things with her in that moment, just like she had. They hadn't said much, but she felt as though they could keep going if she pulled up a chair and settled in, as if they could just bounce thoughts off each other all night.

"I didn't mean to pry," he said. "I just saw you standing up here alone…"

"I'm so sorry," she said, with a jolt of worry, suddenly realizing that she was trespassing. "I didn't think anyone lived here."

"No one does live here." He smiled again, and she felt a flutter at the sight of it. It put her back at ease. It was the way he was looking at her. He certainly had a charming quality about him. She'd already said more to him than she'd said to her own family. "I was just doing some woodwork inside. Would you like to see it?"

"Are you sure it isn't any trouble?" She'd love to go inside, to see how this cottage compared to the old one, but also to pass more time with Jake.

"None at all." Jake unlocked the door and let her enter first. When she did, the smell of new paint and sawdust overwhelmed her. The room was an enormous open space with a vaulted, cedar ceiling, a paddle fan dangling from its center. The white walls were like blank canvases, the only color coming from the floor-to-ceiling windows overlooking the ocean. A few pieces of blue furniture and a cream-colored area rug gave a pop of color against the bare interior. He came in, and she followed him across the highly lacquered hardwoods to the bar that separated the kitchen from the living room. The kitchen cabinets were custom, slats built to hold wine bottles, others for housing plates. They were stained the color of the driftwood siding that she remembered as a kid, and she cleared her throat to keep the emotion from coming back.

"This is beautiful," she said, running her hand along the beveled edge of one of the cabinet doors. She opened it to peer into the empty cabinet and a stab of loss sliced her chest as she remembered that it was this spot that used to house all their board and card games. As a child, it had been a little too high for her, and she'd had to hop up on the counter whenever she needed one. Sometimes the cards would fall as she got them down, scattering along the kitchen floor. Why they hadn't put the games lower, she didn't know, but now, she wished they were still there, that things could still be as simple as they had been then. Faith closed the door and surveyed the cabinets again. They were nothing like the boxy ones that had been in her childhood cottage, but it didn't matter. This place still felt like home.

"Thank you. It's been hard work, but I'm pleased with how it's all turning out." He walked around the bar to join her in the kitchen. "I saw you at Dune Burger, right?" he asked.

"Yes," she said with a smile. She couldn't help but smile at him. He remembered her. She felt so comfortable around him.

"I thought so." He broke eye contact as if he were deciding whether or not to say something, but before she could add anything, he looked up. "I wanted to ask if I could eat with you."

Her smile widened. What an honest admission. She would have been too timid to admit first that she'd wanted him to sit with her. "You did? Then why didn't you ask?"

"I worried you might be in a hurry or something. I didn't want to bother you. You being by yourself made me curious. Are you here on vacation?" he asked.

She wondered what he thought about her. She was eating alone and now wandering around empty cottages all by herself. She must look like a whole heap of fun. "Yes," she answered. "I'm meeting my family, but I'm early. We're celebrating my grandmother's ninetieth birthday."

When she said that, his eyebrows shot up in surprise but then he ironed his expression back out. It was a strange reaction, but the more she thought about it, the more she realized that it did sound odd. Who brings their ninety-year-old grandmother to the beach? What he didn't know was that Nan had the will of an ox, and it had been her idea. She'd been the one who'd pressed everyone, called relentlessly, saying that they'd better come because this was the only time she was going to organize such an event, and, given her age, they'd all feel terrible if they didn't come and she "went to find John." Nan never talked about death. She always described it as finding their grand-father instead. It had always struck Faith as a lovely idea.

Faith had never known her grandfather. He'd died before she was born. Nan had told her stories about him, and she'd seen the black-and-white photos, but she didn't feel like she really knew him. She often wondered about the man that Nan had loved so much.

"Speaking of which, I'd better get going," she said. "Thank you for showing me this. It's beautiful."

"You're welcome," he said, a tiny wrinkle of confusion showing between his eyes.

She wondered what he could be thinking. "It was nice to meet you."

"Likewise." He smiled again, his expression changing. He looked as though he knew something she didn't know. She'd never met this man before but his honesty made her feel as comfortable as coming home after a long trip. She could just feel it. He commanded her at-tention, but in the most wonderful way. She was only concerned with the here and now, just like in a dream. It made pulling away from him to meet her family quite difficult. She wanted to get to know this stranger better, but she knew she had to go. Real life was waiting for her.

But here was her chance to be brave, to take the first step and find out about Jake. To do what she should have done earlier, instead of letting him walk by. She should ask him his opinion for places to get a nice dinner or directions to the real estate office where she was meet-ing her family to get their cottage keys at the very least. She should say something. She could ask him why he'd decided to come to Dune Burger alone. Did he always eat alone? Was he perfectly fine with it like she was?

"Well, I guess I'll be going. Have a great day," she said, turning toward the door. She bit her lip to keep from screaming at herself for not saying more. She knew why she didn't want to remain silent. She was attracted to Jake, and the thought of it scared her to death. She hadn't been interested in anyone since Patrick, and letting someone in could possibly shatter the little world she'd created for herself. A world that she could control, that would never be as painful as what she'd experienced with Casey. While her head told her that one day she would have to give up a little of that control and find a compromise between her work and personal life, she didn't know if she was ready yet because allowing someone in might allow someone to hurt her again. She closed the door behind her without looking back and walked down the stairs to her car.

Chapter Two

Faith should've said something. She should have asked him something—*anything*. Casey would've. It was as if the mere idea of soon being in Casey's presence had sent Faith spiraling back to the person she'd been all those years ago. And she wasn't that person anymore. She was strong, confident. So why hadn't she said something to Jake? In the grand scheme of things, striking up a conversation with a stranger whom she'd never see again wasn't that big of a deal, but the attraction she felt toward him—like the pull of the tide—was something brand new for her. She'd never met anyone before who had made her so curious and interested from the very moment she'd met him.

As Faith pulled onto the bypass, she turned up the volume on her radio and tried to shake the feelings she was having. It was time to refocus. She was about to see her family—her mom, Casey and Scott, and her niece, Isabella, whom she'd only ever been able to see when she was visiting her mother's house before Casey and Scott had moved to Boston. And she was about to see Nan! Faith missed Nan so much. Her grandmother always knew how to reach her. She understood her like no one else could. Life had gotten in the way for quite a while, and Faith hadn't seen her as often as she should have, but she was going to make up for that right now. It was Nan's birthday, and she was going to do whatever she could to make it special for her.

She pulled out the small piece of paper she'd used to jot down the directions to the real estate agency and held it against the steering wheel as she came to a red light. Nan had been insistent that they meet at the agency, get the key to the rental cottage, and arrive at the cottage together. The light turned green and she hit the gas.

In mere minutes, she'd be face-to-face with everyone. She took in a deep breath. It was time to mentally gear up for this. How would she begin a conversation with Casey? She went through the things she'd done recently: She could talk about Teacher of the Year. She was going to make a speech at the beginning of next year to the entire faculty. They could discuss this. Anything to get the focus off the elephant in the room. She could ask about Isabella. She was now five, and would certainly have changed. She couldn't wait to see her.

Faith pulled her car to a stop in front of the real estate agency, the familiar cars of her mother and Casey empty and parked beside each other just across the parking lot. She swallowed, licked her lips, and ran her fingers through her long, dark blond hair one more time to fluff it up. Before she could get up the walk, Casey came out the door, carrying a key in her hand. Faith had replayed this moment over and over in her mind—seeing her sister again, preparing herself for how she'd feel, and here it was. There was no backing down now. It was done. She was about to spend the next two weeks with her sister.

Casey looked up, that perfectly radiant smile spreading across her face. It seemed genuine.

"Hey there!" She waved, the key dangling from her finger. "It's so good to see you!" She shuffled over on her wedge sandals, the delicate straps crossed neatly at her ankles, and threw her arms around

Faith. Their hug was awkward, both of them trying to be as normal as possible, given the circumstances. Isabella was right behind her, looking so much like her mother had at that age. Her niece had gotten Casey's blond hair, her high cheekbones, and her lanky figure. She was beautiful. Casey pulled back to make eye contact. She still looked amazing, her long, tan legs the perfect body type to pull off her cut-off jeans. Casey stepped aside to allow Faith to greet Isabella. Isabella looked up through her lashes, a timid smile on her face.

"You remember your Aunt Faith," Casey said, still smiling. "It's been a while." She looked over at Faith, and that language that only sisters can have flooded her. Casey was telling her how it had been too long, how much she'd missed her, and Faith felt so guilty that she had to work to keep her lips pressed into a cordial expression. She wanted to grab her sister and tell her how sorry she was that she hadn't visited, even though Casey had invited her to Boston several times. She just didn't feel like she could. So much had gone on between them. Casey's actions could be hurtful and selfish, but she was still Faith's sister, and they had a lifetime of other memories that all hit her like a wrecking ball. She realized that she had missed her sister greatly.

Faith was glad to see her mom helping Nan down the steps because she was so overwhelmed by seeing her sister that all those things she'd thought of on the way there had left her now. Her mind was swimming with emotion. She didn't know if she was coming or going. Seeing Casey again and especially Isabella had her confused. She thought she knew what to expect, but now she had new emotions. Nan held on to the railing, holding a handkerchief, the single gold band on her left hand shining in the sunlight. Even after all these years, she still wore that wedding ring.

"Hi, Nan!" Faith nearly shouted, unable to contain herself.

Nan got a firm hold on the railing again, planted her feet on the step, and looked up. "There she is!" she said in her thick, smooth southern accent. "I'd have waited for you in the car—it probably would have been easier on my knees—but it's so damn hot! How's a lady supposed to act ladylike in this heat?" Nan winked at her and dabbed at her forehead with her handkerchief.

Faith laughed despite herself. *Still a firecracker*, she thought. Nan had on a skirt and flats, her legs hidden with thick stockings. No wonder she was hot. Poor thing. She got to the bottom of the steps and Faith rushed up to see her. She embraced her, Nan's flowery scent taking her back to her childhood.

"Hi, Mom," she said, releasing Nan and giving her mom a hug in greeting. Even now, her mother had a youthful appearance, her face milky smooth, as if she'd never spent a minute in the sun, her hair still dark blond like Faith's. She wondered how she was doing, taking care of Nan. Faith knew she'd been struggling a little because Nan refused to give up anything—she still did her own bills, bought her groceries, and cleaned her living area, but it was such a struggle for her now. It was all her mom could do to get Nan to let her take her to the store or help her up and down the stairs.

"So, where is this place, Nan?" Faith asked, unable to stop smiling. Something about being with her grandmother made her so happy. Maybe it was her frank, no-nonsense nature, or the way she didn't seem to care about what people thought. Whatever it was, she loved Nan.

"First surprise." Nan looked around the group, making eye contact with them all. It was just like her to add drama. "The cottage where we're spending two weeks is actually on the old lot!"

That certainly was a surprise. A great one! She'd seen firsthand how gorgeous it was, how much like their old cottage. Excitement bubbled up as she realized that she'd get to spend more time there. She wanted to feel the happiness of her childhood, the closeness with her mother and her sister, and the ease of those times before life had gotten so hard. Nan always just knew how to make Faith happy. Without even trying, she'd given Faith something priceless. She was going to get to spend day after day looking out at the very view she'd had as a child. The view she could still shut her eyes and see as clear as day.

"There's a cottage on that lot?" Martha asked, clearly shocked.

"A brand new one," Nan said, something lurking behind her eyes. Excitement? Was Nan just as happy to have the cottage again as she was? Faith had never thought about Nan's feelings regarding the cottage. Faith had just assumed it wasn't an important part of her life anymore, but, judging by the look on Nan's face, it clearly was. "I arranged for us to be its first guests, the first ones to ever walk the hallways. I can't wait to see that view."

"Isabella," Martha said with the same thrill on her face that she had when they were children and she'd planned something wonderful for them. "You will love this cottage. You know"—her eyes darted over to Faith—"your aunt spent many days building sandcastles there. I'll bet you can build a bigger one than she did!"

Martha had her arm around Isabella just like she'd done with Faith. She would put her arm around Faith and lean in as if she were telling a secret that no one else could know. Sometimes, she'd say nothing in particular—just comment about the weather or what they were having for dinner that night—but it was her unique way of showing affection, and it was nice to see her doing it with Isabella.

At the same time, the obvious ease and love between her mother and her niece, the way the young girl relaxed into her grandmother's frame and took in her every word with such awe, made Faith feel the sting of guilt that she hadn't been around Isabella enough as she was growing up. She didn't have this connection with her niece. For all intents and purposes, she was a stranger to Isabella. Faith had let her issues with Casey get in the way of that bond for too long. She hoped she'd get the chance now to work on that.

"I'll follow you," Martha said, looking up from Isabella and waving at Faith. "You know how to get there, right?"

She nodded. As they got into their cars, Faith hadn't asked, but she'd wondered… Where was Scott? Why wasn't he with Casey? Had he just decided to stay home? Had Casey convinced him that it was a girls' trip, and she'd rather see her family alone?

Once the others were in their cars, Faith made her way onto the bypass, and headed toward the cottage. Jake, the handyman—if that was what he was—had still been building things in there. He'd just finished the cabinets.

Would he still be there? If she'd wanted to think of something interesting to say to him, she'd probably missed her chance with Casey around. Casey would most certainly dominate any conversation. It wasn't her fault. She didn't try to. She was just good at it. Casey was a people person and she could find something interesting to say to anyone. It was a skill that she'd mastered to perfection. Would her sister let her get a word in edgewise with Jake? He was probably gone now anyway.

As Faith drove, Casey stayed on her mind. In high school, Casey had been a cheerleader and had organized the pep rallies on game day. She had planned school dances. She'd run for class president, and, with no experience in leadership at all, she had gotten it. She enjoyed those things and being in the public eye excited her. In contrast, Faith had been on the newspaper staff, where the only interaction at all would come from the small staff when they did layout and the few interviews she had to do with kids around school. It was perfect for her, and she was great at it. The two of them had gone on in very different directions, but it all made sense now, given their personalities. They were both successful, just in different ways. It had taken her a long time to understand this.

She stopped at the stoplight and put on her blinker. The more she thought about this vacation, the more being in close quarters with her sister excited her because maybe they'd have an opportunity to set things straight. They needed time together, forced proximity to finally discuss what had happened so long ago. Faith wasn't mad anymore. It was what it was. Her biggest question now was, why? Why had Casey so blatantly disregarded her sister's feelings? How was she capable of hurting Faith like she had?

When she and Casey had been about eight years old, they'd planned their weddings. They were going to get married on the same day so they could have the biggest cake ever made. Faith wanted a dress with a long train and a veil that covered her face. Casey wanted a tiara and big, puffy dress. They wanted to marry brothers so that they could live next door to each other and never be apart. Now look at them. She hadn't seen her sister in years.

She only realized the radio was on when she pulled into the driveway of the cottage. She'd been thinking about her situation so much she'd not even noticed the music. The sand gritted beneath her tires as she pulled her car up beside the large white work truck, the rest of the family pulling in behind her. Faith was thrilled to see that Jake was still at the cottage, this time on a ladder, nailing wooden shingles to the side of the house. Normally, she'd probably be annoyed that someone was there doing work as she arrived, but not today. She could hardly contain her excitement at seeing Jake again. Would he be around all day? Could she bring him some iced tea and steal a few minutes of his time to talk to him more? Jake climbed down to greet them. He didn't seem surprised to see her, and his expression when she mentioned her Nan's birthday earlier now made sense. He'd already known they were coming.

"You must be Sophia, the renter," he said to Nan, offering her a hand, as she wriggled her way out of the car and stood in front of him. "It's nice to finally meet you." His eyes darted to Faith quickly, a smile surfacing, and then, as quickly as he'd looked at her, he looked away, his attention back on Nan.

Nan tipped her head back to get a look at the cottage, her eyes roaming the entire outside. "It's quite a cottage," she said with an approving smile. "I can't wait to see it."

"I wish I could have finished it before you all came to stay. I still have some work to do."

She shooed the comment away playfully with her hand. "We don't mind. I told that to the real estate office when they said it was currently under construction. I don't want to wait until it's finished. Plus, it'll give me an extra set of strong hands to help me up and down all these stairs you've built. They warned me a hundred times that final touches were still being added, but I wouldn't take no for an answer." She turned slowly until she was facing her family. "The minute I heard this place was livable, I wanted to come. I don't have the luxury of time, so I wanted to get into it as soon as I could—one last beach visit together in our spot. It was good luck that it had been almost completed by my birthday." She looked over her shoulder at Jake. "Do you mind helping me up there?" She raised a knobby finger toward the steps.

"Yes, ma'am." He walked over and offered his arm. Jake certainly was a gentleman.

Faith noticed the ease with which Jake spoke to Nan. He had been chatty at Dune Burger—everyone seemed to know him—and he'd known just the right things to say to Faith when he'd found her on the porch of the cottage. Now, he spoke to Nan as if he'd known her longer than just ten minutes—as if they'd spoken before.

"Did you build this house yourself?" Casey asked Jake as they followed him up the long staircase to the porch overlooking the ocean.

"No," he said, looking back at her while keeping Nan steady step by step. "I didn't build it at all, the construction company did, but I'm doing a few items on the final punch list and some specialty work. I like doing those things. It keeps me busy."

"Sounds like me. I like keeping busy too," Casey said, smiling up in his direction. Faith noticed how effortless it was for Casey to ease into the conversation. It was like turning back the clock: Faith was the quiet one again, walking behind as Casey took the lead. This fact was crawling under her skin uncomfortably as she followed them up the stairs.

They got to the top and Casey pulled Faith aside, motioning for Isabella to follow Martha and Nan into the cottage. Jake helped Nan in. "Let's look at this gorgeous view!" she said. "I've missed it so much!" She grabbed Faith's hand just like she had when they were kids and whisked her over to the same ledge where Faith had been only a little while before. The sailboat was long gone now.

The two women stood in silence, side by side, Casey's long, blond hair blowing in the coastal wind. Casey lifted her hand to hold back her hair, her bangle bracelets clinking together like wind chimes. "Remember when we used to swim through that area right there?" She pointed toward the spot where the waves were breaking, their static sound like music to Faith's ears.

"We'd get past the breaking point—it was so hard, remember that?" Casey looked at Faith, a nostalgic expression on her face. "We'd get knocked around, pushed under. Then, once we got past, it was calm. We'd just bob in the water, the waves swelling under us and then relenting." Her sister looked back out at the ocean, and Faith followed her lead. Faith did remember that. She remembered holding her sister's hand as they walked deeper into the water toward the breaking point, the salty wetness between their fingers as they intertwined. She remembered the burn on her cheeks from the salt, and the relief from the heat as she waded farther in.

"Scott and I are getting a divorce," Casey blurted, her eyes still on the sea. Casey's words took Faith completely by surprise. She turned to look at her sister, only her profile in view. Casey blinked over and over as if she was fighting tears, but if she was, she'd never show it. Faith wanted Casey to turn and look her way. She was speechless. "You're probably happy about it, aren't you?" Casey said quietly.

Faith was floored by this news. She wasn't happy about it at all. She was devastated for so many reasons. Had ruining her relationship with Faith, taking Scott from her own sister, and wrecking Faith's life been for nothing? Scott had been important enough to Casey that she would risk her relationship with her own sister by showing interest in him, knowing that Faith was head over heels for Scott. And now he wasn't even going to be a part of Casey's life?

Years ago, Faith was willing to bet that she'd have had different emotions at this moment—raw, painful, and angry emotions. But now she knew how pointless those feelings were. How they couldn't change the past and what had happened between her and Casey. Back then, she would've felt hopeful that news of Casey and Scott's divorce might mean that Faith could have a chance at happiness again with the man she'd once loved, the man who had broken her heart—her sister's husband.

Scott Robins had been just two years older than Faith. He'd lived next door to her family, and they'd grown up together. Casey, in the same grade at school as Scott, had never shown much interest in him, but Faith loved being with him. They'd spent almost every afternoon together after school, doing homework on the front porch and then staying outside until the sun went down. In the winters, he'd come over to the house, and they'd sit at the kitchen table playing card games and reading. They'd done almost everything together.

So, during the summer just before her seventeenth birthday, when she'd found out she was going to spend the summer at the cottage, Faith had been sad to leave Scott. They were friends—there hadn't ever been any hint of anything more—but Faith knew she'd loved him all her life. And leaving him was hard. While they'd spent time apart in the past, this summer was different because it was the last time she'd see him before he went away to the University of Tennessee. She'd said her goodbyes to him, and they'd even cried that night before she left for the Outer Banks. The fact that Scott, at the young age of nineteen, had cried had impacted her, the significance of it weighing heavily on her as she prepared to go. He didn't want her to leave. It was funny: she'd thought that moment was the end of something when actually it was only the beginning.

After two weeks of missing him and thinking about him every minute that she was at the cottage, they got a knock on the door. Her mom had opened it.

"Good Lord, child! What are you doing here?" she said, hugging the unexpected guest. Scott had driven all the way there just to see Faith. He had no place to stay and he'd been planning to sleep in his car. He didn't care, because, he'd said, he had to see her. He couldn't go away without seeing her again. Scott was like family, so, of course, her mom had ushered him right in and set him up a bed on the sofa.

Faith was so excited to see him that she could hardly breathe. She knew at that point that, without a doubt, she truly loved him. He was her best friend, and she'd missed him so much. The last night before he had to leave, they'd stayed up late to watch a movie after everyone was asleep, eating freshly popped corn and candy. When Faith recalled that memory now it seemed like just yesterday and a thousand years ago at the same time.

"I can't go to Tennessee without telling you this," he'd said, sitting next to her on top of the blankets that her mom had put on the sofa for him. Faith was cross-legged beside him. It felt wonderful to see him again, to be so close to him, and have him with her, even if it was only for a few days. He placed his hands on her face, and she remembered how, in that moment, all the times they'd spent together, all the things they'd done, had a new significance. His long hair feathered across his young forehead as he leaned toward her. "Faith, I love you," he'd said. He kissed her, and she could still remember how his mouth tasted like the watermelon candy they'd been eating. His kiss was eager, his hands moving all over her. And she let him. She kissed him back because she thought, too, how much she loved him.

But Faith still had another two years of high school left, and she knew what would happen. Scott would find new friends, he'd meet other girls, and he'd change. Faith didn't want to be a burden, a weight on his shoulders once he got there and met all the new people he would end up hanging out with. She didn't want him to think back on what they'd had together growing up and have anything but fondness about it. And that night, in a completely selfless act, she'd told him all of that, and he'd left the next morning with a sad look in his eyes.

He didn't come home again until years later, well after graduating. They were in their twenties, and she ran into him at a bar in town when she was out with her girlfriends. She'd thought about him many times over the years, wondered where he was, if he was happy. Faith couldn't even remember whom she'd gone out with that night because she'd spent the whole night talking to Scott. Seeing him again, for her, was like they'd never left each other. He'd given her his number, and she called. After they'd gone out quite a few times, it was clear to her that she still had feelings for him. She couldn't deny them anymore. So, when he invited her to a party, she knew she'd need support. She wanted to tell him that night how she'd always felt, so she'd taken Casey with her. She'd told Casey all about her feelings and explained that it would be Casey's strength that would help her admit how she felt to Scott. She needed her sister.

But Casey hadn't been her support at the party; in fact, Faith had barely seen her or Scott. When they'd arrived, Faith had quickly found Scott and was overcome once more with how she felt about him. But Casey had soon grabbed his attention, and they were chatting and laughing as if they were longtime friends. Casey and Scott had spent that whole night together, and he'd hardly even talked to Faith. Every time he tried, Casey pulled him away, and by the end of the night, Faith had had to catch a ride home without her sister.

After that night, Scott's calls to Faith dwindled. The more he talked to Casey, the more painful it got for Faith until he and Casey were going out almost daily. Days turned into weeks and weeks turned into months, and, before she knew it, she didn't talk to Scott Robins anymore. He was so taken with Casey that he'd moved on. And Casey, too, had allowed it—never sticking up once for her sister, never asking him about it. Casey, who'd always outshone her in childhood, who'd always seemed to be one step ahead of her, one beat in front of her, had done it again.

She could remember the painful moment she'd confronted Casey as clear as if it were happening right in front of her now. "How could you be so cruel, Casey?" she'd said, years of inadequacy boiling in her blood. "I confided in you! I trusted you! And what did you do? You threw yourself at Scott! You don't know how to be a sister. You don't know how to love someone."

"I do know how to love someone! That's just it! I love him! You can't help who you fall in love—"

"Enough! I don't want to hear it," Faith had said, not letting Casey explain herself. "I don't want to hear any more of it. You don't care a thing about me." She'd gotten in her car that day and driven away, tears streaming down her face. The sisterly love between them was clearly one-sided.

She and her sister hadn't spoken very much since, and Faith had never really gotten over her sister's betrayal. Her mother and Nan had tried to get them together to discuss it, but their efforts were in vain. Faith didn't want to talk about a thing. There was nothing that could help in this situation. Casey and Scott had gotten engaged and then married. Against her will, but for her nan, she'd agreed to be in the wedding. Dressed in royal blue satin, and holding a bouquet of daisies, Faith had watched Scott Robins promise to love her sister forever. After the wedding, Faith avoided her sister and Scott whenever possible. When she heard of her sister's pregnancy she couldn't help the jealousy that stirred in her, bringing back the thoughts she'd had of having her own children. Shortly after Isabella's birth, the family had moved to Boston and Faith hadn't tried to repair the distance that had come between them.

Five years later, her feelings for Scott were long gone now, and hearing this news about the divorce only made Faith sad. Sad that Casey had put them into this situation in the first place only to have the whole thing fall apart, sad for the time they'd lost, and sad that Isabella would be caught in the split. Faith didn't know what to say.

"I can't stand it when you don't talk," Casey said, her words slightly broken. "You hate me, don't you? I've ruined everything."

"I don't hate you," Faith said, the words coming out almost reluctantly. It wasn't what she wanted to say, but it was all she could get out. She shook her head at Casey, who somehow expected Faith to make her feel better, despite the fact that their relationship had been completely shattered.

"Then how do you feel towards me?"

"Sad. You risked a lot for that marriage—things you can never get back—and now it's over."

"Things happen, Faith. They just do. Why does it always have to be my fault?"

After everything Casey had put her sister through, did she now want sympathy? It was just too hard to give her that, given what they'd been through. Couldn't she, for one second, think about how Faith might be feeling? No, Casey would never change. But Faith *was* different now, and she wanted things to be better with Casey. She didn't want to hold on to the hurt she felt. Instead of trying to discuss it further, Faith reached over and put her hand on her sister's.

Chapter Three

"What caused this?" Faith asked. Casey and Scott had seemed so happy together. What could've pulled them apart? Since having Isabella they'd always seemed like the perfect family—so happy together. She'd never even heard that they'd argued about anything.

"It was Scott's decision, not mine."

Knowing Scott, Faith couldn't imagine anything ruffling his feathers; he was always so agreeable. Casey was strong-willed and opinionated and she needed someone like Scott to even her out. They were the perfect little family: two loving parents and their adorable little girl.

Faith's mind went back to the day at the hospital when she had gone to see Isabella just after she was born. The excitement at seeing her niece was almost more than she could bear. She couldn't wait to hold this teeny tiny baby in her arms, smell her powdery scent, and feel the grip of the baby's fingers on her hand. She'd raced straight there as soon as her mother had called, because she couldn't wait to see this amazing little baby, even though it meant seeing Scott and Casey. What would she look like? Did she have Scott's eyes? Faith had always loved his eyes.

When she opened the hospital door, her breath caught just for a second. Scott was lying next to Casey, his arms around her, looking down adoringly at her, baby Isabella in Casey's arms. For a moment she felt that same old lurch, recognizing that the way Scott watched his wife was the way he had once looked at her with that same love and emotion. Scott's eyes were wiser than they'd been when he'd looked at her so adoringly all those years ago. His hair was shorter, his face aged a little more—that smooth, soft face that she'd known so well now showing the stubble from a long day. His hand was stroking Isabella's head, and his fingers looked so calm, so careful—nothing like the hands that had moved about her body so frantically that night in the cottage. He wasn't a boy anymore. In that moment, Faith realized that the boy she'd known had grown into a man, and that man was Casey's, not hers. She remembered looking from face to face, and the love that she saw there in that moment was nearly paralyzing. Everything she wanted—a devoted husband, a family of her own— was right there before her, and it wasn't hers to have. She had to be strong. This wasn't about her. It was about baby Isabella.

After she'd seen Isabella, held her, given her auntie-kisses, and congratulated Casey and Scott, she'd spent the rest of the night in her apartment. It was the loneliest she'd ever been. That whole night, all she could see when she closed her eyes was Scott and Casey—the happiness on their faces. It had been like a double-edged sword: she'd felt terribly guilty at the thought of wishing they hadn't been that happy, and she felt angry that her sister, who was capable of being so selfish, could have that kind of happiness at Faith's expense. But then she thought about little Isabella. Isabella deserved to have a family who loved each other.

Faith had grown a lot since those days. She no longer carried around any feelings for Scott—she knew he was good for her sister. What lingered still, however, was the pain of disloyalty. Family had always been the most important thing in Faith's life. They were the people who, no matter what, should be by her side. They knew her failures and her strengths, and they should love her unconditionally. So, when Casey had betrayed Faith's trust, it had knocked her sideways. She'd tried to rationalize that at least it had ended in something meaningful. And it had. Casey had created a family, and Faith could see the importance of this. It had helped soften the blow a little. But now, Casey was getting divorced, and she seemed resigned to the fact that the divorce was imminent. That bothered Faith. It made her angry with Casey all over again despite her attempts to feel sorry for her.

Casey finally turned and looked at her sister, her eyes glassy with emotion. "He says he doesn't feel like he knows me anymore." Faith had never heard Casey's voice like this. It was mild, unsure, nothing like the confident, strong voice she'd always had.

"Why?" She could feel her face crumpling with this news. It made no sense.

"I've been pulling long nights at the firm. Scott works all the time too. When I do have free time, I spend it with Isabella. She needs me. He's a grown man; he can take care of himself. I can't keep him entertained. I don't have time."

How had things turned out like this? Everything had seemed so perfect. Where had it gone wrong? Just then, her sister had sounded scared. Faith could tell.

"How's Isabella handling it?" Faith asked.

Casey took in a long, steadying breath. "He moved out. It's been just the two of us. She misses him. She cries at night. She says I don't read her stories the right way. She asks for him."

Faith bit her lip, trying to make sense of it all. "I'll help you through this," she said. Even after everything, this was still her big sister and she didn't want to see her hurting. It was strange to find herself in this position, but seeing her sister so scared and lost, she knew she'd do whatever she could to make things better.

"Thank you. You're the one person I need in all this."

"Hey, y'all," Martha said, poking her head out the door. "I've got some strawberry margaritas mixed up. I'm thinking frozen. Want me to get the blender going?" Before they could answer, she beckoned them in as she said, "Jake, you're welcome to one yourself before you leave. We won't tell if you're drinking on the job."

Only their mom would invite the handyman she'd just met to have a drink with the family.

"She brought a blender?" Faith said to Casey, unable to control her grin.

"I guess so. You know how she packs. We'd better get in there and have a drink since she's gone to all that trouble. I want to catch her anyway before she adds the alcohol. Isabella might want one."

"Where is Isabella?"

"She's probably with Nan. She loves that woman. Every time we see her, I can't pry Isabella away from her."

The idea of another person understanding Nan like she did filled Faith with happiness. Isabella wasn't a baby anymore. She was a little girl with her own fears and needs. Why hadn't Faith been able to get over herself and be a bigger part of this little girl's life?

She'd thought she could carry on with life and make it just fine without seeing her sister, but that had stolen time away from Isabella as well. Life had moved along regardless of whether she saw Casey, and, although it had never felt comfortable, she'd been able to move along with it. Faith decided that there was no better place to get to know this little girl than this cottage at the beach. It had been her safe haven, the place that had contributed a stockpile of good memories, where nothing could go wrong. And she wanted everything to be right.

Casey walked up beside her. "What do you make of that guy, Jake? I've never seen a handyman with a haircut that perfect. He could be in magazines," Casey pointed out in a whisper as they crossed the porch to the door.

Faith shrugged, befuddled by Jake herself. She thought she'd seen the last of Jake earlier on, but her nan, or fate, had seen to it that wasn't the case. And she couldn't help feeling excited by it. She wasn't about to admit to Casey what she thought about Jake. She was having trouble defining it herself. He had the kind of personality that could pull a person right in, and he had. She was so glad to have the opportunity to go back inside, leave the struggles with her sister behind, and spend some time with him. Being with him eased her away from the burdens of her issues with Casey. She'd only just met him, yet he made her feel happy.

"Right. Time for margaritas!"

Faith balanced the remains of her margarita on the uneven step outside. She'd been keeping Isabella busy most of the time that Jake had been there, and she was glad to finally be outside with him. She hadn't even had a chance to talk to him, so when he excused himself to load the truck once his drink was empty, she followed him out.

"Be careful on this pavement," Jake said, throwing a roll of flooring into the back of his truck. He clapped his hands to rid them of sand. "I haven't swept up yet, and there could be nails. You've got bare feet," he pointed out.

She held on to the railing and pivoted under the stairs to retrieve a pair of flip-flops that she had left at the bottom for her walks to the beach. With a grin, she held them up before slipping them on. Jake was still loading bits and pieces of construction materials into the back of his truck. She picked up an armful of wood—thin slats like the ones on the porch—and began walking them over to the truck. Jake quickly took them from her as if she were holding a mass of bricks. She wondered if he was just being mannerly or if he thought she wasn't capable of holding them.

After looking around for something else to help load and finding nothing that she could manage, she opened the latch door to the small closet under the house and retrieved the broom. It was wide-bristled with a very long handle, and she remembered how they always used to have one to push the water off the pavement after big storms. And even if the water retreated, it would still fill the concrete pavement underneath with sand and debris. She pushed the broom across the surface, looking for nails and any other materials that could be dangerous as she walked. Jake's concern was kind, but it was clear that he had been extra cautious, as there wasn't a thing on the pavement. She finished sweeping and leaned the broom against one of the stilts as he walked up beside her.

"Do you think your family likes the cottage?" he asked.

She nodded. "It's perfect in every way. I love everything about it and couldn't have asked for a better place to spend two weeks."

He smiled. "I'm glad you like it."

She was so glad Nan had made them all come. "This is one of those places that I didn't realize I loved so much until I came back. We haven't been to the Outer Banks since I was a teenager. It has been a while…" She turned toward the wind, allowing it to push against her face, and, like an old friend, it wrapped around her, embracing her as if to say it had been too long.

The slower pace, the simplicity—it was as if she'd needed it to recharge her batteries, and until that moment, she hadn't realized they were so low.

"I remember being here as a boy," he said, and she turned to face him. "There was a time when all I wanted was something else, something different than what I was used to. But then, after I left, I realized that what I really wanted was right here, and I could fill in the gaps in my life myself as long as I was here."

Faith could understand what he meant completely.

"You and your sister seemed pretty caught up earlier. Everything okay?"

Had he seen them talking? Had he watched Casey cry? At the time, the only thing Faith had focused on was Casey. She hadn't given a single thought to who may be watching them from inside. How would she explain to Jake all that had gone on between her and Casey? She took in a deep breath as she tried to find something to say. But he'd already figured it out.

"From the look on your face, things aren't okay."

Once again, they'd managed to slide into unfamiliar territory. How was she supposed to discuss something this serious with him? He didn't know her at all. Yet there was something in his face that showed his concern for her—his head turned to the side as he waited, his brows creased. It seemed genuine, sympathetic, and she was taken aback by the fact that this man could show such worry for a person he'd only just met. The funny thing was, she wanted to tell him. But she was standing outside where anyone could overhear.

"It's complicated," she said finally.

He nodded. "Yeah. I could tell."

"It's okay, though," she lied, trying to find a graceful way to move the conversation forward. She really wanted to sit down in the rocking chairs on the porch and pour her heart out to him. There was something about him that made her feel like she could tell him things, and he seemed to really want to know. He didn't know when he'd asked if she was okay what he was really asking, and she didn't want to weigh him down with a conversation like that. Not here. Not now.

He seemed to read her mind, nodding again as if he'd heard her internal battle. "You don't need to tell me, and I don't want to pry, as long as you're okay. I should probably get going."

She didn't want him to go. She knew he wasn't going to stay all night; that would be imposing. But she wished she could have a little more time to talk. She walked with him to the driver's side of his truck.

As he got in, Faith said, "I'll see you later," hoping that would be true.

He leaned on the open window with his forearms. "You will?" he said with a smile, his eyebrows raised in anticipation. "I hope so."

She laughed, her stomach a mess of nerves. She'd never felt such a rush of excitement over someone before. She took a step back and he started the engine. As he backed out of the drive, he raised his hand to wave. She turned around and headed toward the house, unable to wipe the smile off her face.

"Nan!" Faith said with a gasp as she walked out onto the porch. "Are you drinking a margarita?"

Nan was sitting on one of two rocking chairs, the pink, frozen drink looking out of place in her withered hands. She'd been wondering where Nan had gone for the last half hour. They'd started a card game inside to keep Isabella busy, and Faith had had a hard time breaking away. She'd been thankful for the card game. It took away the pressure on her and Casey, and it managed to lift the earlier mood. It was also fun to see her niece as she smiled, the way her lips pressed together, her eyes showing surprise every time she had a good hand. But if Faith had known her grandmother was outside, she'd have tried to join her a little sooner.

"Is there an age requirement or something?" Nan asked just before she lifted the glass to her lips and took a long, slow sip. "I asked your mother to make me one, although it's so cold, it's freezing me down to the bone. That's why I'd come out here in the first place. The new air conditioner is certainly working well."

Faith pulled the other rocking chair over and sat down next to her nan. She looked past the new-window sticker into the house. Casey, her mom, and Isabella were laughing at something, cards spread across the table.

"Did the carpenter leave?" Nan asked.

"Yes. He only stayed for one drink."

"Mm." She looked down at her margarita, swirling the melting ice around in the glass. "I was hoping to catch him. I have some ideas about improvements. Wouldn't a built-in shelf look just perfect over by the sofa on that wall?" She glanced in through the window. "He could add some cabinets…"

It was good for Jake that he'd left when he had. Faith was sure he didn't need a ninety-year-old renter telling him what improvements to make. It wasn't hers to change, and that fact settled heavy in Faith's chest. She had to keep reminding herself that it wasn't their cottage.

Nan was never worried about offering her opinion. The good thing about that was that one never had to guess what she was thinking. She'd be more than happy to let everyone know—good or bad. She'd made sure to tell Faith what she thought about her attending college so far away, and she'd let them know when she thought they were being obtuse about the whole Scott issue. Nan didn't approve of Casey's behavior—she'd told them both that—but she was determined not to let anything come between the sisters. She'd demanded that Faith come to visit them when Casey had been in town staying with her mother. She looked to find ways to get Faith to drop in, but Faith had conveniently made excuses until the day Casey left to go back to Boston.

"Faith," she'd said afterward, that day, "you have to let it go." It had been easier said than done back then. All her life, Casey had been the center of attention, always getting what she wanted, and Faith had sat in her shadow. Faith hadn't wanted to be around her sister, but as their separation increased, she realized how much she missed Casey. She could see now just how right her grandmother had been. If only she'd listened and tried sooner. Well, she was going to try now.

"You know, your grandfather didn't like me to drink alcohol. He said it wasn't ladylike."

"And what did *you* think?"

"I told him that a lady is a lady whether she's having a drink or not, and how she handles herself is an expression of the type of person she is."

"What did he say to that?"

"He smiled and shook his head at me. He knew I was right." She winked at Faith. "But I still never had a drink in front of him."

"Why?"

"Respect. I loved him. He didn't like to see me having a drink, clearly. So, I didn't bother. I respected his wishes."

"Why are you having one now?" She knew her grandmother's loyalty to her grandfather, so she was quite curious to hear the answer.

"I figured I'd better, if I want one, because in no time at all I'll be looking for John, and, once I find him, I won't be thinking about this drink anymore." She offered a devious smile.

Faith laughed. She longed to have someone in her life that she loved that much. The type of love Nan had for her grandfather seemed unattainable. Faith had had relationships in the past, but she just didn't feel like she'd loved anyone like Nan had loved her husband. Scott had been the first of the relationships she'd had that had actually meant something to her, but it was nothing like what Nan seemed to have had. At the time, she'd thought she loved Scott in this way, but once she met Patrick, she realized she'd been wrong. Patrick had been kind and considerate, and Faith had cared for him, but she hadn't wanted to give up her career for him. She'd been heartbroken when their relationship had ended, but now, looking back, she realized that she'd often had to work hard just to make things run smoothly between them. Had Nan had these types of problems with John? If she had, she'd never mentioned them. It made Faith wonder if, perhaps, the problem wasn't finding the time, it was finding the right person. Maybe one day she'd find someone who would make her so crazy in love that she wouldn't think about anything else.

"I'm glad I did this," Nan said, rocking a little in her chair. Faith watched Nan's eyes as she followed a seagull through the sky. It looked black against the orange sunlight. For the first time, Faith thought about how her grandmother must have felt losing the cottage. It had been a big part of her life too. What memories did she have of her visits? Had she been there with Faith's grandfather? The drive had been tough on her—she'd said so. Her legs and ankles were swollen from sitting so long in the car. She could barely make it up all the stairs once she arrived. Faith was sure she was sore and tired just from the journey. But she'd wanted to come. She'd planned it. And now she sat, drinking a margarita, on the same plot of land she'd run on as a kid. Originally, Faith didn't understand why Nan had put herself through it at ninety years old. But now she did. This might be the last time Nan got to visit this place. A sinking feeling hit Faith in the gut as she thought about life without Nan. She didn't even want to contemplate that, but there was no escaping the fact that she wouldn't be around forever. Suddenly, all the drama with Casey seemed a little silly when faced with that.

"I'm glad you did this too," she said as she put her hand on top of Nan's.

Her mom poked her head out the door. "Y'all seen Casey? Is she out here?"

They both shook their heads.

"Maybe she went out to the car or something. There's no telling. Anyone want more drinks or are we finished for the night?"

"I'm finished, thank you," Faith said. "Nan?" She looked over at her grandmother, chewing on a smile. She had such a young spirit. It was easy to forget that she was ninety, but being with her now, Faith could see some differences in Nan. She was slower, more hesitant. At heart, though, she was the same fiery woman. It was so good to be with her again.

"I've got enough right here," she said.

When her mom went back inside, Faith noticed Casey down on the beach. "Mind if I leave you now?" she asked, nodding toward her sister. Nan followed her gaze, thoughts clearly behind her eyes. She nodded with a pleasant smile.

"But before you go," Nan said as she stood up. Faith stopped and turned toward her. "I don't know what's bothering Casey—she hasn't told me—but you two need to talk it out. Life's too short to tuck important conversations in your pocket for later. You just never know. I had an argument with my sister, Clara. You never met her. We didn't straighten things out, and now it's too late."

Faith started to sit back down, ready to hear about this mystery sister of Nan's, but Nan stopped her. "No, no," she said, waving her hand. "Don't bother with me and my old stories. Go check on Casey. It looks like she may need someone to talk to."

Perhaps it was a story for another time. Faith walked around the corner and headed down the steps. At the bottom, she kicked her flip-flops off and put her toes in the warm sand. It was soft—like powder—under her feet. She padded along the narrow path, through the sea grass, over the dune leading to the beach. It was late afternoon, and the sand, having absorbed the day's heat, burned her feet a little as she made her way across the vast shoreline to reach Casey. Her sister was at the water's edge, barefoot, standing in the waves as the foam crawled across the sand before sliding back out to sea. The wind blew Faith's hair into her face, her T-shirt rippling under its force. She pushed her hair back and held it at the base of her neck as she stepped up next to her sister.

"Whatcha doin'?" she asked Casey the same way she had as a girl. Faith drew a line in the sand with her brightly painted toes and watched it disappear as the tide erased it.

"Just thinking. Trying to clear my head."

The waves were rough, pushing gritty sand around Faith's feet, and she had to move them around to keep them from getting buried. As a child, the waves had scared Faith when they were this big. She'd worried they were giant, gray creatures rolling on their sides. Each one slammed the shore in an eruption of white, bubbly foam then fanned out along the ground like spilled milk. Faith took in a big gulp of the salty air. The smell of it took her right back to her childhood. So many memories were colliding in her mind that she had trouble sorting out which one to let float to her consciousness. Roasting marshmallows, her mom squirting chocolate sauce on them just to make the girls giggle; eating sandwiches with wet, sandy hands; a rainbow of brightly colored beach towels on the line outside; shopping at the local kite store for the perfect kite and flying it—just the three of them at Jockey's Ridge—the wind so strong, Faith could hardly hold on to it...

"I'm glad I came," Casey said, pulling her back to reality. "I wasn't going to."

Faith turned to her sister, waiting for further explanation. She herself had been worried about coming, self-conscious about her decision to stay away from her sister for all of that time, but it had never occurred to her that Casey may be anxious about coming too. For the first time, she realized that perhaps seeing Faith again wasn't easy for Casey either.

It was clear to Faith by Casey's silence over the years that she didn't feel what she'd done was so awful—she had tried to explain it to Faith a few times—but Faith had always cut her short, not wanting to hear Casey's side of things. How could what Casey had done ever be right? But now, as she looked at her sister, the age lines starting to show around her eyes, she realized that she'd been too stubborn. She should have at least heard her sister out. What would Casey have said? Would she have asked for forgiveness? Would she have told her she wanted her sister back? Perhaps she should have talked to her instead of holding on to old grudges.

"Why weren't you going to come?" she asked. Faith was ready to hear her side of things now.

"I didn't want my situation to bring everyone down. This is Nan's time. It's her birthday. I want her to be happy. I told Mom and Nan that Scott was working when I arrived without him. It's the truth. Well, half-truth. I didn't know if it was the right time to tell them…"

How silly of Faith to think that Casey had been worried about seeing her again. Faith acknowledged that Casey's impending divorce from Scott was awful, and it might upset Mom and Nan, but what about the fact that she and Casey hadn't spoken in years? What about that? Faith let out a huff of indignation loud enough to make Casey turn her head.

"What was that for?" Casey said, a twinge of panic on her face. Were Faith's feelings not even in the forefront of her mind? Faith could feel the ache in her throat, the unsaid feelings still right there on the tip of her tongue, but she took in a breath and turned to face the wind.

"What's wrong with you?" Casey said, her words coming out urgently as if she were preparing for a blow, for some sort of confrontation. She knew just as well what was wrong, but she wasn't going to say it, was she?

Well, Faith wasn't staying quiet anymore. She could feel the anger from Casey's selfishness swelling in her chest, and it had to come out. "Weren't you worried at all about dealing with this?" She wagged her finger between them, noticing the tremble in her hands from built-up anger. She wasn't trying to play down the divorce—that was a big deal—but this was a big deal too. Even with their differences, Casey had been Faith's best friend growing up, the one person she knew better than anyone else. And Casey had just let her walk away.

"Of course I was. I just didn't want to bring up old wounds. I just want to move past it," she said, her words coming out controlled and even, like they would in a courtroom. There was a moment as Casey looked at her when her strong expression faltered. Without warning, tears surfaced in her eyes, but she blinked to clear them and then they were gone.

With all her childhood memories at this beach right on the surface, it occurred to Faith that the reason this was such a lovely place was because they'd had *fun* here. That's why she and Casey had been so close. No matter what had happened in the past, Casey needed her now. She'd have to be the bigger person here. Faith hadn't let Casey explain herself because she didn't want to hear Casey's lame excuse for hurting her. She didn't want an excuse then, and she didn't want one now. She simply wanted an apology, an acknowledgment that Casey had hurt her. And if she ever wanted to hear that, she couldn't put Casey in a position where she felt defensive. The only way to feel close again was to try to enjoy themselves.

"I haven't ever let you explain, and I'm sorry. So I have an idea," Faith said, turning the conversation in a totally different direction. It was time for her to take charge for once. She'd never done it before with Casey, but she'd learned to be strong. She knew she could. She'd always followed Casey's lead, but right now, it seemed like, even though Faith had her own trust issues to deal with regarding Casey, they were in the past. Casey was losing a husband and the father of her daughter. "We're on vacation. For two weeks. Let's *act* like we're on vacation. Leave all the baggage behind—the past, work, Scott. I will if you will."

"I don't know if I can."

"Why? Look at this place. It's amazing! It's just like what we had as children. Let's give that to Isabella. Let's take it back for ourselves. We'll deal with the rest in two weeks." She stood still and looked at her sister.

Casey's face showed contemplation. Then, a small smile emerged. "You're right," she said, nodding. Despite her agreement, she was clearly still thinking it over. But, one thing Faith knew about her sister was that when faced with the half-empty, half-full conundrum, Casey always chose half full. "Okay!" She laughed then, and unexpectedly, her laughter sent prickles of excitement up Faith's arms. She hadn't heard Casey's laugh in so many years. It took until that moment to realize how much she'd missed it.

Chapter Four

Tap, tap, tap.

The hum of the paddle fan floated into Faith's consciousness.

Tap, tap, tap.

Was there something wrong with the fan? The tapping came and went, but each time, it was the same—three taps and then silence. Faith rubbed her face to get enough focus to look at the clock. She blinked to try and see the numbers.

Tap, tap, tap.

Nine in the morning! She hadn't slept that long in ages. She threw the covers off her legs, her silky shorts and camisole cool against her skin, and walked over to the window. She pulled back the sheer, gauzy fabric, the only barrier between her and the sun. Before she could focus on the view, she jumped with fright.

"Oh!" she cried, dropping the curtain and covering her mouth. She stood there for a moment, collecting herself.

Tap, tap, tap.

This time, the taps were right on the window. She swallowed, blinked her eyes again to clear them, and ran her fingers through her untamed hair. Self-conscious of her attire, or lack of it, she debated on whether to change quickly, but he'd already seen her. She adjusted her top, tugging it down at the back to make the neckline dip a little less. Slowly, she pulled back the curtain again. Jake was on a ladder, right outside her window, a hammer in his hand. With his free hand, he motioned for her to open the window.

The lock slid back under her fingers and she lifted the pane of glass upward, heat coming at her like an open oven door.

"Mornin'," he said, clearly trying to keep his eyes on her face. She could see the flicker of his gaze as it moved downward, but his manners prevented it from lingering. She squared her shoulders slightly, trying not to think about the fact that it was too hot to grab a blanket and wrap herself up. It was too late for that anyway.

"Good morning."

"I'm so sorry if I woke you. I'm just reinforcing a few loose shingles that I'd missed. I had to get started before it got too hot, but I didn't realize anyone was in there." His gaze flickered again, and he looked at the wooden tiles covering the outside of the house. "When the guys put them up, they do so many so quickly, they aren't as thorough as they should be. I found a few loose ones, so I'm just checking around the door frames and windows." He looked back at her. His eyes were on her face like he was searching for something. Then he smiled. It was a wide, gorgeous smile that was so friendly it felt like she'd known him for years. Without warning, a current buzzed through her as she pictured what that smile would look like in a different setting. Would he smile like that if she sat down next to him in the sand? Or across the table at dinner? Or late at night on the sofa as they talked?

"You okay?" he asked.

She'd been thinking about him, and he'd noticed! The swell of heat in her cheeks was something she'd not felt in a long time. Standing in front of him, wearing next to nothing, and knowing how he made her feel was making her nervous! She took in a discreet breath to steady her pounding heart, but it didn't help. She felt embarrassed, worried that he could read her mind. "I'm fine," she said and cleared her throat.

The corners of his mouth were twitching to hide his grin, and his eyes were trying to tell her something, but, clearly, she wasn't as good at reading people as he was. "What are you up to today? Any big plans?"

"No," she said, still feeling uncomfortable about her attire, but what could she do about it now? She crossed her arms. "The only thing we have planned at all while we are here is a birthday party for my grandmother, but that's not until the end of next week." She took a baby-step backward, trying to be subtle about it. She hadn't brushed her teeth or put on any makeup. Why was she so worried about it? She'd never cared in the slightest what people thought of her, but she'd never had anyone affect her like this either. There was something in Jake's face that caused an undeniable attraction toward him.

"Maybe we could…"

There was a quiet knock at the door and then a creak as Casey poked her head in. "I thought I heard talking," she said, immediately locating Jake at the window. "Mom's made a big breakfast." She looked Faith up and down, trying to hide her astonishment.

I know! Faith wanted to shout at her. *I'm wearing next to nothing, but he caught me like this, and now I'm stuck. Save me!* She pleaded for a way out with her eyes.

"Faith," Casey said, rearranging her smile into a straight position. "I'll keep the food warm if you'd like to go get ready for the day."

Faith could feel the pressure lift off her shoulders. She smiled at Jake as she leaned forward carefully to close the window. "Maybe we could what?" she asked, but Casey was still standing in the doorway.

"I'd like to see you," he said quietly, clearly trying to keep their conversation between them only.

"Faith," Casey called again, obviously trying to save her.

She turned back to Jake. "Okay."

As she slid the window down, Casey called out, "Feel free to join us, Jake! There's plenty of food!" And just like that, Faith wasn't very hungry anymore. Butterflies had filled her stomach instead.

"Why don't you join us?" Casey pressed as her mom stood behind her with a basket of biscuits. It was Nan's recipe—big, buttery, flaky southern rolls, which took a lot of preparation. Faith loved the way they melted in her mouth. She could smell their warm buttermilk scent from her spot at the table. She tried to focus on that rather than the fact that Casey was being relentless about inviting Jake to eat. Okay, maybe not *relentless*, but she was asking him quite a bit, poking her head outside more than once. Regardless of the fact that he was working. He'd probably lose his job if he were found sitting at their breakfast table.

Isabella slid awkwardly onto a chair and scooted to the back of it, leaving an enormous amount of space between her and the table. She tried unsuccessfully to scoot up, and Faith could see the worry on her face as she struggled. That worry looked like more than just not getting her chair into place. She was five, an age where she could understand a lot about what was going on in her life. She was aware, certainly, that her daddy wasn't present. Had anyone asked her how she felt about it all? Had anyone sat down with her and tried to explain what was happening, to ease her fears?

Isabella kept jerking, her little blond ponytail swinging around toward her face, frustration building.

Faith got up and whispered, "Want me to push you up?"

With a serious expression, her thin lips set in a pout, her long eyelashes blinking, Isabella nodded. Faith pushed the chair under the table and then gave her shoulders an affectionate squeeze. While Casey was a wonderful mother, so full of life and love for her daughter, she wasn't the most affectionate person in the world, and Faith felt like Isabella might need a little more right now. She gave her a pat on the arm and returned to her seat across the table.

"Do have some breakfast, Jake," Nan said, wobbling over to a chair at the table and lowering herself slowly as he came inside. Her mom set the biscuits on to the table. "You're too thin."

Faith bit her lip to keep her surprise from showing. Nan didn't need to offer such a personal observation. Jake wasn't thin. He was fit. Perfectly fit—Faith had noticed through his T-shirt when he'd raised his arms to secure a shingle, even though she hadn't wanted to admit to herself that she'd looked. She'd wondered against her will whether he worked out, or if his job was just demanding on his body. Now, he stood in the open space between the kitchen and living area just as he had when it had been the two of them, before her family had come. Again, she wondered what it would be like to be alone with him. It was a ridiculous thought. Why was she sitting there thinking about what they would do if they were alone? She realized her knee was bouncing under the table, and she stilled it.

"Thank you for your hospitality," he said, pulling out a chair and sitting down next to Faith.

"We're doing you a favor!" her mom said, bringing in an egg and sausage casserole. She tossed a potholder onto the table and set the steaming dish on top of it. "My cooking's better than anything you can get at one of these restaurants around here." She winked at him. "Y'all want some juice? I've got coffee too."

"I'll have juice please," Faith said first, afraid if she had caffeine it would make her too jumpy. She was already so happy to have Jake at breakfast that she had to force herself to breathe. Her mom glanced silently at each person, her eyebrows raised, a smile on her face as she waited for their requests. Nothing made her mother happier than looking after her family and guests. Casey, of course, got coffee—Jake didn't rattle her in the slightest. As Faith sat there submerged in her own thoughts, she wondered if her anxiety was not down to Jake being here, but actually because Casey was there, and she worried that Casey would be more interesting than she would. She hadn't had that kind of thought in ages, but it was still there lurking. She didn't want to admit to herself that her old feelings around Casey had surfaced. Nan followed Casey's lead, requesting coffee, but Jake asked for juice.

"Two coffees and two juices. That's easy to remember," her mom said. "Faith, do you mind coming into the kitchen and grabbing the potatoes? Y'all get your plates from the center of the table and dish 'em up. I'll be right back with the drinks."

Faith got up and went into the kitchen for the potatoes, glad to have something to busy her. She returned quickly with the bowl and sat back down. By the time they'd filled their plates, her mom had already returned with everyone's drinks and had taken her seat on the other side of Jake.

"Let's say grace, please," her mother said.

To be honest, Faith hadn't planned on saying grace. She hadn't done it since she was a child. Nan grabbed her hand, and she realized that the others at the table were taking hands as well. They always had, and it had never bothered her before. But then, she'd never had to sit next to Jake Buchanan before. She looked to her right, and Jake was waiting, palm up. Would her hands be too hot? Sweaty? Twitchy? She reached over and placed her hand in his. His fingers swallowed her hand, but they were gentle, still—a perfect fit. Any jitters she had before were calmed instantly when she put her hand in his. It was as if his composure had slid right along his arm into her.

Faith didn't focus on the prayer—she barely heard a word of it. She was consumed with the feeling of Jake's hand in hers. She tried to remember if she'd held hands with anyone she'd dated before. Surely she had, but she couldn't remember the feeling. Something as simple as holding someone's hand was so inconsequential, yet this time, it had made an impression on her. Just like his smile, his grip on her hand was warm, sweet, comfortable. She almost forgot to let go. When she looked up, everyone else had dropped hands. She quickly released Jake's hand and looked down at her egg and sausage casserole. Out of the corner of her eye, she could see that he'd turned to look at her, but then he looked away.

"So, Jake," Casey said. Faith was glad for the chance to sit back and allow her sister to do all the talking. "Do you enjoy the beach as much as the tourists, or do you get tired of it?"

Jake nodded, finishing his bite of food. "Oh, I still enjoy it," he answered once he'd swallowed. He took a sip of juice before he continued. "I could never get tired of the beach." He flashed his smile at Casey, and Faith wondered if she, too, found him attractive.

"We haven't been here since we were kids. What would you suggest for fun in the area?" Casey asked. She wasn't doing anything outwardly flirty, but Faith wondered by her smile, the way she tilted her head, the curiosity in her eyes, if she wanted to find a reason to talk to him just like Faith did. Needing to switch her focus to something else, Faith let her gaze roam to Isabella, who was sitting quietly, picking at her food with her fork.

Isabella looked so much like Casey, yet she seemed nothing like her so far. When they'd sat at the dinner table together as kids, Casey would talk incessantly, her thoughts going in so many directions that Faith would wait silently until dinner was over and Casey had run off to her room, then she would curl up with her mother on the sofa and tell her about her day. Isabella seemed quiet like that. The trouble was, Faith knew that being quiet didn't mean she had nothing to say—the exact opposite usually because it was the quiet ones who noticed everything around them and were always waiting for the right time to get it all off their chests. And Isabella looked like she had a lot weighing on her little mind. Faith's thoughts were interrupted by Jake speaking.

"I don't know if you'd be up for it, but I'm going sailing with a buddy of mine today. The boat has plenty of room. You're welcome to join us. It's the least I can do since you invited me to breakfast."

"You all had better say yes," Nan piped up. "I'd be the first one on that boat if I could get around enough."

Faith looked over at Nan. She didn't want to leave her grandmother all alone while they were out having the time of their lives on a sailboat. That didn't seem like the right thing to do at all. It was Nan's birthday celebration—she'd planned this trip. Perhaps she could help Nan onto the beach or at least sit with her on the porch.

"If you really want to know, it would be quite nice to have some peace and quiet around here for a few hours. Think of it as an early birthday gift," Nan said as if she'd already anticipated what Faith was going to say.

Nan was trying to let them all off the hook. It was very much like her to look out for them and put everyone else first. Growing up, Nan had planned all the beach trips, and she'd said that the reason she'd planned them was because family meant more to her than anything else, and she wanted her family to be close. The bigger picture was becoming clear: Nan had planned this trip not for her but for them, Faith and Casey, to bring them back together again. She was nearly sure of it. And now, they had the chance to go sailing together.

"It sounds like fun," Faith said, breaking the silence.

"Can I go?" Isabella said. Faith couldn't help but smile. *Yep*, she thought. *She's just like me.* She was waiting for the talking to subside, waiting for quiet when she could finally speak. Whatever Isabella was feeling about her parents' split could be eating her up inside, and Faith would be the perfect person to help her handle it—she knew what it felt like to bottle up her sadness, to wait for someone with whom she could share her feelings, only to have no one there to listen.

"Absolutely," Jake said. Then he turned his attention to the others at the table. "Everyone should go. Please come. I think you'll enjoy it. We're leaving at two." He looked at Faith. "I'd love you to come."

How could she say no? Nan was practically forcing them to go, and, as she looked around the table, Casey and her mom had expectant expressions on their faces, as if they were waiting on pins and needles for her answer. But what struck her most was little Isabella. She was on her knees now, her hands on her thighs, chewing on her bottom lip, her golden hair cascading over her shoulders and down her back. She, too, was waiting for an answer, and it was clear she wanted to go. She'd enjoy being there to see Isabella's reaction to sailing.

"I'd love to," Faith said. "What do you all think?"

The table buzzed with excited approval as everyone expressed their opinions about going.

"Fantastic! Why don't you all meet me at the marina at one thirty?" Then, he looked directly at Faith again and said, "I'm excited."

The flutter came back. It surprised her again. She didn't know if she could get used to that feeling, and she didn't have a clue what she was going to do about it. Faith took a sip of her juice and tried to shake the feeling of excitement that thought held.

When they'd finished eating and Jake got up to leave, they were searching for a piece of paper so he could write directions to the marina for them. "I'll see if Isabella has a notebook or something in her room," Casey said, but Jake stopped her.

"I have a pad of paper and a pen in the truck. Faith, why don't you come out with me and I'll write down the directions?"

Faith followed him outside. She watched his strides as he made his way to the truck, how his strong arms swung by his sides, the way his shoulders filled out his T-shirt. He opened the door and pulled a small pad of paper from the glove box and a pen from the center console. The morning wind was still cool, yet the sun's heat was already pounding every surface. Faith shielded her eyes from its relentless rays as Jake leaned on the truck. He shifted to block the sun for her with his body.

"It's nice out. The sea is calm today," she said, looking over his shoulder at the lapping waves behind him. Yesterday's angry, rolling waves were small, gurgling ripples today. "It's a pretty view."

"Yes, it is."

She made eye contact, wondering how he could possibly see behind him, and realized he was looking directly at her. Was he flirting with her? She smiled at the thought of it, and he seemed to notice. "Don't you have directions to write?" she said with mock seriousness.

"Yes. Directions." He set the pad of paper on the hood of the truck. "You know how you came in on the bypass? You're going to get back on…" he began to write, scribbling directions as he spoke, but she wasn't listening to the words. She was noticing the calm way his fingers moved as he held the pages of the pad down when they rippled in the wind, the way his lips pursed just slightly when he wrote, the movement of his features as he spoke. She hadn't even realized he'd finished until he ripped the piece of paper from the pad and held it out to her.

As she went to take it, a gust of wind sent it sailing into the air. She pawed for it, but it floated away from her. She chased it toward the dune, Jake following behind her. It landed in the tall grass at the sand's edge, and she jumped forward to trap it, but as she did, she tripped on a piece of driftwood and fell in the soft sand.

"You okay?" Jake said, arriving at her side in less than a second. He squatted down beside her, but she was already standing up.

"I'm fine, thank you." She felt embarrassed as she brushed the grainy sand from her leg with her free hand. "Got it," she said, holding up the paper. He grinned at her before reaching up and gently wiping sand off her cheek. With one finger, he tucked her hair behind her ear to keep it from blowing in her face. It was a very personal gesture, but she didn't mind at all.

"I could've written it again for you," he said. "You didn't have to go diving into the brush to save it."

"I have strong views about littering," she teased.

His laugh came out in little huffs, his eyes on her as if he wanted to say so much more than what was actually being said. She knew she'd see him soon, but she didn't want him to leave. She wanted to talk more with him, spend time with him, just the two of them. "You sure you're okay?" he asked, letting his gaze slide up and down her legs.

"I'm perfectly fine," she said, dipping her head to catch his line of sight and bring it back up to her face.

"Okay," he grinned at her again. "I'll see you in a bit then."

"See you soon." She walked to the long staircase leading to the cottage door and stood on the bottom step as he got in his truck and started the engine. He gave her one last wave before pulling out of the driveway. She slipped the directions into her pocket and walked up the stairs, her cheek tingling from Jake's gentle touch.

Chapter Five

Casey had taken Isabella to Jockey's Ridge, one of the tallest natural groups of sand dunes on the entire east coast, to climb the mountainous dunes. They'd seemed like a desert of endless sand as Faith had hiked them as a kid. Casey bought Isabella a kite like their mom had done for them when they were little, and Faith was so glad to see Casey carrying on the tradition. Faith had stayed behind in the cottage, and when it occurred to Jake that Isabella might not have a life vest for the boat, it had been Faith who had answered the call from Jake. Now, she found herself shopping for a child-sized life vest with him. She'd insisted on meeting him at the shop, not wanting him to make yet another drive out to the cottage. He was nice enough to take them sailing; the least she could do was meet him in town. And she wanted to spend more time with him.

"I haven't ever taken a child sailing before," he said, his head swiveling from one side of the racks to the other.

Faith stopped to thumb through a few life vests before moving on. The far wall of the store was clad from floor to ceiling with brightly colored surfboards, their patterns and glossy surfaces like artwork. She had to force her eyes from their beautiful designs to keep looking for Isabella's vest. These little shops were quite common along the beach, and she loved going in them. Each one was unique, displaying its wares in its own quirky way. They were small spaces, jammed with all the latest in beachwear, a friendly cashier wearing flip-flops and shorts, with sunglasses on his head, there to help and answer any questions. Her mom had always allowed them to buy a T-shirt as a souvenir when they visited as kids, and there were so many different ones to choose from that it had always taken Faith all week to decide on one. These shops were perfect examples of life here.

As she'd driven into town, Faith had tried not to notice the enormous monstrosities that were now looming over the bypass, big superstores, selling their beach paraphernalia at low prices, and screaming out at her with their bright signs promising her they could meet all her beach needs. There was nothing wrong with those stores in particular; she just didn't want them here. The Outer Banks had always been a place of solitude for her, rich in culture, its small-town beach vibe unique from any other place she'd ever been. As she looked around the shop now, she prayed that those big chain stores wouldn't put stores like this one out of business. She smiled as she caught a glimpse of the locally made jewelry showcased under glass at the checkout counter. Those big stores claimed to have her every need, but she was willing to bet they didn't have what this shop had: charm, personality, warmth. She was so glad that Jake had chosen this place to get Isabella's life vest. She was happy to support the local shops.

"Thank you for helping me out," he said, turning toward her.

"You're welcome."

"I'm glad you're coming sailing today."

"Thank you for inviting my family."

"Well, I already know you well enough to guess that you wouldn't have gone and left them at the cottage. You'd have felt bad about it." He raised his eyebrows as if to say, *I'm right, aren't I?*

He'd only invited them all because he wanted her to go? She smiled. And he was right. "How did you do that?"

"What?"

"How did you know what I was thinking?"

He smiled. "I can see it on your face. Sometimes, it's a quick crease between your eyebrows or movement of your eyes as you're thinking. You give yourself away."

Her ex, Patrick, had never guessed what she was thinking, and they'd been together for two years. The only other person who seemed to be able to do that was Nan. She'd never met anyone else with the ability to see her so clearly, until now. "I think you're just good at reading people. What am I thinking right now?" She looked at him and allowed her bubbling feelings to surface. *I like you so much already,* she thought.

He tipped his head back and laughed then shook his head, amusement on his face.

"What was I thinking?" she pressed, remembering how this little exchange had begun.

He was still smiling, his grin reaching his eyes. "I'm not telling."

"Why? It's *my* thought. You can tell me."

"I'd rather hear you say it."

Her face burned with the idea that he had actually read her mind. Had he guessed how she felt about him? She could feel the heat still in her face as she looked up at him.

That amusement twisted into affection in his eyes. She could almost swear it. She looked at the rack of vests to steady herself. These feelings were happening too fast, and she wanted to slow them down.

Jake followed her lead and held up a tiny pink vest, the buckles swinging free on either side of it. Faith reached over to inspect the size on the tag. It was an extra-small. "I wonder if she's a small," she said, her heart still beating like a snare drum. Jake hung it back on the rack and pushed a few more out of the way before pulling another one out. This one was purple.

"They all look so little to me," he said with a grin. "I can't tell one size from another."

He'd let her off the hook. She was trying to focus, but her head was still swimming. Faith studied the purple vest, squinting her eyes to imagine Isabella wearing it.

Jake seemed to notice her deliberation and took the pink vest back off the rack, holding the two side by side. "I love kids," he admitted, looking down at the vests. "I really enjoy them, and I so rarely get the opportunity to be with them given my line of work."

"What do you like about them?" she asked, genuinely curious. Faith obviously loved kids; she was a kindergarten teacher. She loved their honesty, watching them as they made their way through the world while learning the social etiquette that they'd need as adults. She enjoyed their silliness and their absolute freedom when they were given time to explore. Nothing was off-limits. They hadn't learned enough about the world yet to be wary of things.

"I love their innocence," he said. "I've tried to remember exact moments growing up when life revealed things to hamper that innocence. Sometimes I can remember, and sometimes I can't. I often wish I could see my own child grow so I could learn when it all happens. When does the world finally get a hold of that innocence?"

"Oh, I don't think it happens all at once," she said, tapping the purple vest. Jake slid the pink one back on the rack and handed her the purple one. "It's a slow process. I'd like to watch my own kids too one day." As she said that statement, fear swept through her as she worried that she'd waited too long. She'd spent so much time working that she hadn't put enough effort into her personal life, and now, just entering the dating scene, she may never have that family she wanted.

She walked up to the counter first to get out of the conversation. Faith pulled out her wallet, and Jake, now standing beside her, put his hand on her arm. "I've got it," he said, his wallet already in his other hand. He pulled out the cash before she could stop him, but he seemed to notice her protest. "I'm not going to ask your family to take a boat ride and then make you pay for it in any way. That would be ridiculous."

"But Isabella could use that vest other times as well. It would be like an investment," she said, quietly worrying that Isabella may not visit this beach again with her family. She didn't want to think about that. Maybe she'd be wrong. She hoped she was.

Jake turned back to Faith and smiled, shaking her from her thoughts. "It's my treat." They walked to the door, the sun streaming in through the mass of surfing stickers peppering its glass surface. He opened the door and allowed Faith to exit first. "I'll have it waiting on the boat for her."

The marina was full of the most gorgeous vessels Faith had ever seen. It looked like something from a movie: rows of shiny white boats, their masts gleaming in the sunlight, the lapping of the blue water around them. She walked along the docks, following her mother and Casey. Isabella held Casey's hand and was trying not to step on any of the cracks, her little feet hopping along as Casey tried to hold onto her. Faith paced up beside her.

"What happens if you step on a crack?" Faith asked, careful to keep her feet on solid wood.

"It's water. It'll get you," she said, her head down in concentration. She made another hop. "We don't want to get wet." She finally looked up and smiled. When she did, Faith could see just a little of Scott in her face. It was the movement of her features as she broke into a grin that was like her daddy. Faith had seen it a hundred times on his face. She'd seen it when she'd said something funny. She'd also seen it at his wedding to Casey as he'd looked at her during their vows, and again when he held Isabella as a newborn. It was the first time she'd seen it in Isabella. There'd been a time when it would've made her sad, but today, it made her smile. Scott had a daughter, and she was lovely. It made her feel so happy for him.

When Faith finally swam out of her thoughts, she looked up to find Jake at the end of the dock. He, too, was smiling, his hand raised in greeting. Behind him sat the most amazing sailboat. It was sleek, white with mahogany accents that were so lacquered they reflected the sunlight like a mirror. The hardware was bright silver, every piece gleaming. The sail, a beautiful electric green canvas, was loose as the crew worked it out of its bindings. The whole boat looked as shiny as a pearl, the sail its complementing emerald.

"Thanks for coming," he said, making eye contact with Faith.

The gesture made her a little nervous, so she smiled quickly and then looked down at Isabella. When she did, she noticed her face. Isabella was now standing closer to her mother, her apprehension clear. She was worried about the boat, it seemed like.

Jake must have noticed too because he knelt down in front of her. "Have you ever been on a boat before?" he asked gently, and Faith couldn't take her eyes off him. She watched how his gestures changed—they were slower, more deliberate, careful. "It's just like where you're standing now on this dock. It's the same except for one thing. Do you know what that is?" His voice was so soft and sweet that Faith felt herself hanging on every word, waiting to hear what he'd come up with next. "The boat moves through the water, and it feels like you're flying. But not flying fast. Flying like a fairy, floating, sailing along like magic. That's why they're called *sail*boats."

Isabella kept her eyes on him, her face now exuding wonderment. She was smiling, her eyes big and round as she clearly thought of fairies and magic, and she'd taken a step toward him. What a perfect moment, Faith thought. How lovely he was with children. He'd known exactly what to say and had, in an instant, erased all of her fears. She'd never seen anyone who could be like that—even at the school where she worked, there had never been the opportunity for that kind of magic. She looked over at Casey to get her reaction, and she knew the same thoughts were running through her mind.

"You need something special, though, to really feel like that fairy. Would you like to step over this step with me? It's just over there." Isabella looked back at her mother for approval. Casey nodded and Isabella dropped her hand and followed Jake onto the boat, where he was holding the purple life vest they'd bought earlier.

Faith and the others boarded as he talked to her about her special jacket. Helping her slip it on and buckling the clasps, he eyed the crew over her head. They began to push away from the dock ever so quietly, the motor running at a soft hum, until they were floating in the marina and heading toward the sea. The crew lifted the sail, and it flapped madly until it became taut in the wind. Jake handed the others their life vests, and assisted Isabella with the last buckle. When she was finally finished, he pointed to the vast expanse of blue sea before them and said, "Look. We're flying. Can you see the sparkles in the water? Did you make those with fairy dust?"

A man with a friendly face came up beside them. His skin was dark brown like leather—as if he'd spent every day out in the sun—and his silver hair curled haphazardly as if it were accustomed to fighting the wind. *He must be the boat's owner*, Faith thought.

"This is my friend, Rich Barnes," Jake said.

They went around shaking hands and greeting each other. "Glad to see Jake's made you feel welcome," he asked, clapping his friend on the back. "He's always making friends. Lucky for me, that means I get to meet a lot of great people. Nice to meet you all."

After they'd settled into conversation, Jake began moving around the boat, helping to check that everything was running smoothly. During a lull, Faith made her way to the bow of the boat. She looked out at the sea, the sun on her face and the smell of seaweed and salt in the air around her. The crew behind her made some adjustments to the lines, and their quiet commands mixed with the whooshing of the waves in her ears, and she couldn't imagine a better way to spend her time. It was so nice of Jake to have asked them to do this. In the two days she'd been there, the more she saw of him, the more she liked him. There was something so relaxed about him, so friendly. She decided that she was going to take the initiative. Why not?

From the moment Faith met him, she'd felt different around him compared to anyone else she'd met. She'd never been so open with someone so quickly or been so much herself. She never really enjoyed that beginning time, when she'd just met someone and the two of them had to do a sort of mental dance around each other, trying to keep up the pleasantries and stay within proper etiquette. Jake pushed right through that. He asked real questions, and she told him honest answers. It made her feel like she'd known him longer than she had.

She turned around to go and talk to him. As she did, she stopped in her tracks. Casey was laughing, her hand on his shoulder, her head tipped back, her chest rising and falling from giggling. He was smiling, and Isabella was tugging on his shirttail to tell him something. With the noise in her ears, she couldn't hear them, but the sight was enough to give her pause. Jake was friendly and outgoing. Casey was just the kind of person who could relate to him. She was attractive, witty, sweet.

Her thoughts went back to her lowest when Casey had married Scott. She thought about those lonely nights she'd spent missing him and knowing that he was on his honeymoon with Casey, doing God knows what. It was funny how she'd grown, moved on, gotten over it, but now, seeing how easily things came for Casey when it came to relationships, Faith had to wonder if something within herself was broken. Faith turned back toward the sea and closed her eyes.

"It's a gorgeous view, isn't it?" her mom said, walking up beside her. The boat was cutting through the water, the spray fanning out along the sides. Faith nodded. "Jake mentioned that there's wine and hors d'oeuvres below deck. That's fancy, isn't it?" Her mom smiled, shaking her head. "Jake is a very surprising person," she said before Faith could answer her last question. "He's a handyman who sails on boats the size of yachts in the middle of the day." The skin between her mom's eyes wrinkled as she contemplated this idea. "Who does that?"

Faith didn't answer. She wanted to know more about Jake. She wanted to spend more time with him, but after seeing Casey with him, as much as she wanted to deny it and look on the bright side, she worried it wouldn't happen. And the fact that Jake led such an interesting life only made her feel like perhaps she wasn't the kind of person he'd be interested in anyway. She didn't go sailing with rich friends. She didn't build beautiful cottages. She didn't do a whole lot in life that exciting. Until now, she'd been okay with that.

"Let's go over there with them and find out more about him," her mom suggested with a baiting grin on her face. As Faith thought about it, she realized that her mom was right. She decided to ignore the fears creeping in on her and just enjoy herself.

"Can we go fishing today?" Isabella was asking Jake as Faith and her mom walked up. "Daddy was going to take me fishing but we had to come here to the beach."

Faith looked over at her sister protectively. How awful it must be to carry around unnecessary guilt about things like that. Casey was taking her daughter somewhere wonderful, but in the back of her mind, she had to worry about this missed fishing trip. She knew Isabella didn't mean anything by it, but not being with her dad was clearly playing on her mind. Faith hoped it didn't affect Casey too much. Casey had enough to deal with when it came to her split with Scott; Faith couldn't imagine having to deal with her child's disappointment as well.

"Well, I hadn't planned to go fishing today," he said, squatting down to her eye level like he had at the docks. It was so endearing when he did that. "But I'll bet later this week you and your mommy can meet me on the pier, and we'll go fishing together. I'll be sure to set the time with your mommy." He looked up at Casey for agreement and Faith followed his lead. She wanted to see Casey's reaction. Her sister smiled, agreeing. In a way, she was happy for Casey. She needed something to take her mind off the divorce. She probably needed a little fun more than Faith did. But she worried at that moment because she knew that when given the option of her or Casey, Jake would certainly find Casey more attractive. Their little fishing date bothered her far more than it should. He'd only invited Casey, not everyone. Had she misread his friendliness toward her? He and Casey seemed to be getting along so well. Once again, she was sidelined.

Casey was talkative, like Jake. She had an effortless way of filling conversation, and she was upbeat, generally happy, and agreeable. Even when she disagreed, she could manage to spin her opinion in a way that was so polite and gracious you almost forgot that you'd disagreed in the first place. That was what made her a great lawyer. She could command attention without even trying. Jake, who seemed to be genuinely curious about people, and openly friendly, would surely find Casey interesting.

"The food's ready downstairs," Rich said, only his head and shoulders visible from below deck.

Casey ushered Isabella gently toward the stairs, their mom following behind, leaving Faith standing with Jake. He put out his hand to allow her to go ahead of him. "Oh, no thanks," she smiled, trying her best not to be rude. "I think I'll stay up here. I'm not hungry." Truthfully, the rocking of the boat and thinking again about Casey and Jake had made her stomach a little queasy. She didn't know if wine and food would be her best bet.

"You okay?" he asked.

"I'm fine, thank you," she lied.

He looked at her, thoughts behind his eyes. "Don't move," he said with a grin and began walking away.

Where was he going? Faith sat down on a built-in bench at the end of the boat and tried to focus on the whitecaps at sea. The sky was a gorgeous shade of blue, with white, puffy clouds in the distance. About a mile out, a dolphin fin slipped above the surface of the water and then went back under. She took in a deep breath, the open air and quiet sound of the sail against the wind calming her upset stomach a little.

As Faith waited for Jake to return, she thought again how good he'd been with Isabella. Why hadn't he married and had children? There were so many things about him that she wanted to know.

"Here you go. This should help," he said, emerging from below deck with a can of ginger ale and a small plate of crackers. "The bubbles will help with the nausea, and the crackers will ease your stomach a little. Hopefully." He smiled.

"I didn't say I was feeling ill," she said, not in an accusatory manner, but surprised that he'd figured it out.

"I could tell by your face." He handed her the ginger ale and set the plate on the bench next to her.

"How so?" she pressed. She wanted to know how this stranger, who'd only known her for two days, could read her so easily.

He looked at her, his lips wanting to smile. It was right there waiting, and she wondered how a person could be that happy all the time. "You were blinking more than usual. I thought the sun was in your eyes, but you kept doing it even when the sun went behind a cloud. Your expression had turned serious, and you hadn't been like that quite as much yesterday or today."

"Quite as much?" she asked. She didn't remember being serious. "When was I serious?" Was that her problem? Did she come across too serious?

"You were like that when I first saw you at the cottage and again at breakfast."

"You sure are perceptive," she said, trying not to sound too defensive. The truth was, both times she'd been deep in thought. She'd been contemplating things, and it surprised her that he'd noticed. She could feel the tiniest of emotions at the pit of her stomach—affection for him that she hadn't expected. She could feel a connection with him, and she wondered if he felt it too. Or did he feel that way toward Casey? How odd that two days ago she didn't even know he existed, and now he was dominating her thoughts.

He smiled again, and her queasy stomach fizzled with excitement. "Are you having a good time?" he asked out of the blue.

"Yes. Thank you for inviting me." She was still contemplating her fears about him and Casey. She knew that she shouldn't be, but her old wounds were surfacing without warning.

"You're welcome." He chewed on a smile.

"Why are you smiling like that?" she asked.

"I can tell you're thinking again."

"This is going to get really difficult for you if you stick around because I think all the time," she laughed. "Are you going to read my mind all day?"

"Maybe." He winked at her, and she couldn't help but think how she wanted nothing more than to have him stick around. "Come with me." He took her ginger ale in one hand and held her hand with the other. The gesture was startling, but in that instant she didn't want him to let her go. He led her to an area to the side of the cabin and took a step up, turning to guide her in the same direction. She followed, standing with him on the ceiling of the cabin.

"Can we be up here?"

He chuckled as if her question was silly, but his face was affectionate. "Yes. Just be careful." He walked her to the bow of the boat and sat, motioning for her to sit with him. She stretched her legs out in front of her and crossed them at the ankle while leaning back on her hands. The only thing between her and the ocean was a thin, silver railing. He'd been right: It was like flying. The wind in her hair, the sound of the waves, and the rushing air over her ears so loud that she couldn't get a single thought to process. Her senses were so overwhelmed by what was in front of her. When she finally managed to pull her gaze away from the incredible view in front of her, she looked over at Jake to find he was looking back at her, that smile on his lips.

"Not feeling ill anymore?" he asked loudly over the noise.

She wasn't. It really was like magic. Right there with him, she was fine. And he'd just known how to make her okay. Faith shook her head, that affection for him swelling in her chest. What was happening? She wasn't supposed to feel this way about a person she'd only just met. But there was no denying it.

"I'm glad," he said. "I love sailing. No matter what happens in a day's work, it all fades away out here." He looked out at the ocean.

"I always wanted to go sailing as a kid. This is the first time I've ever been on a sailboat." She didn't know where this thought had come from, but, once again, she just felt able to share everything with Jake.

"Really?" He looked over at her. "I can't say I did a lot of sailing as a kid either, but I do now. I need it. It calms me. And it gives me time to hang out with great people like Rich," he said as she noticed the crew begin to bring the boat to a stop.

Slowly, it glided along the water, cutting through the surface until it was but a bobbing vessel in the gentle swells of the ocean. They lowered the anchor.

"You have your swimsuit underneath your clothes, right?"

"Yes."

"Good. Feel like swimming?"

He stood up, and as he raised his shirt, she realized his shorts were swimming trunks. He slipped his T-shirt over his head, and she quickly turned to look out at the water, although her eyes slid back over to him as if they were under some sort of magnetic pull. Every muscle was perfectly shaped, his wide chest tapering to a fit waist. She took in the curve of his biceps, the flawless square of his shoulders, the ripple of muscle along his stomach.

"Hop up! The water is considerably more refreshing when you get out this far. It's a great escape from this North Carolina heat."

She'd never been so glad that Casey was below deck. There was no way she wanted to stand next to her sister wearing a bikini. She got up slowly, shimmied off her shorts, and suddenly felt nervous standing in front of him in her swimsuit. It was the new one she'd bought before the trip—a black two-piece that tied at the hips. He was taking her in, and it made her feel nervous. She turned around and set the shorts down, checking under her shirt quickly to ensure that everything was where it should be. She adjusted her top. Then, there was nothing else to do but take her shirt off. As she put her shirt beside her shorts, she surveyed the deck floor. She didn't want to look up for some reason. She was right at the edge of the boat, and he was now behind her on deck. She could see him in her peripheral vision if she turned her head just slightly.

She didn't stand there long before there was an enormous splash, water spraying up against her skin. She spun around to find a gurgling circular spray of bubbles, and then Jake's head popped up in the center of it.

"Come in!" He flicked water up in her direction and she dodged it. He was smiling, baiting her. "Come in or I'll come get you," he teased. He didn't stop his eyes this time from moving along her body. The way he was looking at her took away any remaining self-consciousness. She felt pretty. "Stand on the edge right there." He lifted a dripping finger toward the back corner of the boat.

Carefully, Faith stepped over the railing until she was standing precariously on the edge of the boat. "How cold is the water?" she called down to him.

He went under and back up, shaking the water from his hair. "It's perfect."

She debated how to jump in. Feet first? That might take her top off. Should she dive? What if she belly-flopped? That would hardly be the picture of elegance she wanted to paint. Who knew it could be so difficult just getting in the water!

"If you jump, I'll catch you," he called up.

His offer tempted her enough that, without thinking any further, she jumped. The water was startlingly cold as it hit her skin, her whole body sailing right under the water, but almost immediately, she felt the strong warmth of Jake's arms around her. It took what little breath she'd stored in her lungs right away. When she surfaced, she was face to face with him, her body up next to his. They were tangled together, their arms and legs moving to keep them afloat, bumping into each other, their skin touching in all kinds of places. He still had one arm wrapped around her as he looked straight at her, barely blinking. Her wet hair had wrapped around her neck like seaweed and he reached up and slid it over her shoulder, exposing her bare neck. Her skin tingled from his touch. His eyes moved across the surface of her shoulder, up her neck, and to her face, finally meeting her eyes again. Was he going to kiss her?

"How's the water?" she heard from behind her. Faith lurched away from Jake like a teenager caught in a compromising position. She turned around, shielding her eyes with one hand and keeping herself afloat with the other. Casey and her mom were standing at the edge, Isabella already stripping off her cover-up and unbuckling her sandals.

"It's great!" Jake called up to them.

Faith could feel the irritation slithering around inside her. Casey had ruined the moment. Faith knew that Casey had no idea, but it didn't do anything to ease the feeling. She watched as her sister stripped off her clothes confidently, revealing her toned body and shimmery bikini. She swung her long leg over the boat and dipped her toe in the water. "It is nice," she said. Faith kept her eyes on her sister. She didn't dare look at Jake. She didn't want to see him looking at Casey the way he'd looked at her, because with Casey's figure, he certainly would be. Faith wanted that look to be hers only. With a little hop, Casey dove into the water without a splash, her thin body gliding effortlessly below the surface. Faith finally turned to look at Jake but he, too, was underwater, swimming away from them. She couldn't help feeling relieved.

Her mom helped Isabella put her floats on, and with some hesitancy, she jumped in. "Are there any sharks?" she asked, quickly paddling over to her mother.

"You've scared them away," Jake said with a smile. He'd made his way back to them and took Isabella's hands. Kicking his legs, he began to spin her, dragging her little body in circles like a whirlpool. She giggled uncontrollably, and whenever he stopped, she asked him to do it again. Casey offered to take turns, and Faith had to look away so as not to allow the feelings of annoyance to return, looking at the three of them as they laughed and played together.

When they'd gotten tired of swimming, everyone settled down at the back of the boat on their towels to rest, but Faith sat at the ladder, her legs dangling down over the edge. Jake was still in the water, holding on to the handrail. She slid down a step to lower her legs down beside him.

"The water feels like bathwater now," she said.

Jake nodded. "I'm glad you came," he said almost a little too quickly.

"Me too." And she meant it.

"How's your stomach? All better?"

"Yes." But being in close proximity to him in just a swimsuit was making it do somersaults.

He pulled his weight up using the handrail, and Faith had to scoot backward to allow him some space. He was standing on the bottom step, his arms on either side of her, looking down at her. "Hungry?" he asked.

"Actually, now that you say so, I am."

"Let's grab a towel and get a bite to eat then."

The cabin was cool down below deck as Faith shivered in her towel. Without her asking, Jake took a large beach towel from the shelf and switched it out for her damp one. It was shockingly warm against her skin. As he rummaged around in the small fridge, Faith thought about how well he must know Rich. He seemed so relaxed on Rich's boat, and Rich let him have free rein. But then again, it was typical of the relaxed way of life at the coast. She liked how quickly they had befriended Jake, but his relaxed demeanor and friendly nature made it so easy.

He put out crackers and cheese, fruit, and a small platter of assorted vegetables. It all looked delicious after swimming and being in the sun. She felt like she could eat the whole bowl of fruit herself.

"So, your mother had mentioned something about teaching," he said, slicing the leaves off the strawberries and filling a plate. "Is that what you do for a living?"

"Yes. I teach kindergarten."

He grinned.

"What?"

"You look like a kindergarten teacher."

"And what does a kindergarten teacher look like? I didn't know we were a type."

He smiled again, bigger, if that was possible. He was quiet for a second, and, until then, she hadn't seen him at a loss for words. Then, finally, he said, "You have a gentle way about you; you seem very patient and kind. And when you smile, I can tell you mean it."

She smiled. She couldn't help it.

"See? You mean it right now." He handed her a plate with a little bit of everything on it.

She picked up a cracker and topped it with a tiny rectangle of cheese. "Well, thank you. I'll take that as a compliment."

"Good. Because I meant it as such."

His eyes didn't leave her face, as if he wanted to say something else, but he'd fallen silent again. Finally, he looked away and busied himself with his own plate of food. She wondered what he'd wanted to say to her, if anything. She wanted to tell him that she thought he was just the same—kind, genuine—but she too stayed silent. They fell into an easy quiet as they ate.

They spent the rest of the day swimming and lounging on the boat until it was clear that Isabella was getting tired, and they'd all probably had enough sun. As the crew pulled up the anchor, Jake offered everyone another deliciously fluffy white towel. Her mom was helping Isabella dry off, and Casey was below deck getting them some wine. Jake walked up to Faith and rubbed the tops of her arms through the towel.

"I had fun," he said, leaning down to say it into her ear.

"Me too," she said, tipping her head back to make eye contact. When she did, she was too close, his lips so near to hers that she could feel his breath. He lingered there, neither of them moving, and she wanted to kiss him right then. It was surprising. She'd only just met him. But his openness made him so attractive to her that she was feeling things she wasn't used to feeling. He smiled at her and turned her around.

"Warm enough?" he asked, clearly trying to change the subject. Was he brushing her off? It was hard to tell.

She nodded.

"Good." Then, the moment was gone. He'd turned to talk to her mom, leaving Faith a little lightheaded. She sat down and tipped her head back. It was a good day. And with Jake around, she couldn't wait to see what tomorrow would bring.

Chapter Six

"I brought you something," Nan said from the chair in the corner. She waved a finger at a box across the room. "Your mom carried it in for me. Do you mind bringing it over?" Faith picked up the box and took it over to Nan, setting it down with a thud in front of her.

"What is it?" she asked.

"Open it up."

Faith pulled back the flaps of cardboard that were folded in on themselves to stay shut, and inside, she saw a massive pile of photos.

"Close your eyes," Nan said with a smile, and Faith wondered what she had in mind, but she complied. "Now, reach in and grab one."

With her eyes shut, Faith fumbled her way inside the box and lightly moved her fingers around until they came to rest on the smooth surface of a photo. She could tell by the feel of it that it was glossy, so it must not be too old. She pulled it out.

"Open your eyes."

Faith looked down at the photo, and she sat there in silence for quite a while as she took in the memory of the moment that had been captured there. Nan was quiet too. Clearly, she had a reason for doing this, and she was waiting for Faith to process it.

"It's me," Faith said, unable to get her tangled thoughts to come out in a coherent sentence, "…and Casey. We were here. Well, at the old cottage." They were painting seashells to make into jewelry. The photo was slightly aged, but through the fading color, she could make out that they both had had too much sun—their cheeks bright red, their hair golden blond, their eyes tired from a day on the beach. Faith was on the floor, one knee up, her shell in one hand and a paintbrush in the other. It was a typical childhood scene. But what struck her most was that Casey was sitting right next to her, leaning on her shoulder with her chin to see what she was painting. They'd been so close. She could see the love between them.

A pang of sadness shot through her. Casey hadn't leaned on her shoulder like that in a long time. Life had come between them, and now, she could never imagine her sister leaning on her shoulder that way. She wanted to be close with Casey again. She wished things could be as simple as they were when they were kids.

"Pull out another one," Nan said.

Faith dug around for another photo and pulled it out. When she turned it around in her hand, she smiled. It was a photo of a girl sitting cross-legged, an open book in her hands, completely obscuring her face. The only reason she knew it was her was because she could make out the title of the book. It was one of her favorite poetry books by Robert Frost.

"I know what poem I was reading," she said through her smile.

"Which one?"

"It was called 'Come In' and it was my favorite. I read it so much that the cover fell off the book, and then I just read it without the cover."

Nan nodded as if she remembered.

"My other favorite was 'The Gift Outright'."

"I remember that one," Nan said. "He wrote it in Key West. I only remember that because you told me about a thousand times. You were obsessed with Key West."

"I was," she conceded, laughing at the memory of it. "I wanted to go there more than anywhere in the world. I remember thinking how it was the place of poets, of writers. I loved reading so much that it romanticized Key West in my young mind."

"You never went, did you?"

"No." Thinking about it now, Faith realized that she had bestowed her obsession with reading on her students, feeding their love for books and encouraging their passion. It only crossed her mind just now that she'd forgotten what had made *her* enthusiastic about reading. How long had it been since she'd read something just for herself? Since she'd gotten completely lost in a book like she had in her childhood? She wanted to feel that excitement again for herself. "Maybe one day," she said. She dropped the photo back in and took in all of the different photos that were in the box. There were so many.

"Good memories?" Nan asked with a smile.

Faith nodded and reached in again without being prompted. This time, her fingers caught a thick square of paper. She pulled it out and turned it over in her hand. It was a photo of her grandfather, John. On the back, in penciled script, it read, "Sophia and John, 1945."

"I was twenty," Nan said with a smile, shifting in her seat. "That's your grandpa with me."

Nan leaned in closely as Faith held the photo nearer to get a better look. Nan had a white pencil skirt with a white fitted shirt and black belt. She was wearing black open-toed heels, and her dark hair was in pinned-back waves. She looked gorgeous. Standing beside Nan was

Faith's grandfather, who looked familiar to her and like a stranger at the same time. She'd seen countless photos of him over the years—so many that she felt like she knew him—but he was just a frozen image to her, not the real-life warm, kind man Nan had often described.

Faith reached in and found another photo. This one was of Nan and her grandfather grinning together in the chair of a Ferris wheel as their chair sat at the bottom of the platform either before or after the ride. Faith noted her grandfather's arm around Nan, the way his fingers were resting on her shoulder, the tilt of her head toward him, and her smile. Who was this man Nan had loved so much? What was he like? When Faith was just beginning to talk, she couldn't say the word "grandmother." She could only say "Nan," so it had stuck. This man in the photo had never had the opportunity to know his own grandchildren. She didn't have a name for him. He was always just her "grandfather" or "John." Until now, she'd never thought about him really. But now, seeing him with Nan made her wonder about him.

"These are great pictures, Nan," Faith said, her mind going back to that time long ago when Nan had been healthy and happy. Faith looked over at her, and wished she'd made more of an effort to see her. Faith felt guilty because her nan had always been there for her and helped her through difficult times, but Faith had never really talked to Nan about her past, about being without her grandfather. What were those nights like for so many years without her grandfather by Nan's side? How strong her grandmother must be because never once growing up had she seen anything other than happiness in Nan's eyes. Had her grandmother been lonely? Heartbroken? If she had, she'd never let it show.

Faith looked back down at the man in the photo, wishing she had known him. She'd spent her whole life with only women. Her mother had done a wonderful job raising her, and her grandmother was one of her favorite people in the entire world. Even Casey had given her many fond memories of childhood. Faith had wanted for nothing. But deep down inside her, somewhere she'd tucked it away, she wished to have had a grandfather and father like her friends had. When she looked at Nan in those photos, the idea of having her own family slunk its way into her consciousness, especially now after spending time with Isabella—seeing the family bond through the eyes of her little niece.

"May I keep these?" she asked.

"Of course. They're for you."

"Thank you," she said. She didn't want to think about the other photos of her and her family that were probably in the box. When the memories of their childhood took hold in her mind, she almost couldn't bear the fact that she'd stayed away so much. She also didn't want to think about the reason Nan was giving them all away now. It was all so heavy that Faith couldn't let it enter her mind. This was supposed to be fun. And she was nearly sure that Nan felt the same way or she wouldn't have planned it. It was Nan's birthday soon! That was cause for celebration, not sadness.

Nan obviously felt the same way, and changed the subject. "So, how was sailing yesterday? You all were out all day. I assume it was enjoyable."

"It was fantastic. In fact, Jake is so thoughtful and friendly. I'm still amazed that he invited us—complete strangers—to go sailing with him. That was very nice of him, wasn't it?"

"Yes, it was."

"I wonder why he did that?" The question had been playing on her mind.

"You should ask him."

Faith thought about what he'd said at the surf shop, how he'd asked the whole family because he didn't think she'd go on her own. What she really wanted to ask was why he wanted her in particular to go sailing—what did he find so special about her? Especially when he'd turned right around and asked Casey to go fishing.

"I wouldn't ask him, Nan."

"Why not?" Nan was grinning at Faith, her eyes playful, and Faith felt the tingle of heat in her face. Could Nan see something between her and Jake?

"It would be rude to ask him such a question," she said.

"What question?" she heard from behind her and her heart jumped into her throat. Faith hadn't known him long, but she'd known him long enough to recognize his voice. She turned to see her mom standing next to Jake in the open door. He was in his work clothes, so he must have been outside working.

"Oh, Jake, I'm glad you're here," Nan said. "Faith wants to ask you something and I have an idea for some built-ins I'd love to run by you. I think you may like it."

Why was Nan putting her in this position? She didn't want to ask Jake anything. She'd told her that! Nan was all smiles, her eyes darting from Faith to Jake and back, but didn't she realize that she was putting Faith in an embarrassing situation?

Jake grabbed a paper towel off the roll in the kitchen, still looking at Faith as if he was waiting for her to say something. When she didn't, he said, "Well, I'll be out on the porch."

After he left, Faith looked over at Nan, scolding her with her eyes. "Why did you do that?" she asked. It was a direct question, and she wasn't overly harsh about it, but she wanted to know.

"It's important not to let things go unsaid," she said, her expression gentle. Her face was the way it had been when she'd tucked Faith into bed on those nights when her mom was working. It wasn't the same as having her mother tuck her in, but Nan was so warm and loving that she had no problem falling asleep. Nan would read her a story first, and then she always found a way to bring that story around to real life. She'd talk to Faith, her words smooth like silk, as Faith's eyelids would drop. Faith would work to keep them open so that she could hear what Nan was saying, but sleep won every time. Finally, somewhere in the middle of a sentence, as Nan spoke, her eyes would close for the last time, and she'd drift off into dreamland. "He's just a person, Faith. Just someone with insecurities and worries and a yearning to be happy. You don't talk enough to people. You keep all your emotions bottled up. When you let someone in on those thoughts, you're showing that you trust them. But first, you have to trust yourself."

Nan's words calmed her, easing her back to normal. She felt like herself again. Faith knew exactly what Nan was saying. She'd gotten better at talking to people over the years and she'd begun to trust herself. But still, it didn't come easily to her, and instead of taking a leap into the unknown she'd hold back. Nan gave her an encouraging look.

"Make this old woman feel like she's making an impression on you even if she isn't." She winked at her. "Humor me."

Faith huffed out a chuckle and shook her head as she stood up and straightened her clothes. Then, with a grin in Nan's direction, she walked to the door and went outside.

When she rounded the corner of the porch, leading to the long stretch that faced the ocean, she found Jake squatting down near a window, a putty knife in his hand. He was filling in an empty space around a window frame. She noticed the slight golden stubble on his face, almost reddish in the sunlight, and the way the lines on his forehead pulled downward in concentration. He wiped the knife on the paper towel and stood up to greet her.

"Hi," she said.

"Hey." He pulled up one of the rockers and offered her a seat.

She sat down, and he joined her in the other chair. The air was warm on her skin. She looked at the ocean, the sun blazing out over the beach. She put her bare feet up on the rung of the rocker and leaned forward to take in more of the view. A woman was out walking her dog, the surf coming up on its paws. The dog didn't seem to mind as it walked along beside the woman, its tail wagging furiously. Two boys were throwing a Frisbee, and a plane flew overhead, a banner trailing behind it, advertising an all-you-can-eat seafood buffet. She squinted to make out Casey down below, Isabella in her pink swimsuit, building a sandcastle. She smiled to herself.

"Were you going to ask me something?"

"Oh." She looked back at Jake, wondering how to phrase her question. "I had a lot of fun yesterday on the boat," she said, scrambling for words. He smiled, and he seemed genuinely glad to hear it. "I was just wondering"—she broke eye contact in an effort to get out what she wanted to say—"why you would invite a complete stranger to sail with you. It seems like an awfully big thank-you for asking you to breakfast."

He let out a little cough of laugher. "It's really nothing," he said, flashing that smile that sent her heart pattering. "I enjoy meeting new folks, and you and your family seem like great people."

She wanted to ask him why she was so 'great' in particular, but he'd already stood up and was putting the rocking chair back in its place. His answer had been polite and acceptable, but she wondered if there was a reason he was holding back.

"I think your grandmother wanted to talk to me about some suggestions for the cottage," he said.

"Wait," she said, standing to stop him. He turned around. "You could tell when my stomach hurt yesterday." His brows creased in the middle, showing his attempt to make sense of where that comment was going. "You could just tell, right?" He nodded, still clearly unsure of her point. "Well, I can just tell that there's another reason you asked us to go sailing. I can't imagine that you go around being this nice to people all day long. It would be exhausting." She smiled to show her humor. "What is it that made you offer? Tell me." She took a step closer to him, her heart beating so fast she worried he could feel it in the air around them, but it was worth asking.

He smiled, his face gentle. "I like your family in particular," he admitted. "I don't know why—maybe it's your Nan's frankness; it reminds me of my father. Or, maybe it's little Isabella; I've never had any kids, and I love kids. Or maybe…" He stopped.

Maybe what? She was willing him to finish. She'd never met another human being who could cause this kind of intensity in her. She was not going to let him move until he finished that sentence. Maybe he liked being around *her*. That's what she wanted to hear. "Maybe what," she finally verbalized when she realized he wasn't going to say anything more.

He cleared his throat. "It's good getting to know you."

"Me?" It was a question but she stated it rather than asking because she wanted to hear it aloud to make sure she was right. He said it was good getting to know *her*.

"Yeah," he said softly. "You keep a lot of who you are on the inside, and it's fun to see if I can figure you out." His amusement came out as a little puff of air, and he shook his head. Before she could add anything else, he said, "Now, I must see what your grandmother has to say about *improvements*."

"Oh, goodness. Don't feel like you have to listen to her. She's very opinionated," she said, but she was still processing the conversation they'd just had. She wanted to know more about why he enjoyed finding out about her so much. Why did he even care?

He laughed again, making the flutters return. "I don't mind."

She followed him inside. Nan had been right. Talking to Jake was easy. A little too easy. And with that buzzy feeling zinging around inside her, Faith decided to get ready for the beach and join her sister and Isabella. It was a gorgeous day. Best she take full advantage of it. Her fondness for Jake worried her a little, and she'd rather think about something lighter than falling for a guy she hardly knew and who lived a state away. While Jake was chatting with Nan, Faith grabbed the box of photos and took them into her bedroom. She set them down on the bedspread, the bright white wicker of the footboard contrasting with the battered brown edges of the box. She rifled through her suitcase and pulled out her swimsuit.

"Hey there," her mother said from the doorway. "Oh, what is that?" She began walking toward the bed, eyeing the box.

"Nan brought me her photos." Her mother opened the box and peered inside.

"Ha!" she pulled out a photo and turned it around for Faith to view. Faith couldn't help herself; she started giggling. "Remember when you two were dressed up as scarecrows?" she said, looking at the picture and shaking her head, her chest still rising and falling with quiet laughter. "The straw kept falling out of your outfit and, as we walked, I had to tuck it back in. By the time we finished trick-

or-treating, you were 'the Skinny Scarecrow' and Casey was 'the Fat One.'" Then her face sobered. "Oh, sometimes I miss those days. They were tough, but boy were they fun." She put the photo back into the box. "Where're you headed?"

"Casey and Isabella are out on the beach. I'm going to join them."

Her mom smiled. It wasn't her usual smile; it was a proud, motherly smile. It was clear that she was glad her girls were together again. On the outside, that's what it looked like, but on the inside both girls still had a lot to get through if they wanted to be happy like they had been. Faith was doing her best to put the past behind her, but her issues with Casey would never really go away until they'd talked them through. But that would have to wait.

"Wanna go?" Faith asked, setting her swimsuit on the bed and digging around in her suitcase for her cover-up. She looked up to see her mother's response.

"I'll join you in a bit," she said. "I'll stay up with Nan for a little while. I hate leaving her all by herself in the cottage."

"Want me to stay too?"

"No, you go ahead and join Casey. I get to talk to your sister more than you do. Enjoy the time." Then, with an animated look on her face—her eyebrows bouncing upward—she said, "I brought the picnic basket! Maybe I can make everyone a picnic lunch and we can eat it on the beach."

Of course she'd brought a picnic basket. Faith was just glad to have a beach bag, but her mom was prepared for every occasion. She probably had a red-and-white checked tablecloth to sit on, Faith thought with amusement. Her mother's preparation was an indication of her excitement, and it was endearing. She loved her mother so much and was torn between staying there with her and going down to see Casey and Isabella. But then, as she thought more about it, she realized that her mother would probably rather she go and see Casey. They had more reason to spend time together.

She tried to focus on the fact that, even though things weren't perfect between them, Faith had come a long way emotionally. What was left now was the fear that the trust she'd put in her sister had been broken.

After everything that had happened, after the feelings of complete despair, after working through the reality that Scott was going to be her brother-in-law, and finally coming to terms with the whole thing and moving on, it seemed he wasn't even going to be part of the family anymore. Certainly, he was Isabella's father, but with his divorce from Casey imminent, she surely wouldn't see him anymore. It was funny how life played out sometimes.

Chapter Seven

"May I bury your feet?" Isabella asked, as Faith got comfortable in her beach chair.

"Of course." Faith wiggled her toes, her sparkly pedicure shimmering in the bright sunlight. Isabella was on her knees, and the bottom of her pink swimsuit was sandy all the way up to the ruffle around her waist. With her tiny fingers, she dug around Faith's feet, and she could feel the cool sand from underneath the surface against her skin.

Faith looked out at the rolling ocean. On the far left, a sailboat bobbed along, and Faith thought about yesterday. She'd really enjoyed herself. There was something almost magical about being out on the ocean like that, with nothing but blue as far as she could see, the quiet chatter of the crew as they maneuvered the sail, the wind in her hair. And being with Jake.

"I had fun yesterday," Casey said, following her thoughts, and Faith wondered if she, too, was thinking about Jake.

Isabella had finished burying Faith's feet, the sand now up to her ankles. The little girl ran down to the water, squatting on the sand to pick up a shell as the water rushed in around her.

"Me too."

"Jake was so great with Isabella. She looked so scared when we first arrived, but he knew just what to say," Casey said. "I don't know if I could have come up with something like that, and I'm her mother."

Faith remembered Jake saying how much he liked children and even said he'd enjoyed Isabella. She knew what he probably thought of Isabella, but she also wondered what Jake thought of Casey. Did he think Casey was a single mom? Had she made an impression on him? Faith didn't like thinking about it because when she did, it made her remember what had gone wrong between them. When she was around Jake, having Casey present made her slightly uncomfortable and she didn't want to feel like that. She wished they could go back to a time before things had gotten strained between them. She missed the sister who used to lie on her bed with her listening to the radio, the girl who offered her Nancy Drew novels when she was finished with them, the girl who spent all those nights with her outside when the weather was warm like it was now.

Again, she tumbled into her memories. As kids, she and Casey had been inseparable. When she was ten, it was Casey who'd convinced her to hike through the woods to the stream she'd found behind their house just as the sun was slipping below the horizon. Faith would reach out to grab her hand, nervous, as her sister tiptoed across the wet rocks to the other side where a tree had fallen in a storm. Faith was terrified that they'd slip, especially after a good rain when the water was higher, rushing around the rocks, making her a little dizzy as the flow of it zipped past her bare feet. When they got to the other side, Casey would open the jar she'd brought in her backpack, and they'd catch lightning bugs. They were like little stars floating around them in the dark woods. Faith missed those times.

She turned to look at Casey, trying to see past her designer sunglasses. Her face was older, more weathered, but she'd worked hard to keep it youthful, and, if she allowed her vision to blur, Faith could still see that little girl.

"I wonder what Jake's doing up there with Nan," Casey said, shielding her eyes with her hand and craning her neck to view the cottage.

"I think Nan's giving him pointers on the construction of the cottage," Faith giggled.

"She always has to give her two cents. God love her."

"She's great, isn't she?"

"Yeah. I'm so glad she decided to do this. You know, I worry about her and her health, yet at the same time she's doing something like this: planning a trip to the beach." Casey shook her head. "I don't like to think about what things will be like without her. She's the glue for us, you know? She keeps us all together." Casey tilted her head toward the cottage. "We should probably save Jake, though."

"Nah. After seeing how he handled Isabella yesterday on the boat, I don't think he'll need any help."

Both Casey and Faith looked out at Isabella as she stood at the water's edge, filling a bright orange bucket with wet sand. From a distance, she looked just like her mother. It made Faith want to run back to the cottage and dig out a photo of Casey at five years old to see the similarities.

"He's easy to talk to, considering we just met him," Casey said. She sure was bringing Jake up a lot.

"I know." He'd been so sweet to Faith, bringing her ginger ale to settle her stomach and taking her to the front of the boat. From what she'd seen of him, though, he was like that all the time, with everyone. He'd helped Isabella over her worries, he listened to Nan's ramblings about things she didn't know, he joined them for breakfast. No wonder there'd been a crowd around him at Dune Burger when she'd first arrived.

"It's odd that he's single, isn't it?" Casey said.

"Maybe he isn't," Faith said with a shrug. She kicked the sand off her feet.

"I'd date him if I were a single woman," Casey laughed, looking over at Faith, a deviously happy look on her face.

Faith worried about this statement. What if Casey felt the need to get on with her life? She wouldn't... "Yeah, I suppose I would too."

"See if you can get him to offer!"

"What... A date?"

"Yeah!"

When it came to being alluring and exciting, Casey was better than she was. But, on the other hand, there was something about the way Jake had looked at her that made her feel hopeful. And Faith knew that she was capable of having a good time. "He seems like the kind of guy who would easily go out on a date. He'd do it just to be nice," Faith said.

A seagull flew overhead, causing a shadow to trail across the sand. Isabella brought her bucket up to dry ground and dumped it upside down, patting the bottom to pack the wet sand onto its foundation. Faith thought about what it would be like to be on a date with Jake. What would it feel like to be that close to him? Where would he take her? Would they stroll along the beach together or have a nice dinner? It had been a while since she'd been out on a date and she felt rusty, out of practice, her imagination having difficulty coming up with creative ideas. She was willing to bet that Jake would have a ton of ideas.

"I'm actually excited about going fishing with Jake," Casey said.

The initial excitement drained out of her just a little. She'd forgotten that Jake had already asked Casey to go fishing. Granted, it was to appease Isabella, but if he'd not wanted to see her mother, he could've easily gotten out of that situation. They weren't even fishing that day on the boat. He didn't have to offer at all. Casey was starting with the upper hand.

"I'm glad you're enjoying yourself," Faith said, trying to stay positive. "You've had a lot on your plate, and you need a good break. I know what you and Scott are dealing with must be hard," she said, a flock of seagulls flying overhead. "Do you think you will be able to reconcile?"

Casey shook her head and looked out at the ocean. Faith noticed her blinking quite a bit behind her sunglasses, and she felt guilty for bringing up a sore subject. They really hadn't talked about it, though.

"I'm sorry," she said. "I shouldn't have brought it up. I'm just curious. It's a big step, changing a family dynamic like that. Are you sure?"

"No, I'm not sure. I thought everything was fine between us. It blindsided me."

"Was he… Did he… There wasn't another woman or anything, was there?"

"No." Casey picked at a loose thread on the corner of her beach towel. "I asked him." She was quiet for a while. The only sounds were the crashing waves and Isabella's laughter as she chased a sandpiper across the sand before it flew away. "He said he was alone all the time." She adjusted her glasses, but Faith wondered if it was a nervous gesture. Casey hadn't ever really failed at anything. This had to be hard. "He said that it was pointless to live together because he could be alone in his own place without the constant reminder of being alone every time I came home."

"You all didn't spend time together when you were home?" This idea seemed so odd to Faith because she knew how her sister loved being around people. She imagined Casey rushing home to see Scott and Isabella, bursting through the door and dropping her bag right there to reach out her arms and hug them. That would be like her. So why hadn't she been like that?

"My work demands require so much of my time, but Faith, I love my job. I've worked hard to get where I am. When I came home, and work was finished, I sat with Isabella and did what she wanted me to do. Scott was in his office or, if it was late at night, in our bedroom, watching TV. When I finally got ready to go to bed, he was already asleep, and, honestly, I was exhausted myself. We just didn't talk to each other anymore." Casey became quiet again, and this time, Faith could see the gentle rising and falling of her chest as she sat beside her. Casey brushed away a tear that escaped from under her glasses. Her voice broke as she said, "What he didn't realize was that I still loved him. Even though I didn't say it. I still do." She cleared her throat. "We've been separated for a year now, and it still feels like yesterday when he left."

Faith knew what it was like to put work first, and now, here was proof that doing that ruined relationships. Even Casey, who'd always seemed to get everything easily, had let work get in the way of her family, and now she had to face the consequences. "I'm trying to have a fun time while I'm here, but life keeps getting in the way," Faith admitted. "We all need a break. Remember when we used to come here to the cottage as kids? Nothing mattered for that week because we were going to eat Mom's homemade trail mix, stay outside until our skin hurt from too much sun, and turn in after playing board games so late that we could hardly see straight. That was it. That was the expectation for the whole week." Faith fell silent. She missed those times with her sister. And she worried for Casey.

"What should we do for Nan's birthday?" Casey asked, clearly trying to spin the conversation to a more positive subject. "Has she asked for anything in particular?"

Faith shook her head. "Nope. We should probably see if she wants to do something special. We should definitely look for somewhere to buy a cake. Maybe Jake would know."

Isabella came up to them, swinging her empty bucket, tiny droplets of water flinging from it as she walked. The ends of her hair were darker, wet from leaning forward to fill her bucket as the tide came in. Her knees and the backs of her hands were sandy. "Mama," she said, pushing runaway strands of hair away from her face, "I'm ready to go inside."

"Maybe we can get cleaned up and get some ice cream or something," Casey said, her adoration for her daughter clear on her face. She leaned toward Faith. "Wanna go with us?" she asked.

"Absolutely," she said, standing up and folding her chair. She slipped her beach bag over her shoulder and helped with Casey's things as her sister wrapped a towel around Isabella. The little girl slid her sandy feet into a tiny pair of flip-flops that had pink ribbons tied in little bows cascading down each side. Isabella grabbed on to her towel, keeping it around her shoulders, and shuffled over to them as they lugged their belongings back up the dune to the cottage. Once they got to the cottage, they rinsed the sand off their feet in the outside shower.

"What is that noise?" Casey said, tilting her ear upward toward the door of the cottage. The door sat at the top of the long flight of stairs that led from the driveway where they were now standing as they allowed their feet to dry. Jake's work truck was in the driveway with large pieces of wood now tied to the rack at the top.

Faith sharpened her hearing, attempting to make out a foreign sound over the wind in her ears. The house sitting on stilts caused the ocean breeze to whip underneath it like a wind tunnel. She could just make out a shrill whine. "I don't know," she said, following her sister up the stairs. Isabella was sandwiched between them, which she was glad for because the stairs were steep and open, and Faith worried for her niece as she climbed those giant steps. Her legs were working overtime to get up each one.

The whining noise seemed to be getting worse the closer they got but stopped just before they opened the door. When they got inside, Jake was on his knees, wiping dust from the bottom of a giant, rectangular hole in the living room wall. "What is that?" Faith said out loud by accident. She'd meant to keep it to herself, but the sight of the hole sent the words tumbling out of her mouth.

Jake turned around. "Hey," he said, flashing that smile. He had sheetrock dust in his hair, and a pair of safety glasses pushed up onto his forehead. Unbelievably, he still looked good. "I'm putting in a built-in. Your grandmother came up with the idea, and she was absolutely right since there's no storage in this room. Don't worry. It won't take me long. I'll have it all cleaned up by tonight."

It was a good thing he was charming, because anyone else with a buzz saw and a hammer would not be welcome during her beach vacation. But on the other hand, there was something very sweet about Jake and how he took Nan's suggestion so seriously. What in the world was Nan thinking, offering her suggestions anyway? Even if she was right, it wasn't her place to tell the man what to build and what not to build. Faith looked for her sister to see her reaction, but Casey must have headed off to the bathroom with Isabella, probably helping her change out of her wet suit and into some clothes. Nan and her mom were nowhere in sight. They probably couldn't stand the noise.

Faith was dying to know more about Jake. She had so many questions. If she could ever fit those questions into a conversation, she would. Nan would just ask them outright, no matter what they were saying. Maybe she should be more like Nan, she thought with a grin.

Nan seemed to always have it together. She never faltered. She was strong, elegant, and wise, and, even though she didn't wait for pleasantries to get across what she wanted, she was careful with her words. She could make anyone do anything she liked, but she never seemed to take advantage of it. Even as she aged, and her body wasn't as agile as it once was, she was graceful with her movements. She took tiny steps, kept her shoulders strong, and took her time. But she never let on that anything was a struggle. Faith looked up to Nan so much.

"How was the beach?" Jake asked. He slipped his safety glasses down over his eyes and began sanding out the rough edges of the wall.

"It was nice," she said, walking a little closer to get a good look at the damage to the wall. That perfectly white wall. "Isabella wanted to come in. We're going to take her for some ice cream."

"You should take her to Surfin' Spoon," he said. "It's a cool place."

She was willing to bet that Jake knew all the cool places in town. "Have you lived here long?" she asked out of the blue.

"I grew up here." He stood up and took off his glasses, letting them dangle from his fingers. "I bought my first house down here after college." There was a look in his eyes. It felt like… affection. It was hard to tell, as she hadn't known him that long. She'd never met anyone as personable as Jake Buchanan and it was difficult to read what was true fondness and what was part of his general personality. Perhaps she was just overthinking his friendliness.

"I figured you'd been here a while. You seem to know the area so well."

He turned and faced the rectangular hole, stretching a measuring tape across the width of it.

"So, what would you suggest for something fun to do this evening?" she asked.

"Hmm." He measured from top to bottom, a small crease forming between his eyes as he read the length. "Have you ever been to the top of Bodie Island lighthouse? It's got a great view."

"No, I haven't. It sounds nice."

He turned around and looked at her, pocketing the tape measure. "Wanna go? I could come back at around five and take you over."

"I'd love to," she answered honestly, feeling much more excited than she let on. She couldn't wait.

Chapter Eight

"I got a date with Jake." Faith chewed on a grin. She knew Casey would want an immediate explanation. Isabella was pulling her mother toward the ice cream flavors, putting too much distance between them for a response, but Casey's face was all questions. Faith smiled. She knew her sister too well. Faith pulled a cup from a stand nearby and filled it with soft-serve mint chocolate chip frozen yogurt. It was a softball-sized wad of ice-cream-like texture, and, with the summer heat that they'd let in when they'd arrived, it seemed to be melting before she could even get a bite. She handed it, along with a napkin that she'd grabbed, to the cashier who was waiting at a nearby register.

While Isabella pointed out flavors to Casey, Faith walked down the long counter, its surface like the wood of a pier. The whole interior was painted in pastel colors on the inside and out with natural wood accents. When they'd walked up to the place, she'd thought it looked like some sort of boat keeper's dollhouse. It was sea-foam green with a yellow door, fresh pots of flowers on either side of it, their bright pink color contrasting with the light painted siding. Along the side of the place were picnic tables with umbrellas in varying colors that made them look like enormous scoops of ice cream, despite their square shape. She pulled out a few dollar bills and set them on the counter.

Isabella was walking back and forth in front of the various silver handles—each one labeled with a different flavor—dragging her little fingers along the surface of a parallel table whitewashed and then topped with wide stripes in greens and blues.

Casey surveyed their choices. "They have double chocolate, Isabella," she suggested before filling a bowl of vanilla for herself. "How did you manage that?" she asked Faith as she neared her, finally being able to pick up Faith's earlier comment about her date with Jake. Casey's eyes were almost dancing. She seemed genuinely happy for her.

"I was just talking to him. That's all. I asked what he suggested doing for fun. He mentioned Bodie Island lighthouse and then offered to take me there at five o'clock." She couldn't help but be proud of herself. Usually, it was Casey who was the one getting the dates. Faith couldn't remember being in this position growing up.

"I'd like cotton candy," Isabella said, finally deciding, and Casey made a face but tried to straighten it back out.

"Cotton candy flavored ice cream? Are you sure?"

"Yes!"

Isabella's hair was done up in two braids that fell over each shoulder. They were swinging like golden ropes as she wriggled around in excitement. Casey filled a bowl to the brim with pink and blue swirled frozen yogurt and held it out to Isabella. The heavy bowl wobbled in her tiny hands as she attempted to take it from her mother while Casey paid for her ice cream.

Isabella made a scraping sound as she pulled out one of the brightly patterned stools, its silver legs scooting across the floor. Her lips were covered in pink ice cream as she attempted to steal a bite before she sat down. As she licked them, she tipped her head sideways to look at a drip that had fallen onto her hand. She licked that too.

"Use your spoon please, Isabella," Casey said, clearly trying not to laugh. "I'd much rather see a lighthouse than go fishing," she whispered to Faith as they got settled at the table. "That's it. When we get back to the cottage, I'm going to research to find the most fabulous places to visit in the area and then I'll get to work weaving them into the conversation," she said with a wink. It was lighthearted, yet Faith felt a twinge of worry that surprised her.

Faith hadn't planned on going out with someone when she'd packed for this trip. She'd packed for two weeks of sandy feet and days with her family. She hadn't been trying to impress anyone when she'd put her clothes in her suitcase. Now, Faith stood in a towel, her wet hair dripping down her back, staring at her options and biting her lip. With a tiny shake of her head, she pulled out a silky peach-colored tank top and a pair of shorts. It was the best she could do. At least she had earrings to match this one and it would look like she'd tried. She could've borrowed something from Casey, but her clothes were much too fussy and glamorous for Faith's style. And she just wanted to be herself. Faith dried off, dressed, and wrapped her hair up in her towel. As she looked in the mirror, she tried to imagine what to do with her makeup. Should she go with gloss or a light lipstick? Should she choose shimmery powder or flat?

Faith didn't want to overdo it, but she wanted to look like she'd put a little effort into it as well. Jake was nice, and handsome, and she wanted to impress him. After dusting her face with shimmery powder, she added a little pink to her cheeks and some eyeshadow. Finally, she put a little clear gloss on her lips and rubbed them together.

She dried her hair and put on her silver earrings with the dangly peach beads, then looked back in the mirror. As she stared at her complexion, Faith tried to look past the familiar face to see what Jake would see when he looked at her. She had a girl-next-door kind of look to her—nothing like Casey. Faith was shorter, more petite, and cutesier. She wanted to be sexy, interesting. Casey could pull her hair up and downplay her makeup and be adorably cute, but she could also let that gorgeous blond hair down, add some lipstick, and she'd turn heads at a mile away. When Faith figured her look was as good as it would get, she slipped on a pair of sandals and headed for the living area to wait for Jake.

"My. Look at you," Nan said from her chair as Faith entered the room.

"Jake's taking me to see Bodie Island lighthouse."

"Is he, now?" she said, a wry grin on her face.

"Don't get that look, Nan. It's just a friendly offer," she said with a smile, but Nan's comment sent a jolt of excitement through her. She was more excited than she let on. She walked over and knelt down next to Nan.

"I'm just happy you're enjoying yourself," Nan said. "And I'm glad to see you've been out with Casey today. I like seeing you girls back together."

It sounded easy—seeing Casey—and for the most part they fell back in line together like they'd never left each other, but she couldn't deny the feeling of needing to finish things from the past. She'd definitely changed over the years, and she wondered if Casey had too.

"I'm sorry I haven't spent more time with the family until now," Faith said honestly.

Nan put her hand on Faith's wrist, her fingers light and cold. "The past is the past," she said in her wise way. "We're here now. That's all that matters." She smiled and leaned back in her chair. "All the girls are back together."

The girls. It had always been "the girls." Her father had left when she was so young that she couldn't remember him, her grandfather had passed before her birth, and now, both sisters were single. Perhaps they were cursed. Or maybe they were just better as *the girls.* Maybe they weren't meant to find anyone. As she looked at Nan, Faith began to wonder if she should be going out with Jake at all. She should be there, in the cottage, with them all. How insensitive of her to have not considered this earlier.

"Nan," she said. "Do you want me to stay here instead of going out? Would you rather have all us girls together?"

"You mean sit like a bump on a ninety-year-old log?"

"You're making light of it," she smiled affectionately. "We've all been running around like crazy since we got here. Do you want us all to stay together? It's your birthday and this was a trip that you planned after all. I just want to make you happy." She was saying the words, but Faith also knew that staying together in the quiet of the cottage would mean dealing with some of the things Faith didn't really want to delve into. It was easier when they were out at the beach, with people passing by, or getting ice cream. But when they were alone as a family, things would inevitably come out, and Faith didn't really want to deal with them. It was easier to just push it away and move forward.

Nan had laughter in her eyes. "Silly girl," she said. "What makes me happy is not having you sitting here by my feet. I'm aware that I can't move around like I used to, and it may seem to you like I'm just sitting here alone, but when you all are 'running around' as you say, I'm happier than I've ever been because I get to watch you *live*. Life is about taking chances, and I've learned that things can be disastrous if we don't do that. Go see the lighthouse and then come home and tell me all about it. I can't wait to hear."

"You sure?"

"Yes, I'm sure! Now, get up before you get all wrinkled!"

Faith stood up and decided to wait on the porch for Jake to arrive. At this time of day, the sunrays were the color of champagne, and the air wrapped around her like a warm hug. Before she could get to the door, however, there was a knock, and she felt her pulse quicken. She tried to quiet her nerves. *He's just being friendly*, she said to herself. *Stop being so dramatic. Act like you've done this a million times before.* She opened the door.

For the second time since she'd met him, Jake was all cleaned up, and she thought again how handsome he was. When he was working, he had a rugged look to him—scruff on his face, strong hands, his T-shirt tight against his biceps—but when he was spruced up, it was as if he was just as comfortable. Someone who didn't know him would never believe—wearing what he was wearing now—that he worked with his hands. With his pressed shorts, white polo shirt against his slightly tanned skin, and his hair perfectly cut, it looked like he should work some sort of office job.

"Hey," he said with a smile.

His eyes wanted to move away from her face—she could tell because he'd done it before at the window when she'd been in her silky pajamas and again in her swimsuit—but he kept his gaze matched with hers. It made her want to smile, so she swallowed instead.

"Ready?"

"Yep!" she said, grabbing her handbag and throwing up a hand to Nan.

They walked together out to the driveway and Faith gasped. She shouldn't have, but she couldn't help it. She stood with her eyes fixed on what was in front of her. When she was finally able, she tore herself away from it and looked at Jake for an explanation. He only smiled and opened the door of the sleek silver Mercedes. "Well, you didn't think I'd pick you up in the work truck, did you?" he said with a chuckle. Still processing the fact that she was about to slide into this car—its new car smell overtaking even the sea air—she remained silent.

"Have fun…" Casey said from the top of the dune, her words withering to silence as she, too, noticed the vehicle. This wasn't the usual Mercedes—not that any Mercedes would be *usual* in Faith's circles, but this one looked like something out of a car show. The paint finish on the outside was so glossy, Faith wondered if it had been driven very much. She waved to her sister, telling her with her expression how she was just as surprised, and slid farther into the car. Jake shut the door and walked around the back. The black leather interior was spotless—not a speck of dust. Faith tried not to stare at the gorgeous wood-grain console, so she looked up at Jake as he got in.

With only a push of a button, the car purred. It was so quiet, Faith wasn't quite sure it was actually running. "Windows down or air conditioning?" Jake asked as he began pulling onto the road. She buckled her seatbelt.

Faith noticed how comfortable he was driving the car. His shoulders were relaxed, his hand resting on the gearshift in the center console. Did he own this car? Realizing that she hadn't answered his question, she said, "Air conditioning." The last thing she needed was her hair blowing around and sticking to her extra-shiny lip gloss, and she wouldn't dare risk sand getting blown into the black interior.

As Jake drove down Beach Road, the only sound in the car was the hiss of his tires as they rolled through the sand on the surface of the road. Faith was dying to ask him about the car. In only three days, she'd found him to be very friendly, and he seemed to be quite open whenever they'd spoken; yet there was so much—clearly—about him that she didn't know. A handyman with a Mercedes? Friends who owned yacht-sized sailboats? Was he involved in something illegal? She caught herself fiddling with her fingers as her mind spun, so she stilled them on her thighs. Jake looked over at her and flashed a smile, making her glad she'd flattened her fingers out on her shorts. It kept them steady.

"What are you thinking about?" he asked, and she felt the heat in her cheeks.

Faith swallowed, but there was no saliva left in her mouth so the gulp of air and dryness rolled down her throat slowly. She cleared it with a little cough. Scrambling for an answer to his question, she blurted, "How did you meet Rich?"

Oh! That was a terrible question! she scolded herself. What she really wanted to know was how the two men had met and become friends—they seemed to belong to completely different worlds. Now it looked like she might be interested in Rich, for goodness' sake. She was not getting off to a good start. Casey would never have asked such a ridiculous question.

"We went to college together," he said, thoughts behind his eyes, the skin between them puckered in confusion. "We're in the same line of work."

I know. Stupid, stupid question, she wanted to agree with his unspoken thoughts, but as what he said registered, more questions began to swim around in her mind. Same line of work?

"Rich is a handyman?" she asked, the thought tumbling out before she could rein it in.

Jake was quiet for just a moment. Then, out of nowhere, he let out a loud "Ha!" and threw his head back in laughter. His chest was still rising and falling with little bursts of amusement as he looked back at her, and she could see that affection again in his eyes. What had she said? What did he find so funny? The worry from this settled in her stomach, making her feel a little queasy. The very last thing she wanted to do was to insult him in any way.

His smile waned to a grin, and it was clear his thoughts were elsewhere for a moment. "Why the interest in Rich?" he asked very directly.

"I wasn't really asking about Rich," she said. "I was wondering how you'd met someone who clearly has so much…" *Oh, now she was going to look like some kind of golddigger.* She was digging herself into a deeper hole. No wonder Casey was better at getting the guy. She would have never talked herself into such a situation as this.

Jake steered the car around a turn and then looked back at her. "What do you mean, 'has so much'?"

"He has…sailboats," she said, "and…is this car his?"

More laughing. Lots of laughing… What had she said now? Faith reached over and turned the vent so that the air conditioning was blowing right on her face. Her cheeks were on fire with embarrassment.

Once he'd calmed down from his laughing fit, Jake, still smiling, said, "I do carpentry on the side. It's not my full-time job. I do it because I love it. I've always done it with my dad. It makes me feel closer to him. And the car and the boat are mine."

"Yours?" Faith said, trying not to show her complete astonishment.

He smiled.

She struggled to put a sentence together. "Why didn't you tell us?" she asked, wondering why he hadn't pointed that fact out when they'd taken the boat ride.

He laughed again. "What did you want me to say—hello, I'm Jake Buchanan. I own a boat and a car," he teased. "Should I list all my other assets?" He pulled in to the parking lot and turned off the engine. The whole journey had passed and she hadn't even noticed. Her mind still reeling from this bit of information—he'd given her a lot to digest at once—Faith looked out at the massive black-and-white-striped lighthouse, that she'd only ever seen from the road, as Jake got out. She was grateful they were there so she could change the conversation.

He opened her car door and stepped to the side as she swung her legs around. She hopped out, shut the door, and followed Jake to the long, wooden walkway heading to the lighthouse. The walk was made of flat boards, laid side to side, like a low-lying pier, and it stretched for ages. The tall sea grass danced in the wind on either side of it, and, despite it being after five o'clock, the sun's heat was warm on her arms and shoulders as she walked beside him toward the gorgeous structure at the edge of the sea.

The lighthouse looked as though it were all white with a wide belt of black twisting around it like a perfectly horizontal stripe of a candy cane. The black, iron top of it, housing the large glass optic section for the lantern, was so ornamented that it looked as though it were a giant crown. The lantern, housed in a cylinder of glass, sparkled in the sunlight. The whole thing sat on the most gorgeous piece of property—a large expanse of lush green giving way to pond-sized puddles. Each puddle, when seen from this distance, looked like a stepping stone to the sea.

"There's so much space here," Jake said, looking out at the vast stretch of grass that led to the shoreline. "You know what I see when I look at it?"

She shook her head, still taking it all in.

"I see hope and possibilities. All this undeveloped, beautiful land."

Faith knew just what he meant. So much retail space had eaten up the shoreline that this unspoiled landscape was a refreshing change. Looking out at it, it gave her hope too—hope that there would always be some place, some retreat for her when things got crazy in life. She promised herself right then that she'd come back to this place, find a small but perfect spot for solitude and healing, and just soak it in. It really was a perfect view.

"I love the outdoors," she said.

"Me too. At the house where I grew up, it was very wooded. I used to run from backyard to backyard. I'd pretend I was an explorer in the forest."

"Sounds like me," she said with a smile. "I had a creek by my house and a lot of woods. I used to play outside all the time." She followed him along the walk, careful to step over a board that had warped and was jutting out slightly. Things were going more smoothly now; the last thing she wanted was to trip. "Casey and I used to catch lightning bugs."

"So did I!" he said, his voice rising slightly in excitement.

"Did you try to keep them?" she asked.

"I put them in a mason jar. I poked holes in the metal top. I'd keep them in there for about fifteen minutes before I felt sorry for them and let them go. Every time, I swore I was going to keep them as pets."

"That's a very keen observation for a child, to realize they needed to be released."

"I looked out at the woods and I thought how much better it was to run in them than to be shut up in my room, so they needed to have the same freedom. Did you keep yours?"

"No. I didn't think as much about it as you did, but I always let them go."

"Ah." He smiled, sending a current of happiness through her chest. "Maybe it's because you already knew. You didn't have to think about it."

Faith and Jake had let their lightning bugs go, only holding them close to inspect their beauty; their real beauty was when they were out in the world. Perhaps that was how Nan felt about her family. She enjoyed seeing them out instead of shut up in the confines of the house. It hit her at that moment that she hadn't shared much of her social life with Nan in a long time.

Perhaps Nan didn't realize how much she'd changed. Was that why she'd brought them all the way to the Outer Banks for her birthday? Was that why she had all those photos—photos of life being lived? Was Nan hoping to remind them all that they needed to enjoy their lives? No one ever takes photos while sitting at a desk working. Those aren't the memories that matter. That wasn't living. As she walked next to Jake, the wind in her hair, the sun on her skin, the clean, spicy smell of him wafting around her in the breeze, she realized how much of a memory she was making. And this was a memory that mattered.

"So, what do you like to do when you aren't working or building things? What do you do to relax?" she asked, the question coming easily this time. His hand was swinging right next to hers, and she wondered what it would feel like to be able to hold it casually. She wished she could fast forward to a time when she knew him well enough to feel completely at ease around him. He had such a gentle, caring way about him, despite his strong exterior. Would his romantic touch be as light as his words were sometimes?

"I'm up for anything," he said.

"What about if it's raining and you can't go out. What do you do?"

He grinned a crooked grin and shook his head. "You probably wouldn't believe me."

"Why? Do you give yourself facials or something?" She giggled at the thought.

"Ha! No. Definitely not." He chuckled some more and allowed her to hop off the walkway first. On the grounds of the lighthouse was an old farmhouse—white wooden siding with a long country porch. It looked as though it might be a museum. "I sit in my favorite chair and read."

There was something so delicious about thinking of this man beside her, a book in his hands, the quiet hum of the fan or the crackling of a fire the only sound as he devoured the words on the page. What he hadn't realized was that it was the perfect answer. Faith would love nothing more than to sit and read beside him.

"Why is that so hard to believe?" she asked.

"I suppose it is believable. It's just not very exciting."

"Says who?"

"My ex-wife, for one," he said with another huff of laughter, but his face straightened out quickly and Faith could sense the wound that was still there. "Good grief. I'm out of practice."

"What do you mean?"

"First time I take a lady out, and I'm mentioning my ex. Sorry."

His admission warmed her. "It's okay."

"I'm trying not to mess this up," he said in a lighthearted way, but she could feel a seriousness to his words. It was clear that he was trying to make a good impression, meaning that taking her out was a big deal to him. This fact made her so happy.

"I love to read, too," she said in an effort to calm his worry. "It's my favorite thing to do."

He smiled at what she'd said, but there was more behind his smile—a wonder, an interest. He looked a little unsure, which was odd, since he'd been so confident with her family.

"Really?" he asked. Faith sensed that he thought she was just trying to make him feel better, and she was taken with his vulnerability.

"When I was young, I always had a book in my hands. I still do whenever I get a chance, although, with my job, I've been reading a lot of children's books lately."

"I always liked the classics, and my dad said that I was an old soul."

"What was your favorite book?"

"A newer classic, actually. Hemingway. *Old Man and the Sea*. I read it so many times that the binding broke and all the pages were loose inside."

She felt the coincidence in her chest and couldn't believe that it was possible that as kids, the two of them could've been in the same town in the Outer Banks with their noses in a book. "Hemingway? Didn't he have a house in Key West?"

"Yes, I think he did. That's impressive knowledge!"

"I only know because I was obsessed with Key West as a child. I read all of Robert Frost, and he spent time there as well. I wanted so badly to go there."

"Did you ever go?"

"No."

"Why not?"

She took in a breath, relishing the smell of the beach. "I don't know; work commitments, family stuff, I suppose. But deep down, I think I just didn't want to go alone. I'd rather wait until I have someone to go with."

He looked at her for a long time, and she wondered what was going through his mind. It was as if she'd hit a nerve or something. She could sense a little disappointment, maybe? It was hard to tell. "If you wait for things like that," he said gently, "you'll end up having never gone."

It occurred to Faith then that this strong, handsome man, who seemed to have it all together, who had so much free time he could work every day doing something he loved, who had enough money to buy enormous sailboats and luxury cars, and had everything he could ever want—might be missing something. Did he crave the intimacy of a family? Did he want someone to share his life with? Or were those just Faith's wishes coming through?

Reaching the lighthouse, Jake paid the entrance fee and they walked inside. Spiraling upward as far as she could see was a mesh metal staircase. Looking up, the climb seemed daunting as she considered the sandals she was wearing. She'd tried to look pretty, choosing her strappy ones with a slight heel. Now, she wished she had her flip-flops.

"Ladies first." Jake gestured toward the first step. Trying not to think about the journey upward, she put her foot on the step and started the climb to the top. Their feet made clattering sounds as they walked up.

"In my dad's house, there was a crawl space underneath our stairs for storage. My dad cleared it out and made it into a little clubhouse for me. I used to sit in there and read. The only light was my battery-operated book light. I could hear the sound of feet on the steps whenever someone went up. I haven't thought of that in years, but our footsteps reminded me of it."

She looked back at him, wishing they could stop right there on the stairs and talk some more despite the fact that it wasn't the most ideal place to stop. She didn't care. She could be anywhere and talk to him. "You did a lot with your dad, it seems," she said, taking another step.

"Well, growing up, it was just the two of us."

She didn't want to pry, but she wanted to find out everything about Jake. He was like no one else she'd gone on a date with before. He was open, genuine, no nonsense. It was clear that he was just himself. She wanted to know how that little boy, who'd crawled under the stairs as a kid, had grown up to be a wealthy businessman who still did carpentry on the side. What happened in all those years to make him the man who was climbing those stairs with her now? She wanted to know all the things his father had seen as he'd grown up. And she wanted to meet him—the man who'd taught Jake how to be this wonderful, sweet person. "I only ask," she said, "because it was just me, Casey, and my mom. My dad left when we were little."

"Ah. Well, my mom passed away when I was young."

"I'm so sorry, Jake." His loss made her unexpectedly sad.

"It's okay. I have foggy memories of her—like dreams. I remember her kissing my forehead before bed, and I remember her singing me to sleep. The rest of my memories—very good ones—are of my dad."

His words echoed in the hollow space of the lighthouse, but they were the only ones there, so no one heard them.

She stopped and turned around, and he almost bumped into her. His hands were on the railing on either side of her. If he let go, they were close enough that he could put his arms around her. "Thank you for telling me that," she said, seeing him in a new light.

He was eye level, being a step below her, and she could see contemplation on his face. His eyes roamed hers for a moment, as if he, too, had only really seen her for the first time in that moment. The silence was thick around them. She didn't know how to respond to whatever it was zinging between her and this wonderful stranger. The way he was looking at her, it was as if he were going to do something, say something—she wasn't sure.

"It was nothing at all to tell you that," he said quietly, his eyes still intently looking into hers. He pulled in with every word and every look, closer and closer. His face was so near that she could feel his breath, and she swallowed to keep composure. He leaned forward and smiled, just before his lips met hers.

His hands were on her waist, his fingers unstill. She grabbed the railing to keep herself from falling, the feel of his lips making her dizzy. The warmth of his breath as it mixed with hers, the softness of his touch, it was different than anything she'd experienced before. She didn't want to open her eyes or stop the movement of her lips because that would mean it was over, and she didn't want it to end. When she was finally forced into the reality of the moment, and he'd pulled back gently, she opened her eyes to find him smiling.

"Sorry," he said. "I couldn't help myself." He grinned at her, affection showing on his face.

She smiled back at him as he motioned for her to resume heading up the staircase. She had to work to get her legs to move, her brain completely overloaded by the sensation of that kiss.

"I can't wait to show you this."

They'd finally reached the top and the heat from the moment between them and inside the lighthouse had made her feel warm despite her summer clothing. It took all her concentration to keep her mind from reliving that kiss. She needed to get outside into the fresh air.

She walked out onto the circular landing that wrapped around the glass casing for the lantern, and the relentless ocean breeze cooled her skin. She was taken by how large the lantern itself was, but it didn't hold her attention. What nearly took her breath away was the view. She could see nothing but marsh grass and blue ocean as far as her vision could travel. The lighthouse had seemed so big and grand, but compared to the Atlantic it was a tiny thing. She put her hands on the railing, and she could feel Jake beside her as he looked out at the same view. Sharing it with him made it perfect.

"Sit down here," he said, dropping down onto the mesh floor of the overlook. He put his legs between the railings. They barely fit, his feet dangling in midair what seemed like miles above the ground below. Faith followed suit, and, as she looked at her own feet as they swung in the air, the sight made her dizzy. They were so small compared to everything around them.

He pulled a penny from his pocket. "Make a wish."

She had so many wishes: she wished that she and Casey could be closer, she wished that Nan would be around another twenty years, she wished that she could spend every summer here, and she wished that she could kiss Jake again.

"Got it?"

"Yes," she lied, still deciding which one to choose.

Jake flipped the penny off his fingers and she watched it sail down through the air, the sun shimmering off its copper surface. It got smaller and smaller as she tried to keep focus on it, until it disappeared in the marsh grass below.

"It's a long way down," he said, and she nodded. "Don't fall," he said, his words urgent, as he grabbed her by the shoulders, teasing her. She squealed and then laughed.

"Not funny." She cut her eyes at him playfully, but before she could straighten her face out, his lips were on hers again, his hand at the back of her neck. Well, it seemed as if one wish was coming through.

Slowly pulling apart, they both looked back out at the sea.

"I used to come up here as a kid. We would drop pennies and make wishes with all our girlfriends," he said, teasing her. "I'll be honest. I haven't been up here since then. It's kind of fun being back up here."

Faith wondered what that boy was like—the boy who read Hemingway and caught lightning bugs only to let them go. Would she have liked him? More importantly, would he have liked her? It seemed as if she'd have had lots of competition for his affection.

"So you do this with all the girls, then?" Although she'd said it playfully, there was a part of her that wanted to know.

"No. Only the ones I really like."

She laughed.

"It's nice, isn't it?" he asked, standing back up and reaching out his hand. She took it and he helped her stand. She didn't want to leave.

"Yes." Faith imagined what it would be like to sit in a rocking chair day after day with the person she loved, listening to the wind and watching the ocean like she was right then. What a surprising thought to have while standing with someone she barely knew, but being with him calmed her, and, after kissing him, she wasn't concerned anymore with trying to be witty and alluring. She could just stand here and be herself. He made her feel perfectly comfortable.

Out of all the locations Jake could've taken her, he'd chosen the simplest, most natural, lovely place. How did he know that it was exactly the type of thing she loved? There were lots of other places in the Outer Banks—mini golf, go karts, shopping—but he'd chosen Bodie Island Lighthouse. It showcased what the Outer Banks was really about: simplicity. The coastline itself was so amazing that she could sit all day and watch the tide rolling in and out like it had done for generations.

"How could you ever want to sit inside when you could look at a view like this?" he asked.

She smiled. "I was thinking the same thing."

"I don't want to take you home yet," he said. "Are you hungry? Wanna get something to eat?"

"I am hungry," she said, the thrill of his admission that he wanted more time with her lifting in her stomach. She absolutely wanted to do something else with Jake, but she wished she could stay and take in the view a little longer. It was nice being with him. Being up here, completely removed from everything and everyone else, it felt like it was just the two of them.

"Great. I figured you might be. I've already made reservations."

"Oh?" The idea that he'd taken time to work out where to take her, he'd called and made arrangements—it seemed very sweet since they were only out on a casual first date. But that was what she liked about him, how unfussy he seemed. Especially knowing now that he had a lot of money, he didn't flaunt it; it didn't define him. She really loved that he painted and built things, spent time with the other locals. Faith wondered about this place he'd planned to take her. It must be very popular to need reservations. Although most beachside restaurants were quite busy. Perhaps he didn't want to have to wait for a table, although, in her experience, the wait was never longer than forty-five minutes, and they could get a drink at the bar.

"Yep. Somewhere I think you'll really like. But we've still got some time to kill and I have somewhere else I'd like to show you."

She was intrigued and couldn't wait to see where he'd take her.

Chapter Nine

The display windows covered nearly the whole front of the small building. It was shingled, like the cottage, but low to the ground since it was far enough inland to be safe from the floods. Jake held the door open for Faith as she entered, and what she saw was like heaven. Every space was covered in secondhand books, some of them even turned sideways above other books to allow them space on the shelf. There were so many books that she had difficulty knowing where to look first.

Faith wandered along the narrow aisles created by bookshelves, the smell of old wood and used books thrilling her senses. It was a place she'd never been before, but judging by the look of the building, it had probably been there when she'd vacationed at Nan's cottage as a kid. How she would've loved to peruse these shelves back then.

"There's a section at the back that has well-known authors," Jake said over her shoulder into her ear, sending goose bumps down her arm. "I used to buy my copies of Hemingway here. They were only fifty cents and I could use my grass-cutting money to buy them."

She loved the idea of Jake saving up his pocket money to come here and buy books. It sounded like something she would do.

They stopped at the back of the shop and Faith let her eyes roam the shelves. She knew exactly what she was looking for. As she searched, Jake pulled out a few different books, thumbed through them, and put them back on the shelf.

"I haven't been here in ages," he said.

"It's amazing! I love it." She really did. It brought back the desire to read for herself again.

"We don't have enough really good book stores in the Outer Banks."

She nodded in agreement and then, when she looked back at the shelves, she saw it: the Robert Frost section. There were only three books, and one of them she knew like the back of her hand. She turned her head to read the spine—it was newer than her copy. She'd had to tape the cover back on several times, but it had kept falling off. Finally, she'd just left it. It was still at home on her bookshelf. Faith reached over and pulled it off the shelf, opening it to her favorite spot and reading those familiar words. It filled her with the same joy that it used to as a child.

"May I help you?" she heard from behind her and they both turned around.

"How much is this?" She held up the book.

"A dollar."

"I'll take it," she said brightly. Turning to Jake, she added, "I'll bet you can't get Frost for a dollar at that new fancy book store I saw on the bypass. This place is much better than those big stores." Instead of looking amused, however, Jake looked thoughtful, and she wondered what he could be thinking about.

"Where are you taking me for dinner?" Faith asked, not looking back at him but focusing on the steps as she made her way out of the bookstore.

"It's a surprise."

"Why?" She giggled. "I probably haven't been there anyway." She'd never been anywhere at the beach where she'd had to make reservations.

"You definitely haven't been there."

"Is it new?"

"Yes."

"So then you can at least tell me the name."

Jake was quiet long enough that she turned around. He was hiding a smile, the corners of his lips twitching with amusement. Faith allowed the confusion to show on her face.

"It's called Tides Bistro and Wine Bar, but I'm not telling you anything else."

"Is it on the water?"

"Yes."

"You just told me something else." She smiled. It was so easy between them that it brought out her playful side.

She noticed how fondly he was looking at her, the lightness of the fine lines at the edges of his eyes—where he'd probably spent years smiling in the sun—the way his eyes seemed to sparkle, as he focused on her.

"I hope you like it."

"Well, tell me about it then so you don't have to worry!" she teased him.

He laughed, sending her stomach into a somersault. She enjoyed seeing him laugh. It was infectious. She could feel the smile emerging on her own face in response.

She was glad for his dinner suggestion. She wasn't ready to go back to her cottage yet.

***

Wherever Jake's restaurant was, it was a slight drive, he'd said, from the bookstore. They'd been driving for a while, paralleling the beach the whole way. As he drove, they'd been chatting about all sorts of things, and the more they talked, the more she couldn't believe how relaxed she was around him. She was so excited to see where they'd be having dinner. She'd never heard of the restaurant before, and she was quite curious.

Part of the charm of the Outer Banks for her was frequenting the same spots whenever they came. There was a restaurant called Goombays, a small building with a rainbow awning out front that she'd loved as a kid. Inside, the entire ceiling was decorated like the surface of the sea, making her feel like she was eating on the ocean floor. She had fond memories there—good food and funny drinks with plastic sharks floating in them. Would she make new memories at this restaurant Jake had chosen?

They entered Corolla, North Carolina and not long after, he pulled the car onto a little road with short, knobby pine trees on either side. It was so narrow that they'd have to pull over if another car came toward them. They bumped along the stretch of the road. Then, sitting right on the beach, the restaurant, Tides Bistro and Wine Bar, came into view. It was a gigantic structure, all sharp lines and modern minimalism, miles away from the experiences she'd had as a kid. The parking lot swallowed what seemed like acres of land and stretched so far away from the building that the restaurant seemed to need a valet. *Why would anyone need a valet? We're at the beach, for goodness' sake. Wouldn't they want to walk in this gorgeous air?*

She took in the massive building and the super-size parking lot. It was a very odd feeling to have, but she felt uncomfortable. The sight of it was ridiculous given the culture there. It stuck out like a sore thumb. She understood that whoever had designed it was trying to make a glamorous modern structure that took advantage of the amazing views and offered something sophisticated, but this area wasn't about high-end views; it was about tradition and a simple way of life. Restaurants with character, like Dune Burger, that offered laid-back atmospheres, mixed drinks, and casual dinners were what she was used to. They were full of warmth and happy memories from years of visitors and locals.

Faith was delighted when Jake pulled past the valet and parked the car himself. She didn't want to have anything to do with that sort of pretentiousness. He turned off the engine and walked around to let her out. As he held the car door open for her, he looked proud and happy. *What in the world would have drawn Jake to a place like this?* she wondered. *Maybe he just really likes the food.*

He reached out his hand to help her out of the car. As they walked together toward the restaurant, she couldn't help but think again about how this structure was almost imposing on the landscape around it. It was beautiful, certainly, but the Outer Banks was the kind of place where life was stripped down to its most basic elements: sun, sea, sand—and everything else was built with those elements in mind. This building was angular, with glass everywhere she looked—she wondered how in the world it would ever survive a hurricane. Of all the places they could've gone, why did Jake come here? It seemed such a contrast to his personality that it had taken her by surprise.

Jake tugged on the enormous brass door pull, the door—more glass—sliding open. They walked in to be greeted immediately by a member of staff who was wearing all black, a stark white, pressed apron neatly arranged at his waist. He called Jake by name, addressing him as "Mr. Buchanan." The whole place was dark, stacks of wine sprawling their way to the walls of glass overlooking the ocean. More bright white linens were draped on the tables, candles in varying shapes flickering in the centers of each table. Faith tried to smooth out her cotton shorts, and she ran her fingers through her windblown hair, thinking how this kind of place was more Casey's type of restaurant than hers.

The waiter pulled out her chair, and she nervously took a seat. Before she could get comfortable, the man had thrust a menu the size of the table into her hands. She looked over at Jake, and he smiled at her before scanning his own menu.

She followed his lead and began looking at the options for dinner. Her hunger pains quickly turned into apprehension as she read what was in front of her. All the dishes had names she didn't recognize, their descriptions so fancy that she could hardly make out what was in them, and each dish was more money than she'd ever paid for a plate of food before. What were they doing at a place like this? She knew Jake had money, and it was nice that he wanted to spoil her, but it seemed awfully extreme for a first date. Trying to ignore the outrageous prices, she took a deep breath and began again at the top of the menu, reading each description, but by the time she got to the bottom, she had no idea what to order.

This place had stunned her so much that she couldn't stop her mind from circling back to her earlier thought: Was this the kind of lifestyle Jake was really used to living?

"What do you think of this place?" he asked from behind his menu, his delight clearly coming through in his voice.

She looked around, scrambling for something to say, anything positive she could find about the place, but she was coming up empty.

"I wanted to bring you here, because this is mine."

She was completely taken aback. "Sorry?"

"I built this."

Suddenly, she wasn't very hungry. She'd imagined whoever built this to be someone completely out of touch with everything the area stood for, some sort of corporate clone, his mind only on profits and the upper class. The very last person she imagined to be behind this was Jake. Jake, who'd so lovingly worked on the cottage, who'd taken her to the lighthouse to see the views—he knew better.

He'd grown up there! He knew the culture! He knew that the very last thing people wanted when they came to the Outer Banks was something that would remove them from the customs of the area. She'd seen firsthand the growth there, and she'd heard rumblings in news articles and on television about how the locals were resisting this growth. They didn't like it, and neither did she.

"There's nothing like it here. I loved the idea of offering more options. There's so much land here to be developed."

"But do you think that's what people want? When they come to the Outer Banks, do you think they want options or the comfort of those local places that they love?" She couldn't help herself. She was so disappointed.

"There are probably people who still love the quirks of those out-of-the-way places, the little historical treasures. But there are also those who like something new. I definitely believe we have a market for this sort of place here. Otherwise, I wouldn't have built it. I believe people want more options."

Faith looked down at her menu. More options? People who come here don't want more options—they want the local seafood; they want a table full of friends and a band in the corner after the dinner hour. They want a casual, beachy atmosphere with pitchers of strawberry daiquiris and finger foods on brightly colored plates, not this. How could he think this was okay?

"Are you planning on developing more like this one?" she asked, trying to keep the animosity out of her voice.

"I'm always planning," he said, smiling.

Did he really not see what was wrong with this? His comment at Bodie Island about seeing so much hope and potential hit her—did he mean for development? Why did he want to destroy what she'd grown up to love?

The waiter brought a glass, unlabeled bottle of water and two goblets. He filled them half full and then set a basket of something on the table—crackers? She looked at the flat crisps with some sort of seeds protruding from the surface. Before she could reach for one, he set a small ramekin in front of her. It had a pink paste of some sort. Beside it, he placed a bright silver butter knife and then left them alone again. With each passing minute she spent here, she felt uneasier, and she wondered if she knew Jake at all.

"Know what you're going to get?" Jake asked, seemingly oblivious.

She folded her menu and set it down on the corner of the table and shook her head, trying to keep her disappointment in check. Her whole picture of Jake was changing, crashing down around her, and she didn't quite know the best way to handle the situation. What she loved about the Outer Banks was that it had remained true to itself; it hadn't fallen victim to the over-the-top development that had happened in other places. It was a slice of paradise to her.

Her manners told her to just order something and eat it. Then she could leave here and go about her business and finish her vacation without seeing Jake again. But there was a part of her that loved being with the Jake she'd met at the cottage. She wanted more of *him*. Not this.

"There are a lot of choices." She didn't want to admit that she didn't know what any of them were. She tried to look past the overdressed people to the glass wall. On the other side of it was the sea, and the sea gave her calm.

"Are you ready to order?" the waiter said, appearing out of nowhere.

Faith could feel her shallow breathing and the speed of her heart in her chest. She didn't want to be rude to Jake, but she didn't have a clue what to do. "May I have a few more minutes?" she asked. The waiter nodded and disappeared as quickly as he'd come. She looked back at Jake.

"Are you okay?" he asked.

She didn't want to seem ungrateful or rude. She liked him so much but this restaurant had brought her to a new reality that she didn't want to admit to herself. She didn't like any of this. It was too fussy, too expensive, too unlike her in every way. It didn't even fit with the town. Had it not been for the cars outside, she would swear it would never survive, and she still had her doubts.

"You don't like it," he said, an unsure look showing on his face. "I thought this would be perfect."

She didn't know what to say. She was ruining their date, but she was actually upset with him for building this. He was selling out.

He'd grown up here, yet he was falling prey to all the big business that was booming. He, of all people, should recognize what was so beautiful about the Outer Banks, but instead, he'd defaced miles of gorgeous coastline for this restaurant.

"You're uncomfortable here."

She leaned forward, careful not to disturb the pink paste in front of her. "I'm fine," she lied very quietly, forcing a smile, trying not to make a scene. She felt terrible. Her hands were shaking. She saw his eyes change as he noticed, and she slipped them under the table to try and hide the outward signs of her dismay.

The look on Jake's face was a look of complete mortification. She worried she'd hurt his feelings, and she felt bad despite herself. He raised his finger at the waiter, who returned in a flash. "I apologize, but we're going to have to leave unexpectedly. Forgive me." The waiter, of course, nodded in the same way he had when she'd first seen him, and within a few seconds, they were back outside in the daylight.

Faith took in a large breath of salty air, trying to let it calm her.

"I don't understand," Jake said, facing her as they stood beside the valet. The man noticed their conversation and moved a few paces away from his podium to give them space. Jake didn't seem to be worried at all by the valet; he was looking straight at Faith. "I thought this would be a wonderful surprise. We'd have drinks, have fun. I thought you'd love it."

"I'm one of those people who loves the quirks, as you say, of those out-of-the-way places. I'm not alone. My whole family is like that."

He didn't seem offended. "People like you are harder to find these days."

"Do you really think so?" As upset with his view as she was, she still really liked being around him. She even wondered if she could persuade him to think differently. "Let me cook you something. I'm sure you're hungry. I know I am. Let's go back to the cottage, and I'll whip us up something for dinner."

"No, no. *I* asked *you* out. I'm not going to make you cook for me. I'll cook for you. If you don't mind, we can go back to my house and I'll make you dinner. Would that be okay?"

This was the Jake she liked so much. "That sounds wonderful."

The drive this time was much quieter, the air between them now filled with questions on both sides. Faith looked out the window at the cottages that dotted the shoreline as they made their way to Jake's. She wondered what his house would look like. After seeing the restaurant, she wasn't sure she knew who Jake was now. Would his house be showy and grandiose? She hoped not. After a little while, the cottages gave way to grass. The grass thinned out as it met the sand, and, when she finally saw where they were, there was nothing but beach and sea and a sight she'd never seen before. It looked like a cottage-style castle.

Just like her cottage, this one sat on stilts, but with thickly painted white lattice covering the open areas under the house. Along the lattice, contrasting with the starkness of the white, were bright pink roses on green bushes. A wide, wooden staircase—big enough to have at least ten people or more standing shoulder to shoulder as they went up it—was at the front, the treads a natural wood color and the risers painted white to match the lattice. The whole cottage was bright yellow like the sunshine above them, each piece of the trim white. A country porch wrapped all the way around the enormous structure, and every few feet, she saw two white rocking chairs angled toward each other. The home looked big enough to be an inn. It was beautiful, and nothing like that restaurant.

He parked next to a red antique Ford truck that looked like it had been used as a work truck. He'd noticed the truck too, because his eyes went straight from it to the ocean, where she saw a man fishing. They got out of the car, and she followed him to the beach. The shore was so wide at this point that it seemed like a desert, the ocean its mirage.

"Dad?"

The man turned around and put up a hand to shield his eyes. As Faith looked at him, she knew exactly what Jake would look like in thirty years. The man had his eyes, his nose, and his hairline, although his hair was silver in color. He smiled just like Jake, and she smiled back without even meaning to.

"What are you doing?" Jake asked as they got close enough to hear over the wind. The fishing rod was huge—bigger than the ones she'd seen for fresh water. It was sitting in a white pipe-like holder that had been forced down in the sand. Beside it was a cooler and a radio.

"What does it look like I'm doin'?" he teased him, that all-too-familiar grin on his face just like his son's. "I'm catchin' supper."

"Why are you catching supper on my beach?"

"I figured all the fish had probably migrated downstream away from that eyesore you put up."

His father was kidding around, but Jake's face had changed. He obviously didn't find it very funny, and it seemed to almost annoy him. "You're here for something else." She could hear the affection for his father in his words despite his irritation with his comment.

The man ignored his question and turned to Faith. "Jake, son, where're your manners?" He reached out his hand toward Faith. "I'm Charles Buchanan. You can call me Chuck."

"It's nice to meet you, Chuck," she said.

He gave her a grin and then raised his eyebrows at Jake as if to say, "Look at you, bringing home a girl." He was teasing Jake, and she wondered if he'd done the same thing when Jake had brought home girls as a young man. It was playful and silly, but it had embarrassed Jake a little. It was interesting to see his father bring out yet another side of him.

"I'm here because the pier's crowded this time of year with all the tourists, and my own beach is full of people right now too. All the vacationers have spread over to my little corner of the shore. 'Tis the season, I suppose." He turned to Faith. "Now, if he'll let me be, I'll catch us some supper. You hungry?" He winked at his son.

She nodded politely.

"I'm making Faith dinner, Dad. If you catch something, we'll grill it. Otherwise, you know I'll save you some leftovers."

Leftovers? Faith would feel very rude eating up at Jake's house, knowing that his dad was waiting for dinner. "I wouldn't mind if Chuck ate with us," she suggested quietly, looking at Jake for approval. She worried a little about suggesting it, but, to be honest, she couldn't wait to talk with his father and find out more about Jake. Perhaps she and Chuck could even talk some sense into him.

"Okay," Jake said. "Dad, just come up when you're done, and we'll make you a plate. You can eat with us."

"Well, that's kind of ya." He nodded thanks to his son and then winked at Faith the way he might if she were his own daughter.

They left Chuck on the beach and headed back toward the giant cottage of Jake's. He led her up the stairs. As she followed, the sound of the restless sea was at her back, the screech of seagulls overhead. Chuck had switched on the radio as they left, but she couldn't hear it anymore.

She stopped mid-step and took in the thick yard full of wiry grass that was perfectly cut. It eventually gave way to his private beach and the gorgeous, rolling blue water of the Atlantic where Chuck was standing in the incoming tide. Faith forced her eyes from the view to look at Jake. She couldn't imagine why one person would need all this. This was the kind of place that needed a family—a big extended family—with children running in the yard and aunts and uncles filling those rockers.

"You're the only one who lives here?"

He nodded.

"It's huge!" she said before she could think the comment through. After the restaurant fiasco, she worried that it would offend him.

He didn't seem overly bothered by her statement, thank goodness. She didn't want to upset him. Despite what had happened at the restaurant, she wanted to give him the benefit of the doubt. But this house was like something out of a home magazine. It was perfectly landscaped, the porches decorated with potted plants beside the rockers, bright pink and purple flowers flanking the door, and all the way around the porch were hanging ferns.

He opened the front door—an oversized wooden door with etched glass in the center. It was artistic and beautiful, and she could only imagine what it looked like from the inside when the sun came through it. That thought didn't last long, though, as she entered the foyer. The room stretched back, past a formal living room and a dining room, to the other side of the house, where she saw an open kitchen, a second, huge living room, and even a pool table. The whole back side of the house was filled with windows from floor to vaulted ceiling, with a view of nothing but sand and sea beyond them. He gestured for her to walk first, so she made her way down the beautiful hardwoods to the living area, a swimming pool and tables—yes, plural tables—with dark green umbrellas emerging in her view as she looked out at the ocean.

Jake walked up beside her and led her to the kitchen. He pulled out one of the leather stools, neatly lined up at the bar for her. She sat down and rested her forearms on the granite countertop.

"What are you in the mood for?" he asked. His question sounded cautious, and she wondered if he was still upset by her behavior at the restaurant. She really wasn't that hard to please—when she was in a place that made sense to her.

Trying not to gawk at the custom cabinetry and the chef-grade stainless steel six-burner stove, she asked in return, "What are my choices?"

"Ask me. I probably have it."

"I'm not picky," she said, wanting to eat her words immediately. "Why don't you surprise me?" She didn't know what to ask for.

He pulled a pan from one of the cabinets below. It was stainless, just like his appliances, without a single blemish. He set it on a burner and turned on the gas. The room was probably the size of the whole cottage where she was staying. She would never have guessed, meeting him that first day, that he had this much money. A sailboat, Mercedes, a beachside mansion, he built restaurants—what exactly did he do for a living? She had to ask....

"I'm sorry for what happened at the Tides," she said. She was sorry, but she had her own thoughts about the restaurant that she needed to get out somehow. She wanted to love the Tides. She'd loved everything that she'd learned about him so far, and it was killing her that she didn't love his restaurant. She wished she could be thrilled that he'd built one like that, but the truth was that she was mortified. The idea that he could ruin the landscape so carelessly made her question her feelings for him because, clearly, he didn't think at all like she did.

"What did happen at the Tides, Faith?"

She bit her lip to try and get all her thoughts in order. How would she explain to him what she felt without offending him? But then again, they'd been open with each other, and she felt like she had a connection with him. Perhaps she could make him understand. "Do you know what I love about the Outer Banks?" He turned to face her. "Places like Dune Burger."

"You prefer a more casual place? Is that it?"

"Not just that. I like it because it's been a constant; it's been there for me every time I visit."

"So you're opposed to anything new?"

"That's not what I'm saying. I think that anything that maintains that vibe, the feel of this area, is good. The Tides seemed… Forgive me. Out of character for the Outer Banks."

"I think there are things about this area that are stuck in the past. That's the problem around here. They won't open their eyes and give anything new a chance. I had to battle like crazy to get the permits to build the Tides, but I wasn't backing down out of principle. We need to look to the future, and that means being comfortable with change."

"I think there's a difference between being stuck in the past and maintaining the charm of the past. They're two distinct things."

"You sound like the county board of supervisors." He shook his head, clearly getting frustrated by her comments.

She didn't want to frustrate him, but she also didn't agree at all with what he was saying. "Tell me, what did you love about growing up here?" Maybe she could get him to think back to his favorite places. Surely she could remind him of what he loved about this place. It was such a wonderful place.

"The space."

"Why?"

"Because it was a continuous reminder of what I could build here. I've always been a builder. That's what I do."

Before she could respond, Chuck walked through the door, carrying his red and white cooler and radio. He set them both down on the floor and looked back and forth between Faith and Jake as if he were surveying the situation. He had on a navy baseball cap that he hadn't been wearing on the beach, the brim worn from years of wear, the emblem on the front faded beyond recognition. "Got us a flounder," he said, tapping the cooler with his foot. "Let me wash up and I'll get to skinnin' it."

He walked over to the sink, turned it on, and began scrubbing his hands under the stream of water. There was a palpable silence between the three of them, and Faith wondered how the conversation would go from there on out.

"What would you like to drink?" Jake broke the silence. "I have tea, water, lemonade, beer, white wine…" He dug around in the fridge, moving a few bottles.

"An iced tea would be nice."

"I only have sweet tea; are you okay with that?" He pulled out a container of crabmeat and set it on the counter, along with two eggs.

"That's the only tea I drink."

"Ah, that makes two of us."

Chuck eyed the ingredients. "Makin' your famous crab cakes, are ya? Let's fry 'em. We can fry up the flounder with it." He grinned in Faith's direction, the lines on his face white against his tan skin. "I hope you're hungry, Faith. We've got some good food comin'. Jake, son, pour me a tea too, please. That sounds good." Chuck grabbed the kitchen towel to dry his hands, and Faith noticed how delicate it looked in his weathered fingers. "I hope you like sweet tea. It's southern sweet—lots of sugar."

Jake pulled out two glasses, filled them with ice, and topped the cubes with iced tea from a crystal pitcher. "My grandmother believed that if you let it steep in the sunlight when you're making it, it tastes better." He set a bag of breadcrumbs and assorted spices next to the eggs.

"I think she just wanted an excuse to be in the sun," Chuck added with a smile. He'd pulled the large, flat fish out of the cooler and had it lying now on the cutting board.

"Where did she live? Somewhere warm?"

"Mississippi. She was a southern belle," Chuck answered before Jake could get a word in. He slid the knife under the skin of the fish and, with perfect precision, removed the outside. Then he went to work cutting and deboning. "My mother was a beautiful woman in her day."

Faith thought of Nan. She, too, was a southern debutante. Raised by wealthy parents, she had been schooled in the best of everything— how to have the best manners, how to treat people, and how to act with tact and professionalism. While Nan didn't have excessive amounts of money herself, she'd lived well, and she'd made sure to pass along her virtues to Faith's mother and the girls.

"She spent her final years in Florida," Chuck continued, pulling her from her thoughts. "Key West."

"Key West?" Faith looked over at Jake for an explanation, a smile on her face. He smiled back at her, looking at her as if he'd held in a secret.

"I know Key West very well," Jake said. "I've been there quite a few times."

"I'd love to see it," she said for Chuck's benefit. Jake already knew how she felt about it. "So many great authors spent time there. I read so much growing up that I felt like Key West was always present in my life."

"Mmm," Chuck said, agreeing. "Jake used to love reading Ernest Hemingway. My mother showed him all the places around town where Hemingway liked to visit. It's been a while, hasn't it, Jake?" Chuck set a gorgeous slab of bright white flounder onto a plate.

Jake nodded, his hands busy with the preparation of the food.

She smiled, glad to have been let in on this little tidbit about Jake's family. "I loved Robert Frost. Still do," she told Chuck. She took a sip of her tea as Jake combined all the ingredients in a bowl and stirred them together with a wooden spoon.

"My mother liked to read too. She used to read to me, and when Jake spent time with her, she introduced him to all kinds of authors. I sure do miss her," Chuck said, his face reminiscent. He'd washed his hands and lined up asparagus on a cutting board and was chopping the ends at a slant. "She filled in after Jake's mom passed."

She watched how the two of them moved around each other as they prepared her dinner, and she thought about how many years it had been just the two of them. They were perfectly practiced at working together. "Do you have any other family nearby at all?"

Jake shook his head as he lined the asparagus up on a baking pan and rubbed it with butter. "Both Mom and Dad are only children, so I don't have any extended family. It's just the two of us now."

"Oh." Faith looked down at the countertop between her arms. *What a terrible thing*, she thought. *No brothers or sisters, aunts or uncles, nieces or nephews, no cousins, grandparents all gone.* Again, she felt awful for staying away from her own family for so long. This trip was putting everything into perspective for her. It was true, she'd had difficulty with Casey's choices, and her marrying Scott had been painful, but her family was all she had. Nan, her mom, her sister, and Isabella were the most important people in her life, and she should've let them know that every day because life was too short not to. Jake was so accommodating, so sweet, and so open, yet she couldn't help but wonder if he was lonely. This had to be a big house to have all by one's self. No wonder he filled his days with work. It probably kept him busy so he didn't have to think about being alone.

"I have family nearby, but I wish there were more kids around for my niece," Faith said.

"I've always wanted lots of kids," Jake said.

She knew exactly what he meant. Faith, too, had wanted a house full of children.

"I'd love to have children," she said. "I think sometimes that it would be great to hear a tiny voice calling 'Mommy.' I'd be perfectly happy spending days at the local playground or painting at the kitchen table."

"Does the thought ever scare you at all?" Jake asked.

"No." She wanted to read bedtime stories, using silly voices for all the characters just to hear her child laugh. She wanted to be so tired she could hardly manage, knowing that it was all worth it because, when she opened the bedroom door, she could peek in through the faint beam of a nightlight, and see her darling child sprawled on the bed, asleep. "Not at all."

"Me neither," Jake said, his eyes gentle and sweet.

Chuck dumped the bones and scraps into the trash. "They suck all the sleep right out of ya. They make you so crazy you can't get a thought to process. They worry you to death—even when they're grown. But when you look back, there's absolutely nothing better than raising a child."

Faith and Jake both laughed. She was glad for a more upbeat conversation, although her thoughts still went back to that restaurant. Things were so much more relaxed, even in his giant kitchen. She couldn't imagine, watching him now with his father, how laid-back they were, how easy the conversation was, that he could think something like the Tides was a good idea. She worried that perhaps he was only accommodating her with this casual dinner.

"So, how did you two meet?" Chuck asked.

"She's staying at one of the cottages I'm building."

"Jake's been wonderful to my family. He's spent a ton of time with us, and he's been very gracious."

"I like how close you guys all are. It's like you have the perfect family."

"Ha." She shook her head. "No family is perfect."

"People in a family treat each other differently than anyone else. I like seeing you all together. There's a bond there that I really enjoy. You all seem to like each other so much."

"And what are you trying to say, son?" Chuck laughed out loud, clearly just teasing. Jake pretended to ignore his question. There was an ease to how they interacted, and she knew what Jake had meant about how a family treats each other. "Jake and I don't see eye to eye a lot of the time," he explained. "We have a few fundamental differences about what we see for our futures."

"Well, we have things to deal with too, like any other family—difficult things." She thought about Casey, and she could feel her body tense in response.

"Like?" Jake asked, curiosity on his face.

"My sister, Casey, and I don't always agree on things." Her honesty just poured out without warning.

"That's normal, though, isn't it?"

"It is normal to disagree, but Casey has wedged us apart, and I honestly don't think it can be repaired. Ignored, maybe. But not repaired." She didn't want to share her family drama with Jake's father there, so she changed direction. "So, when you're not reading books or sailing boats, or putting in the odd bookcase for Nan, what else do you like to do for fun, Jake?" she asked.

The corners of his mouth pulled up into a subtle, knowing smile, and he stepped away from her, moving back to the prepping area of the kitchen. He'd made little rounds of crabmeat and was now sautéing them in the pan. "I like to travel. I like talking to people. Like you." He smiled.

Her pulse sped up, and she couldn't imagine anything more enjoyable than being with Jake right then at that moment. "Where have you traveled?" she asked, wanting to know more about who he was. Did he like big cities, exotic beaches, famous landmarks? She thought back to her own past, and what she'd accomplished in adulthood. Why hadn't she traveled more? She didn't have any children or a family to help support—she should.

"All over."

"Where's your favorite place to go, Jake?" Chuck piped in, dropping the fish filets into a pan of hot oil after dusting them in a mound of cornmeal. They popped and sizzled, steam rising into the air. "Even I don't know that. I've never asked."

"Hmm." Jake flipped the crab cakes over with a pair of tongs. "There are a million little things that I like about every place."

She eyed him, pressing him for more.

He offered a crooked smile as he tipped the crab cakes up to check that they'd browned. "For example, there's a little café in Boston where I was sitting near the window. It was the only table open, probably because the old wood window frame allowed a draft, and it was frigid outside. I took my coat off but left my scarf, and found it to be warm enough to manage. I was drinking a cup of coffee and reading the newspaper when I looked up and saw snow falling—it was a big, fast snowstorm. People hurried across the street—one woman even held her briefcase over her head. I watched the streets turn from gray to white in a matter of minutes, and the flicker of the candle in the center of the table was such a complement to the cold outside—fire and ice."

He was quiet as he cooked for a while. When the crab cakes were properly browned, he turned the heat off on the stove and got three plates from a cabinet overhead.

"Were you there by yourself?" she asked, genuinely curious about how secure he was with being alone. It was just a state of being for her—one she'd grown accustomed to.

"Yep." When the flounder was finished and lightly fried, Chuck filled a plate and slid it over to her. It looked like something she'd have gotten at a restaurant—a regular restaurant. Then, he filled a glass with the white wine from the fridge and set it next to her.

"Wanna take it outside?" Chuck suggested.

She left her tea and took her plate and glass of wine with her to the back door toward where Jake had nodded as he picked up his own plate. The door was mostly glass, with panes in it, and if one wasn't looking closely, it would've looked like more windows. The sun cast an orange and pink glow in the sky as its light pushed away from the sea. Jake followed with his dinner, cradling his wine between his arm and body as he opened the door and allowed her to go first. She walked out into the heat, and trod carefully along the amazingly landscaped cobbles of his patio. In perfectly edged beds were billowing grasses and flowering bushes. His patio stretched the length of the swimming pool and beyond until it gave way to grass that was so perfectly trimmed that it looked like carpet. At the edge of the property, she could see the dunes of sand and the wire and slatted wood fencing used to keep erosion at bay.

She set her plate down on one of the tables, and Jake and his dad followed suit. As she looked around, she still couldn't believe this was all Jake's. How surreal to be having dinner with this man in his mansion of a home at the beach. She would have never imagined Nan's birthday vacation would have taken such a turn. Her nerves over the Tides Wine Bar had settled a little, although she still had lingering questions. A man who could live out here in this gorgeous, remote location and build a house that reflects that, a man with such respect for his dad—that man couldn't be the corporate bully that she feared. She was enjoying herself again, trying not to think about the fact that the lifestyle she'd seen there could very well be another side of him that he wasn't sharing. She'd clearly demonstrated that she wasn't comfortable with that side of things. And now, things were good. If someone had told her before she'd left for vacation that she'd be here, she'd probably have laughed out loud in disbelief, but Jake was so warm and inviting that he made having dinner at his home with his dad seem normal.

As she sat in the warm evening air, she thought again about Jake's story. North Carolina had very warm summers, but it also had very cold winters. What must this big cottage be like when the sand was covered with snow and all the tourists were gone? It must be cold. "Do you stay here in the winters, or do you go somewhere else?"

He took a sip of his wine and looked out at the ocean. "I stay sometimes. I get a lot of work done in the winter months. It gives me more time to do things like this in the summer." He raised his eyebrows at her with a grin.

She took a bite of her crab cake and was surprised at how delicious it was. She swallowed. "You're a really good cook," she said.

"Thank you."

"He gets it from me," Chuck teased.

She laughed. "Do you get a chance to cook a lot?"

What if he brought women back to his cottage all the time? What if this situation she found herself in right now wasn't unusual for him? Perhaps he wasn't as lonely as she thought? A little stab of jealousy hit her in the stomach.

"I cook sometimes because I enjoy it, but most of the time, I go out so I can meet people and be around others."

"It must be lonely in this big house," she said, hoping her comment hadn't offended him. What if he wanted to be alone?

"Yes," he answered quietly, nodding. "When I bought this house, I hadn't planned on living here alone. I've gotten pretty good at being by myself, though. And Dad comes to visit."

"We've both gotten good at living alone," Chuck said, a loaded grin on his face as he looked at his son. Faith wished she could interpret what it meant.

"Me too," she smiled.

"I'm glad you're here," Chuck said. "It's nice to share this big table with another person."

Faith wondered how this night would go. She hadn't imagined she'd end up at Jake's home. What would he expect of her tonight after his father left? And what did she plan to allow? She didn't really know the answer to that. All she knew was that right now, she didn't want to be anywhere else than right there, under the warm evening sun with Jake.

"I'm surprised Jake didn't take you out for dinner," Chuck said. "I've never seen him cook for anyone but me before."

Faith could feel the heat in her face, and she caught herself as she quickly looked down at her plate. Worrying that Chuck had noticed her discomfort, she looked back up at him to try and play it off, but he'd already caught on, his eyes darting between the two of them.

"I took her to the Tides," Jake confessed.

Chuck sat silently. He was waiting, it seemed, for further explanation. Why would they be eating now if they'd gone to the Tides, he was probably thinking. When neither of them spoke, he turned to Faith. "And what did you think of the Tides?"

It was a direct question, and there was no way around an unpleasant answer. "It was very different than any other place around…," she said, trying with all her might not to show her apprehension.

"Ha!" Chuck tipped his head back, laughter swelling within him, making his shoulders bounce. Then, still smiling uncontrollably, he said another "Ha," but this one wasn't a laugh; it was directed at Jake. "She didn't like it, did she?"

When Jake didn't say anything, Chuck turned back to Faith. "Nobody likes it; don't worry."

"That's absolutely not true," Jake said.

"Yes, I'm sorry. Not *nobody*. Jake likes it. Everyone else hates it." He laughed again. "I can't make him see. It's a waste of land. Nobody wants it here. He thinks that if he builds all these fancy things, the area will boom as a result. But he's wrong."

"It's worked in other cities, Dad. How else do you think I've made so much money? I know what I'm doing. People are already coming here from as far as New York. They didn't used to but now they are. They want more development. They will flock to this area if it's developed correctly. And I plan to do that for them."

"You should see all the ridiculousness he has planned for this area. It's awful. He's going to ruin it."

"You've planned to build more?" she said, unable to eat another bite.

"He wants to build high-rise hotels in Corolla," Chuck said.

Corolla? That was one of the most gorgeous parts of the Outer Banks. She'd just read an article about the wild Mustang ponies that had been there for over five hundred years, brought over by the Spanish when they'd come to the New World. She'd seen them while sitting on the beach. They ran through the surf, galloping wild and free down the shore. The article had condemned the growth in the Outer Banks and how it was squeezing the land down to nothing, leaving the horses in danger. They didn't have anywhere to raise their young; tourists were mistreating them and their habitat. She remembered reading the article several times because it had made her so sad that she couldn't finish it. How could Jake add to that chaos? What was he thinking? She looked up, surfacing from her worries to find Jake watching her, as if he were searching for her reaction.

"That's a terrible idea," she said before she could stop herself. Putting up one ridiculous restaurant was one thing, but destroying a habitat and beautiful coastline was another.

"I have a line of investors that think otherwise." As he said the words, it was as if he was a totally different person, and she could see the powerful businessman emerge. His warmth was gone in that moment, the affection she'd seen in his eyes now absent. He was talking business. If he'd been a cartoon, she'd have seen little dollar signs in his eyes, she was sure of it.

"You can't ruin Corolla."

"I don't think I'm ruining anything. I'm simply changing it. I'm a developer. That's how I make my money. If I don't develop, I don't eat. Simple as that. And I know what I'm doing."

"I'm not debating whether you know your job. But what I am telling you is that you've chosen the wrong place."

"Faith, I've had this conversation hundreds of times regarding hundreds of locations. There's always someone who doesn't like it. But that doesn't mean that it shouldn't happen. I've been very successful with this in the past. I know it will be good."

"I will never believe that it's good. I'm sorry."

"I didn't mean to put a damper on our supper by bringin' all this up," Chuck said. "Faith, you won't change his mind. Believe me, I've tried. He's about as bullheaded as anyone I've ever met. Now tell me, how long are you and your family staying? You here for the summer?"

Just like she had with Casey, she'd eventually allowed the anger to slide away as the night went on. It was the only way she knew how to let go and enjoy herself. It was still there, though. She'd just pushed it down where she couldn't feel it at that moment. They ate and talked until the sun was low on the horizon, and she was enjoying herself

again. Chuck had thanked her for a lovely evening, and he'd gra-
ciously left them alone, claiming he had to get a good night's rest
before a big fishing trip tomorrow.

"More wine?" Jake asked, pouring it anyway. They'd nearly finished the bottle, and it was a big bottle. She grinned, her eyes heavy
with all the conversation of the night and the alcohol. She could feel
the sting of warmth under her skin, and she wondered if it was the
sun or the wine. Jake had set up a continuous stream of beach music
to play on the speakers outside after they'd had dinner, and a reggae
song was playing quietly in the background. She looked at him as the
exterior landscape lighting came on magically. Its low light danced
in his eyes. She noticed the ease with which his smile emerged when
he looked at her, the way his shoulders had relaxed. Their disagreement was behind her for now, and she wanted to pretend it wasn't
there at all.

"How am I supposed to get home?" she asked, taking another
sip of her wine. "We've both had too much to drink." She wasn't
asking to stay. She'd never want to put him in that kind of position.
And, given what had transpired since they'd been at Bodie Island, she
wasn't quite sure where they stood. The restaurant and Jake's plans for
development had changed things for her and maybe for him too. Although it changed how she saw him, she couldn't deny the attraction
and the affection that were still there.

"We could try and walk," he said with a grin just before tipping
the glass up to his lips. His eyes stayed on her as he took a drink.

"It's miles to my cottage!" she said, laughing.

"I'd be okay with that."

"Be serious."

"I am!"

Faith knew the wine had helped along this playful side of both of them. She worried that things may be different in the morning. They'd both let their guards down. She had a glimpse of what it was like to really know this side of him. And she loved it. Jake was funny. He'd told her stories that had made her laugh until she had tears in her eyes. But he could also be serious and sweet. At times, his expressions seemed almost romantic—he looked at her a little longer than he should, and he smiled as if words were right on his lips. It was a very different side than what she'd seen when they'd mentioned his Corolla plans. As they sat in silence, he was looking at her that way right now. He stood up, and she followed his lead.

As they made their way around the table, they stopped side by side. Faith turned to face him. "Thank you for having me," she said, and a current zinged around in her chest. She smiled. She couldn't help it.

"You're welcome."

He was looking down at her. She was so close she could smell his cologne. Coupled with the wine and the sound of the ocean, it made her woozy. There was a slight nervousness to his breathing, a tiny twitch at his lips. He took in another breath. Was he going to kiss her? The wind blew her hair in her face and he started to reach up to move it for her, but it was as if he thought better about it, and quickly dropped his hand. She tucked her hair behind her ear and tried to suppress the overwhelming disappointment she felt. Maybe he'd decided that the differences between them were too significant.

"I'll call a car," he said, breaking eye contact first.

"Wait." She didn't know why she'd asked him to wait. Wait for what? She just knew that she didn't want to leave. He was standing there, waiting as she'd asked him to do. "I…" She swallowed. "I thought maybe we could have another glass of wine."

"We've finished all the wine," he said, but his face said more than that. His face was playful. What was he trying to tell her? Her mind-reading skills clearly weren't as good as his, but the look on his face was giving her the strength to act on her impulses. She took a tiny step toward him and looked up into his eyes. The wind blew around them, whipping her hair back across her face, and this time he didn't hesitate and swept it back with his fingers, his touch so gentle it sent a shiver down her neck. Then, he leaned down and kissed her cheek. "I had a good night. Thank you," he said near her ear, and she had to work to keep her breath steady.

Why had he abruptly ended the conversation like that? Thank you? That didn't sound like someone who wanted to continue things. She didn't want the night to end. He pulled back and looked down at her again. With her eyes, she asked him to let her stay. She didn't want to leave this perfect moment behind. She wanted to put their differences aside because she felt so connected to him. She was sure now what she wanted. She wanted to know what it felt like to wake up to him in the morning, make breakfast together, watch the sunrise over the water. She wanted more time with this side of Jake Buchanan. *Please don't let it end yet*, she thought.

"Faith." He took in a deep breath and let it out. "I wish this night didn't have to end."

For some reason, she knew what he was going to say. He'd read her mind again. There was something new in his face. It was subtle, but she'd noticed it. It wasn't anything like what she'd seen tonight. It was almost apprehension. Was she coming on too strong? Did he not feel for her what she was feeling for him? Or was he, too, worried about that other part of his life where she wouldn't fit?

"But it does. I think you're fantastic. But if you stay, this"—he wagged a finger between them—"this will be different. It's better if we're just friends." His gaze lingered on her for a moment before he finally walked over, grabbed their plates, and headed toward the kitchen.

"How will it be different?" she asked, following him. They'd been so open and honest with each other. How would anything be different than that?

"Believe me. It will. I've been down that road before, and I'm not doing it again."

"Down what road?" She didn't like the way that sounded. Did he see being with her as some sort of sentence? The way he'd made it sound—down that road—made her feel like spending real time with her would be a chore.

"Look, we've had a really great night. I've had a ton of fun. But we both know that when things move beyond what they are now—this one night—neither of us would be happy."

How dare he think for her! He didn't know what would make her happy. Shouldn't she be able to make that determination on her own? But lingering between them in the silence was the real issue: *he* wouldn't be happy.

"I'll call the car."

He put the plates into the sink and turned around. He pulled his cell phone from his pocket. After a few taps on the screen, he put the phone to his ear. "Hello. It's Jake Buchanan. I'm at mile post seventeen and a half." He paused, listening. "Yes. That's me. I was wondering if you could send a car out. I have a lady here who needs a ride back to mile post ten." More silence. "Excellent. See you soon." He ended the call.

Chapter Ten

The Lincoln Town Car pulled into the drive at Faith's cottage. "Thank you," she said, getting out. The driver nodded, and she shut the door. Jake had been pleasant when they'd said their goodbyes, but he'd stood at a distance, a different emotion behind his smile. She kept coming back to the Tides and his plans for development.

"So?" she heard before she'd even gotten through the door. Casey was sitting in the breakfast nook, her laptop open beside her. "How was it? What was the Mercedes all about? Where did you go?"

"Um…" Where should she start? The whole night and all the emotions it had stirred within her were swirling around in her head.

"You okay?" Casey had gone from excited to concerned in a split second.

"Yes," she said, taking a breath in an attempt to clear her head. "It was good."

"Just good?"

It wasn't just good. It was fantastic. Her date with Jake was probably the best first date she'd ever had—even with the disagreement—and she wanted to see him again. She wanted to have his eyes on her like they had been tonight; she wanted to see his smile directed at her. Tonight, she felt something new and interesting—that flutter.

She couldn't deny the way he'd looked at her, the way he'd responded to her. That's what had made that moment when he said they should remain friends so difficult to swallow. Maybe he was right, though. As much as she liked him, and as much as they seemed to fit together at times, the gray cloud lingering over them was their fundamental difference in what they wanted. He wanted to make money, even if it was at the expense of the North Carolina shore and all its serenity—the only place she felt truly at ease. She wanted a quiet place to bring her family, where everyone could have a good time and make memories.

"What about the car? You have to tell me about the car."

"It's his," she said, still trying to make sense of it. "And the sailboat's his too."

"What? It is?"

"He's…" Her mind was elsewhere, but she didn't want to be rude so she pushed the thoughts away and sat down next to her sister. "He's very wealthy."

"What?" she said again. "How?"

"He's a land developer, but he does handyman work for fun."

"This just gets more interesting by the minute!" Casey said, looking full of excitement. Her eyes were glittery, a big smile on her face. Faith felt her dinner sour in her stomach as she looked at Casey's face. This was still a game to her. Faith didn't see it the same way after being with him all night. He'd been vulnerable and honest, and they'd left questions she still wanted to work through. Suddenly, Faith didn't want Casey anywhere near Jake.

"Why do you have your laptop out?" Faith asked, trying to steer the conversation elsewhere. She was tired from the sun and the wine, and attempting to figure Jake out.

Casey's face dropped from excited to somber in a flash. She looked sad, anxious; her brows had pulled together, a deep crease forming between them, her bottom lip trembling just a little before she chewed on the inside of it—probably to keep it steady.

"I got an email from Scott. An informal list of what he wants to keep of ours, and what he thinks I should have. He wants me to check it over before he sends it to his lawyer."

Casey didn't handle tough circumstances well. Things always came easily for her, so when she was faced with something as hard as this, she would want to push it away, ignore the reality of it. When it came to the hard things in life, she struggled, and that's where Faith had the upper hand. Faith had had enough things not go her way in life that she'd figured out how to deal with the situation. Seeing Casey's face told her that her sister needed her right now.

Even though Faith was younger, whenever Casey had a tough time growing up—a boyfriend issue or drama between her and her girlfriends—she'd always find Faith. It was Faith who would comfort Casey, although Casey would only fret about it for a minute or two before sobering up and moving on to more upbeat conversation. When her high school boyfriend broke up with her, Casey had come crying to Faith, lying on her bed, her face in a pillow. Faith had reassured her, telling her that there were other fish in the sea, and she shouldn't worry too much, even though she knew how much it probably hurt. Casey sat up, sniffled a little more, and then went into the bathroom and got her hot pink nail polish. She'd decided that Faith needed a makeover. Faith knew she didn't really need one, but it was Casey's way of dealing with it, and getting over it. She'd let Casey paint her nails, do her makeup, and style her hair that day, and they'd gone shopping together that afternoon. Casey never said another word, or—as far as she knew—shed another tear over that boy, but she knew it had hit her sister harder than she was letting on.

What worried Faith now was that Casey was struggling. She had Isabella to think about, her work, which was quite demanding, and now the divorce. She'd be looking for a distraction for sure. She hoped Casey wouldn't try and make Jake her distraction.

"I'm surprised that Jake hasn't been by to paint that built-in," Nan said as they all sat at the table.

"It's only nine o'clock, Mom," Faith's mother said, pouring more coffee into Faith's cup.

Faith held up a hand to stop her from pouring any more, even though she was exhausted and could do with the jolt of caffeine. She hadn't slept very well last night.

"Thanks, Mom," she said.

Faith worried. Jake had shown up early every day since they'd arrived, but he wasn't there this morning when they'd all gotten up. Was he avoiding her? As the night had turned to dawn, she started to wonder if she'd misread the signs because of the wine. Had he really not been looking at her like she'd thought? What did he really think about her admission that his project to develop Corolla was an awful idea? Had she offended him? And what did he mean by saying he's been down that road before? That still didn't sit well with her. With her mug cradled in both hands, she sat quietly, still pondering it all. If he did stop by, she'd better get up and make herself presentable. She'd only dusted her face with a little powder and brushed her hair. She had no makeup to speak of, and she was wearing an old T-shirt and shorts.

Next to Isabella, Casey sat. There was no sign of the Casey she'd seen last night. Today, she had a brave face on. She was wearing wedge sandals, another of her sundresses—little spaghetti straps showing off her new tan—dangly earrings, her hair curled, lip gloss. Why? What made Casey wake up every morning and do all that to herself? It just wasn't Faith at all. It wasn't that she didn't care about her looks. She just didn't feel the need to spend that much time on it. And, when she really got honest with herself, she didn't even know if she could make herself up the right way. What she'd accomplished getting ready last night had been the extent of her expertise in the area of beauty.

"What do you want to do for your birthday, Nan? Do you want a little party? Cake?" Casey asked.

"Yes! Cake!" Isabella said, nodding vigorously. "I like yellow cake with birthday balloons."

"I want this," Nan said, looking around the table. "And I suppose we should have cake."

Isabella clapped her hands with excitement.

"We want to do something special for you, Mom," Faith's mother said, sitting down beside her. "It would make us feel like we were paying you back for this wonderful vacation."

"If you really want to know, I'd like you to put that box of photos into photo albums so you each can have one or two to remember all the great times we've had as a family. I gave them all to Faith because I figured she'd go through with organizing them, but I'd love it if you all could have them."

Nan was right. Faith had already thought about organizing that box, but she'd been so preoccupied with the goings-on of their vacation that she'd let it slip her mind.

"I'd be happy to do that for you, Nan," Faith said.

"Thank you, Faith. I can always count on you. Maybe you girls could sort through them one of these nights when you're not running the streets," she winked at Faith. Nan was only kidding, but her words made Faith think of Jake.

"Can we go to the beach, Mommy?" Isabella asked. "I want to make a sandcastle."

"Sure we can," Casey said. "I'll walk you down there in a little bit. Did you know, Faith makes amazing castles?"

Faith used to spend hours making sandcastles when she was little. They'd get up at the crack of dawn and go down to the beach. Faith would fill her bucket with water, the chilly morning surf causing goose bumps on her legs. She'd sit on the beach with her shovels and buckets packing sand into them, adding a little water to make it all stick together, and carefully building on to the tops until she'd made a fortress. Casey would plop down next to her, fill one bucket, and then lose interest when she turned it over and half the sand slid down the mound like a mini avalanche. For Faith, it was an act of endurance, of perseverance to make the best castle she could. It didn't bother Faith that it took a long time, or that the tide would eventually wash it away. She worked at it to see the finished product. She was proud of it when it was done.

"I'd be happy to make one with you, Isabella," Faith said. "I can show you how to make a moat around it and everything."

"Yes!" Isabella said, getting up from the table. "I'm getting my swimsuit on right now!"

"Isabella, you haven't finished your breakfast," Casey called out to her, but Isabella had already gone into her bedroom and closed the door. "She's so much like you, Faith."

"You think so?"

"Oh my gosh, yes. Sometimes it's scary. Isabella, you, and Nan are all so much alike. I feel like the odd man out sometimes."

What was Casey talking about? This idea had never crossed Faith's mind. Nan was the leader of the family, the maker of all traditions, the one person who never seemed to falter with anything. How was Faith like her? If anything, Casey should feel most like her. She was a successful lawyer, a mother, and a wife (until recently). Like Nan, she had everything under control. Perhaps the divorce had skewed her view of things.

"I suppose I should get ready to go to the beach, since I'm building a sandcastle today," Faith said, standing up. "Nan, do you want me to help you go down to the beach?"

"No, dear. I'll watch from the porch. The heat is unbearable today. But thank you."

As Faith entered her bedroom, Casey came up behind her. "Thank you for offering to build sandcastles with Isabella. I try to relate to her, but her daddy was always better at it than me."

"You're welcome," she said, glad she could help in some way.

"Do you mind if I stay up here so I can finish divvying out our assets for the divorce? Scott wants the lawyer to draw something up soon, and I guess it doesn't matter that I'm on vacation." She took in a deep breath and let it out. Even with all that was going on, she maintained her composure. Her marriage was dissolving right before her eyes, and she could manage to keep herself calm and collected. Faith had been a total mess when it was clear that Scott had feelings for Casey and had spent many nights crying into her pillow. She wondered if it was healthy for her sister to bottle up her emotions like she was.

"Don't worry about us. I've got Isabella covered. She and I will spend tons of time making our sandcastles. You do what you need to do."

Faith looked past Casey and saw Nan in the hallway, smiling. When she made eye contact, Nan said, "That's what I like to see. Take care of each other. That's the mark of a great family. If only Clara and I could have been like you two…" She looked down at the floor for a moment. "Now, if you'll excuse me, I'm going out to the porch to get comfortable. I want to see some sandcastles."

Faith remembered Nan mentioning her sister, Clara. What had gone on between them? Faith wished she could sit next to Nan and hear her tell the story, but she knew Isabella was waiting.

"Do you mind taking the beach bag down with you?" Casey said. "I'll send Isabella once she's ready."

Faith grabbed the beach bag and a few towels, and walked with Nan onto the porch that wrapped around to the stairs leading down to the driveway. She set them down and helped her grandmother get settled in the rocker. "I'd like to hear about Clara," she said as Nan wriggled into a comfortable position.

"I'd be happy to tell you about her. I miss her and it's nice to talk about her." The mention of Clara had brought a smile to Nan's face.

"Maybe tonight?"

"Yes. Maybe tonight." Nan's smile faded to a more thoughtful expression.

Faith picked up her things and headed down the stairs toward the beach. Even in the morning air, the sun was hot, but it hadn't penetrated the sand yet, and she felt the cool of it on her bare feet as she lugged two chairs to a clear spot. The shore seemed to stretch for miles, only a few people scattered along the coastline. She set the chairs down and opened them up, brushing the sand off the seats of each one.

Faith sat down and faced the sea. She looked back over her shoulder for Isabella, keeping an eye on the part of the cottage steps she could see over the dune. Nan waved from the porch, and she waved back. Then the cottage door opened and Isabella came out, wearing her pink, ruffled swimsuit and pink star-shaped sunglasses. She held the railing as she took each step very slowly, her pink flip-flops wobbling nervously with every step.

That staircase probably seemed huge to her, Faith thought. She remembered that feeling, going up the stairs at the cottage they'd had as kids. Because they were built on stilts, the first floor was raised an entire level and it had felt like she was climbing into the clouds.

Isabella's blond hair disappeared below the dune, so Faith stood up to try and see her. When she did, her heart leapt as she saw Jake's truck pull into the drive. Before she could ponder it further, Isabella was running toward her, a bucket and shovel in her little hands.

"Look what I brought!" she said, plopping down next to Faith. "What should we do?"

"We need to fill a bucket with wet sand. Let's each get one and take them down to the water." As she walked with Isabella, she tried not to think about Jake. She wanted to see him and talk to him about last night, but Isabella needed her. Faith enjoyed spending these precious moments with her niece.

Isabella waited for the tide to retreat back to the sea before she squatted on the wet sand and began filling her bucket. Faith leaned over and filled her own bucket. Another wave rolled in, the foam rushing up around their ankles. Isabella held her bucket up high to keep the surf from stealing it.

"Is this good?" she asked, holding it out toward Faith.

"Yep! I think we have everything we need."

They took their buckets back to a spot close to their chairs. Faith used a shovel to pack down the sand in her bucket. "You have to get it really packed in there. Can you do yours?"

Isabella watched intently, imitating every move Faith made.

"Then, you turn your bucket upside down like this." With a thud, Faith tipped her bucket over onto the sand and patted the sides of it with her hands.

Isabella did the same.

Gently and carefully, Faith removed the bucket to reveal a perfectly round cylinder of sand.

"How did you learn how to make these?" Isabella asked in awe. She'd stood up and was walking around the little mound of wet sand, scrutinizing it. She bent way down and turned her head sideways. Then, she patted her own bucket and lifted it off. It was perfect, just like Faith's.

"I don't know. I just practiced." She picked up a different size bucket and offered the beach bag to Isabella to retrieve more shovels. "We're going to need to fill the buckets again. What shape do you want this time? I'm going to make a smaller one next to this big mound I've just made."

Isabella dug around inside the beach bag until she found the one she wanted. It was a purple bucket with a white handle. They walked back to the water together.

On the way, Isabella stopped short. "Oh!" she said, bending down and picking something up. "Look what I found!"

Faith went over to inspect. It was a twisted little shell that was hollow inside. She turned it over in Isabella's open hand to examine the beautiful stripes of light brown against its creamy colored body. It was in perfect condition. "Do you know what this is?" she asked, lifting it out of Isabella's palm to see it more closely. "You've found a Scotch Bonnet. It's the state shell of North Carolina. Not many people get to find them. How pretty." She handed it back to Isabella. Faith had bought a book about seashells to read on her way to the beach when she was twelve years old. As Faith hunted for shells, she would look them up and see if she could find them in her book. She was surprised that she remembered the name of Isabella's shell after so many years.

"Can we keep it?"

Faith couldn't help but smile at this gorgeous little girl. Casey was right. Her personality was like Faith's. Watching Isabella and seeing how she was like her family members made Faith think about her own children. What would they be like? Would they play with Isabella, build sandcastles with her? Would they be like Faith? She wanted a house full of children to care for, but until then, she was truly enjoying being with Isabella.

"Sure. We'll put it in the beach bag."

They walked, filling bucket after bucket and building their sand-castle. Each time, Faith tipped her head up on the way back to see if Jake's truck was gone yet, and every time, it was still sitting right where it had been. Part of her looked forward to seeing him again. She wanted to feel out the situation, see how he responded to her, continue their discussions from last night. And she just wanted to talk to him again, see him smile at her. But another part of her thought it may be best if she didn't. He'd made it clear that he only wanted to be friends and perhaps he was right. There were obviously some issues between them. She'd been just fine by herself until now. Surely all of these feelings and thoughts she was having were just because she was on vacation. Soon enough, she'd get back to her real

life and she'd be just fine again. There was no need to make her life
any more difficult.

"Hey, y'all," her mom called out, waving to them as Faith helped
Isabella carve out the moat with a shovel. Her mom was at the top of
the dune, a beach towel and a novel under her arm. If Faith squinted
her eyes, from that distance, the new cottage almost looked like the
old one, and her mother like the young mother who had raised them.
It made her homesick for those times before everything had gotten
so complicated.

"Hi, Mom," she called back to her.

Her mom trudged through the sand toward them, stopping at the
western edge of the castle. "Wow, that's wonderful," she said with a
big smile, her cheekbones making her sunglasses rise up on her face
a little higher. "Your Aunt Faith used to make those all the time. Remember that big one you made when we were all here with Nan last
time? It took you all day."

"I do."

Isabella was on her hands and knees, a hot pink shovel in her hand
as she crawled around the edge of their castle digging the moat so
deep that the sediment underneath was a dark gray color. "Do I need
water now to fill it up?" she asked, looking up at Faith.

"You can try, but the water may sink into the sand. You may want
to get two buckets full. That's what I always did."

Isabella grabbed the purple bucket and another green one and ran,
one in each hand, toward the water.

"Faith, honey," her mother said once Isabella was out of earshot.
"I'll watch Isabella. You might want to check on your sister. She hasn't
come out of her room. I knocked, but she didn't answer. She'll talk
to you…"

"What's wrong?"

"I don't know. But what I do know is that whenever Casey is quiet, there's something wrong. And, when you two were younger, she'd never talk to me. I'd have to get the scoop from you. Go up and see if you can figure out what's going on."

Faith nodded, knowing how Casey wasn't the best at divulging her feelings. But her mother was right: She'd talk to Faith. She called goodbye to Isabella, who was already chatting animatedly to her grandmother as Faith crossed over the dune toward the cottage. Jake's truck was still there. She hadn't thought about that when agreeing to come up and talk to Casey. Now, she paused at the bottom of the steps, trying to figure out how she was supposed to greet him if she saw him. He was probably right there in the front room, painting the built-in. Should she be breezy and cool, or should she walk over and make conversation? It made her feel out of control a little bit, and she hadn't felt like that in a long time. She started up the steps, trying to keep herself as calm as possible.

Chapter Eleven

Faith tentatively opened the door. Jake was tapping the lid of the paint can with a mallet. The built-in was beautiful—bookshelves on the top and a double cabinet on the bottom, all painted a glossy white. But her eyes didn't stay on it long. Her attention was on him. She was anxious to talk to him again. She wanted to see him, to look for any sign of how he felt about last night. Jake slipped the paint-filled paintbrush into a plastic bag, the hands that had held a glass of wine last night now spotted with white paint.

"Hey," he said as she walked over to him.

"Hey."

"I'm all done. No more work to do on the cottage, so I'll be out of your hair."

He was finished?

His words surfaced: *I'll be out of your hair.* Faith was hoping the answer was no. She wanted to have more time with him. To get to know the Jake she'd been with at the lighthouse and back at his cottage more. And she wanted to show him what this place meant to her, why she'd reacted how she had to learning about his work and what he was missing out on. Would he give her a chance to do that?

"There's no more work to do? The cottage is complete?" She felt a stab of anxiety at the idea of not having Jake around. She enjoyed him popping by.

"Yep. It's totally finished." His words seemed flat. He wasn't his usual, happy self.

"Oh…" She hadn't meant for her disappointment to slip out.

"I'll be back tomorrow, though, when I pick up Casey and Isabella to go fishing."

With that statement, it was clear that he wasn't planning to see her, in particular, again. And the fact that he was seeing Casey made her chest ache. She would have loved to try and lengthen the conversation to work in the fact that she wanted to see him again, but she had to go check on her sister. That was the whole reason she'd come in.

"I'll see you tomorrow, then," she said, trying to put on a believable smile.

As Jake started to leave, Nan came into the living room, wobbling the box of photos.

Jake immediately took it from her and walked with her over to a chair, where she sat down.

"Thank you, dear. That was kind of you."

"You're welcome. Is this good?" he asked, setting the box on the floor beside her and righting himself next to Faith.

"Yes."

Jake was standing so close his hand brushed Faith's, and her stomach did a little twirl. He didn't seem to notice their proximity. He took a step toward the door. "Do you need anything else before I go?"

"No, Jake. Thank you so much."

He offered his perfect smile and said goodbye, his eyes fluttering over to Faith momentarily and then away. Then, he turned around and headed toward the door. She wanted to run after him and ask him to stay but she watched him let himself out instead.

"I was going to look through these photos," Nan said.

"I want to look at them with you, but I have to check on Casey."

"Yes. Do that first. You know I'll still be here," she said with a wink.

Faith nodded and went down the hall to Casey's door. She knocked twice and then let herself in. Casey was facedown in the pillow, the covers yanked up around her. Gently, Faith lowered herself down onto the edge of the bed. She waited. She waited for Casey to cry a little, sit up, tell her what was bothering her, and get on with the day. That was how Casey operated. But this time, as Faith sat there— the blinds drawn, the room dark, the only light coming from the screensaver on Casey's laptop—Casey didn't move. She cried silent sobs—big and heaving—and she didn't stir one bit.

Faith rubbed her back.

"He sent my list to his attorney," Casey said into her pillow, the words broken by her sobs. "They want to meet when we get back." She started to cry again, louder. "I don't want this," she said as she sat up and faced Faith. "I want to be with Scott. I miss him."

"Do you think he misses you?"

She shook her head. "I don't know."

"You've never asked him?"

"I think the divorce proceedings speak on his behalf. He isn't in- terested in being with me." She sobbed again.

For the first time ever, Casey seemed lost. She didn't look sure of herself like she always had. She looked nervous, defeated, sad, and vulnerable. It was an unexpected sight, and Faith wasn't sure how to handle it. The only thing she knew was that she had to be the strong one; she had to work Casey through this. Faith felt the loss deep within her chest. She ached for her sister. She knew what it was like to love Scott, and she knew what it was like to lose him. She could only imagine what it was like to lose him after experiencing his love in return. Casey and Scott had created a family together, they'd made a life, and they'd become one unit. Now that unit was broken. And so was Casey.

Faith couldn't say it would be okay, because she didn't know if it would be. She knew there was nothing to do but bear this pain with her sister because there was no way to make it any better. She looked at Casey, tears spilling over the rims of her sister's eyes. Casey had always been so confident that now, when faced with something like this, she didn't know how to cope, but Faith did.

"Reach out to him and talk to him. Tell him how you feel. He might not realize you still love him, and I'm sure he wouldn't throw all of this away if he knew," she said carefully. She wanted to get the words just right. "But if it doesn't work out, you'll learn how to manage without him. Then, you'll learn how to be happy without him. And, eventually, he will become a memory like one of Nan's photos—something great that you had for a little while but that you couldn't keep. Remember our cottage? We had a lot of good memories there, but a storm came—one that wrecked it so badly that it couldn't recover—and now it's a memory. The good thing is that we get to keep all those memories and we can think back on them whenever we want to. Life moves forward whether we want it to or not. You are resilient. It hurts. But you'll figure it out."

They sat in silence for quite a while. Casey's sobs subsided, and she sat up. She asked, "Where's Isabella?"

"Mom's got her. They're decorating her sandcastle."

Casey stood up and ran her fingers through her hair. "I'm going to get myself ready, and then I'll go down with her. You know what?" she asked as Faith reached for the doorknob. "There is a quiet determination to her. You've always had it too; I'd just never taken the time to see it until now. Thank you for being there. I've never said that, but thank you."

"You're welcome." She shut the door behind her and went to find Nan.

Nan was sitting in her chair where Faith had left her, a pile of photos in her lap. They were sliding around a little on the baby blue afghan she had draped across her legs. She caught a runaway photo with her hand just as Faith sat down on the floor beside her. She turned it around to show Faith.

"This was when I was twenty."

Faith looked more closely at the photo of two women wearing dresses with fitted waists, heels, and handbags dangling from the crooks of their arms. Their skin was milky white as if it had been airbrushed, both of them so beautiful that she couldn't believe one of them was actually her nan. She could've been a model. Nan had always been lovely, but she saw her differently now. She was a woman with fears, losses, victories... Faith wanted to find out more about the woman Nan had been, what she'd been through in her life, what she'd endured. She realized that she should have done this sooner but there was nothing she could do to change that. She'd just make the most of it now.

"This one's you, right?" Faith pointed to the woman on the left in the photo.

"Yes. And the other woman is Clara. She was twenty-three. It was the last photo taken of her."

It was clear that the two women were sisters, not only because they favored each other, but it was the way they were standing together, their affection for one another evident. "What happened?"

"She died in an accident." Nan shifted in her seat, wincing a little. It seemed to be her hip. She moved around until she looked relaxed. "Her train derailed. We don't know, to this day, where she was headed. I should've known, but I wasn't speaking to her."

What must it have been like to lose a sister? "I'm so sorry," she said. "Why weren't you speaking to her?"

"She'd told me that she didn't think John and I were right for each other. He was known as a sort of playboy, you see. What Clara didn't know, though, was that John told me that the minute he met me, he knew he didn't want to be with anyone else. We understood each other in a way that many people don't. It's a rare thing to find someone who you can spend your years with who makes you so excited every day that you can hardly believe how lucky you are. I found that with John, and the fact that Clara wouldn't accept him had offended me."

Two sisters, arguing over a guy. Faith could certainly relate. While she'd never told Casey not to marry Scott, she had spent a lot of time away from her sister when she should have been with her.

"I refused to speak to her. I was so angry because Clara always seemed to get everything right in life. She had a way about her that made people like her, and I was the one who had to work for everything I had. So finding someone as wonderful as John had taken me by surprise. I was thrilled that he noticed me, and that he liked the person he saw both inside and out. It annoyed me that Clara couldn't be happy for me. She was ruining the one great thing that had happened to me. I should've just ignored her comment and let time tell the story, but I didn't. I was too loyal to John. I didn't want anyone talking badly about him."

Nan reached out for the photo, so Faith handed it to her. She studied the faces in the picture for a few quiet seconds and then shook her head.

"Clara sent me a letter. She said she wanted to talk. I had the chance right then to respond, tell her I'd love to see her, and make it all better again. But I didn't. I let her request go unanswered. I still have her letter at home. I was too proud to admit that I'd overreacted. A few months later, I got word that she'd been killed in the train crash. I wish I'd gone to see her…"

"You'll get to see her again," Faith said, trying to reassure Nan in the best way she knew how. "She's up there with Grandpa. She's with him because now she knows. Time did tell the story, and they're both waiting for you."

Nan smiled, her eyes glassy with emotion. "Yes. And I will tell her I'm so sorry the minute I see her. But she's had to wait an entire lifetime to hear it and I've had to wait an entire lifetime to tell her. That's why I told you that things could be disastrous if we don't take chances. Life is full of them. Don't settle in life. If you do, you may miss a golden opportunity. The very worst feeling to carry with you isn't sadness. It's regret."

Chapter Twelve

"Isabella, are you ready?" Casey called out, grabbing Isabella's sandals. They dangled from her fingers as she slipped her handbag onto her shoulder and slid on her sunglasses. Casey looked amazing. Her outfit was casual but a little over-the-top for fishing with Jake and his friend. It was probably the most dressed down Casey could be for a fishing trip. Faith sat next to Nan in the breakfast nook as Casey gathered things for their day out.

There was a knock at the door and Faith's heart started rattling in her chest. Casey opened the door and Jake walked in, his eyes finding hers immediately. His face lifted and he broke into a brilliant smile. It made her heart beat harder. It was so silly to get flustered around him. He wasn't there for her, though, and he'd made it pretty clear that he wasn't going to ask her out again, so she should just get over it. But for some reason, she couldn't. She remembered the way he'd looked at her, how he'd smiled as she told him stories, that moment when she'd thought he was going to kiss her and what it felt like when he had. Could that feeling be enough to overpower the niggling worry about the rest?

"Hi, Jake!" Isabella said, running into the room. "Where are we fishing today?"

"Well, my buddy couldn't come, so it's just me." He squatted down to her level. "I'm going to take you to a pier down the road. Does that sound like fun?"

"I don't know. I've never done it," she said earnestly.

He chuckled. "Well, I hope you will like it, but if you don't, I'm sure your mom will bring some sand toys and a swimsuit for you and we can go swimming. The water's really nice today."

Faith worried about today when she knew she shouldn't. Casey was just so beautiful and Isabella so adorable. How could anyone not love the two of them? Jake would be the perfect person to make Casey feel at ease, to take her mind off Scott. And sitting on her chest was the nagging thought that Casey had had no problems dating Scott. What would stop her from dating Jake?

Jake greeted Faith.

"Hi," she replied, wishing she could say more, but what could she say?

Jake had already opened the door and was heading out. He had his hand on Casey's back in a guiding way, but their closeness worried Faith. Casey smiled at him, making small talk, but the door was closing. "Have fun!" she said as animatedly as she could.

"Okay!" Casey said with a smile, pulling the door closed.

Jake waved one more time and then they were gone. Faith tipped her head back and took in a deep breath. She didn't want to think about how easily Casey would make conversation with him in the car or how Isabella would melt his heart. She didn't want to ponder whether Casey would delight in his development plans and welcome his wealth. Casey would talk to him, make him laugh, tell him little stories about herself in a way that made her life seem so interesting. She was good at that. Faith tried not to think about it as she grabbed her handbag. She'd decided to spend the day sorting Nan's photos and getting them into albums. She needed something to stop her imagination from running wild and to keep her from dwelling on her thoughts. She'd better get a move on if she wanted to spend any time on the beach this afternoon.

On her way out the door, she peeked her head into her mom's room. "Need anything from town?" she asked. "I'm going to get photo albums for Nan's pictures."

"Why don't you pick up some party supplies," her mom said. "That would be great."

"Party supplies? Like matching paper plates and napkins?"

"Yes. And get some balloons and streamers too."

Faith giggled. "She's ninety years old, Mom. Does she want all that for her birthday?"

"Don't we all want someone to make a fuss over us on our birthday?"

Her mom was good at making a fuss over everyone. She had always tried hard to make the girls feel special, and birthdays were a big deal. She hadn't been able to lavish them with presents or anything, but she'd given them what she could, and she'd made them feel great on that day. On Faith's birthday, she would wake to the floor of her room filled with balloons or her door decorated, paper streamers hanging down from the doorway. Then her mom would make a breakfast of her choice, and, waiting at her spot at the table, Faith would find a birthday card to start her day. When she got home, there would always be something special left on her bed—a new book, a nice sweater, something. Then, when Nan could come over, they would all share a big, fancy cake, with candles. As she blew them out, her mom made everyone sing "Happy Birthday," even when they'd gotten older. They'd eat far too much until their bellies ached, then her mom would tuck her into bed and ask her how her birthday was. She didn't want to know what her favorite part was or if she liked the cake. Instead she'd simply asked, "Did you feel special today? You deserve to feel special."

"Okay, Mom. I'll get the party supplies. Anything in particular?"

"You of all people know what Nan likes."

"I'll see what I can find."

Faith returned with five shopping bags dangling heavily on her arms as she slid the key into the lock and opened the door. Nan was at the kitchen table. She walked over and dropped her arms, the bags falling to the floor with a thud.

"Those got heavy by the fifth step," Faith said, nodding toward the front door. She'd lugged them all the way up the stairs by herself.

"Remember how my house had that big staircase in front?" Nan said.

Faith did remember. Nan had an old house—white with black shutters, and windows so tall that entire trees were visible through them. It had a wrap-around front porch, the boards thick with years of gray paint. She'd played there a lot when she was a child, every day in the afternoons when her mother worked and on weekends when they'd all get together as a family. The house faced west, on a hill, so it had a steep staircase going up to the front door, and on summer nights, Casey and Faith would sit on those steps and watch the sky turn orange as the sun slipped below the pines.

"John used to carry things up the steps for me because I could hardly get up them with just myself." She paused, remembering something.

Faith waited, wishing she could read her mind. "Those are the kinds of things I noticed once he was gone. We'd bought that house when we'd gotten married, and I'd lived in it my entire adult life. I remember one particular night after John died when I stood at the bottom of those steps with an armful of herbs in little pots. I was going to put them inside in my kitchen window. They weren't heavy, but I had quite a few of them—you know how I like rosemary," she said, smiling. "I remember as clear as if it were yesterday. I turned around to hand one to John because he always walked up on my left side. I don't know why he did that, and I hadn't realized it until that moment. I turned, waiting to see his face, and I was alone. He wasn't there, of course. My life after John died is made up of a million little moments like those."

She ached for Nan. She couldn't imagine what it must have been like for her. Faith felt a heaviness in her chest. She'd never loved anyone like that. She wondered how it would feel to know someone so well that something as simple as walking up a staircase could be anticipated down to the very steps he took. But these stories of her grandpa taught her that *that* was the sort of love she wanted to have.

Nan had talked a lot about John lately—more than she ever had. In the past, she'd mentioned him in conversation, but she'd never shared her feelings like she was now. She knew that Nan wanted to be with him, but she ached at the thought of losing her.

"What's in all those bags?" Nan asked.

"Oh. Mom told me to get supplies for your party next week."

"All of that is for me?"

"You know how Mom is."

"Yes. I do. I'll humor her."

"I can hear y'all," her mom said through the screen door in the living area that led to the porch. She was sitting in one of the rocking chairs, her back to them. "I hope you bought paper plates." Faith couldn't see her face, but she could tell by her mother's tone that she wasn't really bothered even though she was pretending to be.

"And matching cups," Faith said, giggling. "I even got us all birthday paper cone hats. They say 'Happy Birthday' in primary colors," she teased.

Her mom didn't respond, but Faith was almost certain that if she could see her mother, she'd be smiling.

Faith reached into one of the bags and pulled out a small photo album. "I also got us a bunch of these." She flipped the pages with her thumb like a deck of cards. "We can start sorting your photos."

"Let's wait until everyone's here."

"Whatever you want. You're the birthday girl." She pulled the bags filled with the albums along the floor until they rested near the box of photos. She'd barely sat down before she heard Isabella's voice.

"We had so much fun!" Casey nearly sang just after bursting through the door ahead of Isabella. "Jake is a great guy."

Faith was glad to see her sister rejuvenated and happy, but there was a feeling gnawing at the back of her mind, making it hard for her to breathe. It took her a minute to place it. It was fear. She tried not to let it come through, but it was getting bigger and bigger, the words loud in her head as she tried unsuccessfully to ignore them—that she wasn't good enough. Scott had chosen Casey. Would Jake do the same?

Jake was easy to like, and Casey would be far better suited to his lavish lifestyle. She probably wouldn't even flinch at it. They'd had a great time together—Casey'd said they had fun, and even if she hadn't, she could tell by Casey's face. This wasn't how Faith had been after her date with Jake. Had Faith been too quiet for him? Had she not shared enough about herself? He'd ended their date with the dreaded "Let's be friends" comment.

"We found common ground when we realized we both had broken relationships. He got divorced two years ago." Casey turned and faced Faith directly. "Did you know that his wife left him because she said he didn't communicate? Jake? Not communicating? I can't imagine that!" Isabella ran to find Martha downstairs to show her a piece of driftwood she'd found that Jake had let her bring home.

Faith forced a smile, but this bit about communication didn't surprise her. It was true that Jake was very open in general conversation, but he'd left her at the end of that night feeling confused and not really understanding what he was thinking, so she could understand why his wife may have felt that way. The problem was, Faith was a listener. She was good at sitting back and letting those around her get out what they needed to say. She was a quiet leader, and she wasn't sure how she was going to handle things, but she wanted to make Jake communicate.

Seeing Casey so full of life, bright, and upbeat after being out with Jake stirred up old emotions inside her, and, unexpectedly, she was angry. Angry with him for not explaining himself more. No. She zeroed in on Casey's perfectly glossed smiling lips. She was angry with Casey. Casey could get on with her life without ever feeling the kind of fear that she'd created in Faith. She'd betrayed her sister in the very worst way, and now, her every move with Jake rubbed Faith the wrong way. She was still furious with Casey, and Jake's actions irritated her as well.

"And! He's invited me to a party tomorrow! A big one!" Casey smiled at Faith, but Faith wasn't smiling. She was scowling—she could feel it. Casey's face dropped. "You okay?"

Not only had Jake spent time with Casey today, he'd had so much fun that he'd wanted to see her for a second time. That was more than he'd offered Faith. It was no different now than when they were kids. Why did this kind of thing happen to Faith? Casey always came out on top. And Casey wasn't doing anything to stop it. What if Jake was the perfect Prince Charming to help Casey get over Scott?

"No."

Nan excused herself, leaving just the two of them in the living room.

"What's wrong?"

Faith dared not admit her early feelings for Jake to Casey. It hadn't ended well the last time she'd tried that. They'd all moved on, but Faith still didn't feel like she could trust Casey. How terrible to not be able to trust her own sister.

Casey's face was full of worry now. "I said you and Mom and Nan should come too."

The idea of crashing Jake's party didn't sound appealing at all. If he'd wanted her there, he would've asked her to come. Her mouth was dry, and she tried to swallow to alleviate it, but she couldn't. She was so angry with Casey still that she couldn't stand it. Again, Casey had stepped on Faith's toes with a man, and being invited to a party when Faith wasn't brought back all her old wounds. Then, she thought, *Why do I have to sit back and let Casey's actions dictate how I feel?* She was stronger than that. Maybe she should go. It would get Nan out of the house, and, perhaps, she could even get a little insight out of Nan. Nan was great at reading people. She'd be able to tell all kinds of things about Jake just by watching him and how he interacted with people at the party. It could be interesting.

"Maybe he doesn't want me there," she said quietly, trying to calm herself down. She could hear Isabella telling her mom stories of her fishing fun today through the screen door, and she still felt a tiny pang of jealousy even though she knew it was ridiculous. She'd only just met the guy. *Oh, who am I kidding*, she thought. *I'm smitten. And a little jealous. Okay, a lot jealous.*

"He had only wonderful things to say about you. I'm sure it's fine."

He had wonderful things to say? She wanted to know what, but dared not ask for fear her sister would see right through her and know what she was feeling. He'd said only nice things about her today; He was having a party tomorrow, and she'd get to see him again. She should go. Maybe she'd even get a chance to pull him aside and talk a little more.

"Nan?" she called. Nan stood up from the kitchen table and walked into the room. She had been very quiet the whole time, and she wondered what her grandmother was thinking. She was looking back and forth between Faith and Casey, a slight curiosity on her face.

"I'd love to go," she said before Faith had even asked the question, her gaze still darting between them. "I can't wait to see how you young people throw a party. I hope I can keep up."

Despite her apprehension, a bolt of excitement shot through Faith at seeing Jake again, overpowering her anger toward Casey. She tried to squelch it. It was silly of her to allow herself to be so eager. The truth was that she hadn't gotten excited like this in a long time, and it made her happy.

Chapter Thirteen

They'd spent the whole evening yesterday sorting photos for Nan. Faith had taken one of the albums into her room last night to look through it once more before bed. She'd left it open at the photos of her and Casey, the sun now casting a glare on the plastic pages. In one photo, they were dressed up in their mother's fancy gowns, wobbling in oversized high heels. In another, they were dangling from the branches of the old maple tree in their back yard, their feet bare, their clothes dirty from playing. It made her think about how much had changed.

Faith thought again about how excited Casey had seemed after seeing Jake. Casey probably wasn't smitten with Jake like Faith was; she was just truly excited to have found common ground with someone. She loved meeting new people and learning about them. She explained it once: the more people she met who seemed in some way like her, the more normal she felt about her experiences.

Faith, on the other hand, had always surrounded herself with a small but tight group of friends. She preferred to be with those people because they were the ones who knew her best. She felt like she could be honest with them, and their sincere care for her made her feel good. She didn't connect with strangers like Casey did. She was quiet around them. That was why she'd been so surprised by Jake. He'd been able to read her, calm her, and bring her out of her comfort zone.

Knowing this fact made her more nervous about seeing him than she should be. It had all hit her pretty hard. She was trying to lessen her fears, not to think the worst. But she worried. She'd go home and never see him again. A long-distance anything would be out of the question, given that she'd only known him for less than a week. She was rational enough to understand all that, but at the same time, she would love to see him again. Then, she thought about this party. Would it be like that restaurant where he'd taken her? Would it make her feel out of place?

Casey came in to borrow Faith's powder. "What's this party for?" Faith asked as she fastened her earring. "Who has a party during the day on a Friday?"

Casey shrugged. She didn't bother to ask, and just dipped right in to Faith's makeup bag, like she'd done when they were kids. It made Faith smile. "I don't know. I think it's pretty big, though. He's having it catered."

"Is it at his house?"

"Yeah." Casey finished powdering her face and dropped the powder back into Faith's makeup bag. "I can't wait to see his house," she said, rooting around for something else.

"Do you not have your own makeup?" Faith laughed.

"I do," she said, not looking up. "I just like your colors."

Was Casey trying to look nice for Jake? She took a few breaths to steady herself. She was trying not to have these thoughts, but it was hard, especially when she saw Casey looking so great.

"I'm going to try and enjoy myself." Casey said.

Casey was right. Faith needed to ease up and just let go. "Me too," Faith said.

The door opened and their mom poked her head in. "Your nan is waiting. She says her hip's starting to hurt from sitting so long," she kidded. Then, her face contorted into a look of concern, and she said, "Should we get Jake a bottle of wine? We shouldn't show up empty-handed."

"He's loaded, Mom," Casey said, swiping Faith's mascara. "I think he can buy his own wine. He's probably got a whole cellar full."

"That's not the point," she said in a motherly voice. Faith turned to look at her as if she were commanding her attention. "We should show our appreciation for being invited, and let him know that we are happy to be there. That's why we buy the wine. I know he can afford it, and truthfully, ours may be too cheap, but it's a nice gesture. It would be considerate."

"I'll help you pick some out," Faith said. She remembered the taste of the wine Jake had poured, and how the fruitiness and smoothness of it had contrasted with his masculine attributes. But then again, he could be gentle and sweet.

"Great! Now"—her mom pointed at Casey playfully—"hurry up your primping so we can go. Isabella's antsy, and your Nan's driving me crazy."

Faith pressed a little harder on the adhesive tab of the giant curly ribbon she'd bought at the Quick Mart in town. It didn't want to stick to the glass wine bottle, and she'd been holding it on the whole ride to Jake's. She'd chosen a white—it was only table wine but at the top of her price range. She knew it probably wouldn't matter, but she wanted to try and make the best impression that she could. Her hands were a little nervous, so she was glad to have the task of keeping the bow in place.

"Good heavens!" her mom cried as they pulled up to Jake's house. "You weren't kidding, Faith. It's a mansion." Her mom's eyes darted over to the wine, clearly wondering if they'd gotten a sufficient gift. Faith pressed her finger on the bow again. Her mom pulled the car to a stop between a BMW and a Lexus. "Careful when you get out. Don't ding their doors! Isabella, Nan, stay put. I'll help you."

Faith grinned to herself when she spotted Chuck's old Ford parked under a tree.

They all wriggled their way out carefully and helped Nan and Isabella to do the same. Isabella walked next to Faith. She was wearing a white sundress with a bright purple sash that tied in the back, a purple bow in her hair, and a delicate gold necklace around her neck. She looked so cute. When she got to the grass that stretched the length of the lawn, she started skipping, her golden hair bouncing with every step.

The house was a far cry from what it had been when Faith had been there with just Jake and his father. The immense yard was littered with bright white tents to keep the sun off, their peaks stretching upward into the sky. The blue sea was calm beyond, its surface glittering in the sun on the other side of all the tents. There must have been over a hundred people there, all holding glasses of wine with little white napkins pressed against the side of their crystal glasses. They were talking to one another, laughing, nodding. From somewhere—she guessed the same outdoor speakers he'd used when it was just them—music was playing softly. Faith steadied her rising nerves by holding onto the bottle of wine, the ribbon pinched between her fingers and the neck of the bottle. Against this backdrop, it seemed out of place.

Faith looked around for Jake, her eyes stopping at the back door to the kitchen off in the distance. Her heart sped up. She remembered the look in his eyes, the way his breathing accelerated, the softness in his features as he looked down at her. Now, seeing that door from so far away, it made her feel like none of it had been real, as if it had all been in her imagination. Funny how time—even a few days—can change perspective. Before she could ponder it any longer, she felt a lift in her hands as Casey took the bottle from them, the ribbon falling to the ground. Martha scooped it up and put it in her pocket. Jake was coming toward them.

"Hi, Jake," Casey said with that flirty smile of hers as she walked ahead of Faith. She held out the bottle. "We brought this for you. Thank you for having us."

Faith had to grit her teeth together to keep herself from snapping at Casey.

"Thank you for this." He peered down at the wine. "And it's no problem. Happy to have you here. How are you, Sophia?" he patted Nan on the shoulder. "Let me know if you need anything. There are chairs under the tents if you'd like to have a seat. Martha, it's nice to see you."

Faith waited to see how he would greet her. She willed him to look her way, hoping she'd see something significant in his face.

He turned to her, and every nerve in her body was on high alert. "Hey," he said with a grin, and she felt like her heart would beat right out of her chest. His eyes were gentle, like they had been the other night, as if he had something more to say. Instead, he turned back to her family, leaving her breathless. *What in the world is happening?* she thought. Faith had always been a no-nonsense kind of person. She'd never been a dreamer, a romantic. She'd always been the levelheaded one. But, being around him, she was a complete mess. The feeling scared her, and she almost wanted to leave. She wished she'd had more than a few seconds with him, that he hadn't said more.

Jake said he'd get them all a glass of wine, and they started walking away from him toward the tents. She could feel every step she took away from him in her ears, her heart still drumming in her chest.

"Why did *you* take the wine and give it to him? You weren't even involved in buying it," she whispered loudly over the chatter to Casey, feeling a lot like her younger self. It was a petty thing to get irritated by, but it bothered her.

Casey looked at her as if she was crazy, and for a second, she wondered if she was. But her irritation won out. If it had been up to Casey, they wouldn't have even brought wine, and now she looked like she'd had the idea in the first place.

"Since I was the one he invited, and you weren't offering it to him yet, I just took it so that we could give it to him in case he got sidetracked by another guest or something. I didn't want to walk around indefinitely, holding a bottle of wine. And he knew it was from all of us," she said.

"But I picked it out. I bought it."

"…As a favor to *all* of us."

Faith let it go, but she didn't want to. She looked out at the ocean and tried to calm down. Her anger was coming back as quickly as the waves were rolling in.

They found a table and Faith helped Nan get comfortable. Jake was still inside, and she wanted so badly to talk to him. "I'm going to go to the little girls' room," she said with a smile to hide the irritation that she felt. They all nodded, and she headed inside.

It was a long walk across the lawn, and as she got closer, her hands became jittery, her heart beating so fast she felt like she'd just sprinted to the house and back. She took in a big, warm breath of salty air and let it out, focusing on the sound of the tide to calm her. It wasn't helping. Casey'd gotten her quite upset, and now, mixed with the buzz of excitement at seeing Jake, she was having trouble calming down. What would she say when she got in there? What did she want to ask first? How was she going to ask it? And would she even get a chance to have that kind of time with him today?

As she passed a group of men wearing dress trousers and pressed shirts, she stopped to get herself together, pretending to look at the flowers nearby. The men's ties flapped in the ocean breeze, and she heard one of them say, "Can you believe Jake's plans for Corolla? Laughable. What a terrible idea."

"I'm not sure it would go over well with the current landowners. They like it the way it is. He'll never get it off the ground. The Board of Supervisors will stop him at every turn," another one said. She understood this, glad someone had some sense on the matter, but their criticizing Jake made her feel a little uncomfortable at the same time. It was true. They didn't need any more Tides Wine Bars going up.

As she moved away and the conversation faded, she just caught one last comment.

"They're outnumbered," the first man said with a laugh. "Jake owns half of the Outer Banks, it seems. I wonder how many he can wine and dine on the Board."

Jake owns half of the Outer Banks... She repeated it in her head. She'd heard it correctly, but she wanted to say it to herself to really understand it. It drove home the fact that he'd made a lot of money doing what he was doing. Although that still didn't make it right. She walked past the table where they'd had dinner together. It was filled with glasses of champagne and wine, more napkins, little hors d'oeuvre plates and silver forks, the chairs askew, some filled with people in fine clothes and designer sunglasses. It was so different from the serene, calm place she'd visited just a few nights before. She liked it better then. She grabbed the doorknob and twisted it open.

The kitchen and living area were full of people standing so close together that Faith had to say "excuse me" to make them step aside. The round kitchen table had been transformed by the caterer with white tablecloths, and silver platters, an enormous chocolate fountain in the center with bright, artful arrangements of fruit on either side. Shrimp and clams and other little seafood bites sat on more platters along the bar where she'd watched Jake cook for her.

The chatter of the crowd faded away as she remembered the quiet of that night. She'd loved getting to know him, hearing his stories, finding out more about the man who worked hard all day just because he loved it, the man who could make her feel at home faster than she'd ever imagined possible, the man who could make her stomach flutter with nerves. As she surfaced from her thoughts, she looked around for Jake but couldn't find him.

"Faith!" Chuck was waving to her as he made his way through the crowd. "Fancy seein' you here," he said as he reached her. His gray hair was combed, although it looked like the wind outside had gotten to it. He had on a button-up shirt and a pair of trousers. Given that most of the men were wearing ties, it was still quite a casual outfit, even though she was willing to bet it was quite formal to him.

"How are you?" she said with a smile, genuinely pleased to see him.

"I'm okay. I'm only here for the free cake," he teased.

She smiled wider.

"How are *you*?"

"I'm fine. I'm looking for Jake. Have you seen him?"

"He may be in the dining room," he said, and, after a quick thank you, she went straight there to see.

The dining room table was covered in light blue linens, with various sized glass vases lining the center. Each one was filled with white seashells and starfish, more white tea candles than she could count sprinkled in between them like stars in the night sky. The rest of the table was covered in more platters, more finger foods. In the corner was a caterer's table, adorned with pleated white linen and displaying an assortment of wines. She walked over to peer at the labels and she was pleased to see that they were all local wines.

"I'm sorry," Jake's voice came from behind her, and she turned around. "I got caught by a group on the way in. I've been stuck over by the pool table." He made a face as if it had been horrible, and she laughed. When she did, she saw that softness again on his face. "You found the wine," he said, after clearing his throat.

"Yes." She turned back toward the wine table as a nervous impulse.

"See any you like?" he asked, walking up behind her and looking over her shoulder.

She could smell his spicy scent, and it made it hard to process his words or find any of her own. He'd never know how she felt if she didn't tell him something. She had to tell him *something*, but the words were all getting jumbled in her head. She turned around to face him. They were so close that it wouldn't take much effort to tip her head up and kiss him. He leaned forward, and she felt a swing of nervousness through her head. She worked to keep her breathing even, and she could feel her mouth drying out, which worried her as he was leaning in toward her, but she didn't want to stop him. At the last second, he reached around her and grabbed a glass off the table and then righted himself.

"I'll fill a glass for your mom and your grandmother if you'll get Casey's."

Faith could not believe she'd just misread that. It took her a minute to collect herself. The more she thought about it, the more ridiculous she felt. Why would he kiss her? He hadn't really seen her since saying he wanted to be friends, so why had she imagined things had changed? She tried to analyze her reasons, but she came up empty. Jake must have noticed her silence because he looked at her again, his eyes roaming her face, and it hit her: She was feeling this way because, when he looked at her, there was something there. She wasn't crazy. She could see it right on his face. He knew it too because as this idea registered in her mind, he caught himself and turned back to the wine.

She knew she had to say something. "Jake?"

"Yes?" He turned back toward her. His "yes" wasn't a question but, rather, a statement, as if to say, "tell me." Was he waiting for her to make the first move?

Without overthinking it, she said the first thing that came into her mind. "I enjoyed being with you the other night."

He nodded, his eyes on her. She was hoping for a response, something to encourage her to go on.

"And I'm glad I'm here now…" She wanted to say more, but she didn't, still worried about his lack of response. Now, looking at him, she worried that he'd closed up. That carefree man she'd seen at Bodie Island, who'd kissed her, joked with her, told her stories—Jake was different now. She'd never had to deal with anything like this before. She liked him so much better when she thought he was a handyman. Was he more of that person or the one standing in front of her now with all the fancy guests and tables of wine? He seemed to notice her thoughts and she worried that he could read them again.

"I think we should get this wine out to your family before they think we've gone missing," he said, turning back toward the table and grabbing a bottle. Faith didn't move at first. She wasn't finished. She wanted to tell him her feelings. But when she finally turned around, he'd filled all four glasses and he was handing two to her. "These are for you and Casey."

Jake gestured for her to go first and she went ahead of him. The moment had passed and she wondered if he'd just wanted to get out of the conversation. They entered the crowd again, and he came up beside her to help her get through. People stopped him to talk, and he politely listened, smiled, and then gracefully left the conversation as he made his way outside.

"What is this party for?" she asked as they stepped into the calmer atmosphere in the backyard.

"I've just broken ground on a resort in Frisco," he said, nodding hello to someone. "They'll have everything money can buy at their fingertips. I've developed a plan with my team that will consist of a neighborhood of sorts, with high-end cottages, all waterfront but with the amenities of a resort."

Frisco was right down the road. It was a small, uncluttered village, a place that offered an escape from the hustle and bustle of growth in the area. All the villages in the Outer Banks backed up to one another, and creating high-traffic areas in one location would certainly impact the others. The Outer Banks was only a slim strip of barrier islands, and one had to go through each village to get to the next. The whole strip was only about thirty miles wide at its widest points. Creating large resorts would certainly clog up the roads and pull in more commerce. Faith's head began to pound.

Another person stopped him to ask where he'd gotten the clams. They were delicious, he'd said. Jake directed him to the caterer.

"There will be high-end bars, swimming pools, a clubhouse with a gym. I'm very excited about the project." He raised a wineglass-filled hand up to another man walking by. "Sorry for the mayhem," he smiled. "All that to say, this is a party to celebrate the start of Whelk Resort, and these are all the people involved—town council, investors, architects—all of them."

Jake's explanation made her sick to her stomach. He'd been so proud of the Tides, having even helped to build it, and now it was really happening: he was building more atrocities. Jake clearly knew how to make money, but even if he was right about this idea that people would flock to these places if they were here, didn't he realize what he was doing? The Outer Banks would lose its charm, and its beautiful natural landscape would be spoiled. She didn't want it to be just another beach location with cookie cutter high-rise hotels and no parking to speak of, with no charm of its own. If he had his way, would he develop the whole area? She hoped not, but it was looking that way. She wanted to give him the benefit of the doubt, and she hoped that maybe he'd thought about what she'd said the other night and been concerned by it, but her views seemed to have little impression on him.

Before they could reach the tent, Isabella came running toward them, her dress ballooning in the breeze as her white sandals pattered along the grass. The purple bow in her hair had come untied, the two ends dangling long on her ponytail. When she reached Faith, she said, out of breath, "I've been down on the beach. It's so pretty!"

Faith tied her bow for her. "It's a pretty place down here."

"Jake," Isabella said, tugging on the elbow of his shirt, sloshing the wine precariously in its glass. He bent down so as not to spill it, beads of condensation from the heat sliding down the glass. "Do you have a bag where I can put some seashells? You have so many on your beach!"

"I do." He smiled at her, tiny creases showing at his eyes. "And you know what else I have? I have a book that shows all the different kinds of shells and tells you their names. Maybe when all this is finished, we can look up the shells you find, and I can tell you what they are."

There were many people out there who had books about shells just like Faith's, but the fact that Jake had a seashell book like her did seem quite the coincidence. *He lives at the beach*, she tried to convince herself; *surely someone got it for him as a gift or something*. But she took it as a sign, a little ray of hope.

"We were wondering where you'd gone off to!" Casey came swishing over, her sundress giving her maddeningly perfect curves. She took one of the glasses from Jake. "I want to show you something on the beach. Do you mind walking with me?" She took the other glass of wine from his hand and gave it to Faith, who now balanced three glasses in her fingers. Casey grabbed Jake by the arm. Then, over her shoulder, she said, "We'll be back in a second."

Faith watched them walk away. Without even realizing it, Casey was doing it again—swooping in and stealing the one person Faith showed interest in! At this point, she didn't care anymore that she'd be leaving next week. She just wanted to have a chance to have her own happiness, however short-lived it was. Why should she have to sit like a bump on a log while Casey had all the fun? She was tired of that. Snapping out of it, she realized she was still holding three glasses of wine. She looked over at Nan, who was already looking in her direction. She'd probably seen the whole thing.

"You doing okay?" Faith asked as she neared Nan, trying to keep things calmer than in her head. She handed her mom and Nan each a glass.

"Yes," Nan said slowly. "You?"

It was a loaded "you." She'd seen for sure.

"I think so." Faith looked toward the beach to see if she could see Casey or Jake. "Do you mind if I excuse myself for just a few more minutes. I want to talk to Casey."

Nan smiled. "Your mom and I have tons to talk about."

"Thank you."

"Chances," Nan said, her grin spreading across her face. "Glad to see you finally taking chances."

She felt her pulse quicken, and she wasn't sure if it was because of Nan's observation, or the fact that she was going to confront Casey, or both. But she turned and started toward the beach. With every step she took, years of pent-up frustration were simmering, heating up. She was still mad at Casey—she just wanted to stand up for herself, tell her sister to back off, and let her know how she felt.

She walked up the wooden steps leading over the dune and spotted them on the beach. Casey was pointing to a tree farther down, and

Jake was talking. Casey laughed, throwing her head back, her hand landing on Jake's arm. Faith stopped, deliberating. Jake didn't know the whole history she had with her sister, and he may not understand if she just burst in and pulled Casey away to talk. It may seem rude. Before she could contemplate it further, Jake had caught her eye, and he waved. They started walking her way.

Casey had her sandals dangling from her fingers, her hair blowing behind her shoulders, and her dress flapping around her legs. She was so beautiful. Faith tucked her hair behind her ears to keep it from blowing around in circles on her head. Then, she smoothed out her own dress and straightened herself up.

"When we were fishing, Jake had promised to show me an area of beach where he liked to fish. I was asking him where it was," Casey said, as she neared her. She looked out at the ocean. "This southern climate is quite a change from Boston. I could sell it all and move here," she said, clearly kidding, but the comment grated on Faith's nerves.

"It's an amazing day. I'll leave you two to enjoy the view," Jake said. "I'm going to get the sand out of my shoes and then head back in to the party." He gave them a wink.

Faith acknowledged his statement with a smile, but inside she was still a mess. Once he was out of earshot, she said, "Casey, what do you think you're doing?" She couldn't hold it in anymore.

"What?"

"What exactly are you doing with Jake?"

"What are you talking about?"

"I've watched you! You're overly flirty, practically yanking the wine out of my hands today to give it to him. Shouldn't you be focused on your husband?"

The skin between Casey's eyes wrinkled, her face crumpling in confusion and resentment.

"You always do this!" Faith said a little too loudly, glad that the distance and the surf drowned out her words for those at the party. "You come waltzing in, doing whatever you please, without once thinking about those around you. You only think about yourself! No wonder Scott left!" She was fuming, saying things she didn't expect to say, but the lid had come off, and it was all coming out. Had she had more time to think about it all, she may have said things in a different manner, but it was too late now, and she'd said it.

"Excuse me?" Casey said indignantly.

"You tell me how much you miss Scott and you're so upset about the divorce, yet you sure don't seem to be missing him when you're off with Jake!"

"Pardon *me* for trying to enjoy myself at a nice party with a gracious host," she spit out. Faith knew she wanted to say more but she was holding her tongue. "You're being dramatic."

"I'm being dramatic? Are you serious?"

"Well, it's either that or you're still hung up on Scott, so you're taking it out on me."

Anger boiled inside her. She knew that was what it would look like to Casey, but it wasn't that at all. It was *Casey*! She was the one ruining everything. "I am *not* hung up on Scott," she said through clenched teeth.

Realization suddenly sheeted over Casey's face. "You have a crush on Jake?" She laughed, making Faith feel ridiculous. As sisters, they had a way of doing this to each other: They could be harsh and downright mean when they were upset, but once it all settled, they'd forgive each other. Forgiveness was far on the horizon today. Casey's laughter caused a blow of fury to Faith's gut, and at that moment she didn't want to ever forgive her sister.

Faith knew what Casey was thinking. She was thinking that they'd only been there for six days and Faith had some kind of schoolgirl crush, and she was throwing a fit over it. But this was more than some schoolgirl crush. She had real feelings for Jake. She was getting out years of frustration over how Casey could always get everything she wanted and Faith had to sit by and watch, even when it hurt her. She'd scarred Faith, betraying her trust. Yes, Faith did think Jake was a great guy, and she did want to spend time with him, but it was Casey's behavior that had caused this outburst. Tears were surfacing, and she blinked to keep them at bay. Her throat was tight with emotion, her chest hurting from the pressure of it.

"I just wish you'd pay attention to other people sometimes," she said quietly. The pain had eaten through the anger. Why hadn't Casey taken the time to notice how she would hurt Faith all those years ago when she'd met Scott? Surely, as Faith's sister, she'd known she should've stopped.

Faith sat down on the bottom step, pushing her feet into the sand. A sandpiper ran along the shoreline, leaving footprints behind it. Casey didn't sit.

"Heaven forbid you notice those around you. But then again, that would put a damper on your perfect little world, wouldn't it?" Faith said, still quiet to keep the sobs from bubbling up. This was by far the wrong place to be having this conversation, but there was no changing it now. The last thing she wanted to do was go back up to the party with watery eyes and a red nose. "You never let yourself feel anything unless it's happiness. You push the uncomfortable feelings away, and in doing so, you never have to deal with the fact that you broke my heart, Casey. You need to stop hurting people. Think about their feelings. Put a little effort in *them*. *Work* for it, if you miss Scott. Show him he's worth your effort. Loving someone takes work, Casey. I've learned that by loving you."

Casey didn't respond. She was looking out at the horizon, her lips pursed in an angry scowl, her breathing steady. Faith knew that this was hard for her too.

"You are so high and mighty," Casey finally said. "You spout off about relationships like you know something about them, when you've had one, maybe two, and they amounted to nothing. Don't you dare try and judge my relationship with Scott. You don't know." Then, without another word, she walked off, leaving Faith alone on the step.

Chapter Fourteen

If she went back to the party, Faith might cry, so she sat on that step, watching the waves. Casey had hurt her. And, truth be told, she'd probably hurt Casey too. Faith was still angry, but she also felt awful. This was the wrong place to bring up her issues with Casey—she hadn't meant to; they'd just bubbled up. She'd taken her built-up feelings too far today, but there was never a good time. One doesn't just set out and say, "Today is a good day to confront my sister." It didn't work that way. She'd gotten out some of what she'd wanted to say today, but their argument was far from over. Casey still hadn't said she was sorry or even admitted to doing anything wrong, so this little outburst had done nothing but get Faith worked up.

She'd sat there on the step until the outward signs of sadness had been erased, but now she just felt empty. Casey was right. What did she know about relationships? What did she know about the life that Casey had with Scott? She'd not even been a part of it. She'd stayed away nearly Isabella's whole life. She had no idea about what the Robins family was like.

"Hey," she heard through the wind behind her.

Faith twisted around to find Jake at the top of the steps that led to the beach. Seeing Jake only made her feel worse because she wanted his comfort, but she knew she probably wouldn't get it. He stepped down, one by one, until he was next to her. Then, he lowered himself down beside her. They were unusually close, given the narrow staircase, so he turned a little to give her more room.

"You okay?" he asked. "You've been down here for a long time."

She nodded, even though she was lying. She wasn't okay at all.

He looked at her as if he saw through it, but he didn't say anything. He leaned back, resting his arm on the step above, and the proximity made it seem like he had his arm around her. She took in a deep breath. She wanted to have his arms around her for real, to rest her head on his shoulder. But she straightened her back to try and look like she had it all together. She was used to getting herself together without the help of anyone else, and she didn't want him to pity her.

"Wanna talk about it?" he asked, looking at her out of the corner of his eye. He was trying to seem casual, she could tell, but he knew something. Had Casey told him what had happened? Her chest felt cold at the idea. Casey wouldn't dare…

"I'm fine. I was just enjoying the view," she said. "You should be up there," she tipped her head back to point at the party, "instead of being down here with me."

"You're a part of my party too," he said, finally turning to look at her. "I couldn't even see you down here! I had no idea where you'd gone until I ran into Casey. I figured you'd come back up and gotten lost in the crowd."

Now she really wondered what Casey might have said. Had Casey put herself in Jake's path on purpose? Faith turned to face him. "Well, thank you," she smiled. "Thank you for checking on me. Sometimes, I like to be away from the crowd, you know?"

He smiled a crooked grin and shifted, their faces too close. "Me too," he said.

"I don't believe that for one minute," she said. "As much as you like to talk to people."

"It's true! I do enjoy meeting new people, getting to know people, but I like my quiet time too. It's hard work doing all that talking. I can't go on like that forever." He chuckled. His face was the same as it was the other night—his eyes looked as though he were drinking her up, taking in every movement she made, every thought she had. She wanted time to stop when he did it because there was nothing she'd ever experienced that was as good as that.

"Thank you," she said sincerely. "Thank you for taking time to come see me down here. You didn't have to."

His face was serious, but the corners of his mouth were turned up into a grin, that fondness pouring through his features. He was so good-looking yet he never acted as if he knew it. Their eyes were locked on one another's, as if they were both thinking the same thing. They were completely alone. No one could see them down here. He was being so gentle and nice. He'd come to check on her, bothered to sit with her when there were so many other people who were surely lining up for his time.

It would be so easy to lean forward and kiss him. She'd never been put in a situation like this before, but right now, she felt as if she would know exactly what to do. This was her moment. *The* moment to take charge and let him know what she wanted. She wanted him—just like this with no pretentiousness or extravagance. He was giving her all the signals she needed; she just had to act on them.

She placed her hand on his chest, over his heart, and he looked down at it.

"Faith…" His words trailed off.

"When I'm teaching and I send one of my five-year-olds on an errand down the hallway, I always ask if they walked back or if they ran. Sometimes they say they've walked, but I know better. Do you know how I can tell that they aren't telling the truth?"

He shook his head.

"I put my hand on their heart. If I can feel it beating wildly, then I know."

He looked down again at her hand, defeat sliding across his face. His heart was beating like crazy, and she knew she'd caught him. For some reason, he'd been trying to play down his feelings for her. She didn't know why, but the idea that he was feeling the same way that she was made her own heart soar.

The moments where he'd laughed at something she'd said the other night, and the way his head turned when he was listening to her, the list of things they had in common—it all went through her mind as she leaned forward. Her heart was beating so fast, she worried it was visible from the outside. Faith put her other hand on the step to steady herself as she moved closer. She was telling him silently that it was okay, that she welcomed anything that may transpire between them. Then, she closed her eyes and pressed her lips to his. The exhilaration of it caused her to lean against him to keep her body steady. His lips were soft and strong at the same time, just like they had been at Bodie Island. Never had she initiated a kiss with anyone. She finally felt in control of her feelings, and it felt wonderful. She knew this was the feeling she wanted to have for the rest of her life with someone. With him?

Then, it all stopped.

Gently, his hands on her shoulders, he pushed her away. For the first time since she'd met him, he looked vulnerable. It was only a second and then it was gone. He stood up. She felt a little frantic, like she wanted to stop him and find out why he'd pushed her away when it was clear that he felt something for her. Whatever the issue was, they could figure it out together.

"I'm sorry," he said. He cleared his throat and took in a slightly jagged breath. "I'm…" He stared blankly out at the ocean as if collecting himself. "I'm sorry."

She sat silently.

"What I've learned in life is that I'm at my happiest when I can be friends with someone—I know how to do that. But when it comes to relationships—day in and day out—I'm terrible at them. I've been down that road before," he said again. "Showing you around is a lot of fun, but when it comes down to real life—who I am and who you are—things will get harder. It's easy to forget when I'm with you, but I can't stop being me and doing what I do.

"What do you mean by that?"

"I'm not going to try and prove myself to anyone. I am who I am, and I'm not going to answer for it. I've had to answer for it my whole marriage, and I'm not doing it again. You don't want me to build up the Outer Banks, but I'm a builder, and I can't be happy unless I'm doing that. I have a totally different vision about what I see for the future. Yes, I want to sit on my porch and read, but only if I know that I've just found land to build a golf course. I can't change who I am or what I do. I'm sorry."

"I'm sorry too," she said, not getting up. Her legs might not have held her if she'd stood up. "I misinterpreted the moment, and I misinterpreted who you are." Had she ever. Clearly, Jake was not going to be persuaded to change his mind about building.

Even putting the issue of Jake's profession aside, he had the upper hand in this argument. He'd known, first-hand, what being in a committed relationship was like. Faith hadn't ever been married. She didn't have a clue about being with someone that long. Casey's words were like daggers inside her head. Her sister was right. What did Faith know about relationships? She'd finally put herself out there, taken a chance like Nan had told her to do, and she'd failed. In the world she'd created back home, she was safe from situations like these. She couldn't get hurt there.

She looked out at the ocean. She didn't know what to say. He was right. Maybe they were better as friends. She was used to living alone, and she, too, had learned to enjoy it. He was reading her again, she could tell, and she tried to push all the thoughts from her mind unsuccessfully.

"I'm glad I met you," she said. "Sometimes in life, there are people who, for whatever reason, make us feel great. You're one of those people for me, but I understand that we are very different. I'd like to stay friends."

"I feel the same way. Friends," he smiled. Then, reaching out to help her up, he said, "Shall we go back to the party?"

Faith grabbed his hand and stood up, letting go to brush the sand off her bottom, and trying to get feeling back in her legs. Her anxiety over the moment had made them wobbly. As she walked up the steps, she thought about how much of a scene she'd made. Her sister had said she was dramatic, and she may have been right. She was at a party, yet she was fighting with her sister and trying to kiss the host.

She was tired. She wanted to go home. She wanted to get in her car and leave. It was all too much. Jake didn't say anything else. He was quiet the whole walk back to the house. As they entered the crowd, the chatter was amplified in Faith's ears, slamming around in her head, giving her a headache.

She walked beside Jake to the tent where Nan was sitting beside her mom, an iced tea in her hands, the wine long gone. Her mom was smiling, unknowing, but Nan focused on her, an unreadable expression on her face. Concern? Confusion? Had Casey come back up spouting her irritation with Faith to all of them? Clearly she hadn't, by the look on her mother's face. Nan was so intuitive, so sharp, that she could always tell. Faith tried to smile, to put on a happy face and play the part.

"I'll see ya later," Jake said as he headed toward a group in the other direction, leaving her with her mom and Nan.

Faith caught sight of Chuck in the crowd and he waved. She thought about how Jake's father felt about his business developments, and she realized that Jake probably didn't want yet another person in his life shooting down his dreams. Even if they were ridiculous. She understood, but it didn't make it any easier. The sadness over their unresolvable differences and the eventual loss of her favorite place were weighing heavily on her. Her head pounded, and the sun and wine were only making it worse.

"Where have you been?" her mom asked with a grin. "We've been having a great time up here. Your nan's been telling me stories about you girls that I'd never heard. Did you know that you two got into her baking flour when you were just a baby and you had it all over her kitchen? She didn't ever tell me that." Her mom laughed, looking over at Nan, but Nan was still eyeing Faith, her gaze appraising.

Her mom's words were barely registering because Faith was still in a fog from what had happened with Jake, and the fact that Nan clearly noticed made her self-conscious. Why had Nan even tried to get them all together? Faith wasn't anything like her sister, and rather than moving forward, the trip had felt like a backward step for them. Her poor mother had packed half her house in preparation, and Faith was ready to leave having used none of what she'd brought. To make matters worse, Isabella was being dragged to adult parties. Where was she anyway? Faith hoped that Casey had her off somewhere playing.

"I'm going in to get some food," her mom said. "If not, I may not be able to drive home!" She held up her wine, probably the same one that Faith had brought her, only half of it gone. Her mom was not a drinker. She usually nursed her glasses all day, making Faith wonder how she could muscle them down once they got warm. Her mom excused herself, leaving her alone with Nan. Faith sat down as she watched her mom heading for the house. Instinctively, she found herself scanning the crowd for Jake, but she stopped herself.

"Would you like to talk about it?" Nan said out of nowhere.

"Not really," she answered, but gave Nan a gentle expression to let her know she wasn't trying to be rude. What was the point in telling her about it? None of it could be changed.

"Well, then. If you're not going to talk about it, I will. Casey came marching up from the beach, looking like a firestorm. Then, she collected herself, got Isabella, and said she was taking a walk. You are nowhere to be found for ages, and when you finally emerge, you look as though someone has put you through the ringer. Jake darted off like a flash. From what I've seen of you and Casey this week, I'm willing to bet that Jake is in the center of your spat."

How does she do that? Faith wondered. Nothing could get by Nan.

"Let me offer you a little advice. I don't care whether you want to hear it or not. I'm telling you anyway. Don't let whatever it is with Jake cloud your issues with Casey. It has nothing to do with him and everything to do with the two of you. You'll never agree—you're too different. But, one day, you'll learn to appreciate your differences. In order to do that, you both have to find your own happiness. And I don't mean a man. You have to be happy in your own skin. You are who you are, Faith. And you are wonderful. I think it every day."

How could she feel wonderful when she'd just made a fool of herself with Jake? She always got it wrong. She always came in second. She didn't want to sit and feel sorry for herself, but the facts were glaring.

"I'd like to tell you something else," Nan said, breaking Faith free from her thoughts. "John was just a boy when I met him. He'd moved in a few streets over when we were in high school, and the teacher had put him at a desk in front of mine in our English class. I remember the sweater he wore on cold days—it was a blue cardigan. As I looked at the back of him every day, I wondered about him. I wondered what it was like moving to a new place. I wondered what he did after school. I didn't love him then. I didn't know him. But I wanted to know him. That's how it starts, Faith. Nobody knows if they're meant for one another—I certainly didn't know back then that this boy sitting in front of me in English class would be the man that I would spend every day wishing to be with again at the age of ninety. I didn't know that he'd be the one who kissed my forehead every night before we went to sleep or the one who wasted away the weekends staying in bed, pulling me back in every time I tried to get up. You won't know, Faith. But if you give up, if you don't try, you might miss it."

Nan made it sound so easy. Faith wondered if she'd ever had the trouble that Faith had experienced. "I can't get it right, Nan," she said, struggling to get the words past the lump in her throat. "I can't get any of it right."

"You don't have to get it right," Nan said, smiling, her gaze wise and experienced. "What fun would that be? What seem like big, difficult hurdles to you now will be a blip when you're my age. It will all be part of your journey to where you're meant to be. At ninety, I finally have it all straight. I know exactly what I want. It's simple. I want my family to understand each other, and I want to know that when I leave here, I can sit with John and feel like I've done something for my family. That's all that matters."

Faith sat quietly, thinking about her grandmother's words. It was difficult to have Nan's perspective, given her age and experience. Faith watched the people around her now, how they talked to each other, how they laughed together, and she wondered what she was doing here with them at this party. She didn't have the kind of money that Jake had. She wasn't used to his lifestyle. She didn't agree with the whole reason for this party or the plans he'd made. Being here was causing old wounds to be opened and making her fight with Casey. None of it seemed to be helpful in any way, and she thought again that maybe she'd better just leave. But then, her gaze fell on Jake. He was standing with a group, a drink in his hand, listening to whoever was talking, but his eyes were on her, all the way across the lawn. He was looking right at her. She smiled. Given what had happened, it wasn't the most obvious choice of response, but it was a natural one. Just like Nan had wondered about John, she wondered about Jake. What if he was like that boy in English class? What if, one day, she'd know him better than he knew himself? Maybe it wouldn't happen, but maybe it would.

Jake looked away, but she kept glancing over at him. But then Casey emerged with Isabella and stood next to him. She said something into his ear, and he bent down to talk to Isabella. Faith was far away from them, but she felt farther and farther away as she watched them. He'd told her they should be just friends and she'd gotten carried away, romanticizing again. She had to face facts: All he wanted was to be friends.

Chapter Fifteen

Faith didn't get to say goodbye when she left the party. With so many people there, she hadn't been able to catch Jake, and Nan was getting hot in the car, so they had to go. Nan had mentioned that she'd said goodbye to him anyway, so at least she could represent them all. Casey wasn't speaking to Faith—she'd given her the silent treatment all the way home, which was fine because Faith wasn't in the mood for any further discussion. Isabella had filled the silence, chattering about anything and everything. Her mom and Nan both responded as if nothing was wrong, but Faith knew they could both tell. And after Isabella and Casey went to bed that night, they wanted to know.

She didn't tell them right away. She was still too upset with Casey. She went straight to her room and closed the door. Once she was alone, and the magnitude of what had transpired was able to finally hit her, she let the tears come. The thing about Casey was that it seemed like she didn't care, when really she did. She cared so much; she just wouldn't admit it to herself. She was the cool, collected one— she'd always been that. Sometimes, she needed to let her guard down.

Even though Faith felt awful, and she just wanted to cry, she got herself together. After using a few tissues, covering the redness under her eyes with powder, and rolling her shoulders to relieve the stress, she went out to face the family. She knew Nan would want to know everything, and she really didn't want to relive the humiliation of the moment with Jake or her insecurities regarding her sister. She really didn't even want to hear what Nan had to say, because the fact that she had figured it all out only made Faith feel like she hadn't. She didn't have years of experiences to fall back on. She barely had any. All she knew was what she felt right now, in the present. She felt like she couldn't live up to Casey, and she never would, because the moment she tried to show someone what she felt it hadn't gone the way she'd planned at all. The embarrassment of it lingered under her skin.

Jake was rich in a kind of way that she had never experienced, the excitement of it sweeping her off her feet but slamming her back down to reality at the same time. He had different views about what the future might look like. And they'd argue about it because she felt that his business decisions were wrong in so many ways. The problem was that she would love a chance to find a happy medium. Why did they have to agree on everything? What kind of life was that? She had a connection with him, and she knew he could feel it too.

She was relieved to find that Casey was in her room, probably still fuming over their argument. Nan was sitting on the sofa with a photo album in her lap.

Ugh. Those damn photo albums! Faith wanted to scream. She was in no mood to look through any more photos of how blissfully happy she and Casey were as children. That was the trouble with photos: They were like sports highlights—only the good stuff. Well, in reality there was a ton of bad stuff too, and painting a picture of their glorious childhood wouldn't help right now. She didn't want to be convinced of how wonderful her life was. There was no changing the way they both felt. And Faith would be glad when she could finish out this vacation and go back to her regular life. If it weren't for Nan's birthday, she'd have already left.

"Have a seat, dear," Nan said, her eyes knowing.

Her mom came in and sat down on the floor, crossing her legs at the ankles and turning around to view the two of them. She looked concerned.

"What's going on?" Nan asked.

"It's complicated," Faith replied. It felt like someone had a tiny hammer banging at her temples from the inside. Just sitting there was exhausting.

"It always is."

"Casey is a very extroverted person," her mom said carefully. She was talking to Nan but looking at Faith out of the corner of her eye. "She'll sometimes steal your thunder. But Faith"—she turned to her daughter—"you're wonderful in different ways."

Her mother was only trying to help, but it was like nails on a chalkboard. It was mother-talk. Her unconditional love was clouding her judgment. How exactly was Faith wonderful? Was she a wonderful teacher? She'd gotten balloons and more mugs than she could house from her students. Was she wonderful at being alone? Perhaps. Maybe that's what she meant.

Nan opened the photo album and Faith let out a sigh. She couldn't help it. She knew she was acting like a child, but after today, she just couldn't take it anymore.

"Maybe I wasn't opening this to show *you*. If you're not going to talk to me, then I'm going to look at the photos. In a week's time, I'll be parting with them so I want to get a good look at all of them."

Faith eyed Nan skeptically. She was up to something. She always was.

"Martha, scoot up here between us. I want to show you something." Her mom complied, and Nan set the book in her mother's lap, which was conveniently located between Nan and Faith.

Nan leaned awkwardly in front of her daughter in an effort to communicate something to Faith. Her fingers shook a little, her knuckles disfigured from arthritis, as she tried unsuccessfully to grab on to the pages. Her mom helped her. They turned pages together until Nan put her hand flat on a photo, a smile emerging as she tipped the book in Faith's direction to view it without the glare of the lights obscuring it. It was a picture of Casey as barely a toddler, cradling a newborn Faith in her arms on the sofa as if Faith were her own baby, Faith's face red, crying the kind of cries only a newborn can produce.

"Oh, yes!" her mom said as she tilted her head to look at the photo. "I'd forgotten about that! Casey used to care for you as if you were her own child. I'd have to pry you away from her. She kept wanting to pick you up! I was so worried she'd hurt you because she insisted on carrying you around and taking care of you." She looked over at Nan, lost in conversation. "I think that lasted a few years, didn't it, Mom?"

Where were they going with this? Faith was waiting for some lesson in it because that's how Nan operated. There was always a lesson in her stories. "Okay, I'll bite. Tell me what you think I should learn from this."

Nan pressed her lips into a pouty frown and shook her head. "Are you implying that you should learn something?"

"Yes. Maybe I should learn that she took care of me and now it's my turn to take care of her or something…"

Nan's chuckle came out breathy as she said, "That's pretty good. I was just going to say that it's natural to love each other. We love our family—even when they drive us crazy. Casey didn't care if you were screaming your head off. She wanted to care for you anyway. I could draw a parallel…"

"Is that what I'm doing? Screaming my head off?" She could feel the anger filling her up. Everyone was against her! She'd done everything she was supposed to! She'd stayed quiet when Casey and Scott had gotten together! She'd stood at their wedding to wish them a happy life! She'd taken chances like Nan had said! How many times could she go over these same facts in her head? There was no other way to look at it! Nothing could be changed. Nothing could be rearranged in a different perspective to make her problems any less. She was meant for the life she had, and she was trying too hard for something else. It was exhausting her. Thank God, she'd get to leave before she could know Jake any more, or he'd hurt her too. He'd said that himself in different words.

"Is that the parallel you want to draw?" Nan said, her face contorting into an expression of sadness.

Why was she being given a lesson when Casey needed this advice equally, if not more? Faith always seemed to be the one who had to compromise, the one to make an effort.

"Don't look at me like that, Nan. Don't feel sorry for me. I've finally figured everything out!"

With that statement, Nan threw her head back and in her southern accent that only surfaced on occasions like these, she said, "Lord, help her!"

"What?" Faith said, her eyes pinned on her grandmother. She had a mixture of emotions. She wanted so badly for Nan to tell her what to do, if there was any way to change things, but she also felt indignant, annoyed that everyone seemed to be ganging up on her.

"Sweet girl, if your life is exactly the way you want it, then that's fine. But I have a sneaking suspicion, given your recent behavior, that this is not the case."

She was irritated, frustrated. Without a word, she got up and walked over to the door leading to the wraparound porch outside. If she didn't get outside right now, she was going to suffocate. Her mom tried to get up, but Nan stopped her. Faith ignored her mother's efforts. She didn't want to talk anymore. She walked out, shut the door behind her, and let the noise of the angry night surf swell in her ears as she took a seat on one of the rockers. The warmth in the air felt heavy around her, settling on her shoulders.

Faith waited for the calm that would inevitably come from being alone. As a child, she'd come out on the porch at night at their beach cottage, cocooning herself in the hammock. Back then, she didn't know anything about worry or sadness, and being alone was a nice change. Now, as she tried to get herself together, she just felt different. Being here had made being alone feel different, and that only added to her agitation.

The door behind her opened, but she didn't look to see who it was. It was probably her mom, ignoring Nan's suggestion, and coming out to check on her. She loved her mother, but she was tired of talking. It wasn't going to change anything. All it would do was point out the obvious.

"I do think about other people," Casey said, walking around to face her. "And, yes, I enjoy being happy. It beats the alternative." She sat in the other rocker and looked down at the floor. Faith followed her line of vision, noticing how the new lumber was a stark contrast to the old wood floors of their childhood cottage. "If you weren't so busy being miserable, you could be happy too. It's a mindset, you know." She looked back up at Faith. "I should be miserable. I never get to see you, and when I do, we fight. I'm trying to be in the present, not dwelling on the past, and—yet again—I've stepped on your toes. We've never really resolved whatever the issues were with Scott, and now I'm losing him. That entitles me to be miserable, but I'm not. You, on the other hand, have had nothing go wrong in your life, apart from a crush that didn't amount to anything, yet you can't be happy to save your life."

"Casey, I don't have feelings for Scott anymore, but I am still hurt, because you should've stopped to look at my face when you left the party with him. You should've taken in what was around you and realized that I was there! But you were so worried about *yourself* that you never even noticed me, or my feelings, nor did you think to ask—not then or after. Why did you think I wanted you to see him? Why did you think I was so excited to get you two together? Not to become a couple! Because I'd found someone I truly enjoyed being with, and I wasn't in your shadow. I trusted you enough to share that with you." She was rambling, and she caught herself, so she stopped. When she looked over at Casey, her sister was crying.

"Do you know why I didn't notice you?" she sniffled. "Because, for the first time in my life, I found that one person who complemented me in a way that no one else ever had. He was so full of life and genuinely interested in me as a person that I fell in love with him instantly that night, and everything else faded away. When I was with him— you're right—I didn't notice you because I didn't notice anyone. He was perfect for me, Faith. I knew you liked him, but it had been years! You hadn't seen him in ages, and all of a sudden you started seeing him again. But as friends. I didn't think it was that serious at the time." She tipped her head back as if the gesture would keep the tears from rolling down her face, but they came anyway. "For me, it was like a lightning strike. He's the man I promised to love for the rest of my life. He's the daddy of my little girl. I miss having coffee with him at the kitchen table in the mornings, even though I had to look at the back of his newspaper," she said, laughing through her tears. "I miss having to pick his book off the floor because he'd leave it there and I'd nearly trip over it. I miss…him. I've tried to move on, and this trip… it all was in an effort to do that, but you know what? It doesn't stop me from crying every night when I go to bed. I miss him so much, Faith." She burst into tears.

Faith stood up, and leaned over to embrace her sister. While she still didn't feel like Casey had gone about it the right way, she understood now. Casey cried, her face against Faith's chest, sobbing, as the crashing waves seemed to be hushing them, pushing them to be better with each other. In that moment, Faith couldn't help but think about that photo in Nan's book. When Faith was a baby, it had been Casey who'd held her to quiet her crying, and now, here they were— the two of them again—but it was Faith who was taking care of her big sister. She realized right then how right Casey and Scott were for each other and how much better they were when they were together. It also made her think about how no one really has it all together. No one's life was perfectly happy.

"You need to tell him," she said as Casey's crying quieted down. "Take a chance." She smiled, thinking about how she sounded a lot like Nan. "He's leaving you because he wants you and he can't have you. You've been too busy. Remember, you just said that there was a time when he was the only thing you noticed. You've changed that, and he feels it. You need to show him how *you* feel."

"Maybe."

"Why wouldn't you?"

"Because I don't know if it will help."

"But what will it hurt, Casey?"

Casey was quiet, clearly thinking it over. Then, unexpectedly, she said, "You seem very sure about your suggestion for me to share my feelings. Have you shared yours?"

"What?"

"By your outburst today, I can tell how you feel about Jake. I'm sorry if I overstepped my bounds at the party at all. It wasn't intentional."

"It's okay. I overreacted, and I'm sorry too."

"So have you told him how you feel?"

"Sort of." She hadn't really told him. She'd tried to plant a kiss on him instead. She needed to take her own advice. "You're right, though. I should be honest with him. And I can see how hard that is. Calling Scott *would* be hard for you to do, I know. If you need me, I'm here."

"Thank you," Casey said, leaning into her sister.

They stayed out on that porch just like they had as kids—the two of them with nothing between them but their past.

Chapter Sixteen

There was a knock at the door as Faith sipped her morning coffee. She'd slept very well after clearing the air some with Casey, and as a result, she was up bright and early. Since she was the only one up, and, consequently, the only one dressed and presentable, she decided to answer it. There was only one person she knew of who would knock on the door of their cottage, and when she opened the door, her guess was confirmed.

"Hey," Jake said.

"Hi." She opened the door wider so he could enter, but he stayed on the porch. It was wonderful to see him again, but she was curious as to why he wouldn't come in.

He held out his fist. "The cleaning crew found this." He turned it over and opened his fingers, revealing Isabella's gold necklace. "Isabella showed it to me. She kept playing with the charm on it." He smiled, his obvious fondness for Isabella filling his whole face.

His smile made Faith feel happy. She was still a little uncomfortable, though. She'd taken a big risk yesterday, and it had backfired. She shouldn't have kissed him. And she was unsure now of how to proceed. Had they settled the issue of the kiss or should she try to apologize further? She figured it would only make things more awkward if she mentioned it. She reached out and took the necklace.

"It looks like the clasp is loose," he said, looking at her hand.

"You can't fix *that*, can you?" she said, trying to lighten the air. There was so much tension between them that she wanted to tease him to help release some of it on her end. She tried to keep her eyes off of his lips, the masculine quality of his hands, the arms that had held her in the water that day…

For an instant, she saw affection in his eyes, and she had to work to push the air in and out of her lungs so she could breathe.

"Nope, sorry."

"Do you want to come in?" Faith didn't know what she wanted to say to him or if, in fact, she wanted to say anything at all—she hadn't thought it through. The only thing she knew was that she wanted to be around him, and she didn't want him to go. It was just like Casey had described it: She didn't notice anyone else when he was around—not even Nan, who was standing behind her.

"Jake," Nan said, putting a hand on Faith's shoulder for support. "Quit trying to be polite and come in. I'm going to make a pot of coffee, and I need someone to drink it with me. Faith and I can't drink it all by ourselves, and no one else in this house seems to get up before nine a.m."

Jake smiled again—warm and friendly—and Faith wanted to turn around and hold onto Nan for support.

"I can only stay for one cup."

"That's one cup less I'll dump down the sink then. Come in."

"What are you up to today?" Nan asked Jake, as she shuffled into the kitchen and reopened the bag of ground coffee. Faith had learned long ago not to offer to help her nan. Nan was insistent on doing everything herself.

"I have a little work to do today. I was actually on my way there. I just stopped to drop off Isabella's necklace."

"Are you building something today?"

"Figuratively. I'm meeting to see if I can get a few old restaurant owners on Beach Road to sell me their businesses. I want their land."

"You don't want their restaurants?" Faith asked from behind them, feeling hopeless and irritated at the same time.

He turned around. "No. I want to build a new one in their place. I need both lots."

The tension returned immediately. "They won't sell," she said, almost to spite him. She hoped they wouldn't sell. He needed to learn a lesson, that people around here liked what they had. They didn't want more giant, unoriginal towers along their beaches. They wanted character.

"If the price is right, they might. If I can secure their retirement, they always sell. And, given what they're probably making with their little shacks, I can recoup what I pay them in a few years with my establishments. I've done it hundreds of times."

"You may have. But you've not done it a hundred times *here*. What if people don't want that?"

"When their property values soar and the smaller businesses start to benefit from the increased tourism, they'll want it."

"It's not always about dollars, Jake." She was arguing with him—she could feel it—and she knew what he meant by the two of them not seeing the future the same way. The only thing was that she didn't let it cloud what she felt for him. It made her want to convince him even more.

"Faith, my feet are starting to ache from standing. The coffee's per-colating. Will you please fill us all mugs of coffee?" Nan interjected.

Jake walked Nan around the bar and over to the table, where she lowered herself into a chair. The coffeemaker was still making coffee, but Faith took the carafe out and filled up three mugs. She slid it back into its holder, and it sizzled on the liquid that had escaped when she'd pulled it out. Faith took two of the mugs over to them.

"Are you going to make an offer today?" Faith asked, sitting down beside Jake and leaving her mug in the kitchen. She didn't want to have any more coffee. Her stomach was already upset from the discussion, and the coffee would only make it worse.

"No. I'm just going to talk to them and look at the land today. I need to really assess it, take measurements, and get a feel for the location before I make an offer."

"What time are you supposed to meet them?"

"Nine o'clock."

"How long will it take?" She had an idea. It was time to take action.

The skin between his eyes wrinkled and he looked at her, clearly trying to figure out her motives. "About two hours."

"Is that all you have to do today?"

"Why?" He took a slow sip of his coffee.

"I want to show you something."

His face was curious, but cautious. "I can pick you up at around eleven."

"Perfect."

"I'll have to have you back at the cottage by one, though. I'm dropping off some supplies for a friend of mine. I'm helping someone build a boat. He needs the supplies by one."

"Ha!" Nan laughed. "I'm glad you don't have too much planned today. Only the purchase of two lots and a boat to build." She winked in his direction. "Well, as you all are making plans, Jake, please keep next Friday free. That's my birthday party."

Would Jake be coming to Nan's birthday? The party was so intimate that having him there would be like including him as part of the family. It would be difficult for her to have him in such close proximity all night.

Jake raised his eyebrows in response. "What time?"

"What time, Faith?"

She hadn't thought it through. She'd mentally prepared for something low-key with Nan—just the family. Having Jake there would add a new dynamic.

"We hadn't decided on a time… How about four o'clock?"

"Great. I'll be there," Jake said.

Faith toyed with Isabella's necklace on the table, thinking about the moment they'd shared when he'd given it back. "What kind of boat are you building?" she asked, still looking at the necklace.

"It's just a small cruiser—a two-seater with a single bench at the back. It's gorgeous, though."

Faith thought to herself that it was too bad Jake wasn't in the boat-building business. He could build as many of those as he wanted, as extravagant as he wanted, and they wouldn't matter at all. Why did he have to be involved in something that she was so completely against? Why couldn't things be easier?

"Hi, Jake!" she heard Isabella call from the other room. She came running down the hallway and stopped at the table, her blond hair fuzzed up on the back from where she'd been sleeping. She climbed into the chair, her long nightgown catching under her legs and winding up around them. The only things sticking out were her two bare feet.

"I found something of yours," Jake said, his voice sweet.

She sat up on her knees and rested her elbows on the table as Jake hooked his finger through her necklace and held it in front of her. "Oh, my necklace!"

"I think the clasp came apart."

"Would you like any breakfast, Isabella?" Faith said.

"Mom said she's going to get me some, but she's talking to Daddy on the phone."

"Is she on the phone right now?" Faith became nervous for her sister. She hoped that Casey was telling Scott how she was feeling. As strong as Casey seemed, this would be hard for her. Faith also wondered if her sister would actually admit being miserable without him.

"Yep." Isabella had pushed the chain of her necklace into the shape of a heart. "Daddy has to go on a trip."

Isabella seemed very upbeat when talking about her father. Clearly, Scott was a good dad, and an important part of her life. And Casey's. Faith hoped they could sort things out.

"Good morning!" her mom said, joining them. "Hi, Jake. Nice to see you again."

As they made pleasantries at the kitchen table, Faith wanted to slip away and check on her sister. What kind of trip was Scott taking? Was it a work trip? Had he met someone else? She was dying to know for Casey's sake. She wanted to be there to hold her sister's hand, to help her through it, to encourage her when she wanted to make light of the situation or brush a difficult discussion under the rug. She needed to be in there with Casey.

"Mom, do you mind getting Isabella some breakfast? I'm just going to check on Casey."

As Faith got up, she looked at Jake, ready to apologize for her early exit, but, before she could say anything, he lightly grabbed her arm, sending tingles all the way up. "Everything okay?"

His concern warmed her. There he was, sitting at the table, as comfortable as if he were one of the family. The odd thing was, he seemed to just fit. They barely knew him, but he already fit. She was willing to bet that if his decisions had been different, and they didn't have their disagreements about development and the type of lifestyle he wanted stacked against them, it would be easy to love him.

"I *hope* everything's okay," she said quietly, trying not to show her feelings. "It was nice to see you." She produced the most casual smile she could.

"You too."

"I'll see you around eleven."

"Okay."

She wanted to stay and talk with Jake, but Casey needed her, so she walked down the hallway to her sister's room, tapped on the door lightly, and pushed it open.

Casey was sitting on the floor, hugging her knees, her chin resting on her arms. The phone sat beside her, not in use. She looked up at Faith and smiled a half smile, as if that was all she could muster. Faith couldn't read into the call at all just from looking at her, and she was dying to know how it went.

"Isabella told me you were talking to Scott," Faith said, sitting down next to Casey. "What did he say?"

"He's going to Colorado. He's flying out Friday."

"What for?"

"To meet with the manager at the Boulder office. I think he's planning to relocate."

Scott was relocating. That meant that he was moving on, starting over without Casey. Faith watched her sister closely for emotion. She wanted to be ready when Casey fell apart, but Casey didn't. Her face was blank, empty.

"What did you say to him?" She wanted to tell Casey to snap out of it, get back on that phone, and scream at Scott not to do it. What about Isabella? Would she have to fly back and forth from state to state to see her parents? Or was he going to just leave them behind? She knew him well enough that she couldn't imagine he'd do that. What was he thinking?

"What *could* I say, Faith?"

They sat in silence, side by side as Faith tried to digest this information. She thought way back to those years she'd known Scott, trying to find some rational reason why he'd go so far away from his wife and child. People did it all the time—she knew that—but *Scott* wouldn't do it. At least the Scott she knew wouldn't do it. …Unless he was running.

She remembered what it felt like to see him after he and Casey were married. She didn't want to have to watch his affection for someone else, let alone her own sister. She didn't want to bump into him in public, have to smile as if nothing bothered her, knowing that her life had been altered. What if he felt the same way about Casey? What if he worried she'd find someone who didn't mind her sporadic work schedule, and the fact that she was never still? What if she started to fall for this new person and he'd have to run into them in public? What if Scott loved Casey too much to endure that?

"You need to tell him to stay. Tell him you don't want him to go."

"It's clear what he wants. I'm not going to grovel. I can stand on my own two feet."

Casey was trying to act as if she was okay with everything. She was too proud to admit defeat, and she wasn't used to not getting what she wanted, so she pretended like this *was* what she wanted. But Faith was determined to get through to her.

"What if he wants you back so badly that he can't stand the idea of seeing you if he can't be with you, Casey? Did you tell him how you felt?"

"He didn't give me a chance."

"Let me call him." She hadn't really spoken to Scott in any significant way since that party so many years ago. She had never thought the idea of calling him would come so easily for her. But it had been long enough. Scott had been her best friend; she'd told him everything at one point in her life. She wanted to find out his side of things.

"What?"

"I want to call Scott. I want to find out what he actually thinks about all this."

Confusion was clear on Casey's face as she looked at Faith.

Her whole life, Faith had thought everything came easily for Casey, that she never had to struggle, yet she, too, had insecurities—Faith was finding that out more and more. Even Casey didn't feel confident enough in her own relationship to tell Scott how she felt. It seemed so silly. Was she worried he wouldn't feel the same about her?

Faith knew what her sister needed and she might be able to fix it all if her hunch was right.

"Let me call him. Mom's getting Isabella's breakfast. You can help her."

"I don't know…"

"Casey. I want to do this as much for me as for you. I'd like to talk to him. I promise not to plead with him or tell him what you think. But I want to hear what he thinks. And he might tell me, Casey."

Still slightly hesitant, Casey reached for her phone on the floor, typed in her passcode, and handed it to Faith. "Come get me when you're done," she said, and then stood up and left the room.

Faith's fingers felt light with anticipation as she tapped the phone icon and typed in Scott's name. His number came up. Seeing his name and number gave her pause. As she stared at his name on the screen, she realized how long it had truly been. This was a big move for her, and she knew it, but just like Nan had said, it was important to take a chance. She needed to finally be supportive of her sister and her brother-in-law. She hit "call" and put the phone to her ear. Her heart pounded as the phone pulsed its ringing signal.

"Casey," he answered on the first ring. Had he been hoping she'd call back?

"It's"—she cleared her throat—"it's Faith, actually."

She heard rustling on the other end of the line, as if he were sitting up. "Faith? Is everything okay?"

"Yes and no."

Chapter Seventeen

It was as if the weight of the world had been taken off Faith's shoulders. She was talking to Scott and she was fine. She was really fine. And she realized that she'd missed having him as her friend. That was what they were best at and what they would always be. She explained that Casey and Isabella were both okay, but the bad news was that she'd heard he was moving away, and she wouldn't get to have all her favorite people together at once anymore. She told him how seeing Nan this week had put it all into perspective, and she felt awful for not spending more time with her family. Now, he was moving away just as she was hoping to have him back. She waited to hear what he had to say.

"I don't want to go," he said. "It's just easier if I do."

"I know what you mean. Casey's a difficult person to love, but it doesn't make me love her any less. I'm sure you feel the same way."

He didn't respond. She waited an excruciatingly long time, but nothing came.

"How will you see Isabella?" she asked.

The hum of the phone was the only sound for a little while and then, finally, he answered, "I want to have her with me. Joint custody at least."

"Traveling like that could be hard on a little girl," she pointed out. She was worried just thinking about it.

"I need a fresh start."

He wasn't saying much. Faith had told Casey that she wouldn't tell him what Casey thought. It was up to Casey to tell him. Was there a way she could do it without breaking that promise? "Do you love Casey?" she asked, point blank.

"Of course," he said without hesitation.

"Then why are you leaving her? I won't tell her." She knew that Scott was aware of how well she could keep secrets. Secrets were like tiny packages entrusted to people. They were wrapped up tightly and only the recipient was able to untie them. She'd been told many secrets over the years, and she'd kept every one of them. Scott knew that about her, so he'd trust her. She was sure of it.

"She doesn't love me anymore. She loves her job. She loves Isabella. But she doesn't love me."

It was killing her. All those wonderful things Casey had told her about how she loved to curl up with Scott after he'd fallen asleep, how she missed him so much… She knew she couldn't tell him. She had to find another way. "Did you know that Casey has never spent longer than a few minutes being sad in front of me? I thought she never got sad. I thought maybe she didn't even care," she said carefully. "What I didn't know was that she doesn't always show her emotions. She's not good at that. She feels so much more than she lets anyone see. Have you ever thought of talking to her about it?"

"I let her actions speak for her love," he said.

"But what I'm saying is, perhaps that's not what you should do. Not with someone like Casey. I think you need to talk to her."

"Why should I talk to her? She doesn't seem the least bit affected by my leaving."

Ugh. That's nearly what Casey had said about *him*. "I promise you. You *need* to talk to her."

"Thank you for trying, Faith. I have to go. Sorry. I have to be somewhere, and I'm a little late. It was good to talk to you. I'm so happy you called. Can we talk again soon?"

"Sure." She said her goodbyes and hung up.

The call had been bittersweet. It had gone by so quickly that it was difficult to register the magnitude of what had actually happened. She'd just talked to Scott, and it had been perfectly fine between the two of them. He'd been understanding and sweet, as she knew he would be. The best part of it all, though, was that, without her feelings clouding her mind, she really enjoyed talking to him, and it felt just the same as it had when they were younger. Being around him would be easy.

But even though she'd made progress with her relationship with Scott, she hadn't changed a thing with him and Casey, which was what she'd set out to do. Both of them thought the same things; they needed to talk to each other. It was their battle to fight; she just hoped they'd fight it instead of letting their pride get in the way.

She sat for a moment in Casey's room, holding the phone. Then she got up, set the phone on the dresser, and went out to be with her family.

"That was nice of Jake to bring Isabella's necklace by," Nan said as she joined them all at the table. Jake had already gone.

"Yes." She was eyeing her sister across the table, wanting to tell her everything but remembering that she'd promised Scott she wouldn't.

So, instead, she continued the conversation about Jake. "He said the clasp must be loose."

"I'll have to get a jeweler to look at it," Casey said. She was leaning forward, her gaze on Faith.

"I want to go to the beach," Isabella said, climbing down off her chair. She'd left a half-eaten waffle and a cup of milk. "Mommy, can we go to the beach?"

"Why don't you take her, Martha? Enjoy yourself. I'm sure the girls will clean up breakfast for you," Nan said.

Her mom looked back and forth between her two girls, and it was clear that she could tell something was going on. "I'd be happy to. But I want to be filled in on anything good when I get back," she said with a grin.

"Yay!" Isabella jumped around in a circle before running off for her flip-flops.

Once she was out of earshot, her mom whispered in Faith's direction, "I heard you talked to Scott. I want to know all about it after Isabella's in bed tonight." Faith nodded. "Okay, Isabella, let's go down and get your sand toys."

"What did he say?" Casey said with urgency as her mom and Isabella left the house.

"Just like I told you I wouldn't tell him what you'd said, I promised him the same. You need to call him, Casey. *You* need to tell him." Nan, who hadn't heard the whole story yet, sat silently. She'd never ask for details; she knew how Casey was. She'd wait for one of them to tell her, but Faith wondered if she already knew. She was a sharp woman; she didn't miss a thing. Faith turned to Nan. "Has Casey heard your 'taking chances' story yet? If not, she needs it."

Nan laughed. "Yes, dear. She's heard it too."

"It's not as easy as just telling him," Casey said, her hopes clearly dashed.

Faith knew Casey was hoping for a grand response, something that would be life-changing, but the truth was, life didn't work like that. It didn't end in a grand finale or some firework-filled moment. It was, like Nan had said, a million tiny moments that when added up made a pretty great life. Faith was only learning that slowly; it was starting to sink in.

"Casey," she said, walking around the table and standing in front of her sister. "Be honest with yourself. What do you want?"

"What do you mean? You know what I want."

"Well, clearly, you don't or you'd go and get it. You always have before." Faith walked back into Casey's room and got her cell phone. When she returned, she set it down in front of her sister.

"Stop being so worried about what he'll think. Stop guessing at his actions because you're too proud to ask him what he feels. If you love him, Casey, tell him. Tell him what you're feeling or he'll never know! Start with just a sentence. It doesn't have to be long. But tell him something. Take a chance!"

Casey sat, her hands in her lap, her eyes on her phone.

"We're here for you, Casey," Nan said. "Just try. It can't hurt a thing."

"I can't do it."

"Yes, you can!" Faith pressed. "He's your husband. You love him, right? You can tell him anything."

"It's different now."

"Why? He's the same person he always was."

Faith could see Casey's face change as the anxiety of the task began to take hold. She was thinking about it. Without warning, she grabbed the phone, opened up the screen, and began typing. When she was finished, she held it in her hands for a few long seconds. Then, she turned the phone around. It said simply, "I love you." With a smile twitching at her lips, Casey hit Send and set it down on the table, her hands shaking just slightly.

Faith clasped her hands together in front of her mouth and tried to hide her smile. Casey had done it. She'd never felt more proud of her sister than she did in that moment, because Casey had let her guard down. Faith threw her arms around her and squeezed her tight.

The three of them waited, their eyes on the phone. Every time the screen went dark, Casey tapped it to keep it open. Then hope fizzled up her spine when Faith saw those three little dots on the screen. Scott had opened the message! He was checking it! The anticipation was nearly overwhelming for her; she couldn't imagine what Casey must be feeling. Maybe it would all be okay. Casey and Scott were so good together, and now, they could get back together where they belonged. Isabella could have her daddy back. Faith hoped that would be the case.

The dots went away and they waited for a message. Faith's knee was bouncing up and down. The time it was taking was making her crazy with anticipation. They sat in silence—all of them—watching that phone, but after the seconds turned to minutes and then the minutes began ticking by, Faith could feel a worry settling in her chest. The screen turned black, and Casey didn't reopen it this time. Scott hadn't texted back. There was nothing.

"He said he was late for something…Maybe he's not somewhere he can text you," Faith said cautiously. "Maybe his phone died."

"Or maybe he doesn't want to know that I love him because he wants a divorce."

Faith shook her head, trying to protest that thought, but she had to wonder if it was too little, too late. Was Scott tired of trying? Before she could wonder any further, Casey had her face in her hands. She was crying.

"This is so hard," she sobbed. "Isabella is killing me. She was up for an hour last night—she misses Scott so much. She cries at night for her daddy, and, honestly, I cry for him too. I don't know how to fix this." She turned to Nan. "Nan. You know everything. What do I do?"

Nan had remained very quiet the whole time. She ran her fingers through the side of her short, white hair and then put her hand on her cheek in bewilderment. Finally, after Casey's wild sobs had quieted, Nan looked as though she had an answer. She said, "Casey, he knows you love him. But what he doesn't know is whether *you* understand why he's left. Give him a reason to come back."

As if Nan's suggestion had finally made it all clear, Casey opened up the screen and texted, "I miss you. I'm sorry I wasn't there enough. I want to make it work. Call me," and hit Send. Then she went into the bathroom, swiped a box of tissues, and returned, tugging a few free from the box to blow her nose.

"Now," Nan said, her voice lighter, "Get yourselves together. Jake will be here to pick up Faith soon. And later, he's going to come and get us after he drops off the supplies for that boat he's building. He and his friend have already finished one, and I told him I'd like to take a ride, since I didn't get to go sailing. He promises to go slowly."

Faith had been thinking about seeing Jake all day. It was ridiculous to even be thinking about him. He'd made it quite clear that he wasn't planning on taking things any further. Pleasant conversation and dinners were all she could hope for. It was fine, really. She'd always been fine on her own. Maybe she'd even be able to help Casey with learning how to live that way. Scott hadn't called. Casey had carried her phone around all morning. She kept expecting to see the phone light up with Scott's name. After hours passed, though, she was losing hope.

Faith had decided to wait for Jake's arrival on the beach. She walked down to the water, leaving her sandals up on the dune. The surf was calm today. It rolled gently toward the shore and left foam on the sand as the tide slid back out to sea. She sank her toes into the soft, wet sand, watching the little bubbles of water as they dipped below the surface around her feet.

The surf could get rough, and it was tough to swim through. Every time she had to face those waves as a kid, though, she got back up, giggling, and squealing, running from them and then to them. Swimming in the ocean was difficult for even an experienced swimmer, yet, as a child, the exertion it took didn't bother her. And, like Casey had always told her, once they got past where the waves break, it was easy. Just like when they were girls, it seemed again to Faith that they were right where the waves were breaking. They couldn't see the other side yet, but they were fighting, pushing, getting knocked down and back up. The difference was that as adults, their will seemed to have lessened. Why was that? Why couldn't they fight harder?

As Faith watched the rolling waves, she noticed those spots where they broke a little softer. That was why they were struggling now to fight—there wasn't a break, nothing to allow them to slip past. In their relationships, they were giving it everything they had and nothing was changing. Faith said a silent prayer that they'd all get a break. Nan needed her family to be happy, Casey needed Scott, Isabella needed her daddy. Even their mom, who loved having her family around, needed everyone around her—Nan wouldn't be there to keep her company forever.

And what did Faith need? What did she really need? At the back of her mind, she knew what she *wanted*. She wanted a family. She wanted a loving husband who she could talk to, who kept her company, who listened to her. She wanted to hear little feet coming down the hallway and to hear the sound of their voices as they called her Mommy… She wanted to be able to come back to this beach and see it. She'd thought before how life wasn't this perfect story, where happy endings were always possible. She had to look on the bright side: She was healthy and happy. She'd be okay.

"Hey," she heard from behind her, and she turned around.

"Hi."

Jake was all spruced up, his hair just perfectly tousled, his face clean-shaven. The smell of his aftershave wafted in her direction, knotting her stomach. He looked positively gorgeous.

"You looked deep in thought just then. You okay?"

"Yep," she lied. She didn't want to bring him down, nor did she want to remove that adorable smile on his face.

"It's nice out today," he said over the waves as he took a step up beside her. She smiled when she realized he didn't have on any shoes. She turned around instinctively to look and smiled wider to find that he'd lined his shoes up right next to hers in the sand. "We didn't visit this particular spot of the beach as a child, but I did go to a beach down the road, and I remember swimming all day. When I came in that night, after I'd had a bath and settled down under my covers, I could still feel the rocking of the waves in my bed."

"I know that feeling."

"It rocked me to sleep," he said, his eyes reminiscent.

She wanted him to look at her, to tell her something else about his past—anything—because standing there with him was making her crazy. She didn't want to think about it, but she remembered the feel of his lips on hers, the warmth of the sun on their faces, and the sound of the waves as he'd kissed her at Bodie Island. She didn't have to try hard to bring that feeling right back up to the surface. She knew why she was feeling this way about him right then. It was because he was talking about the beach he'd experienced as a child, how he would swim all day. It made her feel a closeness to him again, a bond. The fact that he had loved the water and being at this beach—just like she had—showed her he hadn't always been set on changing the Outer Banks. He had once enjoyed its simplicity as much as her—he'd just forgotten—and it gave her hope she could make him remember.

"What did you want to show me?" he asked.

She turned to him, facing the wind so that her hair wouldn't blow into her face. "Hungry?"

"It's a little early, but I could eat."

"Perfect. Let's get in the car. I want you to drive me down Beach Road toward the village of Duck."

"Okay." He looked at her suspiciously, but he had a smile playing at his lips.

As they got in his car, she waited for him to get settled and then she said, "If you're insistent on building up the Outer Banks, then I would like you to take me to a few of my favorite places just in case they aren't here when I get a chance to come back. It'll be my treat."

"Absolutely not."

He pulled onto Beach Road, and she looked at him disbelievingly. If he didn't like the current beach vibe, that was one thing, but he could at least humor her. Was there some reason why he wouldn't take her? "What do you mean, 'absolutely not'?"

"You're not paying. I am."

She smiled, relieved beyond belief. She was so glad that Jake agreed to take her out today. She knew that she probably couldn't change his mind about building, but she could at least show him her side. He grew up there, so his view was clouded because he couldn't see what was in front of him through the eyes of a new visitor. She wanted him to see the charm that she could see. This was her chance to show him.

"Fine. Pay if you want to,'" she teased. "Do you know where Sunset Grille is?"

"Of course."

"I want to go there."

They drove, making small talk, and all she wanted to ask him was what he'd decided about trying to buy those restaurants. Which ones were they? Were they any of her favorites? What was he planning to build there? Finally, when there was a lull, she asked, "Was your meeting this morning successful?"

"They're gonna sleep on it. I told them I'd give them until next week. Then, I'm moving on and my offer will no longer stand. When potential sellers think they have something big to lose, sometimes, the time factor will push things in my favor."

Just talking about it made her uncomfortable, and she was sorry she'd even asked. Jake had put those restaurant owners in a terrible position because they knew what they'd be doing by selling. They knew that they'd be a part of the problem the minute they sold, yet Jake had probably given them such an enticing offer that they could see their future right in front of them. But could they retire wealthy and live with themselves if they knew what he wanted to do with their restaurants? Would they be able to sell, knowing that all the history, all the memories and the stories that could be told about their restaurants, would be lost? She looked out the window, watching the beach emerge between the cottages as they drove. When they finally pulled into the parking lot, she was more than ready to get out and visit one of her favorite places. She'd come there for dinner as a kid with her mom and Nan.

They crossed the road and she took a minute to look at the gorgeous restaurant in front of her. The exterior was wooden, the different extensions painted in pastels—blue, yellow, and turquoise, with pink trim. Palm trees circled it all the way around to the enormous deck that stretched out over the Currituck Sound, a body of water that was separated from the Atlantic by the Outer Banks themselves. Faith loved swimming in the Sound as a kid because she could walk out for miles and still be knee deep, and the waves were tiny ripples that didn't knock her over like the waves of the Atlantic did.

They walked inside and met the hostess. "Can we sit outside today?" Faith asked. She'd never sat outside in the bar area before. Until now, she hadn't been old enough during her visits. The hostess nodded and grabbed two menus before leading them out to the deck.

A long tiki bar sat under a covered porch that stretched the length of the building, Hawaiian-like grass and party lights hanging from the ceiling at the edge to separate it from the wide decking on the other side. People were sitting on stools, having afternoon cocktails— big, colorful drinks with crazy glasses, and all kinds of festive fruit and trinkets dangling from them. The warm breeze rustled the grass over the bar, and the gentle lapping of the Sound could be heard just beyond the quiet conversations of the people seated at tables on the deck. They arrived at a table for two, and the hostess put their menus down.

"Someone will be right with you," she said before walking away.

Faith looked out over the water as Caribbean-style music played, her eyes coming to rest on the long pier that stretched into the Sound. Along the pier were benches painted bright green and a gazebo at the end, painted in matching pastels.

"I'm not driving," she said, "so I'm getting one of those crazy drinks."

"If that's what you want." He was looking around too; she'd caught him. He focused on her face and made eye contact as if to ask what she was thinking.

In her mind, she told him to figure it out for himself, and she wondered if he could read her like he had before. There had been times when he could, but ever since she'd found out about his plans for the Outer Banks, he hadn't tried. The sun was high, casting its rays on the ripples in the water, and, with the soft breeze coming off the Sound, their little lunch date was almost romantic.

A waitress came and took their drink orders. Jake got a beer, but Faith had something different in mind. "I'll have the Castaway Coconut, please."

The waitress scribbled down the order and went to make their drinks. As she did, Jake located the drink on his menu and read aloud, "Vanilla Rum, Pineapple, OJ, and Coconut…," and then squinted toward the page for a second before looking up at her. "It's served in a real carved coconut?"

"Yep." She smiled. "Bet you can't get one of those at the Tides," she teased.

He laughed, but sobered quickly, and she worried that she'd hit a nerve. It had just slipped out, but her point wasn't to draw attention to his choices.

"I'm sorry," she said. "I'm not trying to make you feel bad about what you've chosen to build. I'm just trying to show you why I don't feel comfortable there."

"My ex-wife hated places like this bar," he said, the comment coming out of nowhere.

"Oh?"

"She didn't grow up here like I did, and I had a very hard time making her feel comfortable here. She always seemed unhappy, telling me how things around here could be so much better. I figured there were probably more people like her who would want something different than what we were used to down here. She saw the place as really behind the times. It made me aware of how others might perceive the area. I realized I could make it better, satisfy the people like her and show them that it wasn't inferior to other beaches."

The waitress brought their drinks and set them down on the table. "Are you ready to order?"

Jake nodded to Faith, allowing her to order first. "I'll have the fish tacos," she said, closing her menu and handing it to the waitress.

"Two, please." Jake handed his menu over. When the waitress had gone, he cocked his head at her drink and started laughing. "It's really carved!" he said with a chuckle. "What is that on the front of it? A monkey?"

Faith spun it around to have a look. The drink was enormous, and she had to hold it with both hands because her fingers couldn't stretch around it. "Yep. I think it is," she said as she took a sip. It was delicious and fruity, and she couldn't remember the last time she'd had a drink that good.

"Maybe your ex-wife just needed a drink like this."

"My ex-wife would never have a drink in a coconut," he laughed again. Then, he became serious. "I've been a property developer my whole adult life. I've built developments in Florida, South Carolina, Georgia… I know what I'm doing. Those developments are very successful. When we moved here, I was able to see the Outer Banks through her eyes, and as a developer, I knew what I could do here after she pointed it all out. There are people like her who will come here for the condos and the swimming pools and the golf clubs. That's what they want, and they want it just as badly as you want this."

"But can you have them both here? Is there room for both?" She took a sip off the long, pink straw that jutted out from her coconut.

He chuckled again, that affection in his eyes that she hadn't seen in a while. "I'm sorry. I can't take you seriously when you're drinking from that thing. It's the size of a football! Good thing you're not driving."

He was avoiding the question, but she was happy to see that he hadn't reacted badly to it. That was a step in the right direction.

"Look," she said, seeing a sign by the bar. "There's going to be live music tonight."

He wasn't smiling anymore. There were thoughts behind his eyes, but she couldn't tell what they were.

"Would you come back with me tonight after the boat ride?" she asked, hoping her question would get him talking again.

"Only if you get a different drink," he teased.

"Absolutely! There's one in a fishbowl I'd like to try…"

Jake laughed and Faith was glad that she had lightened the moment between them.

"What made you choose Corolla for your developments?" she asked, trying to sound as casual as possible. She was really upset about it, but she knew that if she dwelled on that, he'd never open up. She had to tread lightly.

"Well, there have been a few successful developments by others in the area. There's still so much space available; there's tons of room to add to what is already a great location, given the wide, clean beaches."

"Corolla's known for its small businesses. Will they be okay?"

"They're not going anywhere. They'll benefit from the increased tourism, like I said."

"Aren't you worried that it'll get too busy and that will drive people away?"

"Other beaches are busy. There's still Coquina Beach if you want open space. That's part of the Cape Hatteras National Seashore, so no one can touch that. I think it's just a matter of organizing the space here."

"I don't think it's as easy as that. What about the wild horses? They won't just magically move themselves. They'll be squeezed out of their habitats," she said. "What will it be like for them if, and when, all the land is finally gone? How many will survive?"

"It is sad, but it's already happening, and it isn't going to get any better. That will happen whether I develop there or not. If I don't build there, someone will."

"It wouldn't bother you that you'd be part of the problem, part of their demise?"

"I don't see it that way at all. Their numbers are dwindling already, and I haven't even begun construction. Why? Because others are building. Who knows, the horses might find a new habitat on their own. They've survived centuries already. How do you know the strong ones won't survive this?"

"What about people? People like me don't want to be forced into squared-off sections of the beach. We want the whole experience, and we won't get that in the shadows of the high-rises."

The waitress returned and set their plates in front of them. Jake thanked her and then looked back at Faith.

"One of the challenges I face in my job is trying to convince people of what they want. You're not seeing the big picture here. You're thinking about a few fond memories you have personally and not the forward movement of the area. People do this all the time, and I have to prove to them that I know what I'm talking about. There are more people who want the high-rises than want the porch swing on that little cottage."

"I disagree."

"Well, you're not making the decisions about it. I am. And I'm tired of trying to make everyone else happy." He looked down at his plate and didn't look back up. Slowly, he cut his tacos with his knife and fork, every slice controlled and even. While he showed no outward signs of being rattled, she had to wonder, given how defensive he seemed, if she'd shaken him up.

They ate quietly, the music mixing with the gentle tapping of the ripples from Sound against the pier. The day was gorgeous, the sky electric blue with no clouds, the sun beating down on them but the breeze of the water keeping the heat away. Faith had finished her coconut drink, and she was finding liquid courage in the silence.

"What if you fell in love with someone again?" she asked, and he looked up at her. "What if you found someone you loved enough to be with for the rest of your life, and she hated what you were doing? What if she hated your developments and she had ideas for something better? What would you do?"

She could see his jaw clench as he tried to keep composure. Then, very quietly, he said, "I had that very issue in my first marriage, but I wasn't moving fast enough, developing big enough resorts—nothing was good enough. I will *never* let that happen again. If I meet someone, and I fall in love again, she will have to accept me for who I am, even if we disagree." He eyed the balled-up napkin by her plate. "All done?" He flagged the waitress for the check.

"Wanna take a ride on the new boat?" Jake asked, coming up behind Faith. From the sound of his voice, he'd cooled down. Faith had been on the beach ever since Jake had brought her home. He'd been quiet the whole ride, and all she could think about was how her little plan to show him something fun had backfired. She turned around and faced him. Perhaps building the boat after dropping her off had helped with his mood.

She made eye contact, hoping that he couldn't see in her eyes what she was thinking. She wanted to talk more about what they'd started at lunch, but she knew he had his guard up and it wouldn't end well. "Sure," she said with a smile. His expression told her that he'd noticed her thoughts. She was terrible at keeping them from showing on her face.

He looked at her a moment, thoughtful. It was as if he were contemplating something.

"How's Casey?" he asked.

Surprised by the change in conversation, and a little disappointed that it had turned away from the two of them, she said, "She's fine."

"She told me about her divorce."

"Oh."

"I can definitely relate," he said with a sad smile. "It's very hard."

Faith didn't say anything. She didn't have any experience with divorce or marriage.

"I hope she'll be okay," he said.

"Me too," she said. "She's got all of us to help her through it."

He nodded. "She's a lucky lady. She has a great family to support her."

Jake was right. Casey was very lucky. And so was Faith. Faith was glad that Jake had pointed out the importance of family; she felt exactly the same way. She wound her hand around his arm. "Let's go see this boat."

Chapter Eighteen

"Careful, Nan," Faith said as Jake helped her step onto the boat. It rocked slightly in the residual waves left from another boat after it had taken off from the dock. Faith held her breath until Nan was safely seated. She couldn't imagine Nan would actually go through with taking a boat ride, but Jake had mentioned a special place he'd like to take everyone, and when he'd described it, Nan had sworn that John had taken her there when they were young. Instantly, she'd wanted to see it. She'd even brave a boat ride for it.

Jake got everyone suited up in life vests. Faith felt a flutter as she watched how gentle he was with Nan as he belted her in, and then turned to do the same for Isabella. He was so good with people. She thought back to the day she'd first seen him. So often, a first impression of someone isn't always the right one, but with him, it had been right on the mark. She attributed that fact to his openness.

Once Jake had finished belting Isabella in and everyone had their vests on, Faith sat down next to Nan. As she settled in, Jake getting situated at the wheel, she finally took a moment to look around the boat. It was sleek with white upholstery and wood grain and silver accents. The wheel was silver, the knobs glimmering against the sunlight. Jake started the engine, the motor purring as he turned the wheel.

"What work have you done on this boat, Jake?" Faith called over the sound of the motor and the water as he drove the boat out to sea.

"I built a large part of the bow," he said, keeping his head facing forward as he steered around a few other boats. "I also helped build parts of the hull. It's a good feeling when I actually get to drive the boats I build."

Once they were on open sea, the wind pushed against them, and Faith worried about Nan. Nan's white curls were dancing around, her eyes squinting in the sun and wind.

"You okay, Nan?" Faith said loudly to be sure her grandmother could hear over the noise. She'd tried to look at Nan, but had to turn back toward the bow to keep her hair out of her face. She tried again to view her grandmother.

"Absolutely!" Nan said, attempting to smile against the speed of the boat. She looked so small sitting there. Faith knew that the seat was most likely uncomfortable, and being exposed to the elements probably wasn't a good idea.

They were headed toward an uninhabited island, created many decades ago by a hurricane, and only accessible by boat. "It probably won't even be around in ten years," Jake had explained. "The hurricanes have almost pushed it completely under water." But when Nan had heard of its location, she was giddier than a teenager, almost bouncing on her toes to go.

Jake pointed out the island as they neared it, and Nan sat up a little straighter. She had her body twisted in the direction of it, her elbow up on the port side of the boat, her fist covering her mouth as if holding in some kind of emotion. The boat gave a tiny lurch as it hit sand and came to a stop on the shore of this small spot in the ocean. It was so tiny that you could see through the trees to the other side, but it had the most gorgeous, silky sand on its beach, the waves rolling in so quietly and subtly that it made the thought of storms seem almost unimaginable. It was like a miniature paradise. Her mom and Casey helped Isabella down onto the beach, but Faith stayed next to Nan.

She'd never seen her like this before. Nan barely moved, her fist so tight against her mouth that it looked as though she'd burst into tears at any moment. Gently, she said, "Nan?"

She tipped her head down, her gaze finally leaving the island, and tears rolled along her aged skin. She nodded, although she was visibly crying. With a sniffle, she sat up and cleared her throat enough to speak. Jake had noticed and was kneeling next to them in concern.

"She's still here," Nan managed. "She's weathered, smaller, but she's still here."

Both Jake and Faith waited for further explanation as Isabella squealed along the side of the boat, running and jumping into the water. Her mom and Casey were chatting, their conversation lost in the wind. They hadn't noticed Nan yet. Perhaps they figured Faith and Jake were helping her out of the boat.

"I've come to the Outer Banks all my life. It is a part of my soul. On the way here last weekend, I tried not to notice how the beach had been obstructed by all those new shops. I tried not to notice the rows of gaudy multicolored umbrellas poking out along the side of the enormous bypass that cut through the once-gorgeous landscape." She wiped another runaway tear and stiffened up as if to fight her own emotions. "I tried not to notice the number of out-of-state license plates there were in the traffic. All those out-of-towners who'd found my little gem. I ignored it all, because I felt that if I could just get to the ocean, if I could just view the sea, it would all be okay. The sea has been the same since before my time, and, God willing, it will remain."

Nan finally collected herself and then she turned back to look at the island again. "John proposed on an island exactly like this. In the haze that is my recollection, it seems like it has to be this is the one." Her eyes became glassy again, and she blinked quite a few times before continuing. "I have moments of panic, moments where I fear that I will go in search for John, and I won't find him," she said, her words thick again with emotion, her voice breaking. "I can't see him, but sometimes I think I can feel him, and like the sea, I pray that he's still here." She leaned on Jake and tried to stand, the slanted surface of the boat making it difficult for her. "He carved my name on a tree somewhere near the shore. I couldn't help but look for it as we pulled up. I doubt I could find it now, even if it was still here. It's probably gone like everything else from that era. I can't see it, but the minute I arrived, I could *feel* it. I don't need to find a marking on a tree to be able to remember. It's as if it were yesterday. I can still feel his hand in mine, hear his words to me. We were so young…" She took a step over to the other side of the boat. "I'll sit here. It's in the shade. Thank you, Jake, for bringing me." She wiped a tear.

"You're welcome," he said solemnly, clearly affected by her story. Nan could always tell a story, but this one was so personal and so honest that it had taken them both by surprise. Jake's eyes were moving along the edges of the boat as if in search of something, but Faith knew it was because he was thinking. She hoped he was thinking about how important loving someone and having family was—more important than all the money in the world.

How lucky Nan was to know that kind of feeling. Faith could honestly say that she'd never felt anything with that amount of depth before, and it made her feel naive. There was so much more to experience, so many more memories to make, she felt as if she hadn't even started her life yet.

"Would you like me to sit up here with you, Sophia?" Jake asked, his face still serious.

Nan smiled. "No, dear. I want you to go down onto the beach and enjoy yourself. That's why you've worn your swimsuits! I'm just happy that I get to be a part of it. I don't need to be down in that hot sand to feel the joy that I see before me. Look at little Isabella. She's having a ball. Go enjoy it."

"You sure?" Faith said, not wanting to leave her.

"Absolutely."

Jake opened the cooler and pulled out a water bottle, the surface of it clouding immediately with condensation in the summer heat. "Here's a water in case you get too warm. Just call down if you need us."

"I will, Jake. Thank you."

Jake hopped down first onto the sand and then held his hand out to steady Faith as she got down. She took his hand, his fingers strong and rough in hers, and went slowly so that she wouldn't have to let go so soon. He looked up at her, contemplation again on his face. That serious, determined expression she'd originally seen at Sunset Grille was long gone now, replaced by this new, thoughtful, deeper look of his. Like he was thinking something over. It made her curious.

"Look, Aunt Faith!" Isabella called, running and jumping over the small wave, landing on her bottom, a splash shooting up around her.

"Isabella," Jake called, "want to swing out really far?"

"Yes!" she said.

"Okay. I'll need your Aunt Faith's help." He turned to Faith, standing beside him, and she nodded. "Come over here, and we'll swing you."

Isabella walked up between them, grabbing their hands with hers. The salty water made them a little slippery, so Faith wrapped her thumb and forefinger around her wrist for leverage.

"One," Jake said, lifting her off the ground. Faith followed. "Two…three!" Isabella swung into the air, and they let go, her giggles like the fizz in the tide, bubbling up loud and wild until, *splash*! Into the water she went. She came out, still giggling, dripping wet, her hair sticking to her face in wet strands.

"Again!" Isabella said, still giggling. They did this until Isabella said her arms were getting tired. Faith couldn't help but think how this might be one of those great memories for her niece.

Jake hopped up onto the boat, checked on Nan, and got a few more chairs. Then, they all sat in a row. The sun was shining off the water, and the sky was bright blue above them. The only sound was a passing boat and the lapping of the waves. Faith, who had a lower chair, stretched her legs out in the sand, feeling the rays of the sun as they reflected off her skin.

"Look!" Isabella shouted from down the beach, her arm stretched out, her finger pointing out to sea.

Faith turned, shielding her eyes from the sun with her hand. There, so close that it seemed they could swim out to them, was a school of dolphins, their fins popping up and then dipping below the surface. There were so many of them! What an amazing thing for Isabella to see.

Unexpectedly, out of nowhere, fear swept through Faith. They probably wouldn't be back all together as a family like this again. Nan wouldn't plan another trip at her age, and they all lived so far away from each other. In a week's time, she'd leave and they'd all go back to their own lives. She wouldn't be back to see Jake, she wouldn't have the cottage, and she wouldn't have this time with her family.

They stayed on the island the rest of the afternoon until evening set in and they all started to get hungry. Faith had asked Nan several times if she was getting uncomfortable, but she'd waved her off, telling her she was just fine. As they loaded everything into the boat, Isabella, wearing her life jacket, curled up on a towel on the floor, her eyes so heavy she could hardly keep them open. Her mom, who'd taken a seat by Jake on the way there, sat down next to Nan, leaving the only open seat in front. Faith sat in the bucket seat at the bow, up front with Jake, everyone else behind them.

As Jake steered the boat, the water spraying up on either side of it, Faith looked out at their gorgeous surroundings. What would this vacation have been like without Jake around? While the cottage was beautiful and the beach was still wonderful, their days would have been a lot less exciting. When she thought back to this vacation years later, she was certain that he would be a part of those memories. They'd just sort of fallen together. How odd it was that it even happened. Never before had she met someone like that. While they had their differences and disagreements, she couldn't imagine having spent the week with anyone else. He'd made it perfect. Did he have this sort of chemistry with everyone? She was sure he got along with everyone, and he was easy to befriend, but for her, there was something more about him, something that would make her very sad when they had to leave.

"What are you thinking about?" he asked over the sound of the engine and the sea.

"Oh, nothing." She didn't know if she should tell Jake about her thoughts. She was worried her growing feelings for him might slip out and he'd made it clear that he didn't want to be anything more than friends. But then she thought about her own advice to Casey. After a few silent minutes of deliberation, she said, "It's awfully nice, what you've done for us this week—the boat rides, fishing, the light-house, the party… You know, since we're just renters."

He smiled, as if she'd said something that amused him. The setting sun gave his skin a warm glow. "I enjoy your family," he said with a smile. Then, he looked back out at the ocean, and she wondered as the smile faded to contentment, what *he* might be thinking about. Had they affected him? Had they even put one little seed of doubt in his head about his plans? Would he miss them as much as she'd miss him? The more she pondered that thought, the more she worried.

When they got back to the dock, Jake scooped Isabella—now asleep—off the boat floor and carried her to the car. Gently, he set her in the seat and fastened the seatbelt around her. Nan had seemed stiff as she walked, and Faith knew how much of a toll that boat ride had prob-ably put on her joints and muscles, but she didn't say a word as she bent over to get into the car. The trip had put a new shine in Nan's eyes. It was special for her and it was nice for Faith to share that with her.

"Thank you, Jake," she said from her seat. "That was lovelier than I could have imagined."

"You're welcome," he said.

Faith got in the other side and shut the door.

"Still up for seeing that band tonight at Sunset Grille?" he said, leaning into the car slightly to make eye contact.

Faith nodded. She was exhausted, and the sun had taken all the energy right out of her, but she wasn't going to say "no" no matter the cost. Being with Jake had given her loads of great memories and she didn't want to miss out on making more.

"I'll pick you up in about an hour." He shut the door gently. Faith waved to him. Her mom and Casey said their goodbyes, and with Jake in their rearview mirror, they pulled off down the road.

Faith had showered and gotten ready to meet Jake, and she came into the kitchen to find her mom and Casey. She sat down at the table. Her mom, who hadn't heard about Faith's phone call to Scott or Casey's text, sat, riveted, as Casey told her everything, and what had transpired.

Casey checked her phone. "Nothing," she said. "I know he's seen it." She opened the text message to check once more, and then closed it. "How could he not respond at all?"

"It seems awfully odd for Scott," her mom said. "Should Faith try to call him again?"

"No!" Casey nearly yelled. She got quiet and looked back at Isabella's bedroom door—she was still sound asleep, and Casey was clearly worried she'd woken her. "Look, he knows. He knows, and he chose not to respond. His silence is loud and clear."

"You're doing it again," Faith said, frustration rising in her veins. "Work for him, Casey. Show him that you're willing to work for him. Tell him until he's tired of hearing it. He's had silence for too long. Fill every moment with words now. Words that tell him what he means to you."

Casey sat for a moment, processing Faith's words. Faith knew it was hard for her sister, and she needed a little push. Faith slid the phone in front of her. With a quiet breath, Casey picked up the phone and dialed his number. It was so quiet, Faith could hear the pulses as the phone rang his line. It rang. And rang. Then, Scott's voice.

"Voicemail," Casey said, disappointed.

"Leave a message." Faith didn't just tell her, she directed her.

"Scott. It's me. I just want to tell you how much I miss you," her voice broke, and she coughed and then swallowed. "I love you so much. I'm sorry I wasn't better at being your wife. I'm not perfect… Please call me," she said in a small voice, and then hung up. The phone sat, dark, on the table as they waited for some kind of response. Faith stared at it, willing it to light up for her sister's sake.

"What if his phone is broken?" her mom said, struggling for some explanation, obviously. Both girls gave her a doubtful look and she shook her head. With a deep breath, she said, "No matter what, we girls stick together. We've always been close. The last few years have been an exception. Let's just help each other out."

Their mom was right. She'd probably want her girls around as Nan aged. Her care would get harder and harder. Casey—even though she'd deny it—would need people around her as she dealt with her divorce. But Faith… Did Faith need anyone? She would've sworn she didn't before coming to the beach house this summer, but now, after only a week, she realized she did need them. She needed them because she loved them, and they made her life fuller.

"Let's take our minds off all this," her mom said. "You know what we should do? Something nice for Jake. He's done so much since we've gotten here, and he didn't need to do any of it. What can we do for him?"

Faith knew her mother was right, but, selfishly, she was just excited at the thought of having yet one more excuse to see him after tonight. "I'll help you plan something tomorrow morning," she said. Then, she got up and patted her sister on the shoulder. "I'm going to wait for Jake on the porch."

***

"You really want to see this band?" Jake asked as he drove toward Duck.

"Yes."

"Have you ever heard of them before?"

"Nope."

He looked over at her and then back at the road. "Then why do you want to go?"

"Because music at the beach is amazing."

"What if it's a heavy metal band?" he teased, the corners of his mouth going up and that playful affection in his eyes.

"Sunset Grille would not have a heavy metal band."

"Okay. You got me. Promise me you won't get the fishbowl drink."

"I'm going to get us both one, and you're going to hold mine while we dance together."

Jake laughed and shook his head.

The sun was setting, and, even though Faith had had a very full day, and she was nearly exhausted, the sight of the pink and blue sky with a blaze of orange slashed through it, the colors dancing on the water below making the pier and gazebo nothing but a black silhouette—they made her feel alive. She was so happy to be there. She could hear the band already—steel drums and maracas, not heavy metal—as they walked up, and she grabbed Jake's arm. He looked down at her hand but then looked back toward Sunset Grille, not saying a word.

He told the hostess they were there for the band, and she sat them outside, close enough that the music penetrated the air all around them but far enough away for them to have a conversation.

"This is nice," he said with a smile, leaning back in his chair a little.

"I thought it would be."

A few couples had gotten up to dance. The breeze of the Sound blew through Faith's hair.

"I'll be back," Jake said, getting up. "You okay for a sec?"

"I'm just fine," she smiled. She watched him go but then turned back around to see the band. The music filled her chest, danced in her ears, and made her tap her foot against the wooden deck. She wanted to get up and sway to the music. She wanted Jake behind her, his arms around her, as they stood with the water and the fiery sunset all around them.

It was so nice to experience the Outer Banks as an adult. There were so many more places to explore, so many things to do that she'd never even considered as a kid. But her thoughts didn't stop there. She wanted to travel. She decided she was going to see Key West. If anything, out of principle. She should get out more, enjoy life, meet people. Life was bigger than her work, and while her job was very important to her, finding a balance was also important.

One song bled into another, until she started to notice that Jake hadn't returned. The waitress had been by several times, bringing water and topping it off, but Faith kept saying she was waiting for him. Now, she wondered what was going on. Was he sick? She scanned the bar—it was full of people—but she couldn't find his familiar frame. She eyed the outdoor hostess station, trying to see if he'd gotten caught talking or something. He wasn't there. She wanted to continue to enjoy the music, but the more she sat, the more she worried. When he finally showed, she was sitting on the edge of her seat.

"I'm so sorry. I had to check my phone—I didn't want to be rude and do it at the table, and then I had an unexpected business call. I had to take it."

He was apologizing, and she knew he was probably very sorry, but sitting there on that deck with no one to enjoy the music with her had made her think. She thought about her ex-boyfriend, Patrick, and how he'd always told her she worked too long. And then she thought about Scott, and how he must feel all by himself when he should be here with the family. This trip had taught her that life wasn't about working.

"I've learned that work doesn't make someone successful, being happy does." She eyed the phone in his hand, trying to drive home the message.

"What if work is what makes me happy?" he challenged her.

"When we first met, I confided in you that I felt like I had to prove to people that I'm happy. Do you remember that? If I recall correctly, you'd said that you knew exactly how I felt."

"And your point?" He looked down at his phone again to check it, and she wanted to grab it and throw it into the ocean.

"I'm not convinced that building your big hotels makes you happy." She only felt happy when she could be with people she enjoyed, making memories, and having fun. She looked up at him, and he was looking at his phone again.

"Well, it does make me happy. And, I've said before, I don't have to prove to you that I am."

She still wasn't convinced.

"But just because my business makes me happy, doesn't mean that I need to be on the phone tonight. If you can sit tight one more sec…" he said. He dropped his phone into his pocket. "I'll be right back, I promise."

She thought again about Scott and Casey. Jake had only taken one work call tonight and had apologized for that, but it had already unsettled Faith. Where had he gone now? Was he sneaking in another business call? What must Scott feel about Casey? No wonder he hadn't responded. If Casey could just make him see that she was serious. She looked around for Jake, and took in a deep breath as she realized she'd lost him again in the crowd. She looked up at the sky to try to calm herself. *Please let him redeem himself after all this*, she prayed. Was it too much to ask him to switch off from work and have a little downtime?

The music was fast—a Bob Marley cover—and she wanted so badly to be able to just relax and enjoy herself. She scanned the bar again but stopped when she saw him, and then she smiled, her heart nearly ready to explode. Sloshing in his arms—straws and fruit skewers bouncing everywhere—were two enormous fishbowls of green liquid. He smiled at her as he wobbled toward her.

Gingerly, he set them down. He knelt in front of her, his eyes meeting hers. "I'm sorry that I left you here," he said. "I put my phone in the car." Right then, she knew that actions spoke so much louder than words, and with that one gesture, he'd made her feel better.

"Thank you for this," she said, still smiling and pointing to her fishbowl.

"You're welcome." He stood up. "Want to dance?"

"Yes," she said, excited.

The band had slowed to gentle rhythm, as Jake led her to the area of deck where the tables had been cleared. He put his arms around her, holding her waist, and she wrapped hers around his neck. He looked down at her, and she wondered what had made him so happy all of a sudden. He seemed so content and comfortable there with her. She put her head on his shoulder, and she could feel his lips against the top of her head. She wanted to feel this way all night; it was simply perfect.

She looked at him. "Thank you for bringing me tonight," she said.

"You're welcome." He locked eyes with her, his face showing deliberation. Then, without warning, he leaned toward her and gently pressed his lips to hers. It was as if they were the only two people there. The music, the breeze, the taste of rum on his lips—it all made her lightheaded, and she was glad to be holding onto him because she didn't trust herself to stand on her own. It felt like the perfect moment and nothing could ruin it.

"I wanted to kiss you at my party," he admitted in her ear after he'd left her lips.

"Why didn't you?"

"I didn't want to get involved again. It's too complicated. You know how I feel about what I do for a living and my plans for the Outer Banks. That's a big deal when it comes to my life. And yet you're here with me, knowing that. As much as I'd like to be friends—it would be easier—I can't help how I feel. I love spending time with you and your family, and this afternoon with your nan just brought home to me how important it is to find someone to share life with. I know we have our differences but I hope in time I can get you to understand the way I see things."

Funny, she was hoping the same, but she was hoping to get him to see her side of things. "I wasn't terribly happy about being left during the phone call," she said honestly. If he was being honest, then she should be too.

"I'd never have done that, but it was an important call."

More important than being with me? she wanted to ask, but was afraid to hear the answer. "What was it?"

"The restaurant owners on Beach Road are ready to sell."

She pulled back and moved off to the side of the deck. "What?" So much for nothing being able to ruin the moment. He just had. As quick as a flash.

"Yep." He smiled.

"That's why you're so happy tonight?"

"Yep," he said again. So it had nothing to do with being with her, enjoying their time together. He was just on a high from having gotten what he wanted.

"I'm sorry," she said, turning and heading back to their table. Their drinks sat, still full. "I can't be happy about this." She sat down and stared at the pineapple wedge and maraschino cherry on the skewer in her drink. "I'm never going to agree with you on this, and it's always going to come between us. Your job defines who you are, and I'm just going to say it: I am wholeheartedly against your decisions."

"I can change your mind."

"So, if I want to change and do what you'd like me to do, it's fine, but you aren't even willing to entertain my point of view? You only want things to work when they're on *your* terms. That's not fair, Jake."

The truth was that, while they had a ton of fun together, when it came down to it, she could see that they were just two very different people. She was never going to change his mind, and he was certainly not going to change hers. She'd better just end things now before they got worse. She didn't want to spend her vacation arguing, and Jake didn't need her nagging him. They'd hit a wall.

"Maybe we should call it a night," Faith suggested. She stood up. Before it had even begun, their night was over.

"Why?"

"I just think it would be better."

"You're avoiding the situation."

"I'd rather not discuss it any further. You aren't going to change my mind."

"You're being stubborn," he said. Why can *you* change *my* mind but I can't change yours?"

She looked out at the ocean. "You know, you're just as stubborn. Casey mentioned that your ex-wife said you didn't communicate. Maybe she was on to something."

Chapter Nineteen

"Want some coffee?" Faith asked Casey, knowing the answer. Both she and her sister were exhausted after having been up with Isabella all night. It had been a long day, and, even though she'd cut the night short with Jake, Faith hadn't gotten settled until late. Isabella had a nightmare that her daddy was missing and she couldn't find him, and she'd gotten them both up in the early hours of the morning. She'd cried for ages, it had seemed. Faith had suggested calling Scott to have him talk to her, but Casey insisted on handling it on her own. She'd said that Scott would be out of the state most of the time, and she'd have to get used to handling Isabella's fears by herself anyway. Plus, Faith wondered if Scott's silence played a part in Casey's decision as well. How dare he get to soothe his little girl when he wouldn't even pick up the phone? Faith was willing to bet that thought had gone through Casey's head.

"Yes, please," Casey sat down at the table and rubbed her face. She looked tired, but not just from last night. She looked overwhelmed.

"Good morning!" their mom said, almost singing the words as she sat down. She was already dressed and ready for the day. Their mom smiled at both of them before realizing that she was the only one smiling. Then, she said more seriously, "How are we this morning?"

"Drained," Casey said. Faith filled the coffee pot and clicked it on. "Isabella kept us up last night. She misses her daddy."

Their mom looked thoughtful, an undecipherable expression lurking below her features. "It'll all work itself out."

Faith poured a cup of coffee for Casey and set it in front of her. "I'm sure it will be okay eventually, but last night was pretty rough." She opened the fridge and pulled out the cream. "Isabella's holding in more than we think."

Their mom stayed quiet. There really wasn't much to say about it.

Faith poured two more cups of coffee and brought them to the table with a few spoons. Without saying a word, the three women stirred their drinks. Faith's eyes burned from lack of sleep, her head heavy with exhaustion. She hadn't slept well after they'd finally settled Isabella back down. She'd been worried about her niece. What would her little life be like now that her daddy would be living so far away? She couldn't believe Scott hadn't even texted Casey. That was so out of character. Were things that bad between them? And she kept replaying last night with Jake. The journey back had been silent and she'd given him the briefest of goodbyes when she'd left. She didn't know what else to do or say. All these thoughts had been swimming around in her mind all night, making her restless.

Before she could ponder any further, Isabella came walking in, her hair wild and bunched up, and her blanket in her hands. She'd slept hard, it looked like.

"Good morning, Isabella," Casey said gently. "I can't believe you're up." She stood and offered her chair to her daughter. "Do you want some breakfast?"

Isabella nodded.

"What are we going to do with Jake today, Mom?" Casey asked, probably trying to steer the conversation away from her and Scott.

Faith felt her shoulders slump. She'd forgotten they were supposed to do something nice for Jake. It had seemed like such a good idea when they'd discussed it yesterday, but now she was hoping she wouldn't have to see him again. It was just too hard. She liked him so much, but they just couldn't make things work. Neither of them would budge.

"I think we should cook for him tonight—make a big seafood dinner," their mom said.

"We've already made him breakfast. Why don't we go out and get drinks or something?" Casey suggested.

Their mom shook her head. "I don't know if Nan wants to do that. I'd like to include her."

"If there's a chair, I'll have drinks," Nan said, coming in. She walked slowly, taking each step with great care. "Good morning," she said, taking a seat.

"Why don't we decide after we all get ready for the day?" their mom said. "Getting freshened up might make everyone feel a little better. I'll make Isabella her breakfast. You two go get yourselves together."

Nan watched her daughter carefully. Mom was up to something, and Nan—ever the observer—could tell. Mom didn't want to go anywhere; she wanted them to get ready... Faith couldn't help the fizzle of excitement that was rising up. It reminded her of the very last time they'd come to their cottage as kids. Her mom, who could always keep a secret, but allowed little clues to leak out all over the place, had told the girls they were going to have a girls' day out. They'd expected to go to the movies or something, but when they got in the car, it was full of car games, snacks, and toys. Their bags already packed, they were headed to the Outer Banks. They hadn't even known they were going. The cottage was destroyed the next year. Faith couldn't help but think how Nan's advice to take a chance rang true that time. Had her mom not decided to take them there that day, they wouldn't have had that last memory—that memory of a time when the real world hadn't begun yet. It had been a good summer—before they'd all gone their separate ways.

Faith decided to follow her mom's lead and get ready for the day. For all she knew, her mother had planned something fantastic. "Casey, I'll let you know when the shower's free," she said, gathering her cup and spoon and walking over to the sink. Casey, clearly thinking the same thing as Faith, had perked up about as much as she could, nodding, her face set in a hopeful expression. Poor Casey needed something to take her mind off of everything.

Her mom's expression had changed over the last few hours. She seemed antsy, edgy, like she wanted to go and do something but didn't at the same time. Faith had suggested the beach, but Mom had claimed she'd already had too much sun, and she wanted to stay in. She'd even whispered that they should all stay in for Nan's sake. What had started as excitement was turning to anxiety as her mom puttered around, clearly trying to fill the time.

"I told Jake that we'd make him dinner tonight," she said, smiling for their benefit. "I know you didn't want to cook for him, but I think he'd like it, and it would give me a chance to cook. I love cooking, you know, and I haven't really had much of a chance. I'd like to try my hand at some seafood dishes."

Both Casey and Faith agreed, more so just to keep the conversation going. Faith was worried about seeing Jake again. She liked him so much, but they just couldn't make things work between them. Faith was also on the edge of her seat, waiting to find out what their mom had planned. Whatever it was, it seemed pretty important, because she'd never seen her mother look this anxious. She kept looking at the door and checking her phone. Isabella was playing with her dolls on the floor by Nan's feet.

Then, there was a knock at the door. Faith hadn't expected a visitor, but she could see her mom's body slump in relief. What was going on? Her mother got up, opened the door just a crack, and then, with a smile like Faith had never seen before, she swung the door open wide. Casey gasped and Faith's jaw nearly hit the floor.

"Daddy!" Isabella dropped her toys and went tearing over to Scott, jumping into his arms. The little girl who had missed her daddy so much last night put her head in the bend between his neck and shoulder, her back hiccupping in quiet sobs. So this was her mom's big secret. It was the very last thing Faith would have ever thought would happen.

"Hey, baby," he said, dropping his suitcase in the doorway and wrapping his arms around her. He looked over at Casey tentatively, meeting her gaze.

When Faith looked at her sister, Casey's relief was palpable. Her eyes were glassy with emotion, her smile trembling in uncertainty. This strong, beautiful woman who could command a courtroom was looking at her husband with so much vulnerability on her face that Faith's conclusion was solidified: Casey was head over heels in love with this man. He could make the most secure, resilient woman she knew become defenseless. Because Casey loved him. Faith hadn't ever loved him like that because she hadn't been able to experience having his love in return. Scott was Casey's whole world, and there were no two people better for each other, and it seemed like things might finally be looking up for them.

"I wanted to respond to your texts and calls," he said, still holding Isabella. She'd stopped crying and had turned her head, resting it on his shoulder. He was rubbing her back, his eyes on his wife. "So I figured I'd stop by…" He smiled, and Casey stood up.

"And?" Casey stood and walked over to him until she was only inches from him, the space between them full of unsaid words.

"That was all I needed to hear."

"Really?" she said, relief on her face.

"We have a lot to talk about," he said. "But if you'll try, I will too."

Casey put her hands on his face, leaned over her daughter, and kissed his lips, tears falling down her cheeks.

"You about killed me, taking so long," her mom said once everyone had settled down, and they all laughed.

"I got stuck in traffic on the way in. Sorry." He bounced Isabella in his arms. He looked over at Faith. "Hey, Faith," he said with a big smile.

She smiled back and gave a little wave. It had been so long.

"It's good to see you," he said.

"You too." And it was good. It was *so* good to see him again.

As Faith looked at Scott, she was taken with how much more mature he looked, how different. It had certainly been a while. His eyes were the same, and his smile, but his face had aged, his haircut a little shorter. What made her the happiest was the fact that she was able to enjoy him and to enjoy his family. *Her* family. Having him there with them was like finding that missing puzzle piece.

***

They'd all spent the day together. Scott had explained that the minute he'd gotten Casey's text, he'd changed his plans, texted their mother from the airport, and headed straight there. He was going to spend the next week with them, and Faith couldn't be happier for her sister. Isabella barely got a breath between the stories she was telling her daddy. She told him about the shells she'd found, about making sandcastles, about Jake's party and her necklace. Faith was full of joy, hearing it all, because she knew that Isabella was making memories just like she had as a girl. And now she got to make new memories with her dad.

Faith stood alone out on the porch, taking in the view. This beach had felt the patter of her little feet as she ran across the hot sand as a baby; it had cradled her when she'd fallen, the ocean knocking her wildly as a girl; and it had seen her grow into a young woman. Now, she looked out at it, feeling sad. In only a week, they'd pack up, leave this place, and someone new would find her beach. Maybe, if they were lucky, they'd get a chance to rent the cottage occasionally, although the cottages booked up so quickly, it would be tricky to get this very one. And, if Jake had his way, the villages would look nothing like her memories when she returned. As she looked at the beach—*her* beach—she wanted to stay there forever. She wanted Isabella to know it like she had. No wonder Nan had dragged them all here. It took seeing it as an adult to really understand the importance of it. Faith hadn't realized as a kid how lucky she'd been to have that beach house, nor could she have imagined how many memories were lying out there in that sand.

She leaned over the railing to see if Scott had gotten the grill set up. He'd brought it in the back of his SUV—it was only a small grill, but the smell of the burning charcoal wafted up toward her, reminding her of all those barefoot days when they'd cooked seafood at the old cottage. Her mom would set the picnic table up for dinners, the paper plates and napkins having to be weighted down with rocks to keep them from blowing away. She and Casey had cleaned and painted about fifteen rocks, and their mom would always pack them. She wondered what had happened to them. Where had they gone? Now, with no picnic table at the new cottage, they'd planned to eat inside, but Faith had stayed on the porch. She wanted to have every minute she could with her view of the beach, and she didn't want to miss a single one by sitting inside. She watched the sky turn from orange to pink, the sun casting long shadows on the sand. It was a perfect night. Jake was due to arrive any minute, however. How would he fit in? Would things be perfect between the two of them tonight too, or would their differences get in the way again? She worried as she waited for him to arrive.

"Hey there." She heard his familiar voice and turned around. Jake was heading up the steps. He walked up beside her and looked out at the ocean. "It's nice tonight."

Faith tried to keep her emotions in check, but now when she was with him, even a comment like that made her want to grab him by the shoulders and ask why they couldn't see eye to eye. It would make things so much easier. She wanted to understand him.

"Do you really think it's nice tonight?" Did he really think it was nice to be with her or just nice outside?

"Yes," he said, that tiny wrinkle forming between his eyes.

"Don't you want to have more nights like this?" Being around Jake still made her pulse speed up, her hands becoming jittery. She'd learned a lot about herself this week. She'd learned that it was easy for her to fall for someone, but that she had to step back and look at the situation carefully before acting.

"Of course."

"How can you when you're sandwiched in a row of high-rises?"

She watched him closing up right before her eyes, and she exhaled in surrender. She hadn't meant it to come out like that. She didn't want to argue with him or debate his work decisions. She didn't want tonight to be ruined by their differing views. She'd taken a risk with Jake by being vocal about her opinions, and he'd made his wishes clear.

"I'm sorry," she said. "I don't want to spend tonight trying to change your mind. I'll let it go for tonight. I promise."

Surprisingly, he looked at her with fondness in his eyes. He didn't look at anyone else that way. She wanted to cut to the chase, to just ask him outright what he thought about her.

"Why are you looking at me like that?" she asked.

"No reason." His expression was serious but the affection was still in his eyes.

"Well, I like it when you look at me like that."

He smiled but didn't offer any response. She wondered what he thought about her admission.

"So Casey's husband is here?" he asked, his eyebrows going up in curiosity. "That's a surprise."

"Yeah," she said. "It's a good thing."

"I know. Given what she told me when we were out, she misses him."

"She told you that?"

"Yep. She misses him a lot. I should go down and help Scott," he said, looking down at Scott grilling below. Her mother had prepared a feast for him to grill.

"Why are you so relaxed around strangers?" she asked with a grin. He'd never even met Scott, yet he was going to go down and help him cook.

He smiled at her, and she felt her limbs go weak. "Strangers are just people. We're all similar in many ways. I enjoy finding those similarities."

"It seems so easy for you."

"It's like chipping away old paint. Sometimes, you find a color you never knew was there. People put up what they want others to see, but if you strip away that façade, you find unexpected pieces of their personalities sometimes."

"I'd never thought of it that way."

He smiled again, that almost doting look showing in his eyes. "See? You just chipped away my paint. You found out why I like to meet new people."

She wished she'd have had a chance to see how many more pieces of paint she'd have been able to chip away, had things gone differently between them.

"Do y'all mind helping me set the table?" her mom called from inside.

"I'd be happy to," Jake said, opening the door wider so that Faith could enter first. She walked under his arm and went inside.

At moments like this Jake was so personable and modest that she forgot all about the lifestyle he had. She could only imagine what he'd paid for the dishes she'd eaten off of at his house, yet here he was, setting the table with paper plates and napkins, not a care in the world. She loved that about him. But it wasn't enough.

After helping her mom, Jake excused himself to go downstairs and cook with Scott. When Faith went back out to the porch to sit with Nan, she could hear them making small talk down below. Jake laughed at something Scott said, and it sent a plume of happiness through her.

Nan looked out toward the ocean. "I couldn't have asked for a more lovely evening."

"The weather is nice," Faith agreed.

"Mmm. I'm not talking entirely about the weather. It's fantastic to have everyone here. I'm so glad you girls are together again."

"Thanks to you," Faith said with a smile.

"It's hard work keeping this family together."

Nan could always keep everyone together. What was her secret?

"When did you know that my grandfather was The One?" Faith asked her.

"Where's this coming from?" she said, her words coming out in an affectionate laugh.

"You seem to know just how to keep us all together, and I just wondered how you made it work so well."

"Oh, I don't know. I suppose that it was the understanding that it won't all be perfect. So the imperfections were what made it great." She turned her rocker to face Faith. "He burned toast," she said. "I don't know how he did it, but he did. It made the whole house smell. I can still remember the swirling smoke floating up around the lamps. It was awful. All he'd had to do was ask, and I'd have made it for him. Instead, John insisted on putting bread in the pan and then busying himself with something. I tried to tell him to stand there with it, but he never did. And then, he'd leave for work and I'd have to smell that smoke all day." She laughed and then became serious. "I'd give anything to smell his burned toast."

Faith grinned, but her heart ached for Nan. "So when did you know?" she asked again.

"I knew quite early on," she said. "There's always that possibility that it won't all work out. It isn't rainbows and fairytales. But I knew right away that when I was around him, I wanted to know more about him, and I liked what I already knew. That was all I needed. I just took it day by day." They rocked a while, the sound of the ocean like a lullaby. "Jake sure does get along with everyone, doesn't he," she said, changing the subject and looking down her nose to peer over at the two men as they steamed clams and grilled fish down below.

"Yes. He does."

"So, Jake," Nan said as they all sat squeezed in around the small dinner table, "what brought you back to the Outer Banks?" They'd been talking for what seemed like hours. Jake was now leaning back in his chair, his arm propped up on the back of it.

"Opportunity." He grinned. "I wanted to build here because the landscape and culture provided a unique obstacle for development. People want large-scale facilities with all the bells and whistles, and I enjoyed the challenge. I love it here."

"I can see why," Nan said.

Faith knew that Nan didn't have the whole story about what Jake saw in the Outer Banks, and he knew that too, but when she said she could see why he loved it, Faith noticed something on his face.

He was thinking about something. Did he feel guilty misleading her? He'd heard her thoughts about the growth of the area when they'd taken their boat ride. He knew how she felt.

Isabella asked for more milk and both Scott and Casey got up at the same time. Casey grinned at him, and sat back down, her face giving away all of her feelings.

When Scott returned with Isabella's drink, her mom said, "Dinner was great, boys." She was right: Dinner was great, but not just the food. For so many years, it'd been just the girls. It was nice to have Jake and Scott there. They added an element to the conversation that had been missing.

After dinner, Scott, Casey, and Isabella went for a walk on the beach, Nan was asleep in the chair in the living room, and Faith and her mom were cleaning up dinner dishes.

"Go hang out with Jake," her mom whispered. "I'll be fine cleaning up. It's rude to leave him sitting on his own." He'd tried to help, but she'd shooed him away too.

Faith looked over at him. He was on the sofa. Any minute he'd get up to leave; she was sure of it. So she walked over and asked if he'd like to sit outside a while. Perhaps he, too, was trying to be polite, because he agreed. They went out to sit in the rocking chairs. They rocked in silence, and in that moment, Faith realized it didn't matter how her life unfolded. She'd take this memory here and now.

Chapter Twenty

Everyone had gone to bed, and she and Jake were still sitting in the rockers. Faith pulled her hair over one shoulder, the texture of it like yarn from the salty air. She wondered why Jake hadn't gotten up to leave, but she didn't mind. She wasn't tired anyway.

"This is what I love about the Outer Banks," he said.

"How can you love sitting on this porch, looking at this beach, when you want to knock everything down and fill the beaches with towering hotels?"

"I meant that I loved the view. And I can have this view from a *towering hotel.*"

As she watched the thoughts surface behind his eyes again, something struck her: Everything she knew about Jake went against this idea that he liked all of the developments he was planning. He did handyman work for fun, he shopped at the local surf shops, he took her family on a boat ride to that little, secluded beach. There wasn't much about his personality that demonstrated that he liked the kinds of places he was building. So, what was driving him? It was the same thing that had driven her to be successful in her job, to build herself up, to be strong. Failure. He was trying to overcome failure. Was he trying to prove a point to his ex-wife that he could do bigger, better things?

"I don't believe that's what you want."

"Sorry?"

"Nothing about those places reminds me of you. There's not a bit of your character in those developments. The Tides? That's not you. You don't eat stuffy meals with cloth napkins. You can, and you have, but you wouldn't choose it. You don't want these high-rise hotels and resorts any more than I do."

"Don't try to tell me what I want. I had enough of that with my ex."

"I'm not telling you what you want. I'm pointing out what I know. You don't have to fluff out your feathers with me. I do think you're good enough. I think you're great, actually. You don't need anything fancy to prove that to me."

Jake didn't say anything. He just turned and looked straight ahead.

Faith looked out into the pitch black of the ocean, the sky like a bowl of stars above them. "I've never been to any other beach and that's okay. I'll get there. All my life, I've wanted to see Key West. But I've only just now realized why I haven't gone. It's because, without someone to share it with, it's just a place like anywhere else. You can turn the Outer Banks into something different, but unless you have someone to share it with, it's just another resort."

He looked at her, his thoughts evident. Then he turned his head back toward the sound of the sea. She could tell that he wasn't angry. He was just taking it all in.

"How long have you been single?" she asked.

"Two years." Then, without warning, he began to talk. It was so surprising that Faith almost didn't take in the words. "My divorce with my ex-wife was final two years ago. I didn't give her enough attention," he admitted. "Rebecca didn't like that. She wanted me to make these grand gestures all the time to show my love for her. She asked me why I never got her flowers and why I didn't have champagne on a random Tuesday. I'm learning what to do to show people I care about them. And I don't always know. I don't know how to be a good husband, necessarily. She pointed that fact out to me every day before we finally divorced."

Faith understood his side of things. She didn't know what to do either. What was so interesting to her, though, was that flowers and champagne would be nice, but she didn't have to have those as a token of a man's affection. Jake had a wonderful ability to see the best in things, and she enjoyed just being with him. It didn't matter what they were doing.

"I don't think you should take her criticisms personally," she said, trying to find the right words. "I think it was more a difference in perspectives. I think you know how to connect with people. You just have to find the right person to be with. And when you do, you'll find that you don't have to work so hard."

He sat quietly, clearly considering what she'd just said. He was contemplating something.

She grabbed onto the arms of the rocker for something to do with her hands in the silence. "Ow!" Faith yelped, pulling her finger to her lips to squelch a sharp pain. Something had just jabbed her finger. As she pulled her hand back to look at it, she realized she'd gotten a pretty big splinter. It must have come off the handle of the rocking chair. When her focus broadened, she realized that Jake had stood up and was now kneeling in front of her, concern on his face.

"I think I got a splinter," she said, holding out her finger for him to view. He took her hand gently to get a better look, and then blew on the reddened area softly. It sent a shiver up her arm. She swallowed.

"We need to get that out so it won't get infected."

"Mom brought a first aid kit," she remembered out loud. "There may be something in there we can use."

"You need to find a needle." He still had her hand in his, and she wished she didn't have to get up because he'd have to let go.

"I know exactly where I can find one." She stood up, and he walked with her inside. With her good hand, she dug around in the front pocket of Nan's handbag. "She always keeps a little sewing kit in here. I know, because I had a button come off once, and she got her little plastic kit out and sewed it back on for me there and then. She told me she never leaves home without it."

A quiet laugh bubbled up in Jake's chest. "She's funny, your nan." He laughed again. "Every day, she totes around a sewing kit in her bag just in case she needs it, but you've only ever used it once in your life."

Faith felt the edge of the kit under her fingers and pulled it out, his comment making her giggle too. "It is funny, isn't it? And I could've gone without that button that day, but she'd sewn it on." She opened the case and pulled a needle from a tiny paper envelope inside. She held it out and, with a grin, Jake took it.

He sat down on the sofa near the lamp and turned her hand over on his thigh under the light, moving her finger back and forth to examine it first. Then, he lowered the needle toward her. "This might poke a little," he said.

The sting of the needle as it penetrated her skin caused her to squeeze her eyes shut. She was stuck in a kneeling position on the floor, leaning her arms on his knees. She rested her chin on one arm, opening her eyes and looking up at him. It was nice. She liked being close to him.

"Sorry," he said, poking her finger again.

"It's okay." She didn't care whether it hurt or not at that moment. She hoped it would take him all night to get that splinter out.

Another poke. "Almost got it. Do you have any tweezers?"

"Yes. I have to get them out of my makeup bag." She hopped up and ran into her room, threw open her makeup bag, and dug around with her good hand until she found them. Then she hurried back. "Here." She sat back down as he took her hand in his again.

He softly rooted around with the tweezers. "Does that hurt?"

"No. You're very gentle," she said with a smile.

"Good." She noticed how his concentration had caused lines to form between his eyes, his brows pulled down, and a focused frown on his face. Then, that relaxed, happy look filtered through his features and he set down her tweezers. "Got it." With her hand still in his, he put her finger to his lips and kissed it. "All better." She wanted so badly to feel that kiss on her lips. He stood up, helping her up as well, and then thumbed through the first aid kit.

"Thank you," she said as he ripped open a packet of cleaning wipes. He pulled out the tiny towelette and shook it free before taking her hand again to wipe her finger. When he was finished, he wrapped a small bandage around it.

"I should sand that rocking chair and repaint the arm."

"You'd probably do it right now if I didn't stop you."

"I don't have my work truck or I would," he grinned.

They were standing together, face to face. He was looking down at her, the corners of his mouth twitching upward in amusement, and even though he wasn't touching her, she had an ache within her to put her hands on his face and feel him next to her. She caught herself urging him with her eyes to touch her, and he seemed to read it perfectly. He reached out and dragged his fingers down her arm, giving her goose bumps. His gaze followed the invisible trail he'd left with his finger and then he made eye contact. He could tell his effect on her.

His breathing was steady as he took a step closer to her and put his hand on her waist. She looked up at him, waiting, hoping he'd kiss her. He looked as though he was deliberating.

"What are you thinking?" she whispered, her body still in the moment, her hands moving up around his neck to help him along.

"I'm thinking how much I want to kiss you, and it's taking all my willpower not to."

"Um-hm." She totally agreed but wasn't using her willpower tonight. She lifted herself up on her tiptoes in an attempt to be face-to-face.

He leaned in, resting his face next to hers—cheek to cheek—his breath near her neck, the corners of their mouths so close that it almost felt like the start of a kiss. "I don't want to screw this up." He pulled back and looked at her, as if waiting for her response to his honesty.

"You won't." Even with a deep breath, she couldn't slow her heartbeat.

"I've messed this up between us a few times now. You deserve for me to do this the right way."

He put his hands on her face and very softly kissed her lips. It took everything she had to be still and not push him down on the sofa. The thought surprised her. It wasn't like her, but she couldn't help it.

"I was wondering, would you like to go on a date with me?" he asked.

"A *date*?" She smiled.

"Yes." His face was playful, almost excited. "A date."

That word "date" had brought to mind her conversation with Casey when they'd first arrived. She'd forgotten all about that until now. That conversation she'd had with Casey seemed like years ago. How far they'd come since they'd arrived. "We've been on a date already, remember? You took me to Bodie Island Lighthouse."

Jake shook his head. "I was thinking about a real date. That was more of a day out."

"Call it what you want," she said. "I'll call it a date."

The way she was feeling at this moment, she knew she could talk to him when things made her uncomfortable. It seemed so easy now. She could feel the excitement bubbling up, but she didn't want to admit to herself how pleased his proposition made her or his reasons for being so happy. Last time he'd been this happy, he'd dropped the bomb on her that he'd be leveling two local restaurants. She was afraid to be too hopeful.

He grinned, a little chuckle of laughter escaping his lips. "Well?"

"Yes. I'd love to go on another date."

"How about I pick you up the day after tomorrow at eight in the morning?"

"Eight in the morning?" She giggled. "Are we going to breakfast?"

"Better." He looked at her a long time, the suspense making her crazy. Then he said, "Well, I should probably go. It's getting late. Thank you for having me over."

She didn't want him to go. She wanted to grab him by the shirttails and drag him back to her room. "You're welcome. You're not going to tell me where we're going?"

He shook his head, a grin playing on his lips. He started toward the door, pausing for Faith to join him.

She walked him down the stairs, and he held her hands as he said goodbye. Then she sat on the last step as he got in his car and backed out of the drive. His headlights caused spots in her eyes, so she stayed there even after he'd gone until they'd cleared. As she took in the sea air, barely noticing the wind anymore after a week there, she closed her eyes, and replayed tonight in her mind. It had been a good night. A great night even. Before it had started, she'd worried about him coming over, wondered where they'd be after what had happened at Sunset Grille, but she was learning to just enjoy the moment.

She sat there a long time until her thoughts had moved from tonight to what it had felt like to sit on that step at her childhood cottage. Those feelings were a part of her that she'd left behind so many years ago, but they were still there, right at her grasp, and she didn't want to let them go. Just like Nan's photographs, the smells, the air—it all told a story, her story. And she wasn't finished yet. She didn't know how, but maybe she could plan the next family trip. Maybe they could all get together regularly. She might even be able to include Jake. With another deep breath, she made her way up to the cottage door and went inside for the night.

"Good morning!" Faith said with surprise as she walked out of her room to find Scott at the kitchen table with the local newspaper. "It's funny to see you sitting there."

"Funny?" he said with a crooked grin, but she knew he understood.

Even when they were younger, Scott always read the newspaper. He had it delivered to his house. She used to tease him because he separated all the sections and reordered them the way he wanted to read them, starting with the Sports section. She huffed out a little laugh as she noticed the paper had been pulled apart and stacked on the table.

"What?" he said, tipping the edge of his page to peer down at the pile in front of him.

"Did you reorder them?"

"Of course. Who wants to start with front-page news? It's so depressing."

Faith laughed. It was like they hadn't skipped a beat. There was absolutely no indication on his face that the years apart had tainted their friendship. With all the stress of her emotions gone, she could just enjoy who he was again. And it came back so easily.

"How are things with Casey?" she asked as she poured them both a glass of juice.

He took the glass, nodding a quick thank-you and setting down the paper. "Things are going well. She wants to try."

"She does. I've seen a side of her this week that's so different than anything I've ever seen from her before."

Faith knew her proximity to Casey, the beach house, their memories, Nan—all of it had changed them this week. She caught a glimpse of the rocking chairs through the glass door as they moved in the wind outside. They looked so new, their runners moving along the yellow wood of the porch. How she wished she'd be able to see those chairs when the paint on the arms had worn, the wood underneath glossy from lotions and tanning oils. She wondered if the porch floor would pucker in places like it had at their cottage. She wondered how long it would take for that yellow wood to weather and turn a deep brown, grains of sand from little feet and well-used towels filling the crevices.

The two cottages were like her friendship with Scott in a way—the old one, warm and comforting, reminded her of younger days but had long been taken by the storms. The new one looked similar and felt similar but it wasn't the same. It wasn't better or worse, just different, and she found it could be just as good as before.

Nan had wanted to sit on the beach today. The whole family had been so worried that she'd fall, trying to walk in the sand, but she'd trudged out there. Then they worried she might get sunburn, so Scott had erected the canopy over the top of their chairs to create shade, and they'd faced Nan's chair toward the cottage so the sun was behind her. Now, they worried about the heat.

"I'm fine. Good grief," Nan said as Faith offered her a bottle of water from the cooler. "You know that I was alive before air conditioning? I survived the heat then, and I'll survive it now."

"I just don't want you to dehydrate." Faith held out the bottle—her final attempt. Nan took it, but Faith wondered if the gesture was just to appease them.

"I don't like facing this direction," she said. "I can't see Isabella playing."

Isabella heard her and gathered her shovels and buckets, dropping them here and there as she wobbled them over in front of Nan. "I can build over here," she said, letting her arms fall by her sides, the colorful pile of plastic toys falling at her feet. She sat down, the sand coating her wet legs as she asked Nan what she wanted her to build.

As Faith watched them, it occurred to her to pull her cell phone out of her bag and snap a photo. She shielded the screen from the sun with her hand to view it. Nan was smiling, the sea behind her.

Isabella's face was animated, her head turned toward her great-grand-mother. She was on her knees, holding a blue shovel in her hand. Faith smiled as she looked at the photo, and she wished she'd taken more since she'd been there. She turned around, walked out from under the canopy, and snapped another. The sun was so bright that she could hardly see what she'd gotten, but when she went back under the canopy to see it, it almost took her breath away. The sky was bright orange, yellow, and blue, the sea showing off its diamonds on the crests of its waves, and two shadows held hands at the water's edge—Scott and Casey. It looked like a postcard. Her mom was sitting under the canopy, her legs stretched out from under it to get sun. She kept fooling with her floppy hat, tipping up the rim of it to people-watch. Faith snapped another photo.

They'd spent the whole day out on the beach. Nan had gone in after a few hours, the heat and sun finally getting to her. Faith had helped her back inside. When she did, she took her phone with her and showed Nan the photos. Nan made her promise to add them to the last photo album, and she said she would. At Nan's direction, she'd opened one of the albums they'd compiled over the last week, and Nan turned to a photo of her and Faith's grandfather. They were on the beach, fully dressed—he was wearing a white shirt, a thin, black tie, and trousers, and Nan had on a dark dress with a fitted waist and a flowing bottom that stopped just a little lower than mid-calf.

"That was taken right out there," she said with a reminiscent smile. "We were going to lunch, and John wanted my mother to take our photo. I tried to hurry him, telling him we should go, but he'd insisted." Nan ran her finger along the surface of the photo. "I'm glad he asked for that photo now." She'd offered Faith a serious look. "I won't be around forever. Promise me you'll keep good records of your memories. You'll be glad you did when you're my age." Faith promised, but Nan didn't have to make her promise; she'd already decided that on her own.

When Faith had gotten Nan settled, she went back out on the beach. Casey and Scott were helping Isabella fill her buckets with seashells. Casey hadn't left Scott's side since he'd arrived, and Faith hoped with everything she had that after the vacation ended, Casey wouldn't go back to the way things were and let work get in the way. One thing was certain: Faith was going to keep in touch with Casey after they left the cottage. She planned to call her sister all the time, ask her how her day was, and hear stories about Isabella.

They'd all decided to go out to dinner tonight. As Faith dressed after her shower, she could feel the slight heat on her skin from a day in the sun. She'd only needed a little powder, her face tan, her cheeks pink. She dabbed on lip gloss and slipped on her sandals. Casey finished up, and the two of them joined the rest of the family as they piled everyone into cars and headed to the restaurant.

Once they got there and were seated, Isabella colored in her kids' menu, Nan showing her how to outline with a crayon and drawing unsteadily on the page. Isabella listened politely like a child twice her age, and then followed Nan's direction, drawing over Nan's lines to make them straight. Scott was relaxed with his arm around Casey, and her mom was sipping her cocktail.

"I'm not relocating," Scott announced as he squeezed Casey's shoulder, his arm still around her but more like a hug than it had been. Casey looked like the world had been lifted off her shoulders. She turned around and kissed him. There was a tiny eruption of excitement, Faith's mom clapping her hands in delight. "I told my boss last night that I had a change of heart, and I'd prefer to stay in Boston. Luckily, I'm able to work remotely and I can stay where I am."

Faith couldn't be happier. She knew Scott well enough to understand what he was saying. He trusted that Casey was going to follow through. He believed she'd be better. It was a huge gesture, given the fact that he'd almost gone through with a divorce, and it showed how much he wanted it to all work out. Scott clearly loved Casey, and Faith knew, after spending time with Casey this week, that her sister loved Scott just as much.

Nan put her hand to her heart and looked down at Isabella. She was thinking the same thing that had just entered Faith's mind: Isabella had her daddy back. As Isabella colored, making small talk with Nan, wriggling around on her knees and sipping her milk, she didn't realize the magnitude of what Scott had just said. Isabella would never again awaken in the night and not have her father.

"I'd like to propose a toast," Casey said, holding up her drink. "To family. May we have many more days like this one in our future."

"Hear, hear!" Nan said, holding up her water. She motioned for Isabella to put her cup of milk into the air. Isabella was more than happy to follow her lead. She raised her drink—a paper cup with a plastic lid and a red and white striped straw. Nan touched hers to Isabella's. "Cheers, my dear," she said with a smile. They all followed, and then settled into the kind of chatter that only families have. It was great to have everyone together, but, to her surprise, it made Faith think about Jake. If only he could be there with them. She wished he were.

Chapter Twenty-one

Faith was giddy with excitement but a little apprehensive at the same time. Today was her date with Jake. He'd asked her out, and that made her so happy that her hands were shaking. But she kept thinking about how things could change in a second whenever they brought up the elephant in the room. She really didn't know how they were going to get over that hurdle, but she knew she wanted to give it another shot. She touched her lips, remembering what it felt like to kiss him. Even though they'd only been apart a day, she missed him. With her handbag on her shoulder, she waved to her mom and Nan on her way out of the cottage and tried to focus on the thrill of seeing him.

She waited outside, this time standing so she wouldn't soil her linen trousers. The sun was so bright in the cloudless sky that she slipped her sunglasses on to avoid squinting. She didn't have to wait long. Jake was soon pulling up in the Mercedes. He got out, the engine still running, walked around the car, and opened her door for her.

"Good morning," he said with a grin as she slid inside.

"Good morning," she returned, pulling her feet in. He shut the door and went around to his side of the car.

They drove down Beach Road, the sand blowing across it, the ocean hidden behind the dunes on Jake's side of the car. She pretended to be waiting for a break to get a glimpse of the morning tide, but really, she was sneaking glances at Jake. He was clean-shaven today, his dark hair showing golden strands from days in the sun. She could see the crease on his cheek from smiling, and it warmed her. He smiled all the time.

"I know you like understated places, and you're not up for a lot of glitz and glamour. But today, since it's a *date*, I wanted to take you to a different beach—one of my favorites. It's a little fancier than what you're used to, though. Tell me you'll humor me."

"Okay. Is it far from here?" She was very curious.

"Not terribly."

He turned onto an exit leaving the Outer Banks and headed across the bridge toward the nearby town of Manteo.

"Are you hungry?"

"I've had breakfast."

"Great. Me too." He looked over at her, his eyes wanting to take her all in like they had that day on the boat—she could tell—but he quickly turned back to the road.

"What beach is it?" she asked, curiosity getting the better of her.

"It's a surprise." He smiled, and her stomach did a flip. Faith loved surprises. She just hoped it wouldn't be a disaster like the Tides. She knew him a little better now, though, and she'd be able to talk to him if she felt uncomfortable.

As they drove, they were getting farther away from the coast, and she couldn't for the life of her figure out where he was going, but then they snaked back around, and, after quite a few minutes' drive, she realized she was at Dare County Municipal Airport. Jake turned the silver Mercedes into a parking spot and cut off the engine. On the runway was a small, white private jet, the steps lowered, awaiting passengers.

"We aren't driving to this beach," he said.

Jake greeted the pilot as they stepped up to the plane. They were talking a bit about the flight path, but Faith didn't hear them. She was too busy looking at the gorgeous aircraft in front of her. She'd never been flown anywhere on a date before, let alone traveled on a private jet.

The pilot gestured for them to head inside, and he followed, taking his seat behind a door at the front. Faith couldn't decide what to look at first—the beaded lighting behind a ledge outlining the top of the plane, the tan leather interior, the wood-grain tables with brass cup holders, the thinly carpeted floors in matching beige, or the televisions throughout. A silver bucket filled with ice sat on one of the tables, the neck of a bottle protruding from its center. Two crystal glasses sat beside it.

"Is this your plane?" she asked as they took a seat on either side of the table and belted themselves in.

"No. I rented it, but I've flown with the pilot many times. I always make sure to get Thomas when I fly. I trust him." The pilot came over the speaker and greeted them. He then said the skies were clear without a lot of turbulence, and he'd get them to their destination as quickly as possible. "You may want to hold on to your glass just until we're in the air. It's fine, but I'd rather not spill anything on you."

Jake looked so relaxed as if this was totally normal, and she wondered if he was really comfortable with all of this. He had so much money that he could rent a jet whenever he pleased, drink champagne first thing in the morning, and fly wherever he wanted to go. Yet he chose to have his primary residence on the rural coast of North Carolina, where he'd grown up. He was so down-to-earth that when he did show his wealth, it was startling.

When they got into the air, he pulled the champagne from the ice and wiped it with a towel. "We should be there in about two hours," he said, the cork making a loud, hollow *pop* as he pulled it from the bottle. "That gives us a lot of time to talk." He reached out for her glass, and she handed it to him.

As he filled her glass, the bubbles nearly jumping out of the top of it and dissipating in the air above, she got a good look at Jake Buchanan. In this setting, pouring champagne, wearing his Lacoste shirt and pressed shorts, his hair perfectly imperfect, his wealth was apparent. This was certainly a far cry from his paint-splattered overalls and tool-filled work truck. Which was more him: that work truck or this plane? She was willing to bet it was the work truck.

Even though she knew he probably didn't care, she was glad she'd worn her most expensive outfit.

She took a sip from her glass, the bubbles fizzing up against her top lip, to try and calm her own nerves. Then, she decided to ask him. "What do you enjoy more: working on cottages and driving your work truck around town or flying to exotic destinations like we are now?"

Although he was more outgoing than she was, and he was open more often, he still hid his feelings sometimes. She felt that all this—the plane, the restaurants, the hard-nosed businessman—it was all in an effort to prove himself. His ex-wife had done a number on him, it seemed, and Faith wondered if he was trying to show her and everyone who knew him how successful he could be. But why? Didn't he realize that he was perfect without all that?

"I like them both."

"That's a cop-out. You have to pick. Which one would you give up?"

He took a swig of his champagne and tipped up the glass as if studying the bubbles, but she knew he was stalling. She knew what he was going to say; she just wanted to hear him admit it. "I'll bet I can guess your answer. You just don't want to say it."

He looked at her, a slight smile on his lips. She knew she had him.

"What's your guess?"

"You'd give up this plane before you gave up working on cottages and driving your work truck."

"And what makes you think that?" He was suppressing a smirk.

"When you chose where you wanted to eat lunch on a regular day before you met me, you chose Dune Burger, but when you wanted to try and impress me, you chose the Tides Wine Bar."

"Are you reading me now?"

"It seems so," she said with a smile. "But it looks like you didn't read me very well after all. You should've known that first day you met me what kind of person I was, because I was at Dune Burger too."

His face showed contemplation but it also showed fondness, and she knew she'd made her point. What she hadn't expected was the kind of look she was getting now. And she knew exactly what he was thinking. He was thinking how right she was, and how good it felt to be with someone like him. She knew that because she felt it too.

By the time they'd finished the bottle of champagne and the small talk had given way to an easy, comfortable quiet, the pilot announced that they were a few minutes out from their destination. Faith looked through her window, and as far as she could see, the ocean stretched before her. It was amazing but she hadn't once thought about her surroundings or taken a look at the view because she was so caught up in Jake. Out her window was the brightest color she'd ever seen, very different from the waters of the Outer Banks. It was a green-blue color, almost turquoise, swirling gray sand showing beneath it in patches. As they neared land, she could see boats scattered along the coastline. They were so small that they looked like snowflakes against a blanket of blue. As the plane descended, she started to make out buildings and trees, the flap on the wing going up and down as they neared them. It was totally silent except for the static noise of the engine as the plane neared the runway. Then, with a gentle bump, they were on the ground.

"Welcome to Key West," the pilot said over the speaker, and Faith locked eyes with Jake, making an effort to keep her mouth from wagging open. He'd taken her to Key West!

"We're in Florida?" she asked, nearly unable to contain her excitement. Her whole life she'd wanted to go to Key West, and now, he'd made her dreams come true.

Jake nodded, that fondness once more in his eyes, and she had to catch her breath.

"Why are you doing all this for me?" She was so overwhelmed. She'd never really had anyone do anything for her and certainly nothing so spectacular.

"You said that you wanted to share it with someone. I've been here tons of times but I've never shared it with anyone. I wanted to share it with you in particular."

"Why?" She was still trying to get her head around it all.

"Because I think you'll see it the way I do. And because I wanted to watch your face when you got here." He grinned at her, and she knew that the day was only going to get better.

By the time they'd disembarked, called a taxi, and arrived in downtown Key West, it was nearly eleven o'clock. "I thought we'd get an early bite to eat," he said. She was glad for that for two reasons: One, she hadn't had anything since breakfast and her tummy was rumbling, and two, the champagne, coupled with the flight and everything that was going on between her and Jake, had made her feel lightheaded.

The taxi pulled up outside a gorgeous old red-brick building that looked almost like an enormous version of the Victorian homes she'd seen in the small towns around her growing up. Its style was unique, however, with its red, textured roof and arched doorways and windows. They walked a block or so before Jake led her down a long pier at the end of which there was a small speedboat bobbing in the swell. Before Faith could ask him what was going on he helped her in and they were heading off into the ocean. He helped her in, and she was glad she'd pulled her hair back as the boat got going. The balmy southern air was different here. It was humid but fresh and clean as it came off the ocean. She took in a deep breath to keep the memory of it. She wondered where on Earth this restaurant was.

They arrived at an island, and Faith had never seen anything so beautiful. A restaurant with a colossal porch stretched out in front of her—tiled floors, white pillars the size of redwood trees, paddle fans whirring above them. There were tables with white linen tablecloths, their edges dancing in the breeze, with wicker chairs pulled up to every table, giving them an unfussy feel. The only color besides the brown of the wicker was the electric blue of the ocean, the white of the shoreline, and the green of the hundreds of palm trees scattered around them. Jake hopped out of the boat and reached over to grab her hand. She took it, and he didn't let go as they walked the short distance to a village of white buildings. The two of them snaked around the buildings until they were seaside, and Faith stopped. She couldn't walk. The view in front of her was breathtaking.

"You like?" he said, smiling down at her, his hand still in hers, and she could hardly pull her eyes from the sight to respond.

When she finally did make eye contact, the look on Jake's face was one she'd never seen before. His eyes were intense, his lips slightly smiling, yet there was a seriousness that made her feel like this was as big a deal to him as it was to her. She let go of his hand and grabbed him by the waistband of his trousers, pulling him toward her. Then he put his hands on her face and kissed her. This kiss was different from the others, slightly more urgent but still gentle. Was he letting his guard down?

It was as if they thought the same thing, and they both pulled away from each other. Jake reluctantly let her go and she turned toward the restaurant that was in front of them. *This,* she thought, *is the kind of fancy restaurant I can live with.* It was perfect.

"This is gorgeous," she finally managed, and she turned to him, pushed herself up on her toes, and kissed his cheek. She felt his hand at her back, as he held on to her. She wished he'd never let go.

He smiled down at her. "I'm glad you like it." Then he eased his hand away from her when a waiter began approaching them.

The waiter promptly introduced himself and took them to their table. She didn't want to know how much a place like this probably cost, let alone the plane, the taxi, and then the boat ride over. But it wasn't the money she was impressed by. It was the fact that Jake had known that this was what she would like and had gone to the trouble of organizing it for her. Jake pulled out her chair.

"You didn't have to do all this," she said.

"I wanted to." He quietly scooted his chair closer to the table and leaned on the white linen with his forearm. Even in this atmosphere, he was still relaxed. "I wanted you to see this beach."

Jake had said himself that things like champagne and flowers didn't occur to him. Yet this did? What was happening between the two of them? Something had changed in Jake.

"Do you come here often?" she asked carefully.

"When I want to get away. It's my favorite place to relax." He was leaning back slightly in his chair now, his arm still on the table, but his shoulders politely squared. "It gets too cold in North Carolina in the winters, and I board up my cottage during hurricane season. I've been lucky not to have too much damage each time."

"And you come here?"

"Yes."

"Why don't you just live here? It's so beautiful."

The waiter brought glasses of water for both of them, the ice cubes clinking together as he set them down. Jake gave him a polite thank-you as he left them alone.

"I don't know. I suppose it's because I like the Outer Banks. I can keep busy there more easily. There are people I know who've been there my whole life, and there's so much to do. I can fill my days with cottage work and boat building."

"But this is amazing," she said, pressing him, her gaze landing on a sailboat in the distance, the sail looking stark against the turquoise water—a very different view from the ones she'd seen at the Outer Banks. She considered his answer, and thought how it spoke to what she loved about the Outer Banks. He didn't say he loved the resort that he was building. He said he loved working on the cottages and boats.

"That's not to say that I don't love this view. I just don't need it all the time." He looked out at the water. "If I see it too much, I worry that it will lose its effect on me. Things are good when they're still new."

Had he meant something else by that comment? Was he worried that she wouldn't affect him the same way once they were settled into a routine?

They ordered lunch, and Faith found that even though she had quite a few questions, conversation was always easy. He had a way about him that made both the times they were chatting and the quiet lulls between comfortable. She didn't have to think about it; the conversation just flowed. When their food came—on fancy white plates with perfect zigzags of drizzle—they settled in and let the conversation slow. The weather was different here, the heat noticeable, the wind gentler up by the restaurant. Even the smell of the air was different. Faith liked it, but she understood what Jake had meant when he said he liked North Carolina too. She did feel after seeing this place that flashy could be fun sometimes, but like Jake, she just wanted to sit somewhere nice and read a book. She thought about how great it would be to do that with him.

After lunch, they walked along the pier that led out over the water. There was so much sea in front of her that it made her feel small. "Thank you," she said, turning toward him. She looked up into his eyes, hoping for that look he'd given her earlier.

He offered a crooked grin. "You're welcome," he said. He grabbed her hand and held it in his. With a smile, he studied their fingers as they moved against each other's, and she felt how perfectly they fit. The jitters were gone. She moved her hand in his, feeling the roughness of his palm under her fingertips and his fingers moved in response. Then he closed his hand around hers.

"Feel like walking around? We could go to Mallory Square and see the street performers or go shopping."

"Whatever you think," she said.

Jake took charge, grabbing a taxi to Mallory Square. It was located along a street with a wide sidewalk that stretched along the coast, palm trees and buildings on one side and ocean on the other. Several cruise ships had come in to dock, and she'd never seen ships as huge as these. The walkway was busy. Jake reached out and grabbed her hand again so they could stay together. It was different this time. His grasp was protective yet light, a perfect physical representation of the way he was in general. She held on to him, glad for all the people so that she'd have reason not to let go. They finally came to a stop at Mallory Square, where a tightrope walker was balancing while juggling fire. She watched as the flames flickered against the water behind him.

"Worst case, he can jump in," Jake teased, his mouth near her ear so she could hear him over the crowd. It sent a tickle down her arm. She laughed at his comment and looked up at him, but his eyes were on the juggler. She followed his gaze, still watching him in her peripheral vision. He seemed so relaxed—he hadn't checked his phone once. He was completely in the moment with her, and he seemed to be enjoying himself.

After the performance, they caught another taxi, and when they pulled up to a house, she wondered where he'd brought her. In front of her was a gorgeous white southern building with a wrought-iron porch going around the second story. The only color against the white and black was the gold of the shutters on either side of the rounded windows and the green of the nearby palm trees. Neatly cut hedges worked their way around the house, and the grass was like a carpet of green.

He looked down at her, affection oozing from his face. "Know where we are?"

"Where?"

"Hemingway's house."

"This is where he lived?" She took in the house again with new eyes.

"Yep." He took her hand again—it was becoming quite a regular thing. She could get used to it. "Wanna go inside?"

"Yes." In that moment, she was so glad that she hadn't been to Key West before because she'd been right: She enjoyed seeing it with Jake.

The rustic interior was very masculine with tiled floors and soft, monotone colors on walls that had the heads of mounted wild game and other relics that looked as though they could have been from Hemingway's travels. They walked from room to room and she marveled at the simplicity of the book-filled shelves and modest wooden furniture. But when they arrived in one particular room, it was as if she could almost feel Hemingway's presence. Sitting in the middle of the room was a small, round table with one chair and an antique typewriter. It looked so solitary to her, but it made her think about the man who'd written those words. That man didn't know when he'd written them that there would be a boy in North Carolina who would read them over and over. She was willing to bet that the boy who caught lightning bugs and read Hemingway was still there in the man standing beside her now.

Back outside, he asked, "Can you guess where we're going next?"

"The Robert Frost cottage?"

"How did you know?" He looked down at her. "I couldn't come to the home of my favorite author without visiting the home of yours."

As they walked down the sidewalk, bicycles lining the walls of buildings along the edge of it, the humidity settled on her skin, making the breeze feel cooler. The sun was so bright, and she wondered if it was shining back in North Carolina at that moment. Was Isabella building sandcastles for her daddy with Casey looking on? Was Nan sitting on the porch while her mom packed a picnic? There was Faith, miles and miles away, walking around Key West. It was surreal. As she looked over at Jake, in this town of unfamiliar shops and restaurants and hotels, he looked so familiar to her now. It seemed so right to have him there by her side.

"I'm so glad we could spend today together," she said.

"Me too."

When they arrived at the Heritage House Museum, they toured the grounds, making their way to the garden where Robert Frost's cottage stood. It was a modest structure, painted a pastel blue—almost turquoise like the sea, with a low roofline and small entryway. Palms and other exotic plants flanked the front door. It looked so small when compared to how she'd imagined it as a kid. The owners didn't allow anyone inside the cottage, so she and Jake stood in the shade of the trees that surrounded it.

"It's amazing to me that those larger-than-life words that I read as a kid could have been written in this tiny place."

"It's a simple little cottage, isn't it?"

She nodded. "I suppose he didn't need a whole lot to be happy."

They spent the rest of the afternoon visiting landmarks where their favorite authors had visited, window shopping, and enjoying the sights. They'd even made it to the southernmost point in the United States. There was a marker to designate the spot. It was an enormous, striped monument, and its shape reminded Faith of one of Nan's sewing thimbles.

"Ninety miles to Cuba," Jake read from the letters scrolled across the top.

He smiled a big, cheesy smile, and she took his picture with her phone. As they stood there together, she thought about how they were making memories, living life just like Nan had said. She wrapped her arms around his waist and thanked him again for bringing her there. He kissed the top of her head.

When Jake mentioned that they needed to get back to the airport, Faith felt a little sad. She'd enjoyed having his company all to herself. She liked being with him. And hanging over her head was the fact that once this trip was over, the realities of life would settle in, and they'd have to figure out what, if anything, to do about each other. She wanted to see him again after this trip. She didn't know how she'd do it, since she lived a state away, and she'd be starting school again in late August. She wanted to see him play with Isabella again, she wanted to hand him a mug of coffee in the mornings, she wanted to sit with him on the porch, she wanted to see *his* pictures in Nan's photo albums.

"We have a few movies to choose from for the way back, if you'd like," he said. "I'm always asked to choose two movies for the flight even though I never watch them. So, let's do it." He grinned at her, the laugh lines at the corners of his eyes creasing upward toward his temples in an adorable way. "We have *Good Will Hunting* or *Office Space*."

"Definitely *Good Will Hunting*," she said, taking a seat on a small sofa at the back of the plane. The television was mounted to the ceiling and could pivot on a hinge. Jake turned it toward her and got the movie ready. When he sat down beside her, their proximity was nice, and she was glad for the movie to give them a chance to just sit together—she was tired after the long day and she only wanted to be beside him. As they got settled, and he clicked on the movie, she leaned on his shoulder, her mind elsewhere. She wanted to stay in that moment forever and never have to face the real world, but all good things must come to an end.

"Faith," came a whisper through the fog of sleep. She couldn't remember being as comfortable and peaceful as she was right then. "Faith?" As she swam out of her sleep, she was aware of the warmth beneath her, the arm around her, and the breath at her forehead. Slowly, she opened her eyes and realized she'd fallen asleep during the movie. When she tipped her head to see where the voice was coming from, she was startled by the look on Jake's face. It was an adoring look. She sat up, blinking to clear her vision.

"I'm sorry," she said. "I didn't see the movie."

He smiled at her. "I know. You fell asleep in the first ten minutes."

"Why didn't you wake me?"

"You looked too peaceful. I didn't want to disturb you." Their faces were so close. She wanted to feel his arms around her, to feel his heart beat against her. He straightened up, pulling his arm from behind her, and said, "We'll be landing in a minute or so."

His words were the ones she'd been dreading hearing all day, marking the end of their date. She wanted this to be it. She didn't care that she'd only just met him. She didn't care that she was leaving the Outer Banks in mere days. She wanted to know what it was like to wake up to *him* in the morning, hold *him*, and kiss *his* lips in the morning. No amount of rationalization could make her feel any differently. Jake was the one she wanted to spend her future learning about, and she didn't care if she was in Florida or North Carolina or the South Pole. She didn't care a thing about how he spent his money or where he lived. She just wanted to be with him. He was that guy in English class with the sweater, like Nan had said. He was the mystery that she wanted to solve.

Chapter Twenty-two

Faith had spent the last two days with her family. They'd gone out to the beach until they couldn't stand the heat anymore and then they'd lazed around the cottage. It had been great because they'd been so busy since they'd arrived that they hadn't really had a chance to relax. Even better, it gave them all time to be together as a family. They turned in early last night after a round of board games, which made Nan happy.

She was glad to be able to spend more time with her grandmother. The cottage was new, but it was starting to feel familiar, the twinge of anxiety filling her every time she thought about leaving it. On the eve of the second full day at the cottage, she decided to spend it on the porch, where she could enjoy the view she'd had for so many years. As she looked out at the sea, she could almost feel her old cottage at her back. Trying not to think too much about missing this place, she focused her attention on tomorrow.

Tomorrow was Nan's birthday party. Her mom had found a bakery in town, and she'd ordered a grand cake. Faith smiled to herself as she remembered worrying about impressing Jake at Nan's party. Now that she knew him better, she realized that she didn't need to impress him. He'd never judge them based on the way they'd chosen to celebrate her grandmother's birthday. Her worries seemed silly now. But her distress over Nan's party had been replaced by a new uneasiness. She hadn't seen Jake since their trip to Key West.

She'd fully expected him to drop by, but he hadn't. She hadn't seen him since he'd left her on the porch after their date. He'd brought her home that evening, walked her up to the door, and they'd had a little chitchat until it was obvious she needed to let him go. She'd put her arms around him and hugged him as she thanked him. His absence had made things feel even more unclear for her. She worried, thinking again how maybe he had just been doing her a favor taking her to a beach she'd never seen. Rich guy to the rescue.

She pulled her feet up into the rocking chair and hugged her knees. The sun was going down behind the cottage, and the blue sky looked as though someone had put it on a dimmer switch. It kept getting darker, her surroundings fading into black. The sound of the tide going in and out and the stars in the sky were all she had left of the evening. The warm breeze blew around her, the air still recovering from the day's heat.

As she sat outside alone, she tried to get her mind off of depressing thoughts like losing her childhood cottage, how the area was going to have changed the next time she would be able to visit, and leaving Jake. She had a lot of great things to be thankful for from this trip. She'd made amends with Casey, and she felt like she understood her so much better. And she'd gotten to know Isabella so much better. She realized that she and Scott could still be friends, and she was so excited to see him back with Casey. She would never have imagined that she'd have that reaction, but it was this trip that had changed it all. She had Nan to thank for that. Nan had planned it and dragged them all there. She always knew just what everyone needed. Her mom was the same way, and Faith expected that when Nan finally went to find John, it would be her mom who would keep them all together. They were so much stronger as a family now.

Before coming on vacation, Faith had looked for just the right present for Nan. What does someone get a person who has lived her entire life, has everything, and wants for nothing? Nan didn't need worldly goods because she wasn't worried about that sort of thing anymore. What was important to her was her family, her health, and eventually meeting back up with the love of her life. So, shopping for Nan had been quite difficult. She'd settled on a gift, knowing that Nan wouldn't need it and may not use it, but now, after spending time with her, and hearing her stories, it seemed perfect. It was small, wrapped in silver paper with a white ribbon, and hidden at the bottom of her suitcase. Faith couldn't wait to give it to her.

The surf gurgled its white foam over her toes as Faith walked along the ocean's edge. The sun was high in the sky now, but she'd been walking since after breakfast. Today was Nan's birthday, the reason they'd all come here. Faith had been excited about it, ready to celebrate the matriarch of the family, happy to have this day with Nan. But now, all she could think about was leaving. Tomorrow, they'd pack up their things, fill their cars, and leave the cottage empty and stark the way they'd found it. It wouldn't have a trace of any of them left, and they'd all go back to their regular lives.

While she had Nan to thank for all these new memories, she also had Jake to thank. He'd provided experiences that she never would have had otherwise. He'd also provided the opportunity for her to have feelings that she would never have had. And now, she had to go back home with all of this in her head. She knew she had to. That was why she was taking a long walk this morning. She needed the time to get herself ready to go back.

Her mom was most likely getting the cake by now. Nan had been puttering around, tidying up, and busying herself. Scott, Casey, and Isabella were on the porch, playing Uno when she'd left. Faith was so far down the beach now that she couldn't even see the cottage anymore, so she turned around to head back.

As she made her way back, she promised herself that she'd see her family more often. She hadn't realized how much she'd missed them until these two weeks. There was nothing magical about their cottage—it could be old or new. What made it magical was the people in it—her family. And the one thing she'd learned this week—more than anything else—was that they were better together. She smiled as she remembered the nameplate on the front of the house: "Better Together." It certainly fit. Even if they had to rent something else in the years to come, she would definitely still drive by this spot and remember how—no matter what changes there were—it always brought them together.

The sand stuck to her feet as she walked, the tide washing them clean as fast as the sand covered them. The water was warm like the air, the breeze blowing against her as she walked back to the cottage. Even though she had to face leaving, she was excited to get back to her family, to have a few hours with them before seeing Jake one last time.

As she neared the cottage, Faith trudged up through the sand, her feet burning from the heat of it as she got farther from the water. The sea had provided relief from the relentless sun as it beat down on the shore. She jogged quickly toward the house and found Isabella sitting beside Casey and Scott right at the sea grass's edge.

"Look, Aunt Faith!" Isabella said, her chest poked out in pride. "I made it all by myself just like you showed me how to do."

Isabella had made a sandcastle with a moat around the edge of it, seashells adorning the roofline.

"It's beautiful!" Faith knelt down to get a better look. "Is this the door?" she said, pointing toward a shell that had been pressed into the side of the castle.

"Yes! And these are the windows," Isabella said, squatting down and pointing to each little shell.

"Scott, do you mind staying with Isabella? I'm going to go up with Faith and check on Mom—make sure she doesn't need any help," Casey said. Scott nodded and Casey stood up, stepping toward Faith.

"Thank you for showing me your castle," Faith said to Isabella. "I can't wait to see what else you do with it!" She wondered what the real intent of Casey's suggestion to help was. It was almost as if she'd been waiting for Faith.

"I'm going to make a town!" Isabella said with excitement.

Faith smiled, her love for her niece filling her up. She was so glad to have had the chance to be with Isabella this week, and she was happy that Isabella had warmed to her.

Once they were over the dune, Casey said, "Faith, I'm so scared."

Faith stopped and turned to her sister. "Why?" She'd never heard Casey say anything like that before, and she wanted to know immediately what was wrong.

"Scott and I have been talking, and he's willing to try if I am... Things are going so well here, but I'm so scared about what may happen when I have to go back to work. What if I fall into the same routine? How can I balance it all? I want to be sure that I'm being the best wife I can be. What do I do?"

Casey was asking Faith for advice. The mere thought of this made her laugh—one quick burst of laughter.

"It's not funny."

"No," she said, becoming serious. "It isn't funny. Casey, you're the strongest person I know. You'll figure it out. You won't fall into the same routine because you're aware that it doesn't work for your family. And the fact that you're worried about it is good! You'll be fine. Because you want it."

"Then why did you laugh?"

"Because you were asking me what to do."

"Ha! That *is* funny," she teased. "I'm just kidding. Faith, you might not have ever been married, and you can't give me the answers I need regarding that, but you're a wonderful listener. You always have been. That's why I asked you what to do. I didn't need a solution. I needed the answer you just gave me. Thank you."

"You're welcome," she said, and they both went up to check on their mom and Nan.

Nan had been sent out to the porch to enjoy the last hours of daylight while they'd set up for her party. Scott kept Isabella busy with a puzzle in the living room as the ladies had worked to prepare. They'd taped streamers to cabinets and lights, careful not to get any tape near the newly painted walls. On the table, Casey had set up Nan's albums full of photos so they could all have a look at them one last time before they were divvied up and taken home. A bouquet of helium balloons bounced around in the center of the table, the breeze from the open door causing them to dance on their strings. Her mom had picked up the cake. It was magnificent—a rectangular sheet cake with three-dimensional waves crashing onto an icing-painted shore. In the corner of it was one candle for Nan to make her wish. Faith set her silver box with the white ribbon on the table next to the cake and the gifts from her mom and Casey. The ribbon had gotten bent on one side in her suitcase, and she was fiddling with it to try and straighten it out.

"Can I come back in now, or are you going to let me dehydrate out here?" Nan said, peeking her head in and holding on to the doorframe for support. "Oh!" she said, her gaze bouncing from one decoration to the other. "It's lovely."

"Come in, Mom," Faith's mom said with a smile.

There was a knock at the door and Faith's heart skipped a beat. She knew exactly who it was. Jake. She ran her fingers through her hair and cleared her throat. Casey opened the door and let him in. He looked as familiar as an old friend, and yet a current of excitement zinged through her at the sight of him. He was all cleaned up again, his clothes clearly expensive but unfussy. He had on a polo shirt and a pair of shorts. She wanted to rush over to him and tell him how she wished he'd stopped by over the last few days, but she stayed put. His eyes fluttered over to her, and he smiled that big, gorgeous smile.

"Well, there he is," Nan said, walking over to him and patting him on the arm. "I've heard a lot about your trip to Florida. Faith really seemed to enjoy it." Nan smiled in her direction, and Faith could feel the heat on her face from embarrassment. She didn't particularly want Jake to know that she'd blabbered on to Nan about her trip. But she had enjoyed it. She'd thought about it a lot over the last few days, and she wanted nothing more than to be with him again. It was so good to see him.

"It was fun," he said, looking over at Faith again. She grabbed the kitchen chair to keep her legs from buckling with anxiety. Maybe it was the fact that she hadn't seen him in two days or perhaps that she was going home tomorrow, but she found herself getting all worked up in his presence.

"I've made some ham biscuits and we have a veggie tray if you're hungry, Jake," her mom said as she brought the tray around and set it down on the table. "And we have drinks. I have beer and wine."

"I'll have a glass of wine," Nan piped up. "Is it white?" She walked over to the kitchen to stand by Martha, who was busy uncorking the bottle.

"Yes," she said to Nan. "I know it's your favorite. Anyone else?"

"I'll have one," Faith said, hoping that the alcohol would settle her nerves a little.

As soon as her mom handed her a glass, she took a giant swig. After that, she started feeling a little better. She tried to avoid the urge to stare at Jake, or, worse still, entertain thoughts of how she could get him into the nearest empty room, so she helped her mom in the kitchen. Before she'd even had half her glass of wine, Scott and Jake were busy drinking beers and talking about the upcoming football season. She was glad for that because it gave her a chance to collect herself.

"Well, I'm not getting any younger. We'd better cut this cake," Nan said.

"You want to do it right away?" Her mom giggled, motioning for Faith to join her at the table. Faith followed, stopping next to Jake. "You don't want to wait?"

"Nope." Nan walked over to the table. "I want to be able to enjoy this night with my family and new, but dear, friend." She winked at Jake. "I don't want to have to stop it all for the formality of blowing out that candle. I'm very thankful for all you've done to prepare for my birthday, but I want to sit down, have a good chat, look at my photos, and eat my cake."

"Well, you're the birthday girl," her mom said, handing out paper hats.

"Put them on!" Isabella said as she stretched the string of hers under her chin, the hat sitting sideways on top of her head.

With a collective laugh, they all put their hats on. They were blue with multicolored balloons on them and said "Happy Birthday" on the front. Her mom lit the candle with a match and started singing "Happy Birthday."

The others all gathered around the table, singing to Nan. The sun was still bright and it poured through the windows like the champagne Faith had had too early in the morning on the way to Key West. As the song ended, they removed their hats but Isabella kept hers on. Faith looked at Jake and quickly looked away when she saw that he was looking at her. She didn't want to look at him for fear that she'd give away all her feelings. She'd completely fallen for him, but not seeing him for a few days had made her trip to Key West with him more like a dream than reality.

As the candle flickered in front of her, Nan closed her eyes and took in a deep breath. Faith wondered what her wish was. Was she wishing something for her family, or to see John again soon, or something special for herself? Somehow, Faith believed that whatever it was Nan had wished for, she'd get it. Nan was not one to sit around and wait. If her wish didn't come to her, she'd certainly go and get it herself. Nan blew out her candle.

Her mom reached over and grabbed a green foil-wrapped present off the table and handed it to Nan. "This is from me," she said. Nan sat down at the table and set it in her lap. With unsteady hands, she slipped her finger under the fold and tore open one end. Then she pulled out the gift. It was a silver frame. "I want Jake or Scott to take a photo of us girls before we leave tonight. Then we can put it in the frame for you."

"Thank you. It's gorgeous." Nan pulled the stand open on the backboard of the frame and set it on the table. She reached over and grabbed a blue package with white polka dots and a white ribbon.

"That's from me…and Isabella and Scott," Casey said with a smile.

Nan grinned in return and opened the present. She held it up so everyone could see it. It was a figurine of an angel. Nan collected angels. She put them out on her mantel every Christmas.

"It's beautiful," she said, turning it around in her hands before setting it next to the frame.

As she reached for Faith's silver-wrapped present, Faith thought about the significance of it. In life, seconds became minutes and minutes became hours and so on, but they needed all of it together to make any sense. Nan had mentioned how, when she was older, Faith would look back on her life and the things that worried her now wouldn't seem so big. They'd be like seconds on a clock, Faith thought to herself. Nan had opened the gift. She held up the crystal clock with silver hands that Faith had kept in her bag all week tied up with that white ribbon. The clock represented time—time Nan had spent over her ninety years making a life, and oh, what a life she'd made. Faith could only hope to have a life like Nan had lived, and maybe, if she was lucky, she'd find herself at a beach house at ninety surrounded by her family.

"This is perfect, Faith," Nan said. "Thank you. It'll go by my bedside."

Her mom pulled out the cake server that she'd dutifully packed from home and brought with her, and began cutting the cake and serving it onto paper plates.

"I'd like to thank you all for making this the best birthday ever," Nan said. "It's been a very long time since I've had such a perfect gift as this: everyone together. I'm so thankful to have been witness to that." Nan stood, walked over to Jake, and grabbed his bicep, looking up at him in a very odd way. She stood with him for a moment without speaking, looking every one of them in the eye. It was very dramatic, and Faith wondered what was going on. Faith could feel the confusion showing on her face despite her attempts to smooth it out. What was Nan going to say about Jake?

"What you all don't know is that I have a present for all of you." Nan waited, her face animated, her eyebrows pushed up and a grin on her face. Nan was clearly making this dramatic on purpose. What in the world would she have to give them that involved Jake? "I've been working for a long time with Jake Buchanan," she said. "This cottage is not a rental. It's mine. I own it."

There was a collective gasp as they all looked at one another. In that moment, like a flash, Faith's reality changed. She envisioned big family vacations with everyone there. Isabella growing up, building sandcastles, a picnic table at the edge of the dunes just like it had been when they were kids. And memories. Lots and lots of memories. She felt the prickle of the news on her arms, and the sting of tears in her eyes.

"When the original cottage was destroyed, I sat on the land, not wanting to get rid of such a gorgeous piece of property. I never told anyone I still had it. I knew that I couldn't take care of it, but I did know that you all could. If you don't want it, I'll sell it. Jake can help me do that. But if you do want it, it's yours. I'm willing it to Martha, but under the condition that we all take care of it. It belongs to our family. You can't leave it for her alone to take care of. Understood?" Nan looked back and forth between Casey and Faith. They agreed.

Everyone started talking at once, their questions and comments turning to laugher and giddy excitement. Faith caught Nan's eye. She was clearly enjoying it all. This was as much a gift for her as it was a gift for her family. Nan loved having everyone together.

Faith leaned over to Jake and quietly whispered under the chatter, "You knew about this the whole time?"

"If I'd have told you, your nan would've killed me," he laughed. And she laughed with him, knowing exactly what he meant.

"Now that the cat's out of the bag, I can tell you that I got you a present," Jake said, turning back toward the group and smiling at Nan. "It's out on the porch. Can I help you walk out to see it?"

Nan nodded, grabbing Jake's arm. The rest of the family followed, and they all collected on the porch facing the beach. Sitting on the floorboards was a brand new wooden bench swing and a pile of chain. It was very much like the porch swing at the old cottage. "I made it myself," he said. "You'll have to show me where you want me to hang it."

For the second time, Faith felt the sting of tears, and she blinked to keep them at bay. Isabella would swing on that swing as she grew up, just like Faith had done. What an amazingly sweet gesture for Jake to have made that for the cottage. She remembered mentioning it to him over dinner, but she never would have expected that he'd have taken the time to build one for them. She wanted to put her arms around him and hug him.

Jake promised to hang it before he left, and, as everyone went back inside to escape the heat, Casey gently grabbed Faith's arm to hold her back. It was clear that she had something to say, and when Nan noticed, being the last in, she shut the door behind her, leaving the two girls outside.

"I can't believe this is ours," Casey said, looking out at the beach. Faith stood beside her, the wonder of it settling in her throat. She was so happy to be able to call this beautiful place hers. But she knew there was something else Casey wanted to say; she could read her sister enough to tell, so she waited. "I'm so sorry," Casey said, turning to her, her skin flushed with remorse. "I'm sorry I hurt you all those years ago. It has always weighed heavily on me, and so I didn't push when you wanted to stay away because until now, I didn't have the guts to say what I'm saying."

While Faith was very happy to hear this from Casey, she realized something at that moment: Casey, who had always seemed so confident to Faith, was actually a lot like her. Casey used her confidence to hide her insecurities. What Faith now understood from Casey's apology was that Faith wasn't necessarily the weaker one; they were both weak in ways. Faith looked up to Casey for her outward strength while Casey needed her sister in times of crisis. Together, they were strong.

Faith shook her head. "It was really silly to have avoided you for so long over that. It makes absolutely no sense to me now."

"I've missed you so much."

"I've missed you too."

"Thank you for helping me with Scott. I couldn't have done it without you." Casey peeked into the cottage and smiled at her husband through the window. He was laughing at something Nan was saying.

"You're welcome." Faith had never felt more confident. In all the years she and Casey had spent together at this beach, it had taken until now for Faith to truly understand her sister. "This is a wonderful beginning, getting this cottage," she said. "It'll be a place where we can always be together." She put her arm around her sister.

They'd spent all evening with Nan, chatting and taking photos, and finally, Isabella, unable to keep her eyes open any longer, asked if she could go to bed. Scott took her to her room and, when he didn't return, Casey went and checked on him. He'd fallen asleep next to his daughter. Casey decided that she, too, was ready for bed, and she joined her little family for the night. Nan was dozing in the chair, and Mom, having just finished cleaning everything up—she never let anyone help her—called out to Faith and Jake on the porch to tell them she was heading to bed as well, leaving them alone.

Jake had come outside to test out the swing he'd hung earlier for Nan. He didn't need to test it, though, because Faith had been swinging on it for a while already and it was perfectly secure. He sat down next to her, and they were so close that, to be comfortable, he put his arm around her, along the back of the swing. She let her feet dangle as he pushed them gently back and forth. Even though he hadn't done anything to prompt it, she put her head on his shoulder.

Faith wished they could spend many nights just like this. But then the truth of the situation set in: She was leaving tomorrow. She may never see him again, even though she hoped he'd keep in touch and, at the very least, stop by when she visited the cottage. But would he? Would their two weeks together fade away in his memory eventually? A sense of urgency washed over her. But what could she do? He hadn't said a thing. Did he have any thoughts on the subject of her leaving at all?

"I go home tomorrow," she said finally.

"I know." He was very quiet, not his usual self.

What else could she say? *Say something!* she wanted to yell out. The more she sat there, the more she wondered if he wasn't saying anything because he didn't have anything to say. Jake had given her signs that her feelings weren't one-sided—those looks he gave her, the way he smiled at her, the softness of his voice compared to the way he spoke to other people, the times he'd kissed her. It all meant something, right?

"Do you care?" she asked, mustering all her inner strength and sitting up to face him. She spread her hands out on her thighs to keep them from trembling.

He turned to her, his face distorted in confusion. He looked almost offended.

"Do you care that I'm leaving?" She was taking a big chance here, because if he truly didn't care then what would he say? She was putting him on the spot and she knew it, but if she didn't, she'd never know. For once, she knew where she wanted her life to go, even if she didn't know how things would turn out. She didn't know if Jake was someone she could be with long-term, but how would she ever get to that point if she didn't take a risk and find out.

"I've thought about it, yes," he said softly, not making eye contact.

She tried to hide the hurt. It wasn't a grand gesture like she'd hoped.

She thought about Nan and what she'd said about those major moments not being as big when she looked back on them. No matter what happened tonight, she'd move on, her life would carry on, and years later, this moment would be but a memory. So, she decided it was time she got on with living her life. She wasn't going home until she had answers.

Before she could say anything, he said, "Faith, you scare me to death. You are the person that I enjoy being around. I can't stand being away from you. I tried. For the last two days, I wanted to see if I could stand being without you and it was the worst two days I've ever had. But when I married Rebecca, I envisioned this perfect life where I grew old with someone and had a family. I worked hard to build something with her and I thought I was doing everything right. But then, when we started seeing things differently regarding my work, she wasn't happy anymore. She wasn't the person I thought she was, and I should've seen it. I tried to build a life, and I hadn't done it right."

"What do you mean, 'done it right'?"

"I know how to build things. That's what I do. I can make magnificent structures, beginning with nothing but dirt. And I'm good at it. But when it comes to building a life with someone, being a husband, I'm clearly *not* good at it. I was just myself, and that wasn't enough. When I got divorced, my life crumbled down around me, and I had to rebuild it. I've done that. I've done it in a way that makes me happy. But when I started talking to you, I could feel that foundation wobble. The very last thing I want is someone trying to change my mind about the life I've created." He took a breath and shook his head.

"Do you know what you're not good at?" she asked, taking another risk. She put her hands around his waist and turned him toward her until they were facing each other.

"What?" he asked, looking at her intently, yet his eyes so gentle that it almost took her breath away.

"You're not good at trusting yourself. Yes. You're good at building. But you're great at being you. How do you know it was *you*? You just believed your ex-wife as if her word was definitive. What if it was *her*?"

He shook his head, clearly unsure.

"I have another question."

He looked up at her.

"Do you like the Tides Wine Bar? Do you enjoy eating there? Honestly?"

He stared at her as if she were reading his mind. A wave of excitement sheeted over her when she realized she had. She could read him too. With a smile, she said, "You don't like it, do you?"

"Rebecca was so excited about that restaurant. She couldn't wait for it to be built. She said we needed something like that in the Outer Banks. So, when I wanted to impress you, I took you there, thinking that's what kind of place a woman might want. She liked high-end places, flowers…"

She'd finally gotten to the truth, that it wasn't about him loving those places, it was about him trying to prove himself after his ex-wife had left. "What if there's someone out there who doesn't even care if she gets a superficial bouquet of flowers because she just wants to be with you, whether you're reading, sailing, or just having something to eat? What if your actions aren't as important as you being there beside her?"

Never before had she been this honest, this open about her feelings. And she knew she was right. It felt so good to get it out. Jake was a wonderful person. Neither of them knew if it would work out or not, but what was the point if they never tried, if they never took a chance?

An undecipherable thought washed over him. A realization. "Like Key West," he said, and she didn't understand what he meant right away. He searched her face as if he were trying to find answers to some perplexing problem. What was he thinking? Then he leaned in toward her. He put his hands on her face and only broke eye contact when he pressed his lips to hers. His hands progressed from her face to her shoulders and down her back, his lips moving on hers, making her legs feel weak. His hands finally came to rest on her back as he kissed her. She held onto him, her own hands unstill, her chest against his, their breathing matched with one another's. She'd kissed people in her life, but she'd never had a kiss like this one.

"I wanted to take you to Key West," he said, his lips still on hers, "just because I thought you'd like it. I wasn't trying to wow you or anything."

"I know," she smiled and kissed him again. "And I loved it."

He pulled back to look at her. "I want to be with you," he said, surprising her. "All I think about is you, lately. When I get up in the morning, when I go to bed at night, you're in my thoughts. I wonder what you're doing when you're away, and I want you there with me." He searched her face for answers, but only for a second. As usual, he'd read her mind, her response plastered across her face. She couldn't stop smiling. He reached down, held her face, and pressed his lips to hers. This kiss was different from all the others. It was gentle and urgent at the same time, their lips moving together perfectly. It was the kind of kiss she'd waited for her entire life and never knew existed.

She could feel it. This was the start of something great, and she couldn't wait to see where it went.

Epilogue

Faith pulled her Land Rover into the drive of the cottage and turned off the engine. The SUV had been far fancier than anything Faith had wanted to drive, but Jake had insisted. The two restaurants that he'd bought were making him so much money that he'd wanted to spend some of it on her. In the end, Jake had decided to buy those restaurants, but instead of knocking them down, he'd repaired them, gave the cooking staff upgraded kitchens, and kept them going. Those two restaurants were keeping him quite busy; so busy, he said, that he'd changed his mind about building in Corolla, but Faith knew better. And her thoughts were confirmed when in the dark one night, while lying next to Faith, he'd whispered in her ear that she'd been right. He'd told her she was right about it all, and he apologized for taking so long to figure it out. He'd fallen in love with the Outer Banks again—*her* Outer Banks.

She opened the back door of the car as Isabella came around the corner. She was fifteen now, lean and lanky like her mother had been, her long hair like strands of gold down her back. She had freckles on her nose, her skin already golden from a few days at the cottage. Her fingernails and toes were painted a matching shade of shell pink, and she was wearing lip gloss. *And so it begins*, Faith thought to herself with a smile. It seemed like only yesterday, Casey had been that age, and Faith had looked up to her, wishing she could be like her sister. The difference was that Isabella was quiet, reserved, and a whole lot like Faith. She'd spent quite a bit of time with her aunt, and Faith was so glad to have had the last few years with her. Thinking about how she'd missed so much of the first part of Isabella's life made her upset, but she'd learned from Nan to pick herself up and keep going.

Nan would've loved to see what they'd done with the place. Even though they could've had a cottage ten times the size of this one, they'd kept it because Nan had bought it for them, and Jake had worked very hard to make it perfect. The porch swing was still hung right where Nan had asked him to hang it, and Jake had done all the upkeep of the cottage, himself. The bookshelves inside that Jake had put in at Nan's suggestion were now filled with Nan's photo albums—they'd all brought them back to keep them in one spot—and they'd added a few new ones as well, but Faith's favorite part of the cottage was just above the rows of albums on the shelf at eye level where they had Nan's silver frame with the last photo they'd all taken together at her birthday party. Beside it was the photo of Nan on the beach that Faith had taken, the water glistening behind her. Between the frames, they'd placed some of Nan's angels. She was among them now, since she'd finally found John. Faith hoped they were watching from above, and every time the family came to the cottage, at least one morning each week the sky turned the most gorgeous shades of pink and purple. And in those moments, Faith felt her grandmother just like Nan had felt John.

"Where's your mama?" Faith asked Isabella as Jake got out of the other side of the Land Rover.

"Inside with Dad and Addison." Isabella walked over to the open car door and helped Sophie out of the car. Sophie, only six, looked up to her cousin, following her everywhere she went. Sophie had been named after Nan, born a year after Nan had passed. Sophie hopped out of the car after Isabella, her brown curls, the color of Jake's hair, bouncing around her shoulders.

"I'm going in with Isabella, Daddy," she said to Jake as she held her cousin's hand and followed her to the long staircase leading to the front door of the cottage.

"Okay," he said as he helped Faith get the suitcases out of the back of the car. "Be careful on the way up."

Every year they met here. Sophie was three years younger than Addison, Scott and Casey's second child, and, just like Faith and Casey, those two girls couldn't be more different. Isabella balanced their differences, being older, wiser, and a good mix of the two. The three girls spent two weeks together every summer, and they had built so many memories already.

Nan would've been proud. She'd been right about everything. Just like how she'd fallen in love with John, Faith could remember falling in love with Jake. It had started on that first day at the cottage, a mutual feeling she felt for him the moment she met him. After she'd left the cottage that summer, he'd driven down to see her more times than she could count until he finally asked her to move in with him. Then one night, while they were curled up under an afghan on the sofa in front of the fire, the snow coming down outside around them, the beach barren and frozen, he'd told her that he loved her. All those moments built, one after another, until one day, she couldn't imagine life without him, and that was when she knew—when she had a million tiny things that made her love him and miss him whenever he was gone. Just as Nan had said.

Jake had told her once about the moment he suspected she was the one. It had happened the day he'd taken them to the island where

Nan thought John had proposed. The story that Nan had told about the man she'd loved had affected Jake. He'd said that he'd never loved anyone like that before, and he wondered if he could love Faith like that. He'd found her attractive and he'd enjoyed her company, but that thought at that moment had taken him by surprise. That wonder had sown a seed in his mind, and when he realized that he loved her, he always went back to that moment as when he'd pinpointed that he'd fallen for her.

Jake had proposed to Faith on that island. He'd taken her there on the boat he'd helped make for her, her eyes closed at his insistence. He led her down the ladder onto the beach, and when she opened her eyes, every single inch of the dry sand and surrounding woods was covered in tiny, flickering tea light candles, making the beach mirror the stars in the sky. With their flames, the bright white moon, and the stars the only light around them, he'd asked her to marry him. He'd carved their names in a tree, and he promised he'd always show her where it was so she'd never have to speculate like Nan had. She'd worried that a storm would push the island underwater. It wouldn't take much to do it, given the hurricanes that hit that area. So, they'd taken a photo of the tree, and they'd placed it in one of the photo albums. It would be their reminder of the moment when they'd decided that they were better together.

The last to arrive at the cottage, they climbed the steps and went inside to join their family. The only sound outside was the rush of the tide and the wind. The cottage stood strong against it, the wood still new-looking, the shingles not yet weathered, and inside was a family—whole and happy, together.

A Letter from Jenny

Thank you so much for reading *Summer by the Sea*. I really hope that you enjoyed the story and it gave you a relaxing summer escape—whatever time of year it is.

If you'd like me to drop you an email when my next book is out, you can sign up here:

www.ItsJennyHale.com/email/jenny-hale-sign-up

I won't share your email with anyone else, and I'll only email you when a new book is released.

If you did enjoy *Summer by the Sea*, I'd love it if you'd write a review. Getting feedback from readers is amazing, and it also helps to persuade other readers to pick up one of my books for the first time.

Until next time!

Jenny

P.S. If you enjoyed this story, I think you'd like my other summer novels—*The Summer House* and *Summer at Firefly Beach*.

Acknowledgments

I'd like to thank my husband, Justin, who continues to surprise me with creative ways to help me meet my deadlines.

Thank you to Oliver Rhodes for his endless patience, creativity, and guidance. I am so very thankful to have his leadership. I am so happy to be surrounded by the talented Bookouture team.

To my editor, Emily Ruston, I have learned so much from her, and am very grateful to have had the opportunity to work with her.

About the Author

Jenny Hale is a *USA Today* bestselling author of romantic fiction. Her novels *Coming Home for Christmas* and *Christmas Wishes and Mistletoe Kisses* have been adapted for television on the Hallmark Channel. Her stories are chock-full of feel-good romance and overflowing with warm settings, great friends, and family. Grab a cup of coffee, settle in, and enjoy the fun!

Don't miss a single spectacular romance from Jenny Hale!